Penelope

A Novel of New Amsterdam

By Jim McFarlane

Twisted Cedar Press

Cover design by Allyson Campbell McFarlane of www.allymacdesign.com

Cover model is Emily Geisen, photographed by Pete Geisen.

Cover painting is "Prototype View of New Amsterdam," circa 1651 from Stokes, I. N. Phelps. *The Iconography of Manhattan Island, 1498-1909, vol 1.* New York : Robert H. Dodd, 1915. Electronic reproduction by Columbia University Libraries, 2008. JPEG use copy available via the World Wide Web.

Published by Twisted Cedar Press, 102 Enoree Circle, Greer, SC 29650

3 5 7 9 10 8 6 4 2

Publisher Cataloging-in-Publication Data
McFarlane, Jim.
    Penelope: A Novel of New Amsterdam / Jim McFarlane-1st ed.
        p. cm.
ISBN 978-0-9851122-0-2
1. New York (N.Y.)—History—Colonial Period ca 1600-1775—Fiction
2. Manhattan (New York, N.Y.)—Fiction   3. British Americans—Fiction
4. Long Island (New York, N.Y.)—Fiction   5. Dutch Americans—Fiction
6. Stout, Penelope, 1622 or 3-1732 or 3   I. Title

Dedication

This book is dedicated to my late father, A. D. McFarlane, who piqued my interest in genealogy, and to my late mother, Beulah, for making me a descendant of Penelope.

Acknowledgements

I wish to give thanks to the Greenville members of South Carolina Writers Workshop for their years of encouragement and advice, especially Barbara, Carole, Marcia, Susan, Valerie A. and Valerie N.

To my daughter Jill, who demonstrated tough love by tossing out my first hundred pages.

To my daughter Sally for removing the boring parts that readers skip.

To my daughter Emily, who persuaded her book club to read and critique an early draft.

To my sister, Broach, who laughed at the right places.

To my wife, Nancy, who allowed me time to write.

To the Judge George W. Armstrong Library in Natchez, MS for owning a copy of *New York Historical Manuscripts Dutch, Volume IV, Council Minutes, 1638-1649*.

Jim McFarlane, February 2012
www.jim-mcfarlane.com

Chapter 1

Amsterdam

Sunday, November 10, 1647

While the rest of the congregation departed and the elders arranged the room for her hearing, Penelope Kent squirmed to relieve muscles that ached from enduring a three-hour sermon on a backless bench. These separatists from the Church of England observed a myriad of prohibitions and she hoped fidgeting didn't compound her crime—whatever it was.

Her betrothed, Matthew Prince, conferred with his father, who moved around the room pinching out the cheap hog-tallow candles with dry, calloused fingers. A chill November breeze from the North Sea swirled the acrid aroma of the smoldering wicks around the drafty room rather than clearing the air.

Again Penelope wondered what she had done, or failed to do. During her three months of attendance, the elders had summoned members almost weekly to the front of the sanctuary to confess and repent of their sins, most often impure thoughts, vain speech and sloth. She knew she was innocent of those vices.

Whereas most of the congregation lived near this church under constant scrutiny by their peers, the elders had scant chances to observe Penelope's behavior because her home was a mile away on the Herengracht, or Gentlemen's Canal, one of the better districts of Amsterdam, even if she was merely a maid living in a tiny room in a garret. She resigned herself to endure a moment of humiliation for some obscure misdemeanor.

The chief elder, Mr. Brown, rustled papers and glared at Penelope as though she were already tried and condemned of murder. She turned her head to avoid his hostility and saw Matthew depart despite his promise to remain and support her. Alone on the bench, she sat up straighter and focused her eyes above the heads of her accusers.

"Miss Kent," Mr. Brown announced sternly. "Present yourself before this inquisition."

She startled at the word but immediately rose to disguise her discomfort. Although her parents were English, she had grown up here in Amsterdam where the Dutch word *inquisitie* was always associated with merciless horrors the Spanish had inflicted upon the Low Countries two generations earlier. An uneasy feeling twitched in her gut but she faced fellow Englishmen, not Spanish priests.

As she stepped sideways between the benches of the women's side toward the aisle, the swish of her velvet dress filled the otherwise silent room. Except for Matthew's aged grandfather, Reverend Prince, who napped in the only chair after his long sermon, she was alone with the elders, separated from them by a table holding a Geneva Bible and two malodorous candles. She faced them with hands clasped meekly in front, her palms damp with sweat.

"Miss Kent." Mr. Brown tilted the paper toward the meager candlelight. "We accuse you of infamous behavior that brings shame and embarrassment upon this congregation. Confess and repent or depart from our midst."

Penelope stifled a gasp. Was this the normal procedure—a vague accusation? One thing was certain. If this congregation ejected her, Matthew would discard her from his life and her plans would be as useless as candle smoke.

Matthew's sister had advised Penelope to plead feminine weakness and deep remorse. Yet it was hypocrisy to apologize for sins she hadn't committed. *To thy own self be true* echoed in her mind. This Puritan-like congregation denounced plays and other worldly entertainment, but these words from *Hamlet* sounded like advice from Proverbs as well.

She took a deep breath and dried her palms against the soft fabric of her cloak, a long-ago gift from her father to her mother. *Think,* she demanded of herself. *Defend yourself.* But how? Two phrases from the morning sermon pushed into her consciousness—a soft answer turns away wrath and pride goes before a fall.

"Sirs." She paused to gain time to organize her defense. Despite fleeing their country and king to save their souls by living in exile, these religious dissidents were still proud of their heritage. "As an Englishwoman, sirs, may I know the details of the charges against me that I may answer them truthfully before God and man?"

The elders exchanged glances. At the end of the bench, Matthew's father said, "Under English custom, she has the right."

Penelope looked at Mr. Prince. Despite three months of betrothal to his son, she still didn't know if the father approved of her or merely acquiesced to his son's awkward circumstances.

Meanwhile the face of Mr. Brown evolved from anger to a poorly contained smirk. Why had he always resented her? He had nearly prevented her acceptance by this congregation, which she had joined as a requirement of the betrothal.

"You are accused of roving the streets of Amsterdam without a guardian and of wearing clothes that mock God and are unbecoming to a member of this congregation."

She involuntarily glanced down at the russet cloak that protected her slender body from the chill of the unheated church but not the harsh glare of the deacons. Fortunately, russet was one of the somber earthen colors, along with the grays of stones, the tans and browns of soil, and the dark green of forest shadows, these former Puritans preferred.

With a look of pleasure, Mr. Brown continued. "Furthermore, you're accused of accepting money from a known philanderer and of kissing him in public."

Speechless and mouth agape, Penelope stared at the elder. He practically accused her of being a harlot. Never in her twenty-one years had anyone so brazenly assaulted her character. Just before she called him a liar, she realized insulting the chief elder would eliminate her from the congregation more quickly than actually being a whore. Jesus had forgiven a prostitute.

Why would the chief elder say such a thing? Surely he had confused her with someone else. She looked around for Matthew even though she knew he wasn't there.

Her attention snapped back into focus when Mr. Brown said, "I take your silence as a confession."

Penelope selected her words with care and almost whispered directly to the chief elder, "No, it isn't. When and where did this alleged activity occur?"

Mr. Brown half rose from the bench and shook a finger in her face. "In the forenoon of Tuesday this week in the Westermarkt, I saw you with that Jew who buys and sells used clothes from a pushcart. He placed coins in your hand, hugged you, and kissed you."

Memories of Tuesday activities swirled through Penelope's head. Yes, she had transacted business with a peddler in the Westermarkt, the crowded marketplace by the western church. The peddler didn't look like a Jew, but Amsterdam's tolerance attracted all kinds.

Her chest heaved in indignation and her face warmed. "What you saw, sir, was me selling mother-of-pearl buttons to a merchant in a public market. When he placed the coins in my hand, he yanked me close and whispered lewd suggestions in my ear."

"So you confess he kissed you?"

With a deep breath she restrained herself from shouting. "No, sir. I confess I slapped his face and stomped his foot to free myself."

Mr. Brown jumped up, almost knocking over a candle. "Do you accuse me of bearing false witness?"

Fearful, as though standing on the edge of a deep abyss, she recalled the scene. The likely location for Mr. Brown would have been the bridge over the Prinzengracht, the Prince's Canal, twenty yards from where Penelope encountered the clothing merchant. "I believe you had a poor vantage point for witnessing a distant altercation and left before the squabble was resolved with my honor intact, if not my pride."

Still standing, Mr. Brown smiled like a cat with a bird in its mouth. "So you admit you were in the Westermarkt without a guardian and you own a dress with gaudy buttons."

Trapped by her own words, Penelope refused to surrender. "I admit I inherited dresses from my mother that are inappropriate for this congregation. That's why I sold the buttons and donated a tithe to this church."

"Were you alone in the Westermarkt?"

Why did he harp on this point of being alone? Thousands of women freely roamed the streets daily. Unlike London, Amsterdam was perfectly safe, at least in daylight, except for pickpockets and the *musico*s near the wharves where mischievous sailors gathered. "I admit to being a housemaid for a righteous Dutch lady who would never tolerate misbehavior."

Mr. Williams loomed over the table and shouted, "Your defense is you're a maid of Amsterdam? Throughout Europe, the maidservants of this immoral city are famed for their brazenness, their freely given kisses to men in alleyways, their hasty journey to damnation in the music halls and brothels along the Damrak."

Waving an accusatory finger with each phrase, he thundered, "The only women more vile than the maids of Amsterdam are their mistresses, who cover their bosoms with lace, redden their lips like harlots, and dance until God's dawn reveals their iniquity. Then they have the audacity to take communion in a former papist church that boasts stained glass windows with idolatrous pictures of Christ."

This denunciation had nothing to do with her, yet she could not refute it, having heard much worse about the women of Amsterdam from neighborhood gossip. She searched for a rebuttal but came up empty. She clutched the fabric of her skirt in disgust at this inability to defend herself and felt her legs tremble as fear crept upward to her heart.

After the speaker ended his harangue, Matthew's grandfather cleared his throat. "Elder Williams, I'm honored you have listened so closely to my sermons about Sodom and Gomorrah. These evils, which you depict so vividly, do indeed flourish in this wicked city. I trust you're describing your fears for what might befall this innocent child and not enumerating her sins."

Reverend Prince's mention of innocence buoyed Penelope's spirits, yet his Cambridge-trained intellect could turn an argument or an opponent upside down in seconds. Into her mind crept a German proverb her father had recited after a voyage across a stormy Baltic Sea: Wealth lost, something lost; honor lost, much lost; courage lost, all lost. Without courage, she could forget her dreams and her future. She clenched her fists to quell her fears and steady her heart.

The aged minister didn't embarrass Mr. Williams by waiting for an answer but rose from his chair, favoring his rheumatic knee as he moved to stand beside Penelope and to face the elders with her. "I'm familiar with the child's history. She was quite young when her mother died. Her father was an Anglican merchant but nevertheless an honorable Englishman, who died in a shipwreck in the Baltic Sea a few years ago, leaving his orphaned daughter penniless. She's an only child with no male relative to serve as guardian whilst she performs her daily chores amidst the numerous temptations of the Dutch."

Penelope lifted her head enough to see Mr. Williams still glowered at her. Matthew's father met her gaze but his face was impenetrable. Did they expect her to grovel for forgiveness for their unfounded suspicions?

Reverend Prince switched from a conversational tone to his sonorous preaching voice. "To preserve her soul from temptation, we should invite her to live with our God-fearing flock here in our neighborhood on Bloom Alley. Who's willing to provide her with a bed and a job?"

Each elder avoided the reverend's eyes and the oblique request for money.

"Ah, there's the rub," said the minister, half turning to cast a sad glance at Penelope. "We're as poor as she is."

Reverend Prince directed his attention to his son. "Thomas, would you like a healthy daughter-in-law to join us and fill our cramped house with more children?"

Penelope scrutinized her future father-in-law, both curious as to how he would answer this intriguing question and discomfited at the prospect of babies. Such responsibilities weren't in her plans.

Mr. Prince shrugged. "Yes, sir, but I'm in no haste for such a blessing."

Was his reply a sign of approval or a polite non-answer? Again she tried to interpret his face but learned nothing except he could out-stare her. The others remained silent. A gusty wind set the candles to flickering. Flickering like her hopes.

Reverend Prince limped a few steps away and stood where he could see both the woman and the five elders. "Miss Kent, that dress you're wearing. Was it your mother's?"

She opened her cloak to display a twenty-year-old dress of tan velvet. Did these men know its original price exceeded their wages for a week of hard labor? "Yes, sir, I removed the ruffles and lace and sold them to a ..." She paused, about to mire herself deeper into this swamp, then quickly rushed on. "To a merchant. Then I added a hem of dark linen." She smoothed her skirts to better display the cheap border brushing the floor.

"Why did you wear that dress today?" Reverend Prince asked.

Penelope lowered her head in guilt. Her mother's ornate dresses clashed with the drabness of this congregation. "Most of my mother's dresses are…are of a prideful color, sir. I would be embarrassed to wear them to this church."

"How many men have you kissed?"

Her head jerked up and she covered her mouth with a hand. Was there no end to their insults? But the reverend had asked and his eyes displayed sympathy not deception. She must trust someone for she couldn't rescue herself from this predicament. *In for a penny, in for a pound* was another of her father's favorite expressions and she feared she was already three shillings deep. She lowered her hand and resumed her diligent study of the floor, praying the truth would set her free. "None, sir. That is, none on the lips, sir."

"Not even your betrothed, my grandson?" Reverend Prince asked gently.

"No sir, only on the cheek. Only twice on the cheek, sir." Her own face grew warm. Those kisses had been from happiness not lust but these old men were too obsessed with sin to understand innocence.

"Elder Williams," said Reverend Prince, more loudly, "perhaps you have some questions." The reverend moved slowly to his chair, which creaked from his weight.

Williams looked to his companions on either side but received no guidance. "These dresses of a prideful color, why do you wear them?"

She swallowed and forced her voice to remain calm. "Sir, I cannot afford new ones."

"Trade them to a respectable merchant for plainer clothes."

"Yes, sir. I'll do that."

The silence stretched toward a minute in length. She dared to raise her eyes enough to see the elders looking dourly at each other.

At last Mr. Williams said, "You're excused, Miss Kent. We'll proceed with budgetary matters."

With lips tightened to prevent uttering a parting remark she would soon regret, she turned away. Exoneration didn't erase the insult. Nor did one victory end this war with Elder Williams. She turned back in surprise when Matthew's father said, "I'll escort the girl to my house."

Penelope and Mr. Prince walked down their separate sides of the church to their separate doors and strode the cobblestoned streets toward the Prince household. Rather than ponder Matthew's absence and his father's presence, she forced her attention to the neighborhood.

A flurry of wind parted the low-lying clouds to give her a glimpse of the city's thirty-foot-high fortifications that both protected and imprisoned her. Only a generation ago, Amsterdam's city walls had leapfrogged a half mile, converting straight rows of orchards into straight rows of houses to accommodate the city's burgeoning population. Changing the French word *jardin* to Jordaan and naming a street Bloemstraat and a canal Rozengracht hadn't made this new section of Amsterdam into a garden. The narrow streets and small houses of low rent contrasted sharply with the prosperous Herengracht, where Penelope had always lived, though not always in the maid's garret.

"My wife's quite skillful at making dresses from whole cloth," said Mr. Prince. "The dye house where I work converts their mistakes into dark shades they sell cheaply. My son must learn a wife comes with expenses."

"Thank you, sir." She studied his countenance but saw only the chill of the weather and the resemblance of three generations of men: Reverend Thomas Prince, Mr. Thomas Prince, and Matthew Prince. "That's kind of you, sir." But every guilder spent on fabric delayed their mission. Maybe his wife could salvage fabric from outmoded clothes and convert them into acceptable garments, though she was reluctant to ask for favors from her future mother-in-law.

"Miss Kent." Mr. Prince hesitated. "Matthew desired to speak on your behalf but I ordered him to stay away. The other elders don't believe in his mission from God and therefore don't trust his judgment on other matters."

Her anger at Matthew's abandonment now transferred to the father. "Do you, sir? Do you believe Matthew heeds a call from God?" Had she spoken too harshly? She half wanted to retract the question and half wanted to hear his answer. She compromised by watching the cobblestones instead of his face. He stopped and she turned back.

Thomas Prince stared in her direction but not at her, his grim face lost in thought. Finally he said, "Before Matthew was born, Mr. Blossom, a friend from the Leiden congregation, invited me to accompany him and his eldest son on a voyage to what turned out to be the Plymouth colony. I was a doubting Thomas. The ship sailed without me."

Why did he tell her this? Before today they had never had a conversation more than two sentences long. Curiosity overwhelmed anger. Did Matthew know his father had once rejected an opportunity to voyage to America?

Penelope searched for a meaningful reply. "Did your friend voyage to America?"

"No. The second ship wasn't seaworthy and a third of the passengers remained behind. Mr. Blossom thought it was the Will of God that he and his son should return home to Leiden."

She spoke reverently, asking him as well as herself, "Who understands the Will of God?"

"Indeed." Mr. Prince now stared at her. "Mr. Blossom's son died in Leiden that winter, not in America. Years later, the man took his wife and younger children to Plymouth."

She didn't know what to say. Did Mr. Prince believe the Blossom boy's death was God's punishment for the father's lack of faith? How does one tell the difference between a coincidence and the Will of God? Or the whispers of the devil? "Why doesn't God protect his faithful?"

"If only the faithful prosper, where's the challenge?" Mr. Prince resumed walking.

She strode beside him, glad she had taken the trouble to sew pebbles into the skirt's hem to prevent the embarrassment of a blustery wind revealing her stockinged ankles.

Half a block from his house Mr. Prince asked, "Miss Kent, do you believe in Matthew's quest?"

This time it was Penelope who halted.

Chapter 2

Amsterdam

Sunday, November 10, 1647

Mr. Prince's question perplexed Penelope. How could she explain why she was willing to sail to the edge of the earth with his son? Love was not the answer. She agreed with the congregation that love between a man and a woman was a vanity that created more harm than good. Shakespeare, the Bible, and neighborhood gossip offered numerous examples.

Reverend Prince had hit the nail on its head: she had no male guardian to accompany her through the streets of Amsterdam and no one to safeguard her across the ocean. She was a poor English girl trapped in a rich Dutch city by the lack of a protector.

Unless she married.

Unless she married Matthew, who dreamed of voyaging to America to fulfill the Will of God but needed someone to believe in him and to assist him. They needed each other.

Multitudes had married for worse reasons.

She might tell Matthew's father that God called her too. But in her dreams the voice of her father whispered, "Follow the waves."

Despite what Reverend Prince believed, the tempestuous Baltic Sea had not swallowed her father. A long-delayed, water-stained letter explained he had embarked on an earlier ship from Danzig and sailed to America to seek his fortune. Four years without an additional word implied he was dead, as did her nightmares that his bones lay abandoned in a distant land, awaiting burial.

She answered Mr. Prince's question with partial honesty. "I believe...I believe I'll serve God by serving Matthew."

Her future father-in-law stared at her. What did he see in her face? Hopefully, not the truth.

After they entered the kitchen, Mr. Prince said, "I'll have Matthew escort you home. I advise not coming to second worship today. Let the elders forget about you for a week."

How serious was her predicament if missing worship was advised to improve it? Perhaps this was a case where the better part of valor was discretion. To spend the remainder of the afternoon reading her father's books of Greek adventures and English dramas, those familiar stories first heard from his lips, would give her a sense of his presence and a sense of belonging.

* * * * *

In the parlor of the Prince home, Matthew waited for Penelope to return from the inquest. Anxiety interfered with his duty to honor God on this Sabbath by studying His Book. He felt remorse that he wasn't present to defend her at her trial. Or did he feel guilt that he had doubted his father's judgment or because he had obeyed his father instead of his own conscience?

What would he do if the elders condemned her? How could they? Years of civil war in England had destroyed any hope for religious toleration there. The king and the Puritans would as soon kill Anabaptist heretics as each other. On the other hand the temptations of Holland lured many of the flock away from the paths of righteousness. Like the Separatists in Plymouth and the Puritans in Massachusetts, the future of the congregation depended upon finding a new home far from Europe, a quest that required Penelope's assistance. Who else in the congregation understood the intricacies of voyaging? Who else had the courage to abandon home and hearth to accompany him across an ocean?

He compelled his eyes to focus again on the margin note beside verse Matthew 7:13 in his Geneva Bible: "we must overcome and mortify our affections, if we will be true disciples of Christ." He understood the need to subdue his emotions to follow the narrow path to Heaven. But which emotions? Certainly lust, greed, and the rest of the seven deadly sins.

His excitement about this mission was evidence of faith in God, not a transgression.

Matthew concentrated anew on the words of Jesus, words that should have special meaning to someone named after the author of the first gospel. Even Jesus had been tempted. Resisting temptation was the true mark of a Christian.

Despite his best intentions, his thoughts drifted back to the day when he had revealed his mission from God to Penelope and she had immediately offered to assist, the day when he had received his first clear sign God approved of his quest to find a new home for the congregation. That God worked in mysterious ways—using an Anglican girl to lead him to the God-forsaken docks of Amsterdam—was never in question. The only miracle was that God approved of Matthew's quest and sent this angel to help him.

Upon the opening of the kitchen door, the sound he had been awaiting, he rose and hurried toward his guide to the New World. His father met him at the doorway between kitchen and parlor and pulled him aside, but Matthew had already glimpsed Penelope slumped like a sack of laundry at the far side of the kitchen.

Father said, "They dropped the accusation."

"Thank Jesus for His mercies," said Matthew. Why then was Penelope so sad?

"Also thank your grandfather. He spoke well." The father gently turned his son's head away from the girl. "However, the elders remain suspicious of a maiden who lives outside this neighborhood where they can't scrutinize her behavior."

Matthew forced his gaze upon his father. "What can we do?"

"Miss Kent mustn't enter or leave the neighborhood unless an honorable person accompanies her. As for her duties as a maid, there's little we can do but trust in God and beg her not to venture near the Westermarkt where someone from the congregation might notice her."

"It's not her fault." Matthew couldn't imagine Penelope ever doing anything immoral.

"Either marry her or forget her."

Matthew drew back. "Forget her? God sent her to me. This inquest was a test of our faith."

Father sighed. "Is your purse full of silver?"

How could anyone think of money at a time like this? Yet Matthew dutifully answered, "I've saved eighty guilders and I have a chest half-filled with carpenter's tools. Penelope advises metal is scarce in America and iron knives sell well to the natives."

Rubbing the back of his neck, Father sat down on a bench. "But you can't sell goods until you get there. Save your money for passage."

His father, who had never encouraged his mission before, now urged him to leave. Surely God had intervened. Everyone should be happy and excited, yet Matthew saw only worry. Father rested his forearms on his knees and studied the floor, and Penelope still leaned listlessly against the doorjamb. What had happened at the inquest?

Without looking up, Father asked, "Does the girl have sufficient wherewithal?"

Matthew recalled a mention of bankruptcy after the sea had swallowed Mr. Kent and his assets. "I think she inherited some jewelry from her mother."

"Ask if it's enough to cover her passage and her needs. Go now and take her home."

"But she'll miss second worship."

"She and the elders need a respite from each other." His father rose and walked away.

Matthew hurried through the kitchen toward Penelope. He wanted to rejoice in thanksgiving but she clutched her cloak tightly around her slender body as though to ward off physical blows and looked so subdued in spirit he hardly recognized her. Softly he said, "Father says it went well and I should walk you home."

She nodded, her gaze seemingly affixed to the floor.

To prepare to go into public, he straightened his stockings, checked that the ribbons of his trousers were securely tied below the knees, and hooked the laces of his boots.

Matthew and Penelope left the house. Side by side they walked east on narrow Bloemstraat, turned right into an even narrower alley called 2nd Bloemdwarsstraat, and joined the crowds on the wide pavement adjacent to the Rozengracht. He ignored the few canal boats that desecrated the Sabbath with work.

Each time he glanced at her, he felt guiltier for all she had done for him and how little he had done for her. He recalled an old argument with his family: he had mentioned Penelope offered to explain shipping and to guide him to the East India Company's shipyard across town in Oostenburg, back when he had thought to become a ship's carpenter.

Mother had said, "It's unseemly for you to go to such a place, especially with a comely young orphan."

Matthew knew he flushed. "Do you doubt me or doubt her?"

"If she walks alone," Mother said, "she risks her reputation. If you walk with her, you risk our family's reputation."

They compromised by having his sister Ruth, two years younger than Penelope, accompany them as a chaperone.

Risk. Matthew risked losing Penelope. Without breaking the Fifth Commandment, when should a man stop blindly obeying his parents and start acting for himself?

Now he said to her, "I should have been there with you."

She didn't look up. "No. The elders were correct. I've much to learn."

He took Penelope's arm to guide her through the happy crowds of vainly dressed Amsterdammers who hoped for sunshine to break through the clouds while they strolled in the cobblestone marketplace surrounding the soaring bulk of Westerkerk. Averting his eyes from the stained glass windows of the church, of which the local populace was sinfully proud, Matthew studied Penelope's face. Frowns of worry and doubt capped her dull and lifeless eyes.

They crossed a crowded stone bridge over the Herengracht and turned north.

He mulled his father's advice. "We should marry now and dispel the elders' concerns." He ignored his father's or-else words. He couldn't bear the risk.

"Now?" she echoed without emotion.

Matthew couldn't see her downcast face hidden beneath her hood. "For your protection."

"For my protection?" Her gray-green eyes briefly met his.

For years, she had been his messenger from God. Until the day he felt lust for her. *All these evil things come from within, and defile a man.*

Later words from the Book of Matthew comforted him: "But at the beginning of the creation God made them male and female. For this cause shall man leave his father and mother, and cleave unto his wife."

Long discussions with his parents and grandfather ensued over the suitability of Penelope as a wife. His mother granted she looked healthy enough for childbirth and was industrious enough. His father allowed no woman in the congregation was likely to marry him if he persisted in this dream of voyaging the world, whereas Penelope was knowledgeable and eager to sail. Grandfather insisted that first she proclaim Jesus as her personal savior and join the congregation.

Penelope did her part, being re-baptized into this congregation of Anabaptists, Brownists, Separatists, Mennonites, or a dozen other heretical names. What had he done besides talk?

As they approached her home, he stopped her and said, "Marriage will protect us both."

She turned her head away from him and toward the house where she lived.

* * * * *

A pair of pigeons perched where the cobblestones of the street abruptly ended at the bank of the Herengracht. They cooed their displeasure but waddled aside as Penelope shuffled backward out of the way of the milk delivery boy and his dog cart. To a life-long Amsterdammer who had never experienced water deeper than a laundry bucket, the stench of the murky canal created a barrier as effective as a stone wall.

Penelope pondered abandoning this ordinary Amsterdam brick house, twenty feet wide, four stories high, home for the entire twenty-one and a quarter years of her life. The extended beam and its pulley wheel for lifting furniture drew her eyes to the westward-facing garret window, from which she gazed each morning toward the distant land of America and the mystery of her father's disappearance. Her view moved downward past the second floor rooms where she and her parents had lived years ago.

A globe, a prized legacy from her father, stood on a table near the first-floor parlor window for the world to notice. Before he had left five autumns ago on that ill-fated voyage to Danzig in the eastern half of the Baltic Sea, her father had spun the globe on its axis. In remembrance of a game they played when she first learned geography, she had closed her eyes and placed a finger on the spinning globe, which slowed from friction and stopped.

When she opened her eyes, her finger lay on the east coast of North America. "The Virginias," she said.

Her father's finger traced a line up the coast as he named the colonies in order: "Florida, Virginia, Maryland, New Sweden, New Netherland, Connecticut, New Haven, Rhode Island and Providence Plantations, Plymouth Plantation, Massachusetts Bay, Canada. If I were a young man again, I would seek my fortune in the Virginias instead of the Baltic. Beavers as numerous as wharf rats. Forests as thick as a wheat field. Oak trees as tall as the sky. A pristine new world without the wars and troubles of this tired old one."

Penelope, then sixteen years old, clapped her hands. "You promised me a voyage when I'm grown. Can we go to America?"

He held her in his arms and kissed the top of her head. "To the Virginias and back would be six months or more. I only promised you a voyage to Lubeck. You might suffer seasickness."

Lubeck was the nearest port in the Baltic, only a week's voyage north to the mouth of the Baltic Sea and southeast through the Danish Sound to the German coast.

She hugged him tightly. "I'm your daughter. How could I get seasick?"

He wrapped an arm around her shoulder and escorted her to the stairs. "You can help me pack. What do I need for an autumn voyage to the Baltic?"

If she had been a son instead of a daughter, she would have packed her own bags. Father and son would have sailed together in the late October winds to the far reaches of the Baltic Sea.

Instead, she remained in Amsterdam and soon learned of Matthew's quest. Six weeks after that, on a dismal December day, news arrived that transformed her into an orphan.

If she had been a son instead of a daughter, father and son would have perished together in the icy Baltic waters. Instead, a daughter's dreams had perished with her father.

So she had believed until a tattered letter from the Massachusetts Bay Colony finally found its way to the

Herengracht a year after it had been written in Boston. A letter that contained more questions than answers. A letter that changed her dream of sailing with her father into a determination to sail to America to find her father. Or at least to discover what had happened to him.

Every morning and evening for the last four years, she had gazed westward from her garret window. For four years she had wondered and waited. Waited for what?

Of course, the original Penelope had waited for Odysseus for twenty years, but that was in the ancient world. This was the modern world with compass, sextant, and charts. This was the middle of the seventeenth century. How could a person vanish without a trace?

Chapter 3

Amsterdam

Sunday, November 10, 1647

A break in the clouds poured sunlight into Penelope's eyes, breaking her trance and transporting her from ancient sadness to current dilemma. She was taken aback to see Matthew standing next to her on the street beside her house. But she wasn't surprised her dreams, her father's dreams, and Matthew's dreams were all tangled together, either weaved thusly by the three Greek fates, predicted by Macbeth's three witches, or predestined by Father, Son, and Holy Ghost.

Matthew stepped in front of Penelope, blocking her view. "We belong together."

Belong? Where did she belong?

Not in Matthew's congregation of Anabaptists, though she had satisfied their queries and participated in their ritual of rebaptism. She was a fraud, scarcely comprehending their philosophy of a personal Jesus and resenting their restrictions on her freedom. Or worse, she was an actor, creating illusions.

Not in England, which she had never seen and which now was engulfed in civil war between the Puritans and the king's supporters. She had written letters announcing her father's death to relatives, mere names and villages in his personal papers, but none had answered.

She belonged on the open sea in pursuit of her father and his dream. Only one path to that goal was discernible.

Matthew was a man of his word. Once he took her unto "death do us part," he wouldn't abandon her despite objections from the church elders. A betrothal was only a proposal, whereas matrimony was a contract. In Amsterdam, a contract was more sacred than a vow to God. A marriage to Matthew would be both.

In London, when a woman wedded, her husband took possession of her money and property and took away her name, whereas in Amsterdam a woman retained her name and her money through childhood, marriage, and widowhood.

Matthew was correct that the loss of her identity in marriage would protect Penelope from the church elders, who still conducted themselves like Englishmen. Instead of chastising a wife directly, they would rebuke the husband and expect him to punish the wife.

But marriage was a two-sided contract. What if Matthew received a new vision from God and renounced his mission to America? As a carpenter, he worked on tall houses. What if a fall from a ladder crippled him?

If she became trapped in Amsterdam as Matthew's wife, she would scrub her mother-in-law's floor forever and never learn the fate of her father. Alone, she was helpless. Wedded, her fate and Matthew's were inseparable.

Her father had often said the greatest risk was to take no risk at all. But he had taken a risk and hadn't returned. She must screw her courage to the sticking point.

Was she afraid of making a decision? Ah, that was the rub. No decision was a decision. If not Matthew, then whom? If not now, then when?

Matthew repeated, "Marriage will protect us."

Her hand crept to her neck to gather reassurance from the chain of the locket that hung between her breasts. She whispered, "The winter solstice."

Matthew's eyebrows lifted. "That's next month."

No, that was five years ago, the day she learned the ship her father was scheduled to be on was lost in a storm in the Baltic Sea. "The twenty-first day of December, the winter solstice, is a fine wedding day."

Matthew grinned broadly. "Any day is fine with me. That's not a Sunday, is it?"

"Anyone can look forward to the future in spring," she said as much to herself as to him. "Only a true believer understands days begin to lengthen and the future brightens after the winter solstice."

"The twenty-first day of December in the year of our Lord sixteen hundred and forty-seven." He said it like a prayer, like a promise to God.

Penelope felt a smile replace her frown, her first smile all day. Mathew's promise to God was better than a promise to her. "And then to America," she said. "Spring's the best weather for crossing the Atlantic. The spring of 1648."

Matthew said, "I've saved eighty guilders. Is that enough for two passages?"

"Almost enough for one. We need ten pounds each."

"Ten pounds?" Having been born and raised in Amsterdam, Matthew had little experience with English money. "Is that one hundred guilders?"

"Yes, ten pounds," she said. "Ten pounds to start a new life."

Matthew frowned. "Then we don't have enough. We'll have to wait."

"No waiting. I have the money," she said and thought *or I'll get it*. She stared at her garret window, mentally inventorying her mother's clothes and the paltry contents of her jewelry box. The bankruptcy lawyers had taken all her father's assets except the globe which she had persuaded them was the landlady's. But a crafty Dutch lawyer had drafted her mother's will to specifically bequeath everything to the daughter at age twenty-one and not to the husband to protect against merciless creditors. Were her mother's possessions worth enough? Probably not, but St. Nicholas's Day was a few weeks away and party-loving neighbors would hire additional help.

To search for her father, she would have to sell everything of her mother's—sacrifice the past for the future.

"Then we sail to the Virginias in the spring," he said. "God willing."

"If God be willing, we sail to New Amsterdam," she corrected. Matthew was indifferent to geography but she wasn't. To most Englishmen, the Virginias encompassed the entire continent between Spanish Florida and French Canada. She only desired that particular part of America that held the secret of her father's disappearance, most likely the island of Manhattan in the Dutch colony of New Netherland. And its port was New Amsterdam.

She stepped closer to this strong, self-absorbed man who would become her husband in a few weeks, her dress fabric brushing his knee. In his jubilation would he hug her on a public street, the elders be damned?

He put his hands on her shoulders and stared into her eyes. "God tested us to determine if we had the necessary faith. God believes in us as much as we believe in Him. Faith can move mountains. And cross oceans. Just look at the Plymouth Colony. If God be for us, who can be against us?"

She shivered and leaned her head against Matthew's shoulder.

Instead of hugging her, Matthew pulled back and took her hands. "Let us pray."

Penelope obediently bowed her head, oblivious of passersby and almost oblivious of Matthew's words of thanks to God. Many years ago, she had prayed for her mother's recovery yet her mother perished. For months she had prayed daily for her father's safe return yet he remained lost. Obviously God had little concern for the prayers of an orphan girl of scanty faith.

Now Penelope believed in the power of silver coins, sturdy ships, and the *Schiffahrkundebuch*, a Dutch seamanship book that had been inscribed to her landlady's eldest son, the lawyer who drafted Penelope's mother's will.

Did Matthew have any idea what awaited them in America? Or how to start a congregation? Or how he would persuade fellow church-goers to sail into the unknown?

On the other hand, what did she know about America, other than her father's dreams, sailors' tales, and a thirty-year-old copy of John Smith's *A Description of New England*?

Homer's *Odyssey* demonstrated the gods helped those who helped themselves. If Matthew's God wanted to aid too, that was fine. They needed all the assistance they could get, for she was a blind woman leading a blind man. Soon they would cross the proverbial Rubicon, after which one could never turn back.

Chapter 4

Amsterdam

Tuesday, December 3, 1647

Penelope lit candles in the wall sconces beside the mirror in her bedroom. Did Matthew's house have a reflecting glass? Surely one was needed not for vanity but to avoid slovenliness, a trait Matthew's younger sister Keziah was often accused of. On the other hand, with Mother Prince's omniscient eyes, why squander money on an expensive luxury?

Penelope, as her mother had long ago instructed, released her hair from its braids tucked under her white cap and brushed one hundred strokes. Dutch schoolgirls, those blue-eyed, flaxen-haired descendants of the Batavian tribe conquered by Julius Caesar, had often teased her with "gray-green eyes like a cat and brown hair like a mouse."

Penelope's father had said her eyes were the color of the storm-tossed waters of the Baltic Sea under a leaden sky. Her dark brown hair with sandy streaks reminded him of the dense forests of Poland in winter, with thickly studded tree trunks interrupted by occasional shafts of muted winter sunlight.

She laid her hairbrush on the dresser next to a copy of *The Unfortunate Voyage of the Ship Batavia,* the most exciting book in Holland that year, with its descriptions of a shipwreck and accompanying murder, debauchery, and aborted mutiny. Unfortunately, she could not discuss the book with Matthew, who would be outraged with such a profane, trivial waste of time, nor with his sister Ruth who couldn't keep such secrets.

Instead, Penelope endured nightmares her father had been caught up in a mutiny and slain in defense of its cargo. She should have ignored the rest of the book but still she read, becoming more and more convinced her father had been murdered. Why did God let evil people live?

She re-braided her hair, curled the plaits into a circle atop her head, and pinned them into place. She poured water from a pitcher into the wash basin, wet a cloth and scrubbed flour from her face. The tiny pockmark on the tip of her nose reminded her of her bout with measles just before her mother's death. She unlaced the neckline of her chemise, shrugged it to the floor, and stood naked before the mirror as she washed her torso, limbs, and private places.

Admittedly she didn't have the plump figure most men associated with health and prosperity nor the face of Helen, worthy of launching a thousand Greek ships. She was interested in the launching of only one, her ship to America. Before the launch was the marriage.

Would Matthew object to her plan to live together in this garret room? Her landlady, Liesbeth, was agreeable, expecting his repairs around the house to compensate for the food he ate, although Liesbeth didn't know big-boned Matthew ate like a bird, that is, like a seagull devouring every edible thing in sight. The alternative was sharing Matthew's pallet near Mother Prince's hearth. The lack of privacy was less abominable than Mother Prince's habit of ordering Penelope to knead dough, scour floors, or scrub laundry on each visit to the Prince household except Sundays, a day free of most physical labor.

Penelope believed she knew enough to be a wife. She had changed diapers on male babies. Most men discreetly urinated in alleyways but some flaunted their anatomy. And of course street mongrels had no shame at all. When a group of hired cooks gathered to prepare a neighbor's feast, they told a myriad of ribald tales about husbands—theirs as well as others. Fellow housemaids offered sly innuendos about their suitors. Nevertheless starting a marriage with a virgin bride and virgin groom in one bed seemed an ill-conceived custom.

Adjacent to a clean chemise in a drawer was a small packet of herbs wrapped in paper, a recent gift from Giesel, a neighbor's maid with an odd sense of both humor and morality, who claimed a decoction at the proper time would prevent pregnancy before marriage. Penelope didn't trust Giesel, who, according to gossip, was well along the slippery path to Hell or at least to the *Spinhuis*, the charitable home where orphans and unwed mothers eked out a bare existence spinning wool and linen fibers into thread. No wealthy father would allow a son to marry Giesel, a lowly household maid, despite a boy's naïve vows of eternal love.

Before the wedding wasn't Penelope's worry. The few times she had observed lust in Matthew's eyes or trousers, she also perceived his immediate embarrassment, reinforced no doubt by Reverend Prince's frequent sermons on the evils of fornication as well as the mortification of confessing intimate sins before the congregation.

The true danger was her husband's lust after the wedding. Traveling was difficult enough without the encumbrance of a child in either womb or arms, not to mention the danger of giving birth in an uncivilized locale.

Noises from downstairs suggested Matthew's arrival. The celebration of a mere birthday, even a seventieth birthday, was too frivolous for Separatists, but not for Liesbeth Rykersz, Penelope's employer.

Penelope quickly donned a clean chemise, a dress, an apron, and a stiffly starched cap. Before racing downstairs barefoot, she verified all strands of hair were carefully concealed beneath her cap as they should be until the wedding night and blew out the candles in the wall sconces. As she descended the stairs, she automatically dusted the banister with a corner of her apron.

* * * * *

A five-decade-old habit of protecting her wedding porcelain from careless maids compelled Liesbeth Rykerz to watch Penelope gently place the good Delft porcelain from the supper table into a tub of warm water and cut slivers of fragrant bath soap, not the common lye soap. What's the use, she thought. Whichever daughter-in-law inherited the dishes would sell them to buy that outrageously expensive and ugly pottery from China. Red dragons, indeed!

Liesbeth glanced at Matthew, the handsome young man seated to her right, who displayed manners, so rare among young people these days.

In a few weeks the girl would marry him. In a few months they would sail away. Instead of feeling happy for Penelope or sad for herself, Liesbeth felt old. Generations come and generations go, and there was nothing she could do about it. Except to stare at Penelope and see Mary of twenty years ago. It wasn't her imagination. More than once, Liesbeth had caught John Kent opening his polished brass locket and comparing the miniature painting of his deceased wife with his living daughter.

The impending marriage reminded the old woman of how many years had passed since her own husband had died and then her three sons had married and moved out of her home. She had rented the main floor to John Kent and his young bride Mary mostly to prevent a daughter-in-law from moving in.

After Penelope was born, Liesbeth taught the little girl to speak Dutch while Mary taught her English. Then Mary and her infant son died from childbed fever even though John hired the best university professors to attend her. A decade later, when John died, Liesbeth hired Penelope as a maid to fulfill a promise to look out for the child if fate took a wrong turn. Also she felt too old to share her house with strangers and didn't need to accumulate more money for those contemptible daughters-in-law to inherit.

Penelope brought to the table the package the confectioner had delivered that afternoon. "Chocolate, *Mevrouw* Liesbeth? You'll be buying a fashionable new dress next."

Liesbeth had worn black since the death of her husband twenty-five years ago. "My fashion taste may be dead but not my tongue or my brain. Geertruid next door assures me I could make as much money speculating in chocolate as I did in tulips. Penelope, your sense of fashion must be dead too. Being wedded in mourning clothes seems uncivilized."

"It's brown like chocolate, not black."

"Mrs. Rykersz," said Matthew, "need I remind you of the words in First Timothy that women should adorn themselves in modest apparel, not with braided hair, or gold, or pearls, or costly array?"

As usual, men quoted Saint Paul. Sometimes, the English words were odd but Liesbeth knew her Dutch Bible as well as Matthew knew his English one because she had forty years more experience. Matthew's views were not so different from her minister's sermons against the wickedness of this city, sermons that were mostly ignored.

Liesbeth fished sewing scissors out of her apron pocket and snipped the wick of a candle to stop an annoying flicker. "Brown isn't the only modest color. Can't you make exceptions for the most important day in a woman's life?"

"But her day of re-baptism was her most important day," Matthew said.

Liesbeth shook her head at such a self-assured young man. If these dissidents and the overly educated Dutch Reformed *domines* argued less about the timing of baptism and whether you needed an education to interpret the Bible, both God and man would be happier.

"Matthew, you've so much to learn about life," said Liesbeth. "And women." She grinned at Penelope.

Matthew sat up straighter. "Jesus only participated in two religious ceremonies: baptism and Holy Communion."

"He attended the wedding in Cana," rejoined Liesbeth.

"As a guest," Matthew said. "And arrived after the ceremony. Jesus approved of marriage, but He didn't consider it religious."

Liesbeth turned to Penelope. "You're so quiet tonight. What do you think?"

Penelope licked her spoon with its residue of dessert. "I fear ministers will add chocolate to that long list of sins."

Liesbeth chuckled and said to Matthew. "When you consider how many lawsuits involve children and inheritance, marriage is mostly a legal arrangement between a man, a woman, their children, and their money."

"Oh, speaking of money," said Penelope. "Matthew, you did bring it, didn't you?"

Matthew removed a heavy pouch from his inner coat pocket and slowly slid it across the table to his betrothed with a frown. "Do you wish to count it?"

"No." She smiled and placed a hand upon Matthew's. "I trust my future husband."

He looked uncertain. "Then why do you pay for our passage now?"

"I've faith in God and in the three of us. As to the rest of the world, there's many a slip twixt the cup and the lip." Penelope raised her beer mug. "To Godspeed on our marriage, our voyage, our destiny."

As the two women clinked mugs, Matthew frowned and shook his head. Penelope lowered her cup without drinking.

Liesbeth drank carefully to prevent spilling a drop and voiding the wish. How could these Mennonites consider a joyous toast to be an affront to God? She had watched this interplay with interest, admiring Penelope's gaining control of the family money well before the marriage ceremony, feeling sorry for the girl's failure to challenge Matthew on other things.

"No wedding dress!" Liesbeth said in a dramatic voice. "No church ceremony! And then you sail away! What else?"

Penelope wrapped an arm tightly around Liesbeth's shoulder either to comfort her or to restrain her. "Remember St. Paul's words about gold?"

"No." Liesbeth stared at Penelope's bare fingers. "You mean you won't have a marriage band?"

"Wedding rings are a pagan superstition endorsed by papists and ancient Romans." She pointed to the moneybag. "The money's better spent on our journey."

Matthew said gently, "God will know we're married."

"How will God know if you don't invite Him to the ceremony?" asked Liesbeth.

Penelope halfway rose from her chair and almost shouted, "Cease, please!"

Liesbeth felt ashamed, goading Matthew at a time when they should be rejoicing.

"I'll be married according to the beliefs of the congregation, my beliefs, as well, now."

Penelope continued in a gentler tone. *"Mevrouw* Liesbeth, will you help me wash my entire body thoroughly with soap. Then I'll take Communion with Matthew and wear a simple dress to the magistrate's. We will take the vows and there will be no ring. Afterwards, there will be a wedding feast. Then my husband and I will go upstairs in this house to my...to our..." Penelope blushed. "To our bridal bed and go to Sabbath services the next morning and go to America in a few months."

Overcoming her embarrassment, Penelope gave Liesbeth a fierce look. "The only question is: will you be there when I say my vows?"

Liesbeth pulled her starched white cap tightly about her head. "I'll be there in sackcloth and covered hair so as not to offend with vanities."

Penelope threw up her hands in surrender. "It's a magistrate's office. Wear anything you wish, but come. I'll not wed unless you come to the marriage ceremony and the wedding feast."

"Of course, I'll be at the wedding feast." Liesbeth grasped Penelope and Matthew firmly by the wrists. "Because it will be held in this house."

"I'm not sure what you intend, Mrs. Rykersz," said Matthew, "but it must be dignified and finished by eleven o'clock. The next day will be the Sabbath. The congregation must be home in bed before midnight."

Liesbeth shuddered at the memory of the two-day wedding celebrations her sons and their profligate brides had thrown a generation ago. And those were mild compared to the current three-day spectacles of some of her neighbors. "I propose a simple feast such as Jesus attended at Cana: good food, good wine, and good cheer. You Mennonites do know how to laugh and rejoice, don't you?"

Matthew nodded. "We're always ready to rejoice at God's blessings. Good food and wine my grandfather will approve of. But no music, no dancing, no toasts, no blasphemy. And your paintings must be taken down."

"Ships, stormy seas, and my late husband are offensive?" She was more curious than insulted, remembering long-ago arguments about Dutch Protestants occupying former Catholic churches with statues of saints and stained-glass windows. At least, the beautiful windows survived.

"Sorry, ma'am. They are considered graven images."

"Young man, 'graven' is from the Dutch word 'to dig' and means incised into a surface or sculpted, not lathered on like paint."

"Please, *mevrouw*." Penelope's voice pleaded for restraint. "Matthew's elder brother was denounced by his family for becoming an artist."

Liesbeth had not heard that before. "I can understand being condemned for living like an artist but denounced for paint?"

Matthew didn't take offense. "Women are rebuked for paint on their faces and lips."

"And rightly so." Liesbeth frowned. "It's so disgusting to see beautiful young girls ruining their complexion with the new craze of cosmetic. You never saw that when I was a girl except on harlots and French women. And Penelope's beautiful globe. Is that graven too?"

"A globe's a tool," said Matthew, "like a construction drawing of a ship. It's not for entertainment. A tool may be beautiful if the beauty's not for the maker's vanity."

Liesbeth sighed. These Mennonites prattled on and on about the danger of vanities, pretty baubles of body and mind that were as significant and long lasting as the morning mist. Certainly the papists had carried vanities too far with golden statues of the Virgin Mary, but these English Puritans strayed too far in the opposite direction to banish all beauty. They made a pride of ugliness. Well, not ugliness but a pride of plainness.

"Matthew." Penelope reached across the table to take Matthew's hand. "I suggest we let Liesbeth and your grandfather negotiate the wedding meal."

Matthew stared at her hand holding his. "My mother will insist on cooking something."

"Certainly." Liesbeth smiled. "We can't expect Penelope to prepare her own wedding feast, can we? Send your mother and your grandfather to negotiate." As a widow who had tripled her money trading tulips with the best of Amsterdam's merchants, she could hold her own against an old preacher and an illiterate English housewife.

After Matthew departed, Liesbeth asked, "Have you paid the *voorleser* to proclaim the marriage banns at Westerkerk."

"Reverend Prince has announced it.".

Was a proclamation at any church other than the Dutch Reformed legal in Amsterdam? Liesbeth decided to pay the fee herself to prevent the vicious gossip that accompanied surprise weddings. A quick calculation revealed only two Sundays before the event. For an extra coin, the *voorleser* would read both the *primo* and *secundus* banns this Sunday and the *tertio* banns next week.

As Penelope swung the candle around, Liesbeth saw beneath the girl's cheerful demeanor. "Do you need a lawyer to prepare the prenuptial contract?"

"Oh, *Mevrouw* Liesbeth." Penelope hugged her. "A lawyer would charge more than we will possess after I pay for our journey."

From a few inches away, Liesbeth stared into the girl's eyes, eyes that didn't sparkle with happiness of a bride but dimmed with worry. "Child, I've watched you since birth. Do you truly know what you're doing?"

Penelope rubbed the locket beneath her dress like a good-luck charm. Liesbeth knew it was inherited from the girl's mother and was identical to her father's—brass like all good nautical equipment with a tiny painting inside.

The girl sighed. "As a young child, I dreamed of voyaging the world with my father. Later, I dreamed of marrying a sea captain as you did or a rich young merchant and sailing the globe. After my father died, after war broke out in England, after I realized how complicated the world is, after I realized I'm a woman without money or family... I don't know where I belong."

"You appear to be escaping from the pot of poverty into the fire of these zealots." The world was filled with fanatics, good and bad. Liesbeth's father had been one of the Sea Beggars, common Dutch sailors in small fishing boats, who risked their lives to drive the hated Spaniards from Holland, even joining the English in attacking the Spanish Armada, not that the English gave them credit.

Liesbeth eyed the girl critically. She had a faraway look again, the same gaze as when her father stared at his globe for minutes at a time. How could a woman be the physical image of her mother and mental image of her father?

"Do you love the young man?" asked Liesbeth. Many people said love of money or love of power was the root of all evil and love of another person was the root of all happiness and unhappiness. Moderation was the key, but young people never understood moderation.

"Matthew and America, America and Matthew. I can't separate the two. Living with Matthew in the bosom of his family is fearful. Going to America without Matthew is frightening. Going there with him is my destiny."

"Ah, the innocence and naiveté of youth." Liesbeth marveled at her own life—marrying the dashing son of a fishing boat captain and now being a rich widow with grasping daughters-in-law and ungrateful grandchildren. "Do you have enough money?"

"Yes, barely." Penelope kissed Liesbeth on the cheek. "All I need from you are prayers for good sailing weather."

No, Liesbeth thought, you need much more than that but you would never ask for help.

Chapter 5

Amsterdam

Wednesday, December 4, 1647

After the next morning's chores Penelope walked a mile north to the Herenmarkt, the market square at the juncture of the Herengracht with the Brouwergracht, or Brewers' Canal. A few hundred yards ahead lay the harbor, a flotilla of ships and the ever-present seagulls. She stopped to admire the masts stretching above the seawall.

She located the red-brick building of the *Geoctroyeerde Westindische Compagnie*, or Chartered West Indian Company, called the GWC by the Dutch. This organization held responsibility for the trade and defense of all Dutch colonies bordering the Atlantic Ocean.

Penelope entered the three-story building with a central courtyard, a tiny imitation of the sprawling offices of the prosperous East India Company on the other side of town.

"Passage for two to New Amsterdam in the spring, *mevrouw?*" echoed the clerk, who looked younger than she did and whose breath reeked of *nagelkaas*, a Friesian cheese made with cloves. The Dutch used *mevrouw* for both "miss" and "ma'am."

The clerk consulted his documents. "The schedule lists a provisions ship for Curaçao in the Caribbean in early March, but it immediately returns here with a load of salt. From Curaçao, you'll transfer to the next available ship to New Amsterdam."

"How long do we wait in Curaçao?"

He grinned. "Probably a few weeks. Freight for passengers to New Amsterdam is thirty-two florins per adult, half-price for children. Food is seven stuivers per day, payable in advance for one hundred days. Freight for baggage is five florins per hundredweight."

Penelope noted the GWC still called a guilder by its old name of florin, also the English word for a two-shilling coin. "Seven stuivers per day for one hundred days? That's as much money for food as for the passenger."

The young clerk shrugged. "Food is optional. You may bring your own, pay freight on it, cook it yourself, or eat it raw. Be sure to bring enough. The hundred days is an estimate. You settle for the exact cost at the end of the voyage."

In her head, Penelope computed the fare for two passengers, one hundred days of food each, and six hundredweights of baggage to be 164 guilders, slightly more than she expected and two guilders more than she had. Not to mention unexpected expenses. According to her father, long journeys always generated unforeseen cost.

Fortunately tomorrow was the fifth of December, the day before St. Nicholas's Day. Instead of a gaily wrapped gift left in her shoe, she expected payment from the housewives who had hired extra help during the previous weeks of holiday feasts and parties, a godsend for maids and cooks who needed extra money.

"Do you want insurance on the freight?" asked the clerk. "Only 10 percentum of its value."

Although many Amsterdam merchants routinely insured shipments, her father had claimed he, as the superintendent of cargo, was the insurance for his consignment.

The loud scrape of a chair on the floor distracted her and she locked eyes with an older man at a desk near a window. His piercing glance and bushy eyebrows made her shiver. She imagined him to be one of the murdering sailors from *The Unfortunate Voyage of the Ship Batavia*— now thirty years older but still bloodthirsty.

Contemplation of pirates and shipwrecks made her think again of insurance, but that expense would require more money than she could obtain.

"No." She smiled. "We'll trust in God."

"Your choice. As the proverb says: More people drown in a wineglass than in the sea."

She spelled the name Matthew Prince for the young clerk, so it wouldn't appear as the Dutch name Mathias Princen. She watched his laborious efforts, thinking she could handle the job twice as fast. No respectable company would hire a female even though many women did equivalent work within the protection of a family business.

"Your name?" the young clerk asked without looking up.

Penelope spelled it for him, for she had never heard of a Dutch woman with her name.

"Last name?" he asked.

She almost said "Kent" but paused.

In London, a clerk would assume she was Mrs. Matthew Prince and wonder why her husband wasn't arranging passage. The streets there were too dangerous for a girl to walk alone a mile across town with two guilders, to say nothing of nearly two hundred guilders.

The clerk looked up. "Last name?"

A premonition warned her not to announce to the world that Penelope Kent sought the whereabouts of John Kent. "Prince," she said to take advantage of being English in a Dutch world. Let the clerk think Matthew Prince and Penelope Prince were brother and sister.

The clerk calculated her fare three times and waved the paper gently in the air for the ink to dry. "The invoice is exactly 164 florins."

Penelope pondered turning her entire fortune over to the GWC versus stuffing the mass of silver back under a loose floorboard held down by one of her bedposts. What if the GWC went bankrupt? What if Lisbeth's house burned down? What if she or Matthew grew ill? Was she afraid to commit herself to this voyage? No, she persuaded herself, she was reluctant to entrust all her money to a stranger.

Within the confines of her apron, she hefted her 162 guilders of silver coins, wrapped in old newspaper like a lump of cheese. She hoped the clerk didn't hear the muted clink of money. "Do I accrue interest if I pay now?"

"Interest?" He glanced briefly at the old clerk by the window and chuckled. "No."

"Then why should I pay early?"

The clerk shrugged. "If you don't pay in full within a fortnight of departure, then your names are removed from the list."

Where was the harm in waiting? "When further details are available on the ship and departure date, please send notification to Liesbeth Rykersz on the *Herengracht*. You won't forget, will you?"

He widened his eyes. "I remember all the young ladies who book passage with me."

Outside the GWC building, Penelope collapsed onto a bench in the garden to recover her wits. She had suspected a tired old man to be a murderer and had revealed her name and address to a young, underpaid clerk.

What kind of spy was she?

If her father had died of illness or accident, the authorities would have notified someone. But if her father was the victim of foul play, then the murderer would be apt to kill anyone investigating the disappearance of John Kent. She thanked her quick wit at calling herself Penelope Prince, a temporary lie. This would be her English name in a few weeks. She resolved to be more discreet in the future.

During the walk home from the GWC office, Penelope absent-mindedly followed two rich businessmen dressed in silk, one in black and one in bright colors. The crowds parted before them like the Red Sea because in Amsterdam wealth was royalty.

She reviewed in her mind the letter from her father, the letter she had long ago memorized and hidden:

Boston in the Mass. Bay Colony, 26th of March, 1643
My dearest daughter,
   Don't worry. I expect to be home in six months with wealth enough to astound even the landlady.
   I trust Master Nicolsen has shown you the accounts of the voyage to Danzig and you impressed him with your knowledge of ledgers as I had boasted. I did indeed retain 5 percentum to undertake this trip to America. Why? Because soon after departing Texel for Danzig, we discovered a German stowaway, whom I befriended when I learned he had spent years in America. Eventually I gained his trust and he told me an amazing story I dare not entrust to paper. Cherish this little talisman as a symbol of our future success, but show it to no one.

A drawing of an oval with ragged edges interrupted the words.

   The first part of my plan—pretending to be a distressed Puritan—was easy enough because the Puritan war had already begun by the time I concluded my transactions in Danzig and returned on an earlier ship, leaving my goods and instructions with Master Nicolsen.
   The second part—crossing the northern Atlantic in stormy winter weather—was ill advised. I feared the ship would be lost a half-dozen times.
   By good fortune, I made the acquaintance of a convivial Englishman, who has a plantation grant from the Dutch governor on the mainland adjacent to an uninhabited part of Manhattan Island, where riches of the earth await a knowledgeable hand to scoop them up. His first name is the same as mine and his last name the

*same as the tall, lean gentleman with the short, fat wife
who dined with us before my spring voyage to Lubeck.*

*With good fortune and God's grace, this successful
venture may land me on dry land for the rest of my life,
except for the voyage I promised my beautiful daughter.
With some of Master Nicolsen's profits, buy yourself a
gown of fine fabric so that you may celebrate my arrival
and impress some handsome young swain.*

Your loving father.

Again Penelope puzzled over the clues in the letter.
What kind of talisman, or good-luck charm, was an oval
with zigzag edges? A precious gem? As a penniless maid,
her only experience with rubies and emeralds was five
minutes browsing in a goldsmith's shop before being
evicted.

To extract wealth from the earth surely meant gold,
silver, or gems although no one had ever reported finding
such riches in any of the Virginias despite innumerable
attempts.

The German and Englishman were unnamed, as were
she and her father. The letter was even addressed to her
landlady, although Penelope had recognized her father's
handwriting and intercepted the correspondence as she
paid the messenger.

Her only usable clue was the reference to the English
planter. She remembered the odd couple because of the
political doggerel about Jack Sprat. But what was the
man's real name? Morton, no, Throckmorton. Had this
John Throckmorton guided John Kent or had he murdered
him? The German's tale had merely transferred her father's death from the Baltic Sea to an unknown locality
across the ocean, a spot she was determined to find.

She ignored the dichotomy of hoping he was alive and
wanting to find his grave.

The rich gentlemen entered the Exchange building on
the Dam, a large plaza at the center of town, before she
noticed where she was. This was a good omen because her

father's voyages truly began and ended at this building with the signing and fulfilling of contracts and transfers of money. With a hand on the jamb of the Exchange's doorway she felt her father's presence amidst the tumult of commerce.

*****

On Saturday morning, December 21, Liesbeth admonished the neighbor's cook not to burn the fowl—a fatted goose was frightfully expensive but appropriate for a wedding feast—and instructed two hired maids concerning separation of the Englishmen from the Dutch neighbors, "You can recognize these Mennonites by their clothes. They dress like starving ministers."

She now waited for Penelope and Matthew to return from Communion at the Separatist Church. Liesbeth wouldn't have attended even if invited. Those Mennonites took religion too seriously.

Noises at the kitchen door interrupted Liesbeth. She hugged Penelope, met Matthew's two cheerful sisters and his gloomy-faced mother, and showed them where to place the food they brought.

From the tower of the Westerkerk a few blocks away, the bell rang eleven times.

Matthew said, "The Stadhuis closes at one o'clock." The Stadhuis, or City Hall, was located a few blocks away on the Dam.

Liesbeth listened as the local magistrate read the wedding ceremony in Dutch from the Dutch Reformed prayer book and was somewhat disappointed at the simplicity of the five-minute ceremony. What did she expect? It was just another minor contract to them. No need for music or flowers. What was the purpose of a church if not to host beautiful weddings? Yet Penelope seemed satisfied, rather than happy, as though she had concluded a complex business transaction.

Back at Liesbeth's house, the neighbors came early and left soon after congratulating Penelope and learning there was no entertainment and the food was ordinary. After the

Separatist men completed their half-day of Saturday work, members of the congregation drifted in.

Liesbeth had the serving girls roll out a little wagon containing her gift—a ten-gallon keg of light red wine. Liesbeth asked Reverend Prince to say a prayer of thanksgiving before the maids filled the glasses from the anker of Spanish claret. This was as much of a toast as Liesbeth reckoned she would get.

Reverend Prince presented the couple an English Bible, emphasizing it was the latest Geneva version, not the king's version that the Anglican Church used. Wasn't a Bible a Bible?

The Mennonites offered prayers to the bride and groom while enjoying their Spanish wine with more enthusiasm than Liesbeth had expected from the dour group. She accepted the sound of happy voices babbling in English as proof of her success as a hostess.

Chapter 6

Amsterdam

Saturday, February 1, 1648

Six weeks later, Penelope raced down the cobblestones alongside the Rozengracht. Clutching her cap, she skidded around the corner into the narrow alley of 2nd Bloemdwarsstraat and almost collided with an old woman. Breathless, Penelope burst into the kitchen of the Prince household, waved a freshly printed broadsheet, and shouted, "Look!"

Mother Prince gaped. "I see a doxy with her cap askew and her bodice crooked."

Penelope tried to straighten her clothes with one hand as she continued to wave the single sheet of newsprint. "Did you hear the news?"

"News is no excuse for slovenliness and poor manners." Mother Prince stomped toward the cold draft blowing through the open door. "Did you come here alone? How many inquests will it take to teach you proper behavior?"

Penelope resisted the urge to retort and said quietly, "They agreed upon the peace treaty two days ago. Do you want to see?"

She offered the paper to Mother Prince, who turned away, and then to Ruth, who shook her head and wiped floured hands on her apron before attending to the renegade hair escaping down the nape of Penelope's neck. The younger sister, Keziah, quietly swept up the trash that had blown through the doorway with Penelope's entrance.

Mother Prince started to say more but the sound of Reverend Prince's cane in the hallway stayed her tongue. Penelope edged around the shrew and toward the hallway.

"Who's making enough noise to raise Lazarus?" asked Reverend Prince cheerfully as he entered the kitchen.

Penelope offered him the broadsheet. "The Spanish have signed the peace treaty."

"A peace treaty, at last? I'd given up hope for that in my lifetime." He patted his pockets. "You read it. I must have left my glasses in my closet," he said, referring to the small room where he studied and prepared sermons.

She trembled with excitement as she recited the news that washed across Amsterdam like a wave, "January 30, 1648. At Munster, in the province of Westphalia..."

"What's that to do with us?" interrupted Mother Prince, nodding to Ruth and Keziah to resume kneading dough. "The Spanish have behaved themselves for years."

"Ah, but do the papists acknowledge Dutch sovereignty?" asked the reverend.

The Dutch people's bitter struggle for independence from Spain had ended with the Twelve Year Truce of 1609. During the next four decades, Spanish kings claimed to be the rightful ruler of the land that now called itself the Republic of the Seven United Netherlands. Penelope had heard many tales of hostilities between Dutch and Spanish vessels on the high seas.

Penelope reclaimed her confidence. "Yes. And both countries renounce privateering. Don't you see? It's safe—"

"Safe?" Mother Prince scowled. "Nay, it's a fantasy instigated by the Devil to lure my son. He belongs here."

That Matthew should be sleeping in this house and Penelope kneading dough in this kitchen was what the older woman really meant.

Penelope, having grown up in the freedom of prosperous Amsterdam, pitied the woman constrained by a neighborhood that was fearful of anything new. These poor Brownists believed in freedom of thought but only the freedom to think what they already thought. They professed God's love for mankind but restricted God's love to themselves.

The young wife stared back. "It's now safe for Matthew to journey to America to fulfill his destiny." She placed a hand on Reverend Prince's arm. "Surely this is a sign that God approves of Matthew's mission."

Her eyes searched for reassurance in the reverend's weathered face. Sometimes Penelope had nightmares wherein she and Matthew sailed directly west, the route favored by the English across the treacherous North Atlantic Ocean, and were lost in a storm. Sometimes the nightmare took them southwestward where their throats were slit by Spanish pirates.

Reverend Prince patted her hand and beamed. "Yes, child. Our God of peace surely smiles upon you and Matthew. Let's have a prayer of thanksgiving."

Mother Prince glared at her father-in-law and then at her daughter-in-law.

The Westerkerk clock struck eleven as Reverend Prince intoned amen.

Penelope said, "There's still time to check on our ship." She almost knocked down Keziah on her way out, ignored Mother Prince's reprimands, and hurried alone the two miles to the Herenmarkt and the GWC building, not even pausing at the entrance to catch her breath.

The young clerk recognized her and answered her question before she asked. "*De Melckmeyt* arrived two days ago and is being unladed at Haarlem Point, before three weeks of repairs. Scheduled to depart for Curaçao on the first day of March."

Two days ago was the same day the treaty was approved—another sign from God.

She gasped her thanks to the clerk and sprinted out of the building north to Haarlem Point, dodging barrels, carts, and pedestrians to climb the steps to the top of the seawall overlooking the Zuiderzee where she studied the lines and the rigging of *de Melckmeyt, or The Milkmaid*.

The long, narrow, three-masted flyboat was the new simple design that, according to her father, made Dutch shipping the cheapest in the world. A flyboat needed only a master, one mate, and ten crewmen—half the number of a comparable English ship—and could sail closer to the wind. The hull curved in the middle, like a fat-bellied merchant, to create more cargo space with less deck, because the King of Denmark assessed tolls through the Sound at the entrance to the Baltic Sea on the width and the breadth of the deck.

De Melckmeyt was a full-sized ship of about three hundred tons, Penelope estimated, worn but not abused, a tough ship that had survived bad weather but not so old that shipworm damage would cause the vessel to leak or fall apart in a storm. From the mast fluttered a banner, three broad stripes of orange, white, and blue, the flag of Holland but adorned with the letters GWC superimposed on the central white stripe.

She could hardly wait to tell Matthew the sailing date. As Penelope adroitly dodged dog-carts and businessmen on their way to the Exchange, the name of the ship struck her: *The Milkmaid*. Why did the Dutch give their ships such meek names as *Crow* and *Swallow* whereas the English boasted brave names such as *Golden Hind, Lion,* and *Tiger* or inspiring ones such as *Adventure, Defiance,* and *Mermaid*? She remembered Liesbeth's fairy tales of Reynard the sly fox, who used his weakness to outwit his stronger enemies—lion, bear, and wolf. By assuming an unpretentious manner to deceive the enemy into overconfidence, the Dutch gave themselves an advantage.

Penelope smiled as she contemplated her ship's understated name.

Then she rejoiced even more thinking about her imminent departure from Amsterdam. No longer would Mother Prince hint Matthew deserved an English breakfast of hot porridge, bacon, and sausage instead of a Dutch breakfast of cheese, butter, and cold bread. No longer would the goodwives in the congregation scrutinize each article of clothing as though it revealed whether the soul of Matthew's wife was pure enough to journey to heaven. No longer would she be scolded for walking alone through the streets of Amsterdam as she did now.

Soon she would leave behind the Old World and venture to the New World where her father's spirit beckoned. She breathed a quick prayer of thanks to God that her destiny and Matthew's destiny were one and the same.

* * * * *

Monday morning, the third day of February, dawned clear and cold. Penelope hurried to get Matthew fed and off to work and the house cleaned. Upstairs, she shoved the bedpost off her hiding place and carefully counted out 164 guilders of silver coins and wrapped them tightly in a kerchief so they didn't jingle. Robbery was rare in Amsterdam but the clink of metal would attract pickpockets in any city. She stuffed six extra guilders into pockets sewn into the lining of her cloak in case the price had changed.

During the interminable mile walk to the GWC building at the Herenmarkt, she studied each barge on the canal and each house on the street as though to bid them goodbye. She pushed through a jam of pedestrians gawking at a busted barrel of beer and a city watchman arresting two vagrants lapping up the spoilage like dogs.

Outside her red-brick destination, she hesitated. In December she had lied to Matthew, telling him she had paid for their passages upon her first visit to the GWC. She had wanted Matthew and his family to believe the money was irrevocably committed and she and Matthew were irreversibly destined to voyage to America.

Should she wait until the final two weeks before departure? What if other passengers plunked down coin and filled up the ship despite the clerk's promises?

Hardly realizing where her footsteps led, she approached the harbor at Haarlem Point, climbed the steps to the top of the wide seawall that protected the city, and closed her eyes. Voices of strangers called to each other, seagulls squawked, wooden ships creaked. A chill breeze struggled against the pins that fastened her cap to her hair and wafted the aromas of tar, pitch, and spices to tease her nose. She pictured her father standing at the bowsprit of a Dutch flyboat, his coat open and blowing in the wind, his eyes fastened on the setting sun, a smile on his face. Was she as brave as her father? She had to be for his sake.

She opened her eyes to a mundane scene of sailors mending ropes and sails, porters handling barrels and crates, and vagrants looking for opportunities. One idler stared openly at her. With a black patch over one eye, he looked like a Cyclops.

Inside her apron pocket beneath her cloak, Penelope gently hefted two pounds of silver coins, a lump of metal that would purchase three months and six thousand English miles of travel. But not if she were robbed.

Penelope strode into the red-brick building, straightened her body to its maximum height, and stacked 164 guilders onto the zinc counter. She protected the coins with her hands and told the clove-scented clerk, "After the chief cashier has signed the voucher, if you please."

He stammered, "You...you don't trust me?"

"Even if you were my brother," she said, "I would still insist upon the chief cashier's signature."

The clerk approached the bushy-browed old man at a desk beneath a window and waited for him to abandon his quill and look up. Penelope pretended to study notices for a ship's carpenter for a voyage to the GWC colony of Pernambuco in Brazil and for seamen to Danzig.

Her father had often told stories of his trips to the Baltic region, where Protestant armies from Sweden or Catholic armies from Austria had swept across the land, leaving behind ten years of famine and pestilence for the surviving peasants of both religions. Those stories had been like the Trojan War, of faraway people, of faraway times.

The Puritan War in England was different, flooding her own Amsterdam with desperate exiles from her parents' homeland. For each soldier killed or maimed, an English woman became a widow or lost her chance to marry. Matthew had no reason to fight in this war because both Puritans and Anglicans despised Separatists.

The man she had imagined to be a former pirate limped toward her with stiff joints. "This is highly irregular."

Wasn't the job of a head cashier to be suspicious of everyone? "Is it prohibited?" she asked with a smile.

"No. But we have procedures." The old man was not impressed with smiles.

Penelope clinked her stacks of coins and locked eyes with the chief cashier. "*Meijnheer*, will you sign the voucher now or must I have my grandmother"—a small white lie about Liesbeth—"complain to one of the Nineteen Gentlemen who will ask why you caused so much trouble when this could be settled in a half-minute?"

The cashier frowned and stroked his chin.

Perhaps people often threatened to complain to the Nineteen Gentlemen, known as the *Heren XIX*, who were the directors of the GWC. She decided to make the threat more believable. "My grandmother bought more shares of GWC stock with her dividend when Admiral Heyn captured the Spanish treasure fleet in Cuba in '28. She would have done better to have invested in the East India Company instead."

The head cashier counted the coins, signed the voucher, and stalked back to his desk.

Apparently pleased to see the old man discomfited, the young clerk whispered, "You're fortunate to journey on a provisions ship. Curaçao often lacks food and has to reduce victuals." He winked as he handed her the voucher, "How many of the Nineteen Gentlemen does your grandmother truly know?"

Without looking up from the paper she studied like Matthew studied his Bible, Penelope said, "If she doesn't know all eight from here and two from Friesland, her friends do."

* * * * *

A few days before departure, Penelope sorted her meager possessions, deciding what to pack and what to sell. Liesbeth's slow footsteps echoed on the stairs to the garret.

"Dear child," Liesbeth said. "I've said too many farewells on windy piers over the years. I want to say 'God be with you' where it's quiet and warm."

Penelope's eyes sparkled with tears as they hugged. "I love you too."

Liesbeth reached into her apron pocket. "Take this little bag and secure it in your chest, next to your father's globe. I know that's packed safely. There's a note and a small remembrance. Don't open it until you're far to sea."

Deeply incised into the worn leather of the musty drawstring bag was a sailing ship. Surely this money pouch had voyaged often with Liesbeth's seagoing husband.

Penelope opened the secret compartment under the wooden framework of the globe and inserted the bag next to her father's letter. Her tears and embraces were thanks to the woman in whose home she had spent her entire life, the woman who filled the role of grandmother, the only person in Amsterdam she would care about after she left the only home she had ever known.

Chapter 7

Amsterdam

Monday, March 16, 1648

Repairs on *de Melckmeyt* took longer than expected, delaying the ship's departure by two weeks. Due to the intense activity in the busiest port in the world, the ship lost its prime place at Haarlem Point and anchored in the harbor awaiting final errands, crew, and passengers.

At last, Penelope stood on the pier below the seawall, basking in excitement and anticipation, surrounded by Matthew's kin and a few members of the congregation, who gawked at the ships. Refusing to allow her mother-in-law to spoil her joy, Penelope ignored the shrewish woman's scowls and breathed deeply of sea stenches and cargo aromas that recalled her father's frequent departures to faraway destinations. With the cliff of the massive seawall blocking her view of Amsterdam and water in front of her, the pier felt like an island. Her journey had begun.

Matthew's grandfather hugged Penelope and whispered, "I entrust Matthew's soul to God but his earthly body to you. You must be his father and mother as well as his wife."

"I promise to take good care of him," she whispered back. Here was a second person besides Liesbeth whom she would miss.

Matthew gripped his grandfather by the arms. "Until we meet again."

Grandfather Prince's eyes had a far-away look. "Until we meet again. Whether it be in Heaven or on Earth."

On a flat cargo net sat their two wooden chests, a heavy one of carpenter tools well sealed with pitch and another with clothes, books, and a globe, adjacent to the baggage of other passengers: ten Dutch soldiers, their corporal, and a farm family of husband, wife, and two young children.

Penelope kept a watchful eye on two idlers talking to the gantry operator. Were they looking for work or a chance to pilfer?

Matthew's sister Ruth whispered to Penelope, "I can't believe this is finally happening."

Penelope turned away from the scene of Mother Prince offering Matthew some honeyed oatcakes and begging him to forget this mad journey into the unknown. If Matthew succumbed to this lure—like Odysseus's men eating lotus leaves and forgetting their duty—then Penelope would rather go to America alone than become a slave in Mother Prince's household. Mother Prince hugged her son and refused to let go.

A bosun blew a whistle and proclaimed the barge was coming and the tide would not wait. Penelope signaled to Matthew, who gently pushed himself away from his mother. Turning away from her son, Mother Prince buried her face in her husband's shoulder. Mr. Prince's eyes were directed far beyond the ships, probably toward the voyaging opportunity he had missed three decades earlier.

At one end of the flat-bottomed barge the bosun lined up the passengers while at the other end the gantry operator cranked a windlass to raise the cargo net. Matthew's family and friends offered a hail of "Fare thee well" and "God speed you on your journey."

Soon Penelope lost sight of Matthew's family amid the multitude of vessels in the harbor. When the barge gently nudged against *de Melckmeyt*, seamen draped a rope ladder over the side. The senior oarsman told the soldiers to climb the swaying cables.

Trijn, the farmwife who was as plump as a dairy cow yet looked strong enough to lift one, stammered, "Do they...do they expect me to ascend such a flimsy rope?"

An oarsman laughed and called to a sailor above. "Drop the chair for the ladies."

A sturdy armchair dangled from a gantry above their heads and descended as three seamen manipulated ropes and pulleys.

Trijn backed away from the chair as though it were a wild animal. "Am I to entrust the lives of myself and my child to that contrivance?"

"Would you rather climb?" Penelope gathered her skirts and seated herself. "They call it the master's chair. The master of the ship." With a jerk, the chair rose and her body slid forward. She clutched the rough hempen ropes that passed through holes in the arms of the chair and hoped the gantry operator was free of distractions.

Despite the feeling she might fall out at any moment as the chair lurched skyward, Penelope released the rope from one hand and waved to Trijn and Matthew below. Seamen pushed the other end of a boom to swing the chair over the deck and loosened ropes to lower the chair. A sailor assisted her onto the solid planking of the deck.

Meanwhile, six-year-old Jan broke free from the hand of his farmer-father and scurried up the ropes like a wharf rat, forcing his father to follow. The chair descended and returned with Trijn and her daughter, Sophie.

Two sailors attached a hook from a second gantry to the cargo net containing the passengers' chests. Matthew climbed the ropes like the other men had done.

A well-dressed man of about forty years of age with sharp eyes and impatient gestures introduced himself as Master Pietersz and warned them not to interfere with the crew. Penelope maneuvered to the front of the clump of passengers and observed seamen attach a rope from the barge to a capstan near the bow and winch up the anchor.

With the rowers straining against their oars, the little barge tugged the ship away from the adjacent well-traveled vessels. The crew released the tow-barge and set one small sail. The helmsman guided the craft slowly through the waterfront where ships were as crowded as the houses of Amsterdam. Once clear of the harbor, seamen raised more canvas. Soon they lost sight of Amsterdam and sailed with the tide through the Zuiderzee toward the Noordzee, or North Sea.

The driver of a bullock cart waved to them from a road atop the wide, grass-covered levee that restrained the water, his head about even with the deck of the ship. Penelope looked down at the low-lying farmland on either side of the river.

Near a drainage ditch, four sails on a windmill revolved lazily, lifting water up into the river. As far as she could see, ditches crossed and re-crossed the muddy fields like canals through a city. She looked at Dirck, a tall sturdy farmer with a sun-reddened neck. "It hasn't rained for several days. Where does all the water come from?"

"Water seeps through the dike," Dirck said. "You can't stop it so you just pump it back into the river. Otherwise, the land's too wet to farm."

"Pump it forever?" Penelope asked.

"Forever is the life of a farmer."

When the Zuiderzee widened, the ship veered away from land. Windmills faded into the distance. The ship-master announced the weather was good, the moon was bright, and they would sail through the evening into the Waddenzee and on to the island of Texel, the last stop before the Atlantic Ocean, where they would wait for good breezes.

Penelope's father had told her Dutch vessels were fa-mous among sailors for their ample food. The crew consid-ered a ship to be merely a floating part of Holland and expected to be treated like Dutchmen. The GWC obeyed the naval guidelines for provisions per man per week: five pounds of meat, five pounds of bread, half-pound of cheese, half-pound of butter, two pounds of dried peas and beans, a quart of vinegar to thwart scurvy, and ample beer—more than sufficient for the strenuous hours of labor expected of the seamen. Unfortunately, fresh bread would be soon replaced by virtually indestructible ship biscuits, what her father had called hardtack, manufactured in huge quantities in Amsterdam's busy bakeries.

After a plain but generous supper of Amsterdam bread, cheese, and beer, Penelope and the other passengers retired to their hold with its metal-enclosed candles. The corporal organized his soldiers at one end of the hold. The six civilians milled at the other end. Penelope looked around in confusion. Her father had never described the details of setting up housekeeping in the ship's hold.

Two sailors appeared and opened a storage locker that in the dim light looked like any other part of the wall. They stretched out sailcloth partitions and fastened the grommets on obscurely located hooks in the ceiling beams. Within fifteen minutes, half of the open hold was partitioned into private rooms with hammocks dangling from the low beams.

From the top of the ladderway, the last sailor said, "This hatch cover will be fastened from the outside at night for your safety and unlocked at dawn. Bang loudly if there's an emergency. Oh, I almost forgot. Be sure to keep the dung buckets securely fastened to the bulkheads and empty them before the seas get rough. I advise you to reserve a couple for seasickness." Then he was gone and the hatch cover banged down.

Why had her father never discussed chamber pots?

In the dim hold, made even darker by the partitions, Penelope and Matthew prepared for bed by simply taking off their woolen outer garments and wrapping themselves in blankets against the March chill.

Matthew's slumping hammock reminded Penelope of their wedding night. Her old bedstead had creaked and groaned at triple the customary weight when Matthew joined her on the down-filled mattress. The ancient ropes beneath the mattress sagged so much she feared the two of them had rolled into a feather-lined pit. By the time they extricated themselves and pulled the mattress onto the floor, bells of the Westerkerk announced the arrival of the Sabbath and Matthew's insistence upon abstinence from carnal activities.

The next several evenings Matthew had disassembled the bed and shimmed, glued, and clamped the joints before lacing new rope through the holes and pulling it tight.

Now, to sleep alone after ten weeks of marriage was strange, as well as lonely even though Matthew was only an arm's length away. She reached out a hand, rested it on his shoulder, and fell asleep with dreams of following in her father's footsteps, or rather following in his wake.

* * * * *

In the morning, noisy activities on the wooden deck above as well as the unlocking of the hatch aroused the passengers of *de Melckmeyt*. Afraid to miss a minute of the ship's activities, Penelope was the first passenger on deck, opting to use the open-air perch under the bowsprit rather than wait her turn for a chamber pot.

Sailors rowed to the sparsely populated island of Texel to take on barrels of fresh water, uncontaminated by the urban wastes of Amsterdam. The shipmaster frowned at the steady winds from the south. Several of the other dozen ships at anchor on the lee side of Texel buzzed with activity, obviously preparing to travel north, probably to the Baltic. Surely her father had often had mornings like this, preparing to leave on a gentle southern breeze.

That afternoon Penelope's wishes came true when the fickle winds of early spring shifted and the tide was compliant. The ship raised its anchor, tacked into the Oceanus Germanicus, as her Dutch globe called it, or the North Sea according to the English, and headed southwest.

At last she understood why her father had risked his life on sea voyages—the rhythmic slap of waves against the hull, the creak of wood and rope, the smell of pitch, the taste of sea salt in the air, the wind that threatened to steal her cap but allowed sea birds to fly without flapping their wings, the wonderment of what the next hour would bring. The ship continually moved south and west among the mild waves, tacking now and then, obeying the will of the winds. With reluctance she abandoned the view to join the others for supper.

After two bites sturdy Matthew, who never missed a meal, complained of an upset stomach and excused himself from the table. He loitered at the ship's rail for a few moments before staggering down the ladderway. Penelope followed but he shooed her away.

The odors of sickness from the hold encouraged her to remain upon the deck as much as possible. She reached into her apron pocket for the *schiffahrkundebuch*, or seamanship book, but was surprised to retrieve *The Tempest*. Penelope laughed, imagining Liesbeth going to a used book dealer and asking for anything in English about ship voyages. The play opened with a storm sinking a ship and stranding a family on an island, not the best gift for a voyager. But the old woman had meant well, having watched as Penelope, agonizing over what books to take, had finally selected two slim volumes of Homer over voluminous Shakespeare.

The Tempest could wait. Penelope opened the seamanship book and started to study.

Master Pietersz's voice startled her. "Oh, a seaman recruit, is it? A new recruit is entitled to one question a day."

Penelope asked the first question that came to mind. "What's our route to Curaçao?"

He replied, "South until butter melts. Then west into the sunset."

On the chilly deck of a ship in the North Sea in March, the young wife from Amsterdam marveled that the earth could be as warm as a steaming loaf of fresh bread.

She could already box the compass—that is, recite the thirty-two points of the compass: north, east of north, northnortheast, *et cetera*—because her globe had such a diagram in the otherwise blank spaces of the South Pacific Ocean. This knowledge did her little good. The ship's compass was obscured in a sturdy wooden box near the helm, a location the passengers were forbidden to visit. Each half hour, the helmsman called out the course and the speed. Pegs were placed into the proper holes of the traverse board, which she couldn't see either.

Such minor disappointments didn't diminish her joy at all the things she could observe. She went below to tell Matthew what he was missing.

He refused to leave his hammock. "I can't walk if the floor tilts a different way each second. I'll break a leg."

"You have to eat something. I saved bread and cheese from breakfast."

He covered his mouth with a hand and mumbled, "Don't talk of food."

"Very well." She decided to interest him in something mechanical. "When the helmsman turns over the half-hour glass, he rings the ship's bell. At the first half hour of the watch, it's one bell. After an hour it's two bells. They start over after eight bells, which marks the end of each four-hour watch." She refused to waste a daily question to ask why a double ding was called a single bell when she might think of something more important.

Matthew leaned over the edge of the hammock and spat. "Can't they find a quieter bell?"

"The whole ship must hear the bell, because the crew unstows the log and throws it over the stern. It's a triangular piece of wood with a lead weight"—she ignored his groan of misery—"so it mostly sinks into the water and sticks there. It's attached to a long rope with a knot every seven fathoms. When they turn the half-minute glass—actually it's only twenty-eight seconds because the number of rope knots in twenty-eight seconds is the ship's speed in knots. A knot—"

"Stop moving around," he said. "It makes me sick."

"I'm not moving. The ship is."

"Then make the ship stop moving."

Penelope stifled a chuckle. In his hammock he was a reverse pendulum. Instead of being the bob that moved in a stationary clock, he was a stationary bob in a swaying ship. "Close your eyes and nothing will move."

He closed his eyes. His hammock rocked gently as the ship dipped and plunged, creaked and groaned, rolled and righted its way through the seas. He removed his hand from his mouth.

"A knot is one English nautical mile or one-third of a Dutch *zeemijl*. So if five knots pass over the gunwale, the ship is traveling five nautical miles per hour."

"Where's my Bible?"

"You can't read with your eyes closed."

"It will give me comfort just to hold it."

She dug into their chest, found the wedding gift from Grandfather Prince, and handed Matthew the Bible. She also retrieved her father's globe. "One degree of latitude is sixty English nautical miles. In a full day at five knots due south, we would travel exactly two degrees of latitude." She didn't confuse him by mentioning that Rotterdam lay due south of their current position.

He clutched the Bible and began to mumble verses.

Penelope carried the globe onto the deck. She attempted to explain the ships' speed to two soldiers but they hung their heads over the rail and vainly attempted to expel their seasickness into the ocean. When the ship lurched, she almost dropped the globe. The honor of possibly being the first passenger on *de Melckmeyt* with her own globe would not compensate for the ignominy of being the first person to lose one overboard.

Carrying the sphere back to her trunk, she remembered Liesbeth's bag hidden inside. She dumped out three small copper coins wrapped inside a sheet of paper and read Liesbeth's shaky, spidery words: "Dearest Penelope, These three gold coins—"

Gold! She had thought the coins were copper.

She began anew. "These three gold coins always remind me of you because they were minted in Mexico in 1626, the year of your birth. They were a part of the Spanish treasure fleet captured in 1628 by Master Piet Heyn, a friend of my late husband. It's only fitting you take them with you to America. Together, they are worth sixty guilders, the bargain price Pieter Minuet paid for the island of the Manhatans. Spend them on something of lasting value like Herr Minuet did. Love, Liesbeth."

The coins indeed had the date 1626 and a portrait of Spain's King Phillip. What strange coincidences there were in life! As she refolded the envelope with her father's letter to insert into the protection of Liesbeth's leather bag, a dried leaf fell out. Why would Liesbeth keep a twig?

She leaned closer to blow it away and stopped. Something about its shape nagged at her memory. The twig was a stem with five leaves. Each leaf was three times as long as wide and had finely serrated edges. She opened her father's letter and laid a leaf atop the drawing of an oval. They matched. This was the talisman.

What did a twig have to do with extracting riches from the earth? Or was it a symbol of something else?

She felt guilty to keep a secret from her husband and glanced his way to see if he watched her. He was either asleep, praying, or dead from seasickness. The sound of footsteps encouraged her to stuff the mystery back into the drawer disguised as part of the globe's base.

Every hour, that is, at two, four, six, and eight bells, she returned to offer him a sip of water or a bite of bread and to slosh a bucket of seawater over the planks to sluice vomit into the bilges. Nevertheless, the stench of bile and urine permeated the hold and increased daily.

Between bells, she studied the thirty-two points of direction relative to the ship: dead ahead, one point on the starboard bow, *et cetera*. When the watch in the crow's nest called out, "Sail, two points on the starboard bow," she turned to the right front of the ship and saw a distant sail silhouetted against the setting sun.

In the fiery orb's last gloaming, she sucked in a deep breath of fresh air and climbed down the ladderway into the hatch to check on her miserable husband.

Chapter 8

The Atlantic Ocean

March 1648

The next day's fickle winds were mostly adverse. After each log measurement, *de Melckmeyt* tacked in a different direction to Penelope's delight. As mariners hauled on the rigging to adjust sails, she tried to match a myriad of actual ropes to tiny drawings and obscure names in her seamanship book. Meanwhile, she tried not to laugh at Dirck, who practiced walking on the shifting deck.

"Dirck," she called. "Keep your knees flexible and anticipate the movement of the deck. Feel the ship through your legs." She stood, balanced a book on her head, and glided smoothly across the rolling deck. "The trick is to keep your head from bobbing up, down, or sideways."

Dirck muttered to himself, "Knees bent, like jumping off a wagon. Anticipate the movement, like preventing a goat from escaping past you through a gate. Walk with my head still, the opposite of a chicken." When he swaggered across the deck like an old sailor, the ship tacked and destroyed his rhythm and he had to learn anew.

Trijn watched her husband rub his sore bottom after a hard fall. "How long until we reach land again?"

Penelope swept her arms in a broad gesture of joy. "Who cares? I could sail forever." How could her companions be tired of the ocean already?

Dirck muttered, "Forever? Maybe I can learn to walk by then."

At eight bells, Penelope observed the master and mate use the astrolabe to measure the angle of the sun above the horizon. Following in her book as they corrected for the sun's declination to compute the latitude, she was pleased to agree with their computations, although she longed to dangle the flat circle of brass from its leather strap and align the alidade herself. Reading about it was one thing, but doing was better.

Trijn waited until Penelope closed her book. "Why bother with such tedious numbers?"

Penelope grinned. "I like to prove myself capable, even if no one else knows. Imagine baking the most delicious cobbler in the world and eating it all by yourself."

Trijn licked her lips. "Now I understand. Too much pride is a sin, yet I hunger for my own cooking."

On the fourth day, the ship passed between Calais and Dover, entered the Oceanus Brittanicus, or English Channel, and presented the passengers a distant view of the white chalk cliffs of England. Penelope invited Matthew to come see but he mumbled God had cursed England with a civil war and had cursed this ship.

Penelope stared at her parents' homeland with a strange mix of feelings: welcome, farewell, fatherland, foreign land. The other passengers sighed with boredom once they passed the chalk cliffs and learned land was not expected for three weeks.

The seas became calmer as they left behind the English Channel and entered the Atlantic Ocean proper. After several days of near fasting, Matthew began to join them for meals although he ate only a fifth of his usual quantity of food and took back to his hammock a handful of ship biscuits. He claimed the regularity of a swaying hammock was his only prevention for seasickness and spent most of his time there, his unopened Bible clutched in his fingers.

* * * * *

Each evening, Penelope sat on the deck of *de Melckmeyt* as the sun sank below the ocean horizon and stars leaped into the sky. She never tired of observing the planets and constellations because the smoke- and fog-filled skies in Amsterdam could hide a full moon. Although their ship seemed to be the only one on the ocean and Matthew was below decks, she didn't feel alone beneath the immense sweep of the sparkling stars, especially when six-year-old Jan sprawled beside her and created new constellations of farm animals. His constellations made as much as sense as the ancient Greek ones the sailors taught her.

Penelope marked the spring equinox on March 21. The other passengers anticipated the arrival of Easter as the moon slowly changed phases from new moon on March 22 to full moon on April 5, bringing the holy day the following Sunday. Like the Puritans, Matthew ignored Easter as he ignored Christmas. To demonstrate solidarity with her husband, Penelope remained below decks when Master Pieterz conducted an Easter sunrise service.

Sometimes, Penelope entertained the farm family and soldiers with the adventures of heroic Odysseus, trying to find his way home to his faithful wife, Penelope. The wide, empty, dark ocean was the perfect setting for the classic stories of exotic ocean danger. At the end of each adventure, she reassured young Jan that Odysseus did indeed find his home at last, but it took a long time.

The next morning at four bells, Penelope brought another bucket of seawater to sluice the deck under Matthew's hammock and relieve a tiny bit of the miasma in the hold.

Matthew whispered, "I overheard two soldiers talking. Did you tell the farm boy those heathen stories last night?"

Penelope said, "He enjoys the tales of the *Odyssey*. Are you feeling better?" She hoped so. He had lost weight during a week of seasickness. "Come topside. It's a sunny, cheerful day."

"You shouldn't corrupt his soul with non-Christian legends."

"Your grandfather studied it at Cambridge." She stood with bucket in hand. He was correct the ancient Greek stories were pre-Christian and therefore heathen. If they really corrupted the soul, the papists would have banned them long before the Reformation.

"Yes, before he abandoned the Church of England for the true faith."

"Jan's parents don't object. They enjoy the stories too."

Matthew thumped the Bible. "You spend too much time with people outside of our congregation."

Penelope noticed no new stains on the deck near Matthew. She slung the saltwater under his hammock anyway before she was tempted to douse him. "Matthew, what am I supposed to do? We are a congregation of two on this ship and you don't care for my company these days."

"You could study the Bible."

Penelope placed a hand on her husband's brow to determine if his utterance of nonsense meant he was feverish. He was cool and clammy but that described most of the space between decks. "Elder Williams says I'm not qualified to interpret the Bible."

"Most women aren't but you could still draw comfort and inspiration from it."

Although St. Paul deserved the blame for this attitude, she worried about Matthew because he had never said such things to her before. Was illness causing him to babble? If so, did he truly believe what he had said? "Are you hungry? I saved biscuits and cheese from breakfast."

"Biscuits, yes but no cheese."

He nibbled on a piece of hardtack she retrieved from her apron pocket, then sipped water from a goat skin.

"Can I get you anything else?"

"Jonah survived a fish. This too shall pass."

She thought he had fallen asleep until he gnawed on the hardtack again. She tiptoed away.

Topside she plopped herself next to Trijn who cuddled Sophie as usual. The little girl tolerated seasickness as poorly as Matthew.

Trijn said, "You don't act like it's a lovely day for a sail."

Penelope sighed as she glanced at a bright, blue sky and sails comfortably filled with wind. "Matthew's as cranky as a baby and talks nonsense. I don't know if he's feverish or having nightmares or what."

"I like it when Dirck talks in his sleep. Then I know what he worries about. He sleep-talked about this voyage for weeks before he discussed it out loud."

"For weeks? What did you do?" Penelope held onto her cap as a stray gust of wind caused the rigging to creak.

"At first I was horrified to think of leaving family and friends. But soon it made sense. Then when he argued with himself in the night, I whispered suggestions to encourage the right choice. And here we are."

Penelope agreed a man was more receptive to new ideas before he announced a decision.

Trijn tried to play patty-cake with Sophie but her baby was listless. "Has anyone ever died from seasickness?"

Penelope chuckled. "My father claimed to know a man who jumped overboard to end his misery."

"If you don't mind my curiosity, your Matthew doesn't seem the adventuring type."

"It's complicated."

"Life usually is."

How much should she share with Trijn? The farmwife was a practical person who didn't seem prone to gossip, not that this ship held many people to spill secrets to. "You don't look adventurous either."

Trijn gave a hearty chuckle. "So true. But Dirck has the misfortune to be the third son of a third son."

Orphaned Penelope rubbed the locket around her neck. "A large family sounds nice."

"When Dirck's grandfather died, Dirck's father inherited only nine *morgen*s of land. Dirck will inherit only three *morgen*s." Trijn snorted. "Three *morgen*s, indeed. In thirty years when his father dies."

"How big is a *morgen*?" Penelope briefly studied the ocean after an odd wave disturbed the customary slap of water on wood. Probably a stray wave from a distant storm. Nothing to worry about.

Trijn looked at the surrounding ocean with its absence of landmarks and shrugged. "A *morgen* is as big as …as big as…as much land as one man with one ox can plow in a morning."

Morgen was also the Dutch word for morning but this answer didn't help Penelope. "Couldn't you buy more land? Aren't they creating new polders by diking the sea?"

"The price of land rose faster than we could save money. And the Republic doesn't create new farm land as fast as farm mothers create sons."

Penelope considered her parents, who moved from England to Amsterdam because her father was the second son of a second son in a country where the first son inherited all the land. "Why America?"

"They say the *patroon* of Rensselaerswyck owns one hundred thousand *morgen*s along the North River. Can you imagine such a thing?

"He will lease us as much land as we can work. Dirck can lease twenty *morgen*s. When Jan grows up, he can lease twenty *morgen*s. If I have more sons, each can lease twenty *morgen*s. In thirty years my family could be plowing a hundred *morgen*s instead of three."

Trijn held up her young daughter to face the trackless ocean as though it were farmland and laughed. "And Sophie's husband can lease twenty *morgen*s to plow."

The wind shifted a few points. The first mate shouted orders and sailors hauled on ropes to optimize the sails.

Should she and Matthew buy land, not twenty *morgen*s, but enough for him to build them a house and her to plant a small garden? How soon after they arrived in America and where? Then she realized they had never discussed what to do first. Merely leaving Amsterdam had occupied all her attention. How, step by step, would Matthew accomplish his mission from God?

* * * * *

"Mrs. Prince, I forbid you to associate ..."

A bucket thudded on the deck and seawater splashed the planks under Matthew's hammock as Penelope clamped a hand over her husband's mouth. "Matthew, please don't finish that sentence. Don't speak something you can't unsay."

Through her fingers his words sounded like "But I'm your husband."

She spoke in soft tones as though to a sick child, "Yes, you're the husband and the chief elder of our congregation of two. But we can't withdraw from the world. We'll need help to find our place on this new continent. We'll need a job for you and a place to live. Just like in Amsterdam, the congregation must interact with outsiders." She removed her hand from his mouth and stroked his cool and clammy forehead.

"Only the men need to go outside the congregation."

With a corner of her apron dampened with spilt seawater she wiped his brow and worried if he suffered alternate bouts of chills and fevers. "Matthew, your mother had a dozen women in the congregation to rely on. I'm only one person. I can't do everything by myself. I need help."

"God will provide."

"Yes, God will provide help in the form of people. You don't expect God to solve our problems with angels and burning bushes, do you?" She shouldn't have asked the question. What if he said yes?

"If we are worthy, God will provide for our needs."

According to the church elders, most of the residents of Amsterdam were unworthy yet their needs were provided for. She crooned as much to herself as to him, "God tests us to see if we are worthy. Endure this to glorify God."

Trijn was right. A sick husband was more of a nuisance than a sick child. But Penelope had promised both God and Reverend Prince to care for her husband in both sickness and in health. Matthew seemed asleep so she tiptoed away for fresh air and reminded herself again it wasn't Matthew's fault he couldn't tolerate sea travel.

She emerged from the dim hold into the bright sunlight. Why was she belittling him for not knowing how to establish a new home for the congregation when she was equally naïve about how to investigate the disappearance of her father?

Chapter 9

The Atlantic Ocean

April 1648

Three weeks south of the white cliffs of Dover, the watch on the *de Melckmeyt* called out "Teide." Penelope only saw a bright glint on the horizon. Swallowing her pride, she asked Master Pietersz, who explained Teide was a snow-capped mountain on the island of Tenerife, one of the Canaries. Hour by hour, they approached the apparent contradiction of snow almost in the tropics. By mid-afternoon a white blob, two-hands-breadth tall, floated above the distant horizon, its snowy summit glistening in the sunlight, impossible to miss.

A young seaman on his first voyage looked in awe. "They say it's the tallest mountain in the world."

"An excellent choice for the prime meridian," said Master Pietersz, though it was not marked as such on Penelope's old globe. To the mate, he called, "Change the course to westsouthwest."

Penelope recalled the shipmaster's answer to her long-ago question. The weather was indeed hot enough to melt butter, but they had eaten the last of it a week ago, before it turned rancid in the heat.

Master Pietersz was in a mellow mood. "Every navigator loves Teide, because you know your exact location and the trade winds here are quite reliable. On this course in twenty-three or so days we reach 13° north latitude. Then we'll be only two or three days east of Barbados, the easternmost island of the Caribbean."

"Why not aim exactly for Barbados?"

"If we're off course even slightly, we'll never know we missed it. I can only guess at my longitude. Between the sun and the North Star, we can always find 13°. Then by sailing due west, we are certain to spy one of the Windward Islands. Once we know where we are, we drop to 12°, locate Grenada, and sail to Curaçao."

Penelope tried to explain ocean navigation to the other passengers. All they understood was twenty-five more days of open ocean, after which they would see islands but not stop until they arrived at Curaçao a week later. But Penelope enjoyed day after day of sailing.

When they reached the Tropic of Cancer, at 23 ½° latitude, the official delineation of the tropics, the crew changed from long-sleeved linen shirts into loose-fitting cotton ones. Penelope had seen cloth made from Egyptian cotton in Amsterdam shops but linen was so much cheaper.

No one had suggested tropical clothes for the passengers because their goal of New Amsterdam lay at latitude 41°.

A strong gust of wind whipped her skirts. In hopes the breeze might cool her legs, she held down her dress the least amount that modesty required while she looked astern at the dark storm clouds and the log line bobbing in heavy swells. The shipmaster looked more pleased than concerned when a sailor called out six knots.

As the afternoon progressed, the storm overtook the ship. Finally the master ordered the passengers below and some of the sails reefed.

Sailors locked down the hatch cover. Even though she knew the purpose was to keep seawater out of the hold, she felt imprisoned. What if the ship sank? However, if she were on deck and the ship sank, she would still drown.

Dirck asked, "Does everyone know how to swim?"

"You can swim?" asked Penelope. In Amsterdam the canals remained filthy despite the city's efforts to flush the waterways by coordinating the flow of the Amstel River with weak ocean tides.

"Sure. Jan and I swim like ducks." He tucked his arms next to his body and wiggled his fingers, pantomiming a duck's feet paddling underwater. "Because we learned in the duck pond on the farm."

Penelope said, "I hope you can swim like a herring because we're a thousand *zeemijls* from land."

A gust of wind buffeted the ship and almost knocked Penelope off her feet. She stared at Matthew swinging in his hammock. "I wonder if my husband has the right idea." But his greenish-colored face indicated otherwise.

Trijn called Penelope to join her in a corner. Dirck held his two children, Trijn held Dirck, and Penelope held onto Trijn. The soldiers had prepared better and clung to a thick rope stretched from bulwark to bulwark.

The wind howled and the waves crashed into the hull. Wooden planks creaked. The deck tilted until the clump of passengers slid across the floor and into a deep puddle of stinky water. Sophie screamed and Trijn called out to her. Matthew clambered out of his hammock, crept over the slippery floor on hands and knees, and grabbed his wife. The deck leveled as the ship righted itself and then tilted in the opposite direction. Between Dirck bracing one side of their corner and Matthew bracing the other, the cluster of six passengers managed to retain a precarious position.

Matthew's assistance and strength despite weeks of skimpy food and little exercise both surprised and pleased Penelope even though he frequently retched into the water that continually sloshed around them—water already contaminated with bilge residues and the overturned chamber pot. Fortunately Matthew's stomach had little to contribute and an additional stench was preferable to bruises or broken bones.

For hours the ship acted, as Dirck said, like an angry bull. It bucked, rolled, dipped, snorted like thunder, and knocked things around. Waves sloshed over the deck. Rivulets of salt water dripped from the ceiling onto their heads.

While Matthew prayed, Penelope shuddered at lines she recalled from *King Lear*:

> "*Blow, winds, and crack your cheeks! rage! blow!*
> *You cataracts and hurricanoes, spout*
> *Till you have drench'd our steeples, drown'd the cocks!*"

She tried to imagine a wave rolling over the roof of the house next to Liesbeth's, washing over the bronze weathervane rooster she had often admired from her garret window. Surely waves didn't get that huge.

Now she understood how Odysseus felt when his sailors released the captured winds from Aeolus's bag and the resulting storm drove them far from home. At least this tempest drove them toward their destination.

At last the waves and winds subsided and the sailors unlocked the passengers from the hold. The ship's bell indicated only three hours had elapsed. On deck sailors acted like nothing had happened. Wet wood sparkled in the late afternoon sun. Or was that just a contrast to the darkness of the hold.

"Was that a hurricano?' she asked the master, who appeared pleased his ship suffered no ill effects.

"Ha," he laughed. "Merely a thunderstorm."

Merely a thunderstorm like the ones that washed refuse from the streets of Amsterdam into the canals and cleared soot from the air. "What would a hurricano be like?" She recalled the playwright's fearful description and tried to picture riding out a worse storm while locked in the hold. What a difference between a brick house on land and a floating wooden box!

"The hurricano is a Spanish legend to keep foreigners away from their colonies," said Master Pietersz. "They claim the West Indies has the hurricano and the East Indies has the typhoon. Neither compare to a blizzard from the North Pole. When I was a cabin boy on a voyage to Iceland, we tarried too late in the season. The rigging was sheathed in ice. Visibility was less than twenty fathoms. We nearly smashed into an iceberg. That was a storm!"

Meanwhile soldiers hauled up buckets of seawater and doused each other as well as Dirck and Matthew. With a full bucket in each meaty hand Trijn called to Penelope to join her in privacy below.

Penelope followed her down into the hold. It was better to smell like a wet dog for a few hours than a dung bucket all day, even if the seawater left her hair hard to brush.

* * * * *

On the twenty-third day, they reached 13° and turned a few points toward due west. Barbados and Grenada were exactly where Master Pietersz expected them to be. In six more days, the master pointed out the island of Bonaire where the ship would pick up a load of salt after discharging the passengers and cargo in Curaçao.

"Have you ever been to New Amsterdam?" she asked.

"No. There's no profit in my meeting Pieter Stuyvesant again," replied Master Pietersz.

"You know the Director-General?" she asked.

"Back in '44 when Stuyvesant led the attack on the island of Sint Maarten, a cannon ball mangled his leg so badly the chirurgeon had to amputated much of it. Only one soldier in three survives an amputation. Stuyvesant likely ordered God not to let him die. But God has a sense of justice because the wound never healed properly, as often happens in the Indies. It festered and pained him greatly."

Penelope shivered at the image of cutting off a man's leg as though it were a haunch of pork.

The master's eyes scanned the sails, the skies, the decks. "When Stuyvesant tried to command my ship. I explained to him that while he was upon my vessel, he was merely a common passenger and had two masters: his Savior and me. And I was not far below Jesus."

Penelope knew the master was in charge of the ship, the crew, and the common passengers. She had never considered uncommon passenger. "Did he accept his position?"

The ship's bell dinged. The master studied the rigging, snapped his finger at the helmsman, and pointed to a corner of sail that flapped slightly. The helmsman relayed an order to a sailor who tightened a rope. The flapping ceased.

"I explained it in military terms." The master grinned. "Stuyvesant was alone, whereas I commanded ten sailors. If he disobeyed me again, I would declare him in mutiny and try him. As the shipmaster, I'm also the judge. After I proclaimed him guilty of mutiny, I would either make him walk the plank or cut off his other leg. I suspect a man with his pride would endure the plank rather than grovel legless for the remainder of his life."

"Sir, I pray I haven't offended you on this voyage."

"Indeed, *mevrouw*." The master bowed slightly to her. "Your presence has been entertaining. I wish more passengers took your interest in the ship and navigation." Then he grinned. "And possessed your resistance to seasickness."

Penelope took advantage of the master's compliment. "I have another question concerning navigation. When we leave Curaçao on our next voyage, do we merely sail a point or two west of north to reach New Amsterdam?"

"Four and one half knots," sang out a sailor retrieving the log.

"There are two difficulties with that route." Master Pietersz laughed. "First the island of Hispaniola is north of Curaçao. You must go either east or west of it. Secondly, due north of Hispaniola is the Sargasso Sea."

Penelope was determined to learn as much as she could while the master was in a talkative mood. Longitudes on her old globe were poor guesses. "Is sargasso a poison?"

"It's the Portuguese word for seaweed. The few sailors who ever returned from that region of the sea said it has seaweed and nothing else—no tides, no wind, no hope of leaving."

A little flattery never hurt. "How would a smart master such as yourself navigate to New Amsterdam?"

"Since the Spanish are no longer our enemies, the best route is between Hispaniola and Cuba." Master Pietersz drew the route in the air with a finger. "Then northwest between the Bahamas and Florida, then follow the curve of the American main to the northnortheast being sure to give a wide berth to Cape Hatteras. Then due north to New Netherland."

She visualized his finger tracing the route on her globe. "To zigzag around the ocean seems so much further."

"Further in miles but shorter in time. The winds and tides favor that route north. Only God knows why."

The mate arrived with papers in his hand. A nod from the master dismissed Penelope.

"Thank you, sir." She went below to trace the shipmaster's sailing directions on her globe. Matthew watched her with little interest, his bleary eyes barely open.

"Can I get you anything?" she asked softly.

He shoved the Geneva Bible into her hands. "Read the Twenty-third Psalm. It sounds better when spoken aloud."

Several times she read the verses, carefully pronouncing "adversaries" and "doubtless" instead of "enemies" and "surely" to avoid upsetting Matthew with differences between his Geneva Bible and the king's Bible she had learned as a girl in the Anglican Church.

She kissed his forehead, thankful Matthew in his fitful sleep had listened to her suggestions of tolerance for other people who might help them and thus assist his mission from God and her mission of discovery.

Chapter 10

In the Caribbean Sea

Friday, 15 May 1648

Life on board *de* Melckmeyt had satisfied Penelope's utmost expectations—for a month. Now, even she looked forward to solid land again.

The rare sunshine in Amsterdam was always enjoyable but the intensity of the tropical sun, even in late afternoon, sapped her energy. She squirmed a few inches to remain in the shade cast by the foresail. Would she ever get used to the heat? It was worse than reaching into an oven to remove a dozen pies.

A river of perspiration dripped down from sodden hair trapped inside her airless cap. It ran down her back to soak her linen clothes and dripped down her nose to plunk upon the deck. She was too lethargic to wipe the sweat except when it blurred her vision.

She plucked at her sleeveless vest every few minutes in a futile attempt to let fresh air flow between fabric and skin, but her clothes fit snugly around the trunk of her body as intended. Allowing the top two eyelets of her chemise to remain unlaced was little help. The calendar said the month was May. Surely Amsterdam had never suffered a day as hot as this, even in August.

At the cry of "Land, ho" from the crow's nest, Penelope overcame her torpor to stand near the bow of the ship for her first view of the island of Curaçao and its large, protected harbor in Sint Anna Bay. Something was missing.

"Where are the trees?" Penelope had expected lush tropical rain forests.

Matthew, frail and wan from weeks in a hammock, clung to the railing beside her. "Who cares about trees? I'm happy just to see land, thank the Lord." He looked sick instead of happy.

She envied him the male prerogative to loosen the strings of his linen shirt and to let his breeches flap, untied at the knees. If he complained about her lack of stockings, she would counter with his lack too. At least his clothes moved in the breeze. She looked again at his baggy garments. How much weight had he lost during this voyage?

A large ship lay on its side on the shore with workers repairing its keel. She shaded her eyes with a hand and strained to see better. "It looks like a desert."

A sailor laughed. "The Spanish claimed all the good places long ago. Welcome to Fort New Amsterdam."

"A desert?" Dirck stood a few feet away. "No one told us about a desert."

"Who cares?" said Trijn. "We'll only stay a few days."

"How can anything grow in this heat?" asked Dirck.

De Melckmeyt was owned by the GWC. The soldiers, who were also owned by the GWC, disembarked first and quickly marched away to their new home, or perhaps hell, as some of their mutterings implied.

The six passengers organized their baggage and presented themselves to a company clerk. Penelope wished he wore an eye patch so that she wouldn't have to stare at an ugly scar that caused one eye to droop. The clerk pronounced their documents satisfactory and promised placement upon the next ship.

Penelope asked, "When will the next ship arrive?"

The clerk didn't bother to look up. "Soon."

She glanced at Matthew and Dirck, who both shrugged. "Do we have other choices?"

"How well do you swim?" The clerk laughed until he had to wipe his nose on his sleeve.

Penelope spun on her heel and walked away a few feet. She hated to play the fool but declined to antagonize this stranger in a position of power. Yet she remained close enough to hear anything useful he might say.

An Angolan shuffled down the gangplank with a heavy bale of cargo and trudged toward a distant building. Three others followed him. Penelope had seen an occasional *neger,* or black man, in the distance in Amsterdam but never one five feet away.

Dirck, the large sturdy farmer, blew out a breath. "Did you see that first man? He's carrying more weight than even my big brother could lift."

The clerk returned papers to the two men. "Fortunately for you, we never have enough soldiers to fill all the *barracas,* so one is reserved for visitors." He called for a junior clerk and more black slaves to carry their baggage. This second clerk, a gangly youth with bad skin and a frequent smile, led them to the ground floor of a building and opened a storage room of ship hammocks and other sundries.

Dirck said, "Hammocks again. Do you have any beds?"

The clerk laughed. "You don't want a bed."

"Yes, I do."

Penelope agreed with Dirck. A flat bed should remove the kinks from her back, surely caused by sleeping curved into a semicircle. Even the hard, flat floor looked inviting.

"To be more accurate, you don't want to share a bed with the creatures on this island."

"What creatures?" Trijn swished her skirts as though making sure rats hadn't followed them from the ship.

The clerk pointed. In a nearby corner, a pair of foot-long lizards walked on the wall several feet above the floor.

Jan shouted with glee, "Are they baby dragons?"

Trijn scooped up Sophie and Jan, ready to stomp on any lizard or dragon that threatened her children. Penelope stared, trying to match these peculiar animals with any of the dangers faced by Odysseus during his long voyage.

"What on God's green earth?" Dirck outweighed the lizards a hundred-fold but didn't approach.

"The Spanish call them *geckos*," said the clerk. "They're harmless. But I can't say the same for the scorpions, tarantulas, and snakes that haunt this island."

"You mean a scorpion like the constellation Scorpio?" asked Penelope.

"What's a tarantula?" asked Trijn.

"A tarantula is a big hairy spider." The lanky clerk held his thumb and forefinger apart to form a circle as big as Penelope's wrist. "Scorpions and tarantulas love to hide in dark places like boots and mattresses and inject poison into whatever disturbs them."

Penelope sighed. "We'll take the hammocks." Why hadn't her father ever complained about sleeping in the equivalent of a fishnet?

"Jan!" said his mother. "Did you hear that? The snakes and bugs here will kill you. They're not playthings like garter snakes in the field or eels in the canal."

The clerk explained families usually stretched their unneeded blankets from the ceiling to create the semblance of private rooms. The new residents paid careful attention to the numerous crevices of the roughly plastered wall but found no other surprises. Penelope debated closing the windows in the stifling building to discourage the vermin but discovered the windows had no glass, only louvered shutters.

* * * * *

Within two days *de Melckmeyt* deposited a year's supply of provisions for the garrison and departed Curaçao for Bonaire to pick up a load of salt to carry to Holland where it would be combined with fresh cod to create stockfish.

Penelope watched the ship depart. Not only were they marooned on the hot, dry island until another ship arrived but she and Matthew were each being charged seven stuivers a day for food yet they got no closer to their destination. At least, Matthew now ate enough to get his money's worth, regaining weight lost on a seasickness diet.

After a few days of solid land and solid food, Matthew wandered over to examine the ship careened on the beach for major repairs. Despite being a mere house carpenter, he was hired to chisel mortises at the outrageous wage of a guilder a day, nearly twice what he made in Amsterdam. He returned each evening tired but happy.

Penelope was also happy for Matthew to be out of the *barraca*. After a few days on land Jan and Sophie frolicked all day in the heat wearing only a thin shift, whereas merely sweeping up the dust that continually sifted through the shutters of the glassless windows exhausted well-clothed Penelope and Trijn, who hated to let a man see them idle most of the day.

At least they didn't have to cook but Penelope had expected a better variety of food once on land. The company mess hall served the same ample but monotonous fare as on the ship: cheese, olive oil, bread, and beer for breakfast; either salted fish, salted pork or salted beef for lunch with vinegar, beer, and boiled peas; and some combination for supper. What could one expect in a desert?

Dirck made friends with a retired soldier who kept horses and farmed in a valley where the scant winter rainfall soaked more deeply into the soil. Dirck said the island was a grassland not a desert and happily explained the details of water management: too much in Holland, not enough here. In exchange for his labor, he received fresh vegetables to supplement the company rations.

One day Dirck laughed as he came through the doorway. "You'll never guess what delicacy I have today." He dumped several gnarly, oddly shaped roots onto the table.

"Turnips? Rutabagas?" Matthew guessed.

Penelope retrieved a root and sniffed twice. "I've smelled this at the docks, in cargo from the East Indies. Nutmeg? Tumeric?"

Dirck grinned. "Ginger."

Trijn asked, "Where did you get it?"

Her husband said, "The farmer grows it in the marshes next to his spring. Says it grows like a weed. We're drying a barrel of it to ship to New Amsterdam. I got this for Matthew. They claim it prevents seasickness."

Penelope fondled a root. "What's the dose? Do you steep it? Boil it?"

"Think of it as a hand." Dirck flexed the joint of his little finger. "Break off a small finger-joint and chew it."

* * * * *

A few days later, Matthew returned from work with a big grin. "Did you know the history of the ship I'm repairing?"

"*De Groote Gerrit?*" Penelope asked.

"Yes. It and two smaller ships, *de Kath* and *de Liefde,* were dispatched from New Amsterdam in February to raid Spanish ships."

Cat? Love? What silly names for the ships of privateers! Penelope thought.

"They couldn't do that." Trijn looked at Penelope. "You told me the peace treaty between Holland and Spain was signed at the end of January."

"Yes," said Penelope. "But a treaty is a piece of paper. It can't travel faster than a ship. His High Mightiness Stuyvesant in Manhattan hadn't heard the news when he dispatched them. Not did his Mightiness Rodenborch in Curaçao know."

Penelope had carefully noted the distinction in title between the Director-General of all New Netherland and the mere vice-Director of Curaçao. Who could explain why men were so enamored with fancy titles? Just a vanity. As substantial as a breath of air and disappeared with death, as Grandfather Prince would say.

Matthew said, "All three ships left New Amsterdam together and were scattered by a storm. *De Groote Gerrit* took on water and almost sank. To lighten the load, the master threw most of the provisions overboard. The garrison was on half rations before we arrived."

"The other two ships?" asked Penelope.

"They both limped into port with crews decimated by pestilence. And Curacao had no way to send word to Manhattan about the situation."

What a predicament. All three ships out of service. Little wood on this island for repairs.

Dirck said, "When we arrived, the clerk said two ships had sailed off a month ago to go privateering. I guess the crews recovered."

"You mean legal piracy," said Penelope. Like her merchant-father, she could see no difference between pirates and privateers.

"How can piracy ever be legal?" Dirck shook his head.

Penelope said, "The GWC's charter authorizes it to conduct warfare against all enemies of the Dutch Republic. Holland and Spain have been at war ever since the Twelve Year Truce of 1609 expired."

Trijn said, "We've been at war with Spain my entire life? I never knew that."

"Here's the embarrassing part." Matthew grinned. "A ship from Salem in Massachusetts came to buy salt. The Dutch commander begged the English ship master to deliver an urgent letter to Manhattan."

Dirck asked, "Is it legal to be a privateer after the war is over, even if you don't know the war is over?"

A former ship's bell rang for the evening meal.

Penelope shrugged. "That's what lawyers are for."

Chapter 11

Curaçao

Thursday, July 16, 1648

In the mornings and afternoons, Trijn and Penelope sat in the shade of the buildings with their backs toward the ten-to fifteen-knot trade winds. More dust than air penetrated their linen clothes. During the siesta hours, a Spanish custom which the Dutch garrison had adopted, the two women sat on the floor in the least hot corner of the *barraca*, gossiped, and watched the children.

After more than five weeks on the island, Penelope despaired of ever escaping from the heat of Curaçao. It was hot enough to fry eggs on the rough-laid cobblestones, if they had any eggs.

What else could she have done? Only a ship or two a year made the quest from Amsterdam to New Amsterdam compared to dozens heading for the riches of the East Indies. What did this desolate island offer besides a few pounds of ginger, hides, and green turtles?

God, give me patience. And give it now. The old jest was sad instead of humorous.

Boom! A rumble came from the harbor.

"What was that?" Trijn looked to see where her children were. "A thunderstom?"

"Sounded like a cannon," said Penelope.

"Is it a battle?"

Penelope jumped up. "Maybe it's the signal of a ship arriving. Let's go see."

"It might be dangerous," said Trijn.

"If it's a battle, we'll all know soon enough." Penelope started to re-lace her chemise.

She missed a hole but just pulled the laces tighter at the top. Clutching her stockings and shoes in her hands, she hurried barefoot to the stairs and climbed to the wall overlooking the harbor. A ship approached cautiously, most of its sails furled. A cloud of blackish smoke slowly drifted away from a forward cannon.

While all the men's eyes were on the ship, Penelope found a secluded corner to tug on her stockings, lace her shoes, and watch the ship. When properly dressed, she approached two clerks and eavesdropped.

The younger clerk pointed a telescope at the ship. "But, Thijs, she flies a Dutch flag."

"Flags are cheap," said Thijs, scratching his salt-and-pepper beard.

"Could it be a pirate trying to trick us?" The first clerk returned the glass and shielded his eyes from the overhead sun as he stared south. "Does every Spaniard on every ship and every island in the world know the war is over?"

Dutch flag or not, Penelope noted, the ship wasn't a fly-boat like *de Melckmeyt*. This vessel was much smaller and bulged less in the center like an English ship. The masts were too tall, as though designed by a pirate or a privateer for maximum speed.

Jan raced up the steps far ahead of Trijn and Sophie. "Did he say pirates?" Jan clambered on the wall overlooking the sea and Penelope grasped the back of his shirt to ensure he didn't tumble over. He pointed at the ship. "Why would a pirate sail like a lazy goose?"

Penelope thought Jan's observation was accurate even though she had never seen a goose swim. Any tasty bird in an Amsterdam canal would swim for its life.

Thijs peered through the glass. "I see the company emblem on the flag. The ship looks familiar. I count fourteen guns." He headed with the telescope toward a distinguished older gentleman, whom Penelope recognized as Paulus Leendersz, the man Matthew worked for.

"Mijnheer," Thijs said respectfully, offering the telescope, "I think it might be *de Kath*."

Leendersz scanned the approaching ship for a full minute. "Yes, it's *de Kath*. She rides high in the water. The shipmaster is not Hans Weier." He handed the glass to Thijs and started toward the quay.

The younger clerk asked Thijs, "What does he mean?"

Thijs hesitated until Leendersz was out of earshot. "When *de Kath* sailed out four months ago, the master was Hans Weier—an old friend of Meijnheer Leendersz and an excellent seaman. This ship's master is cautious and inexperienced. Where is Master Weier now?"

Penelope followed the crowds to the wharf, where she spied His Mightiness Lucas Rodenborch, vice-director of Curaçao. She squirmed through the crowd to get close enough to the man in charge of the island to eavesdrop.

A man strutted across the gangplank and saluted Rodenborch. "Your Mightiness, Master Juriaan Andriessen brings orders from his High Mightiness Director-General Petrus Stuyvesant in New Amsterdam."

Rodenborch returned the salute. "Andriessen, you were the chief gunner on this ship when she embarked. I pray Master Hans Weier is not at the bottom of the sea."

"No, your Mightiness." Andriessen grinned from ear to ear. "We captured a Spanish ship and took it to Manhattan. Hans Weier is on his way to Amsterdam with a master's share of the prize money."

"That's good news indeed." Lucas Rodenborch grinned.

Paulus Leendersz pounded the new master on the back.

According to the rules of privateering, as her father had once explained to Penelope, the entire prize was the property of the owners of the successful ship, in this case the GWC. The GWC would appraise the captured vessel, its cargo, and valuables and divide the value of the prize according to a formula, wherein the owner got a major share, the master received a large share, and a tithe was divided among the crew.

"His High Mightiness Stuyvesant," said Andriessen in a formal manner, "orders us to return to New Amsterdam at once with as much salt and dyewood as we can carry."

"He damn well knows—." Rodenborch frowned. "Come to my office. We'll discuss company business there."

Andiressen's grin evaporated. He saluted. "Yes, Your Mightiness."

The high officials headed out of the mid-day sun toward offices inside the masonry walls of the fort.

Penelope positioned herself where Thijs could see and hear her but she spoke to Trijn. "This ship returns to New Amsterdam. I wonder if we can sail with them."

Thijs immediately answered. "You might as well. The six of you eat more than you're worth, and we have no dyewood to fill the ship, only salt." Thijs greeted friends who walked down the gangplank.

Penelope hugged Trijn in excitement, then again spoke loudly enough for Thijs to hear if he wanted to, "I wonder how soon the ship will depart?"

Thijs ignored her until the last sailor reached the quay and was out of earshot, then turned and said softly, "If Andriessen says his High Mightiness Stuyvesant wants salt as soon as possible, you'd better go pack. He'd sell his grandmother to a brothel to keep even half a Mightiness happy."

* * * * *

By the time Shipmaster Andriessen returned to the pier, six passengers, their trunks, and one small chest of ginger waited on the dock adjacent to *de Kath*. The mate had loaded the company cargo but waited for Andriessen's approval before allowing passengers or private freight aboard. The ship left the harbor in a few minutes for the four-hour journey westward to Bonaire. No one gave the excellent harbor at Sint Anna Bay a farewell glance.

Dirck stood at the bottom of the ladderway to the hold and said to Trijn. "Watch your step, dear. This ladder is steep and there's no handrail, just a rope."

Penelope followed Matthew, who followed Trijn, who carried Sophie in one arm. As Trijn neared the bottom step, an unseen voice said, "Now there's a hammock warmer I approve of."

Penelope froze. Dirck helped Trijn to reach the deck safely, then turned, grabbed a sailor by his shirtfront, and yanked him into the light streaming down the hatch.

Dirck said, "If you insult my wife again or even look at her twice, I'll toss you overboard."

The sailor grasped Dirck's thick wrist with both hands to wrench himself free. "Yeah, you and who else?"

Because of frequent climbs up the rigging, seamen tended to be lean and wiry with strong arms. Penelope feared Dirck was tangling with a handful.

"Me and Fredrick." Dirck lifted a handful of fabric and the seaman's chin rose a few inches.

Because the seaman's hands wrestled futilely with Dirck's wrist, the sailor jerked his head at Matthew, still on the ladderway. "Is he Fredrick?"

"No." Dirck grinned and raised his hand further. "Fredrick is a yearling bull that I castrated." Either the other man was off the ground or had long toes. "By myself."

The seaman gurgled something that Dirck took to be an apology. He released the seaman, who disappeared back into the shadows.

"That wasn't necessary, dear," Trijn said. "I could have tossed the scrawny little thing overboard myself."

"And likewise for the rest of the passengers," Dirck called after the coughing seaman.

Penelope murmured thanks to Dirck. What would Matthew have done? Turned the other cheek, or threatened the man, or ignored the affair? How well did she know her husband? She had never seen him lose his temper.

She glanced around the dim but commodious hold and followed Trijn toward the side opposite to where the sailors had slung their hammocks. There wasn't much to do until their chests were delivered so she promptly went topside again into the sunlight and clean air.

Penelope stood at the bow of *de Kath*, straining ahead to see the island of Bonaire. She almost laughed out loud for the happiness of sailing again. Soon her journey would be over. Then her new life in America and the search for her father would begin. She had pushed her father's disappearance to the back of her mind for months as she concentrated on arranging the voyage, growing accustomed to marriage, and then enjoying the journey.

Traveling from thirteen degrees north latitude to forty-one degrees should take two weeks plus several days for detours around Cuba, the Sargasso Sea, and Cape Hatteras. Three weeks or so to figure out how to find an invisible man. In the meantime, she followed in her father's footsteps and leaned forward over the rail. She clamped a hand onto her head to keep her cap from blowing off.

"What are you doing on deck?" A sailor's gruff voice interrupted her reverie.

She laughed. "Enjoying the wind in my face."

"You should be below decks and out of our way."

The first mate barked an order from afar and the seaman abandoned her with a glare. But she sought a less visible spot between two of the deck cannon from which to watch the waves.

The ship tacked northeast and southeast against the prevailing easterlies as the helmsman approached the southern shore of Bonaire cautiously in the twilight. The land, scarcely above sea level, was almost indistinguishable from the water. A slight error would poke a hole in the ship's bottom. The crew furled the sails, launched two rowboats with sturdy ropes, and towed the ship into a protected but rocky anchorage. Adjacent were the pitiful garrison, an almost new warehouse, and dilapidated huts.

In the morning, *neger* slaves shoveled salt into wooden barrels and rolled them up the gangplank. Sailors positioned the heavy barrels in the hold, periodically building walls of heavy plank to hold them in place.

Penelope wished to see more of the loading, the responsibility of her late father, a supercargo, that is, superintendent of the cargo. If freight broke loose during a storm, it could be damaged or could smash into other shipments. Or too much weight could shift to one side of the ship causing it to keel over and sink.

The passengers were ejected from the ship because they were in way of the work. They congregated on the pier, reluctant to wander too far away and be left behind.

Dirck stood with his hands on his hips and stared at the barrels. "Maybe I should be a businessman instead of a farmer. Did you hear what the first mate said? Fifty *last*s of salt, worth eighteen or twenty guilders per *last* to New England fisherman. A thousand guilders for free."

Similar to an English ton, a *last* was two thousand Dutch pounds.

Penelope looked at him askance. "It's not free. There's the cost of the workers, their food, soldiers to guard them, this ship and its crew for six weeks." Her father had often discussed the difficulties of buying goods at a low price and selling them high enough to cover the numerous costs of transportation and still make a profit.

"Never mind the company's money. How long will it take to load fifty *last*s?" asked Matthew.

Dirck muttered to himself, "A hundred thousand pounds at three hundred pounds per barrel, that will be..."

Penelope said, "About 333 barrels."

Matthew sighed. "At the rate they're working, that'll take all day."

The first mate overheard him. "Two days is more likely. Go explore the island."

The passengers looked at the mate and then looked at each other.

Trijn asked, "What could be worth seeing on this dismal island?"

"You'd be surprised," the mate said. "Be back before dark."

Between the work and the ship, only one direction beckoned. The passengers picked their way among rocks and water in search of dry footing. The shore was mostly an interlocking series of pools that were filled by tides and storms and slowly drained back to the ocean. Higher up the beach, slaves had cleaned and dammed some of the natural pools to form salt pans which winter storms filled with seawater. Summer sun evaporated the water to leave tons of salt crystals waiting to be shoveled up.

Lower on the beach natural tidal pools ebbed and flowed with the waves. The children chased crabs across sand and rock. Jan scooped up a three-inch fish flip-flopping in a puddle and held it up for all to see.

Trijn pointed to a pool. "Look. The water is pink."

"It's all slimy and full of bugs." Penelope also noted the dirty water smelled nearly as bad as the ship's hold.

Jan shouted, "There! A pink stork! Two of them."

Indeed the big birds with long, impossibly thin legs and rigid stance did look like storks, favored in Amsterdam as signs of good luck and fertility and encouraged to nest in the summer on unused chimney stacks. These fowl were not barely pink, but flaming pink. Penelope laughed at pink storks on a Caribbean island.

Dirck said, "I see a few dozen more in the next pool."

Beyond the next pool and its birds a small rise in the land blocked the view. Even standing on her toes, Penelope couldn't spy what lay ahead.

Jan asked his father, "What's that stork doing?"

"I suppose it's waiting for fish to swim by like our storks do at home."

Trijn said, "Its bill is crooked, not like a stork's at all. And its feet look odd."

Matthew said. "See how it raises its head to swallow."

With a small gasping fish outstretched in his hand, Jan slowly approached the nearest bird. "Here, storkie, storkie. Want a nice fish?"

With an ungainly flutter of wings, the bird took to the air and settled amid a small flock fifty feet away. Jan chased until that flock of pink storks rose to safety, honking and hissing loudly. Jan pursued them too, shouting, "Look. I have a fish for you."

Trijn yelled after her son, "Jan, come back! Not so far!"

The air beyond the knoll filled with hundreds of flaming pink birds, each crying as though Jan were yanking its feathers. Not hundreds but thousands. Tens of thousands.

Jan ran back and hid behind his mother.

"What on God's green earth?" asked Dirck.

Within fifteen minutes the birds settled down. The sky was quiet and empty again.

The six visitors crept to the knoll and peered at the next stretch of beach. Large pink birds filled pools of pink water as far as the eye could see.

"Not a green earth, but a pink earth," Penelope whispered.

Chapter 12

Caribbean Sea

Sunday, July 19, 1648

"We're sailing north." Trijn wiped sweat from her forehead with a sleeve one day after leaving Bonaire. "When will it get cooler?"

"It won't." With a linen handkerchief Penelope patted away beads of perspiration that continuously formed under her once-starched cap and dripped downward. "We're headed toward the noon-day sun." She knew it was hopeless to try to explain that four weeks past the summer solstice, the sun was still near the Tropic of Cancer. They would sail north toward that imaginary line of latitude for the next several days. Even after they passed it, the calendar would still show July and the weather would still be stifling.

"Breakfast is over," said Eriksen, the first mate. "All passengers must stay below decks until the noon meal."

"It's hot as Hades below decks," said Dirck.

"Master's orders," said Eriksen. "It's a small ship. Passengers interfere with the crew."

With grumbling, the passengers descended the ladderway into *de Kath*'s only available hold where both passen-

gers and crew slept—on opposite sides of the cramped
space not occupied by fifty lasts of salt. Penelope plucked
at her clothes, trying to let air circulate near her skin,
knowing it would get hotter each hour.

Hades, Dirck had said. Odysseus had visited the place
too and survived. Surely sitting in the steamy hold
wouldn't be as bad as crossing the river Styx.

As usual, Matthew sprawled in a hammock. Penelope
sat nearby, leaned against the side of the ladderway, and
bent her knees so that Jan could sit on her skirt hem and
lean against her shins. Together they rocked gently with
the movement of the ship. Traveling with a six-year-old
wasn't too bad. He was more entertaining than Matthew.

Three-year-old Sophie was peevish and climbed all over
her mother's warm, plump body. Penelope invited the child
to sit with her, but she shook her little head. Penelope
couldn't blame the girl. Sitting with slim Penelope was like
sitting in a wooden chair compared to the upholstered
softness of Trijn.

Jan asked, "Will we see any more birds?"

Penelope shook her head. "Maybe a few seagulls but no
birds like the ones on Bonaire. What a wondrous sight."

Jan stared at the square of bluish-white sky far above
his head. "I'm bored."

Several sailors who had just finished their watch scoot-
ed down the ladderway. They were now due four hours of
rest. Among them Penelope recognized Beanpole, a sailor
several inches shorter than she and heavyset, the opposite
of a beanpole. These sailors called each other by derogatory
nicknames, such as Stinky or Four-toes. One had a German accent. Could he possibly be the man who had lured
her father across the ocean?

Beanpole pulled a small knife from an ankle scabbard
and whittled on a piece of wood, tiny curls of shavings
falling relentlessly from a nearly completed project.

Jan asked the whittler, "Can you carve me a pirate
ship?"

"You don't need a toy for that, lad," Beanpole said. "You're riding on a pirate ship."

"What?" Penelope looked closely at Beanpole. Had she heard right?

"This very ship was a privateer on our last voyage." Beanpole squatted in the sunlight near Jan. "Here, lad. Would you like a snake?"

Jan examined the toy. "That's not a snake." The carving looked like a coil of rope with a big mouth at one end. "Snakes are long and skinny, not round."

"That's no Dutch snake, lad. That's a snake from Brazil. I seen it coil itself like that around a pig, squeeze the life out of the squealing animal, and swallow it whole."

Jan stuck his finger through the coils of the wooden snake. "On our farm, water snakes grab frogs and swallow them whole."

"Be telling of mermaids next." Out of the shadows appeared another sailor, nicknamed Rusty, because of the reddish shade of hair reminiscent of harlots strolling the Damrak at twilight. Rusty slouched against a bulkhead, just out of the sunlight.

"The Portuguese call it *anacanda*," said Beanpole. "It's God's truth. Truer than the lady's story of a thousand ships sailing after one woman."

Penelope had told Jan and Sophie a bedtime story from the *Iliad* the previous evening but didn't realize the sailors listened too. They were only a few feet away on the other side of the cramped hold, an embarrassing circumstance especially at bedtime. To give the seamen credit, or perhaps the credit was due to Dirck's threats, they had mostly ignored the passengers.

"Were you really pirates?" Jan asked.

Penelope hesitated, trying to decide what to do if they were truly pirates but also curious.

Beanpole squinted up at the open hold. "I got to talk softly. Our new shipmaster is part of the story and ships got ears."

"Not like Hans Weier," interrupted Rusty.

Penelope didn't care for the way the red-headed sailor looked at her and heat-stressed Trijn, who was often careless at letting a stocking-less ankle peek out from under her skirts. Instinctively, Penelope shoved her own shoe out of sight.

Frequent trips to the Amsterdam docks should have inured her to such glances from a sailor. These seamen acted apprehensive. No, that was too strong a word— uneasy—but certainly not contented like the ones on *de Melckmeyt*.

Maybe the difference was these seamen had been privateers. What did she know? This was only her second voyage. Surely by now every ship in the Caribbean had heard of the peace treaty signed in January and pirates were no longer a danger. She shuddered at the image of pirates—or privateers, no difference—boarding her ship.

"Now Hans Weier was a great ship master," Beanpole said. "I'd call him an admiral after the way he captured *Nuestra Senora Rosario*."

"Masterful strategy," added Rusty, who kept an eye on Beanpole as though he were jealous of the attention his friend received.

Penelope scrutinized Rusty, trying to decide if he fit the rumors—innuendo really—about sailors who had ship wives. She understood loneliness on long voyages but not how two men could be husband and wife. Such things had to be immoral because men looked around furtively when they talked about it.

"It started back in January in Manhattan. His High Mightniness, the Director-General himself..." Beanpole turned his head and spat, apparently expressing his opinion of the man, "begged us sailors to become privateers, to sail to the warm Caribbean, and prey on the papists."

Rusty coughed and spat into a corner. "Awfully cold in Manhattan in January."

"Were you pirates?" asked Jan.

"We was patriots, continuing the war against the Spanish enemy." Beanpole pulled a fresh scrap of wood from his pocket.

Jan looked disappointed as he studied his new toy. "I'd like a pig to fit inside the snake."

Beanpole grinned, to reveal several teeth missing. "A pig don't much look like a pig after an *anacanda* squashes the breath out of it. A fellow what sailed with Abel Tasman told me about a red rabbit bigger than a man. Lives on an island east of the East Indies. I'll carve one of them."

Penelope smiled at the phrase "east of the East Indies." A book she had read the previous year about the wreck of the ship *Batavia* east of Indonesia described plenty of islands but didn't mention giant red rabbits. But Beanpole hadn't claimed to have seen one, only to have heard a story of one. The sailors in Amsterdam's Damrak were full of strange stories. Her father had often cautioned her that only one sea tale in ten contained even a smidgeon of truth. She wouldn't have believed ten thousand pink storks if she hadn't seen them herself.

Rusty immediately stood up straight and stared when a sailor rolling dice on the other side of the hold shouted out. What did he fear?

Jan held up the coiled snake like a telescope. "Sophie might like a giant red rabbit, but I want a squashed pig."

Then Rusty slouched back against the bulkhead, looking like he was asleep on his feet.

Beanpole turned the block of wood around and around as though trying to spy a red rabbit in the grain. "We was on this very ship—*de Kath*—with Hans Weier as our shipmaster. Only had bad luck at first. The whole ship caught a fever straight out of New Amsterdam. Two Spaniards in a rowboat could have overpowered us. We was lucky to arrive at Curaçao, where we laid up a month or so to recover."

"What a boring place," Rusty said.

Penelope agreed with Rusty and hoped they weren't still contagious. Rusty looked rather pale.

"Then our luck changed." Beanpole grinned. "Master Weier picked a strait running east-west only sixty *zeemijlen* from Curaçao and thirty *zeemijlen* from Caracas."

Ninety English nautical miles from the large Spanish port of Caracas seemed rather daring until Penelope realized Curaçao was the same distance from Caracas.

"We anchored betwixt two tiny islands just south of Isla de Margarita. The master sent lookouts to the flank of the huge peak atop Margarita with a telescope and a mirror. About the sixth afternoon we got a signal from the glass: a ship coming from the east down the center of the strait."

"The seventh afternoon," said Rusty, "not the sixth."

"That don't matter. It weren't long to wait."

"Hate waiting."

She agreed with Rusty again and smiled as Jan's fascinated eyes shifted from one sailor to the other. She also checked that Trijn was still dozing and couldn't object to Jan hearing this intriguing pirate tale.

"Master Weier sailed us out into the strait and dawdled so that when we sailed east in the late afternoon, we came out of the sun headed straight toward this Spanish ship."

"The *Nuestra Senora Rosario*," said Rusty.

Beanpole squinted at the carving. "But we didn't know her name then."

"Didn't even need false colors," said Rusty in his usual brusque fashion.

Jan asked, "What are false colors?"

Beanpole pointed up through the open hatch to the mast even though they couldn't see the ship's flag from their position. "Suppose a ship with a Dutch tricolor of orange, white, and blue approaches a Spanish ship, then the Spaniard gets all skittish. But suppose the Dutch ship flies a Spanish flag, then the Spaniard will be all friendly like."

Jan asked, "Isn't that cheating."

Beanpole winked. "Aye lad, in love and war all's fair."

Penelope hoped the wink wasn't intended for her. She was curious about privateers, feeling more knowledge would protect her in the future, despite the current war being over. "Why didn't you need false colors?"

In the darkened hold, Beanpole pretended to shade his eyes with a hand. "Because the Spaniard couldn't see our ship against the glare of the sun, not even with a glass."

"Looking at the sun through a glass can burn out your eyeball."

Beanpole frowned at Rusty. "The lad knows that. He ain't no fool."

"Never know with a young one."

Beanpole held the future giant red rabbit to the light and studied it for half a minute. "Only three hundred fathoms away, the Spaniard got suspicions on us but it were too late. Andriessen put a warning shot through the canvas. Our new master was the chief gunner then. To give him his due, he's a fair shot."

"Fair shot with a cannon." Rusty emphasized the last word.

What was the unspoken history of this odd group of seamen? Beanpole had an open, honest face but Rusty's eyes darted continually as though he mistrusted the world. She distrusted him.

"We was ready with six cannon, grappling hooks, muskets, and swords."

"Did you cut off a Spaniard's head?" asked Jan.

"Jan!" Penelope whispered. Trijn still dozed in the heat.

Beanpole grinned. "Not this time. That danged Spanish deck cleared like a church after amen. The Spaniard struck his colors soon enough and lowered his sails. We grappled and boarded but had no cause to shed blood."

Privateers were no better than highwaymen.

"A wretched little ship with hides." Rusty coughed again and spat noisily into the shadows. "That was the cargo— cow hides from Trinidad and a little tobacco."

"You expected a treasure ship?" asked Jan.

"Turned out to be one," said Rusty. "Well, sort of."

"Not at first." Beanpole shook his head. "Master Weier split the crew and cargo between *Rosario* and *de Kath*, recovered our lookouts, and dropped off the Spaniards on the beach with one longboat and some food."

"Tricked those papists," said Rusty. "Told them we were returning to Pernambuco."

Pernambuco, thought Penelope. Brazil. Land of coiled snakes and sugar plantations. How would the citizens of Amsterdam enjoy fancy desserts without the thousands of lasts of Pernambuco sugar imported each year?

"Why," asked Jan.

"Master Weier don't want the papists to be angry at Curaçao."

"Sailed out that very night," said Rusty.

"We had to have a master for the captured ship. Master Weier picked Andriessen."

"Why Andriessen?" Penelope's curiosity surprised her.

Beanpole shook his head. "I suppose because he's smart with numbers. Decent navigator."

"Kisses arses, he does," Rusty added.

Penelope put her hands over Jan's ears. She had trained him not to ask questions about what sailors had just said when she did that. Rusty's comment echoed what the clerk at the pier had hinted about this shipmaster.

Rusty straightened up and stared when two dice-players began to argue.

Beanpole carved the rabbit's ears small and the tail long and huge. "Selling a pirated Spanish ship and cargo only thirty *zeemijlen* from Caracas, now that's nothing but foolish. We set sail for New Amsterdam."

Rusty slouched again.

"Master Weier worked us six hours on and two hours off until we finally got to the straits of Florida. Then we could relax."

"Never did catch up on my sleep." Rusty looked like he was asleep now, leaning against a bulkhead.

"Our friend Joris, he was as sure as sin this fancy-pants merchant on *Nuestra Senora Rosario* done hid his valuables. Joris took his knife and pried at every plank on the ship." With his little whittling knife, Beanpole demonstrated probing between the deck planks.

"Finally found a loose one," Rusty said.

"Loose what?" asked Jan.

Beanpole explained in more detail. "Joris found a loose plank in a cabin, reached into the crevice, and pulled out a leather bag. The dang bag held a pearl necklace and silver coins—pieces of eight."

Penelope's father had once shown her a few Spanish *reales de a ocho,* large silver coins worth two and a half guilders, called pieces of eight because they were often cut into eight bits to be used as smaller coins.

"Nearly two hundred of them." Rusty sighed. "Such a pretty sight."

Beanpole spat into a dark corner. "Joris lost half of them coins gambling with us but he kept the pearl necklace."

"Until he reached Manhattan."

Beanpole sighed in despair. "Damn fool. He goes and sells the pearls to a friend of the *schout*, who knew a common sailor must have stolen such valuables. They done arrested us all."

In Amsterdam, a *schout* was sheriff and prosecutor. Penelope assumed the same was true in New Amsterdam.

Beanpole spread his hands wide in a gesture of futility. "Master Weier steals a ship from the Spanish and is a hero. We sailors find silver and pearls hidden on that same stolen ship and they threaten to hang us as pirates."

"Not fair," said Rusty.

Penelope asked, "Were you tried in court?"

"Confessed," said Rusty.

Beanpole clasped his hands in prayer. "The Director-General shoulda been a minister. He believes confession is good for the soul."

"Get a lighter sentence if you confess." At a faint noise Rusty glanced up the ladderway.

Beanpole shifted his body to get better light for the carving. "Because of a lack of sailors, the Director-General pardoned our piracy if we agreed to fetch a boatload of salt for him."

Penelope shook her head in confusion. "They trusted you enough to let you be sailors again?"

Rusty shrugged. "Nothing to steal but salt. No place to escape to."

"We only stopped at Curaçao and Bonaire. Now we go straight back to Manhattan."

Penelope asked, "Why is Andriessen still a master? Surely a criminal can't be one."

"We sure as sin didn't tell Andriessen of no treasure because we don't trust him. But Captain Weier, he's a rich man now. He's done gone home to Amsterdam."

"No other choice for master but Andriessen."

Jan frowned. "That doesn't look like a rabbit."

Beanpole handed the carving to the boy. "That's the way the man described it. Big hind legs. Big tummy. Short front legs. Sits up like a begging dog. Huge tail. Leaps over bushes."

Jan held it up to the light and laughed. "I'll keep it because it looks like a dragon. Sophie can have the next one. She likes kittens."

A giant red rabbit is as likely as a dragon or a mermaid or a pink stork, Penelope thought. But she asked, "What happened to the pearls and pieces of eight?"

Beanpole snorted. "The *schout* confiscated the pearls and silver but he couldn't keep all of them for hisself and prosecute us too. Thus the company got most of the Spaniard's treasure plus our share of the prize."

"Not that a common seaman gets much of a share. A tithe split among an entire crew."

Jan asked, "Will you carve Sophie's kitten now?"

Beanpole slid his knife back into its ankle sheath. "Later boy, I need my sleep."

Rusty said, "Sell him a toy so you can pay me the guilder you owe me."

Beanpole threw up his hands in disgust. "That's my life. Peace breaks out when I'm broke. The days of privateering are done for. The best way to make money now is to own a tavern in Manhattan."

Rusty spat again. "Have to be a friend of the *schout* to do that. Or pay him off."

"They say his price is cheap." Beanpole shrugged. "I wonder if he holds a grudge."

"Why would he?" Rusty yawned. "We made him rich."

The sailors drifted to their side of the hold and bedded down.

Penelope glanced around. Waiting was hard. Two or three weeks of sweaty boredom in this stinky hold with nothing to see or do except think about the future.

When they arrived in New Amsterdam, would she seek out the *schout* and ask him about John Kent? But, according to the two seamen, the schout in New Amsterdam couldn't be trusted. Not trusted by anyone or not trusted by thieving sailors?

How much money would a man kill for? Or die for? She looked at sailors dozing on the far side of the hold. For a hammock, three meals a day, and a few guilders a month these seamen risked their necks climbing high in the rigging on an ordinary day and were expected to risk life and limb to defend this ship or to attack another ship for plunder. She stared at Beanpole. Could he be a murderer?

Murder was quite common in Shakespeare's plays. But how easy was it for real people?

Could she locate her father's murderer without putting herself in danger? What would wily Odysseus do? Obviously, what he did when he finally arrived home in Ithaca—go in disguise to evaluate the situation before revealing his true identity. Penelope had the perfect disguise: Mrs. Matthew Prince. Who in New Amsterdam could link that name to John Kent?

To forget about murder, Penelope contemplated what she might do in New Amsterdam for her twenty-second birthday next month on August 13. Half a lifetime ago she learned Julius Caesar died on an exotic date, the ides of March, and wished her birthday was the same.

Her father explained the ides was the fifteenth day in only four Roman months; in the other eight, including August, the ides was the thirteenth. It was so easy to be happy when one was eleven years old. Or six years old. She stroked Jan's tousled hair and he smiled up at her.

Matthew didn't believe in birthday presents but Penelope had saved herself a silver half-guilder. What shops, besides taverns, would she discover in Manhattan? A confectionary shop perhaps? New Amsterdam was closer to the sugar plantations of Brazil than Amsterdam was. After months of GWC food, fresh cheese or fresh fruit would be a treat. Even a fresh carrot would be delicious.

Jan asked, "When will we get there?"

Most of the sailors had gone to sleep. Sophie clung to her mother. Dirck and two sailors gambled with seashells picked up on the rocky beach of Bonaire. Matthew mumbled Bible verses. What would occupy Jan for two weeks?

Penelope asked, "Would you like to learn to read?"

Stinky passed by on another trip to the dung bucket. "Hey, boy. Them books won't teach you to reef a mainsail in a storm."

Chapter 13

The Atlantic Ocean

Thursday, Aug 6, 1648

During her few minutes of freedom to stretch her legs after lunch, Penelope stood near first mate Eriksen when he took a noon measurement of the sun. After weeks of disappointment, she still hoped for an opportunity to use the astrolabe and this might be her last chance.

"Thirty-seven degrees, the latitude of Virginia," Eriksen said to no one in particular, even though she was the only one close enough to hear. "It's always good to be well north of Cape Hatteras. Only four degrees and two days from New Amsterdam."

Penelope glanced astern as though to confirm the ship was safely away from Cape Hatteras, a dangerous region because land stuck so far out into the ocean, and noticed the skies to the south. "I've never seen clouds of that grayish-green color. Nor that shape."

Ericksen nodded. "Won't get a sighting tomorrow with a storm coming."

Contemplation of another storm made her stomach twist in knots like seasick Matthew's.

The master came on deck to check the mate's calculations. They discussed the winds and clouds. Soon a stream of orders flowed, one directing all passengers to go below.

Throughout the afternoon, a stronger and less predictable rocking replaced the gentle motion of the ship. Merely walking was dangerous. Penelope clung to a post to keep from sliding across the floor. The odor of vomit floated in the air. Until this weather, Penelope's fellow passengers on this second trip had been doing better in their ongoing battle with seasickness. Was it experience or the ginger? Would chewing the aromatic root overcome the noxious aromas that began to fill the stuffy hold?

Matthew sat up in his hammock. "Dirck, do you have more ginger?"

"Here's my last piece," Dirck said. "You've been gobbling it like fried eel all day."

* * * * *

After a sparsely attended lunch the next day, Penelope held onto a line of rigging to keep her balance as she delayed her return to the vomit-encrusted hold. She half-listened to the helmsman curse the blustery winds that attempted to push the ship northwestward toward land.

The helmsman shouted to the first mate only a few feet away. "Does Andriessen want to try for the South River?"

The South River, called the Delaware by Virginians, marked the southern extreme of the colony of New Netherland. No safe harbors existed between there and New Amsterdam.

The first mate called back, "No, he's in a hurry to get to New Amsterdam. It's less than a day away with this extra knot of speed the storm gives us." He left to check the forward sails.

The helmsman muttered, "Wouldn't want Andriessen to get a scolding for being a day late. Instead we risk our necks for salt in August? Bah."

Penelope agreed with the helmsmen. She too was anxious to reach her destination but not at risk of shipwreck.

The passengers were ordered from the deck into the safety of the hold. The winds increased during the afternoon and became more erratic. The waves crested higher. Penelope sat at the top of the ladderway with her head in the fresh air, hoping no one on deck would notice her.

From her restricted view at the level of the deck, the rolling of the ship presented a panorama of boisterous greenish waves and billowing gray clouds. She slid down a step when the ship master stalked by then poked her head up again like a mouse in its hole.

Not far away, the ship master conferred with the helmsman and the first mate. She eavesdropped on their conversation despite the wind that blew some words away.

Master Andriessen, the partially deaf former cannoneer, shouted, "It's a...thunderstorm. It'll be gone...morning."

The helmsman shouted back, "No, it's a hurricano. It'll...worse and last for days." Beanpole had said the helmsman was quite experienced.

Master Andriessen shouted, "...hurricano never strays beyond Florida and we passed there days ago."

The first mate said, "Whatever...this washtub of a ship doesn't like..."

The helmsman said. "I can't take her through the *hoofden* in...erratic winds."

A sailor nicknamed Stinky had explained yesterday the last obstacle before the placid waters of the Upper Bay and the fine harbor of Manhattan was The Narrows. Two *hoofden,* or headlands, constricted the channel where the combined waters of the North River and Upper Bay struggled to enter the Atlantic Ocean, similar to Odysseus's challenge of navigating between Scylla and Charybdis. She prayed for better fortune than the ancient seaman's.

Andriessen said, "But we can make it to the Lower Bay."

The Lower Bay offered a wide entrance between the jutting peninsula of Sandy Hook, also called Godyn's Point, on the west side and the stones of Rockaway Point on the east.

"The Lower Bay...," the mate said. "Which part is the safest?"

"The winds...southeast," shipmaster Andriessen said. "Enter the bay and turn southwest. Put Sandy Hook between us and the storm."

"...tacking crosswind to the storm," said the helmsman, "but...hug the lee shore of Sandy Hook. Then anchor and ride it out."

Penelope diagrammed the discussion in her head. Andriessen's scheme would place the barrier island, into which the southeast wind was now trying to drive the ship, as a shield from the same wind. All they had to do was make a loop to the far side of Sandy Hook.

She moved to allow a sailor down the ladderway.

"Take this. It's supper." Molasses, the fat cook, handed her a pail of ship biscuits and lumbered back to the galley.

She almost fell as she lugged the pail to a lower tread and waved a hard, stale biscuit in the air. Matthew groaned and looked away. Odors of seasickness and urine came and went as gusts of air swirled around her. How awful would it become when they closed the hatch for the night?

Four-toes, Dog's Breath, and Bucket—who used to be called Gimpy until his unfortunate encounter with a vomit pail—came forward and took a handful of biscuits.

* * * * *

Penelope endured a long, fitful night, loosely tied into her hammock. Sailors, on two-hour watches, came and went, the hatch cover banging in the wind, streams of rainwater and seawater sloshing down the ladderway. At least the water washed the vomit into the bilge, where the pumps squeaked all night as shifts of seamen pumped saltwater back into the sea. The steady pump noise was more comforting than the erratic howl of winds and creaking of ship timbers.

Dim morning light seeped into the hold and proved they had survived the night.

"Land, Ho!" rang down faintly from the crow's nest.

"Thank the Lord," whispered Matthew.

"Where are we?" Penelope asked Four-toes coming down the ladder.

"Too close to the shore in this storm," said the drenched sailor.

Penelope didn't like the sound of that and started to extricate herself from the hammock.

"Don't bother," the sailor said. "Can't see a damn thing." He stumbled away, stripping off his oiled-cloth coat on the way. Water dripped from his hammock for several minutes.

At the end of another shift, Stinky stumbled down. He smiled at Penelope. "Now, there's land worth seeing."

She poked her head out of the hatch and peered around. The long-awaited land proved disappointing, merely low gray shapes on the horizon. The ship still tossed as much as ever. Sea foam sloshed around her as waves burst over the ship. Ever so slowly, the ship crawled forward until the gray land-shapes were definitely astern and the helmsman made the larboard turn around Sandy Hook.

The wind felt as blustery as ever. Did the waves grow smaller? Yes, she could feel it. The ship didn't roll as far. Waves crashed over the beam less often.

She turned to tell the others the good news but stopped at the sound of voices.

Shipmaster Andriessen said, "An excellent execution of my excellent plan."

The helmsman said, "Look. The wind's still shifting. Coming more from the east."

"Then we arrived in time," Andriessen said. "A few hours later and an east wind would've made it trickier to round the Hook."

The helmsman said, "A shifting wind is more evidence of a hurricano."

"Damn your blasted hurricano," shouted Andriessen. "Any idiot knows God reserves that particular wrath for the dominions of the accursed Spanish not good Protestants. We're safe now."

Who knew more about the hurricane: Playwright or seaman? Experienced helmsman or novice ship master? England had never seen a hurricano—a Spanish word—so the playwright's forty-foot wave was surely an exaggeration. The Spanish had sailed these waters for a century and a half and they feared the hurricano although Penelope had doubts about winds that traveled in a circle as the helmsman described. A waterspout maybe but not a storm ten thousand times stronger. Yet she had seen one pink stork and then thousands more.

She shook her head in exasperation. Whether this was a hurricano or not, any storm was dangerous. She wouldn't rest easy until clouds dissipated and skies turned blue.

The mate said, "The waves are smaller here. Would you prefer to still be in the ocean?"

The helmsman had no answer. The few sails still aloft alternated between full and loose in the blustery wind.

"How long is this Sandy Hook island?" asked the master.

"It's a peninsula," said the helmsman. "Two or three zeemijlen long."

Andriessen sounded confident. "Go halfway and anchor. It'll blow over by tomorrow."

Penelope retreated down the stairs and waited. An hour later she felt the ship slow as sails were reefed and heard the anchor chain rattle. Tired sailors trudged down the steps and fell into their hammocks.

She crept topside into the gale and clung to the lower ropes. If questioned, she would claim they needed more biscuits. Sandy Hook was half an English mile away on the larboard beam, a low-slung beach. Several miles ahead— south or southwest, she thought—lay the mainland, a dim blur in the distance. The deck was nearly deserted. One sailor on watch stared intently from the stern into the distance as though searching for taverns in Manhattan.

On the deserted deck in the late afternoon she grew bolder. She was tired of the dark, stinking hold. With her back to a mast, her clothes sopping wet, her loose hair blowing in the storm winds, she stared at the blurry shape of the distant mainland, the land called America.

Penelope lingered at the mast, captivated by the winds and clouds, drenched by gusts of rain, anxious to see distant forests. She understood why Odysseus had chained himself to a ship's mast to listen to the sirens. She couldn't resist the lure of a land covered with forests—tall trees like her father had described along the coasts of the Baltic Sea. She had to see for herself, comprehend it in her soul.

Although she didn't move her head from its position tight against a mast, her view of the distant shore slowly changed. She asked Stinky—not a bad fellow on a gusty day—why the ship turned on its anchor chain. He went to find the mate, who checked the wind and the sea and went to find the master, who was already coming topside. They conferred quietly a few feet away from Penelope, who hoped to remain invisible in a brown dress behind the mast, despite craning her neck to eavesdrop on the conversation.

Erkisen, the mate, looked over the side. "The waves are higher."

The helmsman held up a cloth by a corner. "Northeast by east. It's shifted two points in two hours. Thirty-five, forty knots?"

"Is this wind going in circles?" the mate asked.

"Damn it," the ship master said. "Storms don't go in circles. We'll be safe here. This storm can't change direction any further than it already has."

"You can't predict the course of a hurricano," the helmsman said. "It will follow you like a demon and turn on you like a snake."

Eriksen held out his hands in helplessness. "The winds started out from the southeast, then the east, and now are veering more to the northeast. What do we do if the winds shift more to the north?"

"If you're so afraid, go below with the women and children. I'll find another mate." The shipmaster strode angrily back to his cabin.

After the master had gone, the helmsman said, "The hurricano does go in circles. It will blow water up your nose and sand up your arse."

The mate repeated, "What do we do if the winds shift more to the north?"

The helmsman stared at the skies for a long time. "We pray."

The winds continued to shift direction. The dreary sky darkened even more. Violent gusts from the north pounded *de Kath*. For a quarter-hour rain fell as though God poured it from buckets. Storm-tossed waves crashed upon the invisible shore.

Matthew came to reason with her, but Penelope wouldn't listen. He knelt and prayed for deliverance.

Ship master Andriessen emerged from his cabin again and conferred with the mate and helmsman. They studied dark swift clouds, ugly waves, and rain squalls blowing in from two points west of north. The ship creaked and groaned, jerking on its anchor chain.

The master shook his head. "How can winds change so rapidly? This anchorage is a trap."

The helmsman cursed the hurricano.

The mate asked, "Do we try for Arthur Kill behind Staten Eilant? Or the Raritan River?"

"Either one is better than staying here," the master said. "Raise the anchor."

The mate blew his whistle. The crew stumbled out of their hammocks and sprang into action. Two sailors armed with axes took up position next to the mast. Penelope and Matthew fled down the ladderway into the darkness and wet stench of the hold. How much danger were they in if the master was ready to chop down the main mast?

Six passengers huddled on the floor in a corner, Jan and Sophie in relative safety in the middle of the adults. They prayed in English and Dutch.

Even below decks, Penelope heard the mate bellow, "Raise the..." The anchor chain rattled and the ship lurched, knocking the passengers around. "Unfurl the bottom..." The wind must have caught the sail as the ship heeled ten degrees, then fifteen and twenty. The passengers braced themselves. Why didn't the ship right herself?

All around her, wood groaned from the struggle between the forces of nature and the will of man. Timbers twisted. Water, seeping through the distorted planks, dripped onto her head and sloshed around the deck. The ship heeled, rolled, bucked. Frantic shouts floated through the air as the ship tried to overcome nature.

Sluggishly, the ship righted herself and picked up speed.

As Matthew whispered, "...through the valley of the shadow of death," during his fiftieth repetition of the Lord's Prayer, a massive jolt sent a shudder through the ship and tumbled the passengers across the hold. Timbers screeched. Winds wailed. Barrels of salt crashed against bulkheads that groaned and shrieked. Matthew threw his body over his wife to protect her.

Dirck said, "If this ship was an oxcart, I'd say the wheel hit a rock."

"No. The ship has grounded." Penelope prayed it was stuck on a sandbar and not destroying itself on sharp rocks.

Afraid to move, the six passengers waited for the vessel to right itself. Instead the ship lurched forward again with even more force. Timbers split with terrifying clamor. A heavy beam crashed to the deck of the hold beside Penelope, the wallop echoing in her ear that pressed against the thick wooden planking.

Matthew bellowed in pain. Water gushed into the hold from all directions.

The cry, "Abandon ship!" came from above and other voices repeated it.

"Matthew," she shouted into his ear. "Get up. The ship is falling apart."

"My leg's broken," he gasped. "Leave me. Save yourself."

Two sailors jumped down the stairs, splashed through the water, grabbed Trijn and the children, and pushed them up the ladderway into the heart of the storm. Dirck followed.

Penelope grabbed Matthew's hand and half-dragged him across the sloshing, sloping planks to the ladderway of the doomed ship. A sailor insisted, "Save yourself. Climb."

"No!" she screamed. "Not without him."

Pulled from above by his wife and pushed from below by a sailor, Matthew hauled himself up the steps into slashing rain, fierce winds, and scant daylight.

On deck another sailor pointed. "Land! Over there. Jump! The water's shallow."

Through the raging noise, Penelope heard the helmsman cursing the hurricano, or maybe it was a memory from earlier.

Crawling, sliding, slipping down the tilted deck, hand in hand, they plunged overboard. She was already so wet with rain she scarcely worried about drowning.

Spitting saltwater, Penelope struggled to her feet in the chest-deep sea, her clothes having absorbed fifty pounds of ocean. Matthew floundered nearby.

"Lean your weight on me," she said. They stumbled through wind, waves, and treacherous bottom. They fell and went under. Water sucked them backwards. A wave lifted and pushed them toward the shore. Penelope stood. Waves sloshed around her waist. With a broken leg, Matthew could go no further without deeper water to support his weight.

"Stay here. I'll get help."

Her calls couldn't penetrate the wind. She trudged onto the beach and shouted into the ears of two sailors. One on each side, they worked Matthew out of the surf and onto the beach. Torrents of rain had made the sand dunes as wet as the ocean. Now wind instead of waves attempted to knock her down.

The sailors called the cook who performed the role of chirugeon for he knew how to saw limbs off livestock or people. He gently cradled Matthew's leg and suddenly yanked it into position, the screams lost in the wind, the jagged ends of broken bone now invisible under the bloody skin. Seamen bandaged his leg with scraps of sailcloth and splinted it with driftwood. Penelope lay half on top of him in the sand, her face sheltered in his chest, his face sheltered in her long, blowing hair, her missing cap unnoticed.

During a wet, howling night, they heard, rather than saw, the ship break apart. Cargo, flotsam, and jetsam washed onto the shore or slammed together in the surf. Heavy barrels of salt crashed into one another, split themselves open, and made the sea saltier.

Chapter 14

Sandy Hook

Saturday, August 8, 1648

In the meager light of dawn, First Mate Eriksen surveyed the refuse-strewn sand and wondered how Master Andriessen would explain the loss of his first command to his High Mightiness, Director-General Stuyvesant. Would he tell the truth: he had done everything he knew how to do, yet still calamity struck?

A disheveled array of cargo, rigging, and personal possessions littered the storm-line of the beach. The sky promised a bright, cloudless day. The fickleness of weather and sea—deathly storms followed by beautiful calm—never ceased to astonish him, like a quiet sailor armed only with a marlin spike, who became a screaming banshee when boarding a Spanish ship.

The cook, Molasses, dutifully started a fire and retrieved utensils, barrels of food, and water. The man's hopeful attendance to his daily tasks reminded Eriksen an officer could still redeem himself with strong leadership despite yesterday's misadventure. As his grandmother's proverb said: every herring must hang by its own gill. Or maybe Fate was warning Erkisen his time was at hand, that he should return home with his profits while he still could. He knew sailors who had survived several shipwrecks and others who had died in the first one.

Master Andriessen interrupted Eriksen's thoughts with a speech to the survivors, who stood blank-eyed, waited for sizzling pork, or salvaged beer from a leaky barrel.

"Gentlemen and ladies," Andriessen began in a strong, clear voice. "By the grace of Almighty God, we all live and we have only one serious injury." He waved a hand in the Englishman's direction but didn't look at him.

"New Amsterdam is ten *zeemijlen* in that direction." All eyes followed his hand as he pointed northeastwards along the deserted beach. "Thirty English miles," he added for the injured man's benefit.

"We are on the far side of the point, where ships seldom come. Our only course of action is to walk in a large circle around the bay, a distance of about twenty or so *zeemijlen*, to reach Manhattan."

Eriksen was glad the shipmaster didn't add, "If we remain here, we die," because someone's conscience might object to the abandonment of the injured man. A quick retreat was the best way for the majority to survive.

Andriessen stretched out his other arm in the opposite direction. Again all eyes followed his gesture. "We'll start our circle southwest—away from New Amsterdam. With God's help, we'll meet friendly aboriginals or perhaps fur traders. It will be a difficult, dangerous, wearisome trek, but we *will* make it."

Several heads nodded. Some still looked dazed.

Andriessen paused and surveyed the group. "Gather whatever you can find to carry food and beer. God helps those who help themselves, so let's get busy."

Andriessen had spoken with more much assurance than Erkisen felt. In a state of confusion, an authoritative voice could lead men anywhere—into battle, through danger, toward the jaws of hell. Where was Andriessen leading this band of survivors?

Safety in numbers, Erkisen whispered to himself. *Safety in healthy numbers. Sacrifice the weak and save the strong.*

People shuffled away and began to pick through the remnants half-buried in the sand.

Andriessen signaled Eriksen and spoke softly. "Have the men salvage whatever they can, especially muskets, shot, and powder. Fetch the chest of trade goods with iron hatchets we can use for firewood and rafts. Have the sail maker prepare two harnesses so each child can be carried on a man's back."

Eriksen barked out specific orders. The crew rounded up intact barrels of salt, wrapped them in sailcloth for protection, and buried them in the sand. They knew that no cargo meant no pay for them.

Then Eriksen turned to the injured Englishman. "*Mijnheer* Prince, to carry you would require four men in shifts and we can't spare them. Furthermore, travel in your state would be wretched agony." He didn't add, *and kill you more quickly than remaining here.* "We'll take good care of your wife."

Mijnheer Prince nodded solemnly. "Thank you. God will look after me."

"No!" the wife shouted. "God sent me to look after you."

Husband and wife faced each other. Eriksen glanced from one to the other, seeing both concern and fear in their eyes. "You've a quarter hour to decide."

The wife stared wide-eyed at her husband. "You'll die without me."

"You must leave," the husband said. "You will die if you stay."

In a gesture that reminded Eriksen of his grandmother, God rest her soul, the wife put her hands on her hips and jutted out her jaw. "'Until death do us part.' I'm not leaving you!"

With regret, the mate realized no woman had ever felt such concern for him. His pity for the man was now tinged with envy, but he had no time for passion or regret.

Andriessen approached. Eriksen rehearsed his arguments in the unlikely event the master proposed to endanger them all by dragging along this nearly-dead weight.

Andriessen spoke softly to the husband still in the embrace of his wife. "*Mijnheer* Prince, if we reach New Amsterdam quickly, you should expect rescue in about ten days, maybe a fortnight. If you aren't rescued within three weeks, then you'll know we're done for. If you spy a ship, make a smoky fire so they can find you. May God have mercy on your souls."

Eriksen thought, may God have mercy on all of us.

In the ensuing silence, Eriksen saw in the Englishman's eyes an understanding of his state, a lack of choices that would result in his death. And now, the death of his wife.

The Englishman said, "God bless and preserve you."

The master walked away as the farm family came over to say goodbye with lengthy shaking of hands and brave words but Eriksen lingered behind.

The farm boy said with earnest conviction to the Englishman's wife, "Odysseus will come and rescue you."

"Yes, Jan." The Englishman's wife spoke to the boy but looked at the ship master. "Master Odysseus will come back for us as soon as possible."

Eriksen prided himself on his ability to understand and control people. But this strange woman was too well educated to be the wife of a carpenter, too interested in ships, and too friendly with his crew. He would never understand her. Especially after she elected to die on this God-forsaken beach with her injured husband.

The work progressed uncommonly fast. Eriksen had great respect, but only temperate fear, of the sea for he had seen it at its worst and had survived. Yet the unimaginable perils of this strange wilderness of land struck mortal fear into his sea-faring heart.

"Could you please have the men fetch my chest of carpenter tools?" the Englishman asked.

"It's at the bottom of the sea." Eriksen feigned the pose of a calm, brooding leader, his hands clasped behind him.

"No, the storm washed it ashore. I saw it half-buried in the surf."

"We don't have time." Eriksen continued to look away.

The woman said, "My husband needs his tools if we are to survive in this wilderness."

Silence lay heavily upon the nearby crew and passengers. Eriksen turned and stared at the woman. She had an odd name: Penelope. She stared back, not flinching. Her husband lowered his head to signal submission. At least, the man understood a second demand in this crisis was as good as mutiny. Who did this infernal woman think she was to challenge the first mate?

Hearing the shuffle of several sailors leaving to fetch the chest, he realized he had hesitated too long. To maintain a semblance of command, the mate half turned away and called to the sailors' backs, "Hurry it up!" If he survived, Eriksen promised himself he would quit the sea.

He shouted to prove he was still in charge. "Each man to carry one hatchet, two if he wants and has no musket. No personal possessions, except your stoutest shoes, one blanket, and one change of clothes."

He ignored the woman and spoke to her husband, "*Mijnheer* Prince, there should be hatchets left over. Make gifts to any *wilden* who come by."

Wilden—wild men—the heathen barbarians of America, friendly or fierce, naïve or vicious. The only thing predictable about them, Eriksen had been told, was their unpredictability. His one encounter with them had proven that. Now whenever he ventured into the woods of Manhattan, he brought a loaded and primed musket and several armed comrades.

Three sailors dragged the heavy chest of carpenter tools through the sand to a group of stunted pine trees. The

Englishman declined the offer of a musket, saying he had no experience.

Apparently believing the devil would take the hindmost, the frenzied horde of crew, soldiers, and farm family organized themselves for the march. Eriksen didn't ask the Englishman about the wife's intentions for he had no time to waste on people as good as dead. He ignored the several cries of farewell and the answers of "Godspeed" as he looked ahead to a week or more in this devil-infested wilderness. He was prepared for a few people to die on this trek as long as he wasn't one of them.

*****

On the silent beach Penelope waved until her last contact with civilization vanished around a bend in the shoreline. In a moment of panic, she wanted to abandon her husband and flee after the crew. *Get thee behind me, Satan.*

Then she turned away and stared at the scattered remains of the hurried departure. She trudged through the sand and collected anything she could carry including what the passengers had thrown away.

Matthew broke the silence. "Please fetch a drawknife from the tool chest and that straight piece of driftwood so I can fashion a crutch."

Penelope slogged through the sand again and tugged on the chest's lid. It didn't budge. "How much tar did you use to seal this?" She recalled his many evening hours in Amsterdam sharpening and greasing the iron implements before stowing them in the chest.

"A gallon. I didn't want my tools to rust during an ocean voyage."

"I can't move either you or the chest. I'll fetch a couple of those little axes for you to pry it open with."

While Matthew dragged himself through the sand to rescue his tools, Penelope searched the beach. Except for the jungle of tall masts in Amsterdam harbor, she had never seen a forest but the thicket of little pine trees behind the dunes was not worthy of the title. Those trees did earn her respect when bristly limbs threatened to rip her garment to shreds as she penetrated the undergrowth.

She had never before walked on a beach, except for the rocky shore of Bonaire. In amazement, she studied the multitude of shells half-buried in the sand. She picked up a pretty one to examine and threw it down in alarm when a living creature emerged. The tiny beast looked ugly but harmless. What other surprises awaited her in this strange land?

Gossip had said rich Amsterdammers traveled to the coastal villages of Friesland to enjoy swimming and frolicking in the water. How and why does one frolic in the ocean? Water was for ships, not people. And dangerous for both.

She didn't venture far from the fire and returned often to pile up more driftwood and to ensure her husband didn't attempt overmuch and injure himself more.

The ship master had advised to create a smoky fire to signal a ship, whereas previously she had always strived to make smokeless kitchen fires. A damp cloth would do the trick. What if a passing thunderstorm quenched the fire?

Although noon was hours away, the heat of the August sun beat upon them. Together, they rigged a sail fragment into a canopy with the otherwise worthless pines serving as two corner posts of the shelter.

At noon they nibbled on ship biscuits. Penelope glanced upward at the sun, automatically estimating its height in the sky. What good was knowledge of latitude now? She wasn't going anywhere.

In early afternoon, Penelope scolded Matthew for his foolishness. He had tested his crutch and learned that walking in loose sand was dangerous even with a support. He didn't complain of his pain but she saw it in his face.

In mid-afternoon Penelope called to Matthew. "Look at this enormous log I'm standing on." Tall sea grasses rustled at her ankles.

She held her arms in a five-foot circle. "It's partly buried in the sand. Inside it's hollow and big enough to climb into. Surely, it's an oak. Father said oaks could be gigantic."

"I can't see it." Matthew started to rise.

"Matthew, sit down! I'll flatten the grass with a stick so you can get a glimpse." She released the branch she clung to and jumped down to the sand.

"Can you comprehend a living tree that big?" she asked.

Matthew nodded. "I wonder how many planks such a massive tree would yield?"

Chapter 15

Sandy Hook

Saturday, August 8, 1648

In the shade of the canvas awning an hour later, Penelope watched the small hot fire burn wood at an alarming rate. It popped and spat sparks whereas peat burned slowly and evenly in the fireplaces of Amsterdam. The idea of the fire dying in the middle of the night was unimaginable. Or rather her imagination was too active concerning a night without fire. While Matthew dozed, she crept away to find more wood before dark.

Before the ocean tried to drown her, the infinity of the sea was inspiring. Now, the bay frightened her. No, not today's bay, but the memories of yesterday's bay.

"Have courage," she whispered. She removed her shoes and stockings, lifted her skirts, and waded until cool water covered her ankles. She itched all over from the storm-blown beach sand embedded in every pore of her clothing.

She had often scoured Liesbeth's floor in Amsterdam with sand to remove grime and to make the wood shine. Gently she rubbed her arms and ankles with wet sand, marveling that human skin could be so dirty. A washcloth like she formerly used in the privacy of her bedroom would be more comfortable but not any more effective.

Thoughts of scouring a floor brought up memories of home. She wept and pretended tears were seawater. Practical Penelope had been entrusted by Grandfather Prince with taking care of dreamy Matthew. Her name itself was a byword for constancy, for the perseverance of a faithful wife waiting twenty years for her husband's return from the Trojan War despite "the slings and arrows of outrageous fortune."

She smiled through her tears, for having mixed English books with Greek ones. She mustn't allow distress to affect her mind, for clarity of thought was her only defense. Plus her literary knowledge of weapons used in the Trojan War and the battles of Julius Caesar. So far, her only enemy had been a two-inch beast hiding in a shell.

Without her cap, hair cascaded around her face, like a harlot strolling the Damrak. Her tresses were too tangled to braid or to comb, even if she had a comb. She chuckled for worrying over such minor nuisances. She and Matthew were alive and rescue would arrive in a week or two.

Late afternoon brought little relief from the day's heat to the two survivors from higher latitudes, sweltering under the canvas. Penelope worried about Matthew's reddening cheeks and nose. How long would her pile of driftwood last?

She stood and stared west across the calm waters of the bay toward the low-hung sun, somewhat obscured by distant clouds, thin and reddish.

She paused to listen to the silence. In Amsterdam, a city of a hundred thousand people, she had often felt lonely but never alone for the noises of civilization surrounded her.

"Penelope, what are you thinking about?"

"Bottomry bonds," she answered in due course.

"Bottomry bonds?" Matthew echoed.

She turned to look at her husband next to the fire. "I'm thinking about how much I know and how worthless it is. If this fire goes out, I don't know how to make another." At home in Amsterdam, flint and steel always hung by the fireplace. She no longer had a home.

He didn't look worried. "Wood is plentiful. We can keep the fire going."

She stared at the flame. "At the Amsterdam beast market I ordered my choice of meats. The butcher sent the account to Liesbeth and she paid. Here we have a few pounds of salt pork. When it's gone... There's no market in this wilderness."

She turned away from her husband, wanting to silence her voice but unable to control it. "I know how the Trojans and Greeks slaughtered each other, but I don't know how to kill an animal. A butcher killed, gutted, and skinned a rabbit in two minutes while I gossiped with his daughter."

Matthew answered, "God will provide for us, for we are his faithful servants."

How many of God's faithful servants had been martyred in recent wars? She forced the blasphemous thought from her mind. Despair filled the void.

"I grew vegetables in Liesbeth's garden. I haven't seen any carrots, radishes, or peas here. I don't know what wheat looks like in the field." She plucked a handful of sea grasses and examined the tiny seeds. "Is this plant edible?"

Matthew said, "'For in the multitude of wisdom is much grief, and he that increases knowledge increases sorrow.'" His voice was lifeless as though the Bible verses emerged from his mouth on their own volition like her worries did.

She surveyed the desolate shore, devoid of cities, devoid of civilization. "I know how to write contracts and arrange shipments. Yet buried over there are hundreds of barrels of salt. I don't even know who owns them now: the master who buried them, we who sit beside them, or our rescuers?"

Her husband's posture slumped like butter in the tropical sun. "Avarice is a deadly sin."

She eyed the disturbed landscape where ship timbers covered the sand that covered the sails that covered the barrels that held the salt. "I know what a bottomry bond is. If a ship is stranded in a distant port, the master can borrow money in the name of the ship. If the ship is wrecked, the bond holders have rights to the ship as long as the bottom, or keel, exists. I look at my own shipwreck and don't know whether the keel remains intact."

"There is profit in wisdom, more than in folly." His fingers carved "wisdom" and "folly" in the sand.

She ignored the words of Solomon. The setting sun peeked through pink clouds. A faltering breeze stirred the grass. Sweat dripped from her nose.

"I understand sin arising from pride of money or pride of beauty. Has God punished me because I was too proud of my knowledge?"

"'Pride goes before destruction and a high mind before the fall.'" Matthew's hand wiped away his earlier symbols and replaced them with "pride" and "fall."

She stared at the words in the sand. "If pride were truly a deadly sin, surely Amsterdam would've been drowned by the sea long ago."

Tears formed in her eyes because she knew she was guilty of pride of knowledge, guilty thereby of causing the hurricano to wreck the ship and to injure her husband.

"Here my only useful knowledge comes from a book I was ashamed to show you. Survivors of a shipwreck ate anything they could find: vermin, dead beasts, crawly things on the beach.

"Once, I was proud of being civilized. Now, I contemplate eating slimy things without names. How pompous was I to fall this far this fast?"

"No!" Matthew shouted and sat up straight. His eyes bored into hers. "Job suffered even more, but he was innocent of wrong-doing. God tests us, like he did Job, assessing our faith to see if we're worthy."

She turned away from her husband. "I know I'm unworthy. Why does God punish you for my sins? What lesson is He trying to teach me?"

"Teach us," he said. "This journey was my prideful mission."

She faced her husband, who offered to share her guilt equally, even though he only deserved a hundredth part of it. "Why does God make life and faith so hard?"

Matthew reached up and squeezed her hand. "If God sent gentle rains to the believers and hailstones to the non-believers, where would the challenge be?"

His faith was so big, hers so small. She might as well be a heathen as a Christian. "How can I believe like you do?"

"Faith starts as a tiny mustard seed but grows into a large tree."

She plucked debris clinging to her arm. "A tiny seed can also grow into a weed." She flung the kernel into the ragged grasses surrounding them.

"Trust in Jesus," he said.

She had always trusted in Jesus even though she didn't possess Matthew's utter faith that reached to the marrow of his bones. She had never felt her physical existence depended upon that faith. Until now.

Was this God's purpose—to demonstrate the futility of believing in man's knowledge instead of divine grace? Was this what accepting Jesus as your personal savior meant?

She knelt down and held Matthew's hand while he prayed aloud for many minutes. He pursued comfort in the familiar story of Job, innocent Job who suffered so much, faithful Job who refused to curse God, loyal Job who was at last restored to prosperity.

Penelope gathered no hope from these words because God destroyed Job's wife and children during the ordeal and then provided a new family.

Together husband and wife recited the Twenty-third Psalm. He concluded, "God tests us to determine if we're worthy to live in this new land. Our faith will sustain us. Amen."

She tried to pray. "I'm guilty. I'm sorry. Forgive me." It sounded like a papist prayer, rote words that the Separatists despised. Reverend Prince had taught an effective prayer must be an original plea from the soul, not a ceremonial formula.

Faith would certainly sustain Matthew. Yet she couldn't even create a simple prayer. *Jesus, have mercy on my soul.*

The sun threatened to dip below the western bay. Penelope cooked supper to sustain their spirits, to keep busy, to prove she still possessed one useful skill. She soaked salt pork in hot water, drained it twice, and cooked it an abandoned pan. With a hammer from Matthew's tool chest, she pounded the indestructible ship biscuits back into crude flour and cooked lumpy pancakes. They scattered the tasteless crumbs for the familiar gulls, those memories of home, of happier times spent looking at ships on the docks of Amsterdam, only five months ago, a lifetime ago.

After supper, Matthew implored God again with a long prayer of hope for rescue and thanksgiving for their lives.

"Is the pain bearable?" she asked.

"A little worse than hitting my thumb with a hammer."

She accepted this fib, perhaps the first he had ever told her, a lie contradicted by his grimaces. Fearful stories of festering wounds that poisoned the blood reminded her she had no knowledge and skill to counter them. Even the leg of His High Mightiness Pieter Stuyvesant had been amputated to save his life.

How does a chirugeon amputate a leg? How does the patient survive? Comparing the dismemberment of a chicken carcass to Matthew's body caused her to shudder.

In the fading sunlight she opened the bandage to examine the wound. It was black, red, purple, and ugly. What did she know? Might salt preserve his flesh as it did the pig meat. But the pig meat would never live again. She restored the bandage as well as she could.

To pass the time, Penelope told Matthew a shortened version of the wreck of the *Batavia*. She skipped the attempted mutiny, the rape of the female passengers, and the murder of half the sailors. Instead she described how survivors found food and water on a barren island and how the second mate steered a tiny boat by the moon and stars to reach civilization and safety.

There was no moon yet tonight. When was the last time anyone in foggy Amsterdam had noticed the skies? The moon was important on ships at sea and on lonely beaches.

She felt alone and far from home. Except she no longer had a home. How could her husband be so close and yet feel so far away?

Matthew twitched in his sleep, each movement making him moan. Penelope slept fitfully, frequently feeding the fire and worrying about Matthew, fire, food, water, firewood, weather, God, rescue, fire, Job, tomorrow, firewood, and Jesus.

Would the light of morning ever arrive?

She lay on her back and stared around the edge of the canvas shelter at the bright crescent moon high in the sky, a day or two before its last quarter. Toward the east the stars slowly dimmed until only Venus was visible above the pine thickets on the sand dune. A light breeze wafted the aroma of pine, as though she visited a carpenter's shop. She heard Matthew's regular breathing.

"Jesus," she whispered to the heavens, "preserve Matthew. He lives only to serve You."

She rose because it was morning, brushed sand from the dress she had slept in, and combed her matted hair with fingers. Without thinking, she looked for her cap, which the sea had consumed in the shipwreck. She picked up a linen stocking, felt the gritty sand in the weave, and shoved the stocking back into a shoe.

That the heap of firewood had diminished by only a third as she blindly fed it during the night brought a smile to her face. She placed two logs on the low flame and then surveyed her world, mostly the scattered detritus of the hurried departure. She ought to straighten the mess, salvage what was useful, and burn the rest. That's what any housewife ought to do.

She walked barefoot twenty feet away, squatted down, passed water, and kicked sand over it.

Back at the shelter, she envied Matthew and his slumber. Every minute of sleep was one less minute of worry.

A half-barrel of ship biscuits, a hunk of cheese, a few pounds of salt pork. Then what? She stood as still as the piece of driftwood holding up the canvas and watched Matthew breath. His chest rose and fell, rose and fell.

Having spent her entire life in a seaport, Penelope noted the absence of sea gulls. The morning silence was broken only by the buzz of flies and the faint lap of tiny waves. She stared at the empty, lonely, deserted beach. What if her husband died? She tried to comprehend total aloneness.

She jumped. Matthew's hand had slapped a fly on his broken leg and he grunted at the self-inflicted pain.

"Good morning." She forced cheerfulness into her voice. "Would you like bacon for breakfast?"

Matthew looked at his leg, around the shelter, then up at her. "Bacon would be good."

She shooed flies off the cheesecloth that covered the hunk of salt pork, sliced the meat, and dropped carvings of bacon into a skillet on the coals. She dipped a mug into the water barrel, replaced the top loosely, and handed the mug to her husband. A sand-colored bird with a black neck flew in and pecked at the remaining pork. She looked around for a way to protect the meat from flying thieves.

What was that motion to the east? She shielded her eyes from the brightness of the sun rising over the dunes.

"Matthew! Somebody's coming. We're rescued!"

Chapter 16

Sandy Hook

Sunday, August 9, 1648

"Rescued? So soon?" Matthew staggered to his feet. His clumsiness knocked the skillet of bacon into the sand.

"We're saved." Penelope moved beside him and gripped his arm to support him. She bent down to retrieve his crutch and looked toward their rescuer. Silhouetted against the rising sun, a human walked toward them, a body that looked like a child's drawing of a stick person with skinny arms and skinny legs.

Was she seeing things? She rubbed her eyes against the brightness of the sun. "Matthew, who is it?"

"I don't know." Matthew shielded his eyes. "Two, three, four of them. Half a dozen. More."

A dozen men converged upon them from all directions. Bare arms, bare legs, naked except for skimpy cloths that wrapped their loins. And thin shoes on their feet.

She shoved the crutch into his hand and grasped both arm and crutch. "Matthew, they're *wilden!*" Her father had talked of the wild aborigines of America. But she expected them to be like a circus performer's tame bear on a chain, not to stride like they owned the beach with stone knives and hatchets in their belts. Bows dangled from their shoulders.

She moved a little behind Matthew then realized she was supposed to protect him. She shuffled up next to her husband. Why had Matthew declined a musket? What good would a single weapon be against a dozen men?

The *wilden* stopped fifteen feet away, formed a semicircle before the two Europeans. They stared at one another.

"They look young, like children." Penelope estimated their ages at fourteen to eighteen. Their bodies were much leaner than Matthew's but some were as tall as he.

"Children with weapons are even more dangerous."

"They don't act dangerous." She thought they looked curious. Nevertheless, she shivered.

One native, a little taller and perhaps older than the rest, stepped forward. He held up an empty hand and spoke some words.

Matthew raised his hand in a similar manner. "God bless you this fine morning."

"What do they want?" she asked.

"Who knows?" Matthew gripped her hand. "Don't show fear."

Her father had once said those same words when they confronted a snarling dog in an alley. When he clapped his hands, the dog ran away.

The *wilden* broke ranks and wandered the campsite, fingering the discarded goods that littered the area, but taking nothing.

Penelope's eyes darted as she tried to watch all of them simultaneously. "The master said to trade with them."

"Trade what?"

She looked around. Two large wooden chests caught her eye. "Trade the hatchets."

"Give them weapons?"

She hesitated. "They already have bows, arrows, knives, and stone hatchets. What difference will an iron one make?"

Penelope started to move forward.

Matthew held her back. "It's too dangerous."

She pried his fingers loose. "Doing nothing is more dangerous."

She walked hesitantly toward the chest of trade goods. The *wilden* gave way before her. One reached out a finger to touch her hair. She shifted away from him in fright and almost bumped into another. The second one touched her dress, stroked the fabric lightly with his fingers. Sweat beaded on her forehead. She wanted to slap his hand. Or run. But Matthew had said not to show fear.

She gathered her courage and walked forward. The linen fabric slid through the aborigine's fingers. She flinched as another reached for her dress but she continued onward.

At the trade chest, she stopped herself from flinging open the lid. Instead she opened it the smallest amount, reached in her arm, pretended to stretch to the bottom, and withdrew an item from the half-full chest.

She turned around, her body half sitting on the lid to protect it, and looked at the young men. They stood tall and fondled the hilts of the knives in their belts. She froze.

Matthew called to her, "Don't hold it like a weapon."

She looked down at the small ax that she clutched in her hand like a hammer ready to strike a nail. Her fingers moved away from the handle to the iron head. The *wilden* relaxed.

She recognized the tall one, the one who had gestured to Matthew. The bodies of two small animals dangled from his belt along with a knife and other weapons.

"You, sir." The handle of her hatchet pointed to the two animals at his waist.

The leader approached and stroked the iron blade with a single finger. Then he looked down at his belt, shrugged, and displayed empty hands.

Penelope slowly stretched out the handle of the little ax and lifted the head of an animal. It looked like a rabbit. She waggled the iron hatchet in her right hand and waggled two fingers of her left hand at the two rabbits. An iron hatchet for a meal was a poor trade. But she had more iron than food and she was anxious to make these *wilden* happy—happy enough to go away.

The native grinned. He quickly jerked two rabbits from his belt and dangled them in front of her. She stretched out a hand for the animals. He stretched for the iron weapon. For a moment both held iron and meat. Then she released the hatchet and took the rabbits.

The aborigine waved the iron weapon in the air and shouted to his companions. Penelope tiptoed behind the other *wilden* and sneaked back to Matthew and the canvas awning, where she deposited the rabbits beside the pork.

"Well done," Matthew whispered.

A tiny smile formed on her lips. Let the young man celebrate. He could probably catch two rabbits in two minutes. She couldn't catch two rabbits in two weeks.

A scar-faced native stomped up to the Europeans. He removed an ugly necklace of bones and shells from his neck and thrust it toward them, pointing with his other hand alternately at the native with the iron hatchet and at the chest of weapons. He spoke rapidly, angrily in his incomprehensible language.

With a step forward, Matthew placed his body between Penelope and the aborigine. "What do you want, you rude beggar?"

She peered around her husband's shoulder. "I think he wants to trade." What else could he want?

"For a hatchet?" Matthew asked. "That necklace isn't worth anything."

"I don't care. The first mate said to keep the *wilden* happy." What would the savages do if they became unhappy? She didn't want to find out.

"Will they go away after they trade?"

"I hope so." Penelope eased forward.

The young man stopped scowling. He led the way and dropped the necklace atop the chest. She picked it up gingerly. What kind of bones did it contain? She started to drop it into her apron pocket but she wasn't wearing an apron. The hurricano had stolen it.

Again Penelope opened the lid the least distance and pretended to search the bottom for a hatchet. She held one up. The native yanked it from her hand and ran toward the first customer, waving his prize high in the air.

Before she could slink back to Matthew, several natives confronted her on the path and dangled various things for trade. Even in the foreign tongue, she could detect their impatience. Matthew looked distressed. She grinned at the jealous little children and returned to the chest.

One by one, she examined whatever a native offered, accepted it, and handed him an iron hatchet. Matthew took a step closer to her with each trade, watching her like a guard dog, even though the young natives seemed as dangerous as a flock of pigeons.

As she prepared to exchange another hatchet for a stone knife, she heard a distinctive clunk of iron against iron and looked up. Not far from where Matthew stood, two *wilden* argued over the opened chest of carpenter tools. With an upraised hatchet, the native she had traded with first threatened the scar-faced man who held one of Matthew's chisels.

"Stop that," she shouted. "Those tools belong to us."

The two thieves froze and stared at her. Matthew turned toward them and took a step.

"That's our property you're stealing." She waggled the stone knife in her hand in warning. "Now drop it and close our chest," she said in the voice she used with naughty neighborhood children in Amsterdam.

The two aborigines ignored her and returned their attention to their own dispute.

Matthew moved toward his trunk to protect his tools. His crutch caught in the sand but his leg continued forward. His full weight pressed upon his broken limb. He screamed and began to fall.

As though time stood still, Penelope watched Matthew's body pitch forward toward the two thieves. The native leader, his arm and weapon already raised, turned at the sudden scream and brought his hatchet down upon the leading part of Matthew's body.

The iron cleaved her husband's skull. He collapsed and lay motionless in the sand.

The sand turned red. Sunlight glinted off the shiny weapon protruding from Matthew's skull.

The murderer stumbled back. The second aborigine stepped forward and knelt beside the body.

"No!" screamed Penelope. Without thinking and without noticing the hatchet and knife in her hands, she raced toward Matthew and his murderer.

The second aborigine, startled by her ferocious charge, backhanded her with the chisel. The sharp blade cut across her abdomen. She dropped her weapons, clutched her intestines, and staggered sideways. A shadow descended from above and behind. A hatchet grazed her skull and bit deeply into her shoulder.

She fell to her knees. "No," she whispered to the man with the chisel as she fell at his feet. "No" was her last thought.

Chapter 17

Sandy Hook

Sunday, August 9, 1648

Hours later, Penelope regained consciousness. Her head ached and her left shoulder was afire with pain. She lay on her back. Every movement increased the agony. She remained motionless. Nothing made sense. The bright sun blinded her. Why was she lying in the sun?

She shifted her eyes downward. They didn't focus well but she saw red and white. She didn't own a red and white dress. The congregation would never approve. Her eyes focused better. The white part of the dress was her bare skin. The elders would never approve of her nakedness.

A throbbing near her left ear and in her left shoulder confused her. Her right hand felt wet and dirty. At least the fingers moved, but they looked reddish. Red gloves? She had no red gloves. Matthew would never approve. She raised her hand a few inches and focused on her fingers. They were bloody. She lowered her hand and rested it on her abdomen. Her skin felt sticky and irregular, not clean and smooth like it should be. A cut. A long cut. A soft slippery mass in the cut.

She should...she should... She fainted.

Waking up, she inventoried her body. The half-dried blood on her abdomen indicated the bleeding had stopped. Her right hand and arm worked. Something was badly wrong with her left arm. Her right hand probed her aching shoulder and detected a deep gash, the skin gaping open a half inch. Why didn't it hurt more? A wound that deep should scream with pain.

She wiggled her toes, flexed her knees, and stretched her leg muscles. Everything below her waist worked, yet she had no strength. The tiniest movement jarred her brain. Her neck had a thin trickle of drying blood. She whimpered when her fingers reached toward the left ear and touched a lump like a ball of wet yarn.

The top of her head tingled as though scalded with boiling water but she feared it was as tender as the last spot she touched.

Where was Matthew? Why wasn't he here to help her? Was he injured too? Did he need her help? She wanted to lie in the sand and ignore her injuries. If Matthew was not helping her, then she must help him. Where was he?

She swiveled her eyes but saw nothing but sea grasses. Moving her head the smallest amount generated waves of pain. Telling her body to be steady and to ignore the pain, she planned her movements.

She turned her body onto her right side, leveraged her elbow, and pushed to a sitting position. Her screams rattled her brain inside her skull. With eyes tightly shut, she waited for pain, nausea, and fear to subside.

From the higher vantage of a sitting position, Penelope saw a bare, motionless leg. The rest of the body was out of sight behind a small dune. It must be the leg of an aborigine because Matthew wore clothes, like she did. She looked at her pale, bare skin and the pale, bare skin of the unknown leg with a splint wrapped around it.

It had to be Matthew. The idea that Matthew was dead paralyzed her. No, surely her body had been just as still a few minutes ago. Matthew was unconscious as she had been.

How badly was he hurt?

She started to rise but had no strength. She couldn't crawl on hands and knees with only one good arm. Inch by inch, she dragged her body across the beach, ignoring the scraping of sand on bare thigh.

Matthew's bloody matted hair indicated a head injury. Was it bad? His chest felt warm to her touch. She knew he must still be alive and put her head to his chest to hear the affirming sound of his heart and feel the rise and fall of his breathing. There was neither. Nothing but the heat of the sun.

She lay with her head on his chest. She had been unable to cry for herself. Now she cried for both of them and for a vanished dream of a new life. She ought to say a prayer for his body but words wouldn't come. Matthew's congregation didn't indulge in funeral rites. Death meant a trip to Heaven and a happy union with Jesus. She cried again.

In her loneliness and grief, she prepared to lie down and die too. Was this how her father had died? Without a grave? Without words said over him? Like Matthew, she was Anabaptist now and didn't deserve any final words. But her father was still Anglican. He deserved kind words to commend his soul to God.

The concluding words of Matthew's prayer from the previous evening came to her, "We put our faith in our Lord and Savior, Jesus Christ, and pray, 'Yeah, though I should walk through the valley of the shadow of death, I will fear no evil, for thou art with me; thy rod and thy staff, they comfort me.'" Her hand rested on Matthew's crutch. She grasped it. With trembling limbs, she arose and leaned on the staff. She should stand to honor her father's memory.

"Thou doest prepare a table before me, in the sight of mine adversaries; thou doest anoint mine head with oil, and my cup runneth over." She looked around. Near the canvas awning, she saw a keg.

Even stronger than thirst, she felt a need to dip a cloth into the water and cleanse Matthew's body. Even though they didn't say words of grief, surely the Separatists cleaned the body even though the soul had gone to Heaven.

Slowly she shuffled the immense distance of ten feet through the sand. The overturned water keg retained a quart of liquid. She sank down around the crutch, stretched her face into the keg, and lapped water like an animal.

She clumsily brushed her head against the broken wood and squealed with pain. The scream echoed behind her and she whirled around on her knees to face this new danger. Two huge black birds the size of geese flapped ungainly, backed away from half-eaten rabbits, and then stared at her with their evil red eyes. Never had she seen such ugly creatures. Were they Greek Harpies or the devil's minions come to claim her soul? She cringed away from them.

In the silence, a smaller black bird joined these cronies of Satan, walked to Matthew's leg, and pecked at it. She waited for Matthew to slap the impertinent bird, until she remembered he would never move again. She cursed at the bird like a sailor and collapsed in the sand, fearful of losing her soul for the curses and her mind from the trauma.

The throbbing inside her head matched the cadence of the Twenty-third Psalm, as she had relearned it from Matthew's Geneva Bible, "The Lord is my Shepherd; I shall not want. He maketh me to rest in green pasture." Ahead was a pasture of tan sea grasses.

"And leadeth me by the still waters." Between the grass and the surf was a quiet tidal pool. "He restoreth my soul and leadeth me in the paths of righteousness for his name's sake." A path through the tan pasture led to the hollow trunk.

"Yea, though I walk through the valley of the shadow of death, I will fear no evil, for thou art with me." Slowly, with the aid of Matthew's crutch, she shuffled in a meandering line toward the hollow log "... in the sight of mine adversaries..." The evil-eyed harpies backed out of her way. Black-as-the-devil birds watched sullenly.

Words of the psalm looped through her fuzzy brain. The feathered cronies of Satan watched her pass amid their ranks, waited, and then resumed their approach to the body in the sand.

She crawled inside the log, stretched out on her back, her good hand restraining her intestines, her wounded shouldered cushioned by a bed of sand.

"Doubtless kindness and mercy shall follow me all the days of my life, and I shall remain a long season in the house of the Lord."

* * * * *

Only sluggish breathing and a slow weak heartbeat proved the woman still lived, barely, perhaps not for long.

Late in the afternoon of the third day after the attack, a small thunderstorm drenched the beach of Sandy Hook for half an hour. An outstretched tree limb intercepted rain droplets and directed a trickle through a crack to the floor of the wooden cave where mushrooms grew. Cool rain on the comatose woman's outstretched arm half aroused her. She moved restlessly in the hollow log.

In her restiveness, her hot cheek contacted the refreshing water. She turned her face in semi-awareness and lapped the water from its shallow pool. Her coma receded, replaced by a fever throughout the night in her wooden cave, soon, perhaps, to become her coffin.

The morning light of the fourth day aroused her to semi-consciousness. Her mouth sought the previous day's water but found only mushrooms and damp sand. The mushrooms were moist. She chewed one and then another and fell asleep again with a third in her hand. A few hours later she awoke more fully. Her hand brought the mushroom to her mouth. She bit a piece and chewed.

She looked at the thing she nibbled and recognized it as a mushroom. She took another nibble. Her brain asked her mouth why it was eating a mushroom. The mouth said it was moist and good. Her hand reached and found another one and she nibbled. Her brain said you've never eaten a mushroom before. The mouth said it was hungry and the mushrooms were here. The brain asked if they were poisonous. The stomach said not yet.

She slept fitfully until the throbbing in her head and shoulder awakened her. She remembered a dream that Matthew had been attacked and killed. It wasn't a dream. Matthew's body lay dead in the sand. She must go to him. She must bury him. She must pray for his soul. She must...

Chapter 18

Sandy Hook

mid-August, 1648

"Mother, Mother, don't leave me alone." Penelope, feeling five years old again, stretched out her right hand toward the image of her dying mother's face in the small halo of light shining into her eyes. Her knuckles hit the edge of the knothole in the hollow log. She scarcely remembered crawling there after...after...

Be strong, her mother's spirit said.

"Mother, don't leave me. I'm dying. I need you."

Be strong for your father.

"Be strong," Penelope whispered. She lowered her hand and flinched when her elbow bumped against the hollow log and her hand touched her head.

The halo of light dimmed. Another figure seemed to move in the shadows.

"Odysseus, is that you? Your faithful Penelope has waited twenty years."

She fell into a fitful sleep to be awakened by the patter of raindrops on the log and the drip, drip, drip of water through the knothole onto her hand. She inserted wet fingers between cracked lips and sucked the moisture.

"Thank you, Matthew. Tell Jesus I'm ready."

Her head throbbed. She tried to move her left hand but it stuck to her abdomen. She closed her eyes. Old memories flowed through her mind. "Father, I'll never be seasick. I promise. Take me to America. It's my destiny."

Hoof beats awakened her. Through the entrance hole in the side of the log, she saw a brown animal speed by. From the distance came shouts of exhilaration.

Odysseus on horseback had come to save his Penelope!

She struggled to extricate herself from the log, clambered atop it, and shouted hoarsely, "Odysseus, I'm here! I've waited for you for so long!"

It wasn't Odysseus. It was more naked *wilden.*

She screamed hoarsely, "Come, you heathen savages. Come kill me. End my misery. O death, where is thy sting? By all that's holy, let me join my father in Heaven."

* * * * *

Two Algonquians, Tisquantum and his nephew Shonto, members of a nearby Lenni Lenape tribe, had heard third-hand stories of the recent exploits of a band of young Susquehanna braves. Tisquantum decided to hunt in the coastal area as well as search for more boxes of iron tools.

Shonto released a hasty arrow at too great a distance, and a wounded deer fled across the beach. They shouted as they chased the frightened animal, forcing it to leave an easy track to follow. Now, they came face to face with a wondrous sight—a dirty, naked white woman twice as tall as a normal person screaming at them.

The natives stopped and stared at the apparition. Or was it a spirit of the dead?

After the woman jumped down from her perch, Tisquantum saw she was a woman of ordinary height, with smears of dirt and blood and a dangling arm. She approached them with a fierce eagerness. Shonto raised his stone hatchet as though facing the charge of a wild boar.

Tisquantum cautioned his nephew in their native Algonquian language, "Hold, Shonto. She's crazy. The spirits teach us to be kind to such people." Especially to ones who might have a fortune in iron tools.

Shonto held his position.

Obviously, a naked woman with a mutilated arm attacking two armed warriors was mad. To the woman, Tisquantum held out his hand with the palm spread and said loudly in Algonquian, "Stop, Crazy Woman. We will help you." She halted at his cry, trembled, and collapsed to the ground.

Tisquantum was surprised the woman had survived her wounds—intestines poked through a cut in her abdomen and a hatchet had glanced off her head, biting deeply into her shoulder. Whoever had scalped the woman had taken only a small strip of hair—a half scalping. What could one expect from a Susquehanna? Botching the kill as well as the scalping.

The man opened a pouch of herbs and ointments, crumbled the dried leaves into the wounds, and applied salve as he had often seen the tribe's medicine woman do.

He positioned her arms alongside her ribs with her hands covering her abdominal wound to hold her bowels inside and then wrapped leather straps around her chest and stomach to hold her all together.

"Uncle?" asked Shonto. "Why do you bother?"

"Did you see any iron tools on this beach?" the older man asked.

"Nothing but a stout cloth flapping in the wind."

"Someone will be grateful if we save her life. Either she will reveal her treasure or the white men across the bay will reward us. Either way, she and I win or lose together."

While Shonto fetched the cloth from the pine thicket, Tisquantum searched for treasure within the hollow log the white woman had stood upon. The log was a white oak of mature size with the common rottenness of old age in its center, the sort favored by yearling bears in winter. Forest mushrooms shouldn't grow on a beach but the moist, shady spot in the rotting wood was similar to their usual home in the leaf litter of the forest floor. There was no iron. Tisquantum wrapped the woman in the white man's stout cloth, and forced some water into her mouth. His concern was not her weight but whether they would reach his village before dark. Each night without the healing knowledge of the medicine woman worsened the victim's chances of survival. The aborigine flung the limp body over his shoulder and started home.

Alternating his burden with his nephew, they achieved the distance in a comfortable six hours, arriving in mid-afternoon at their village a few thousand paces from the southern shore of the bay.

Tisquantum carried the feverish woman to the raised platform outside the hut of Sho-na-goh, the medicine woman. He called his wife, Abba, to come clean the woman and called the nearest girl to bring him food and drink.

Sho-na-goh emerged from her hut and glanced at the patient. "She's a white woman."

Tisquantum said, "She's badly injured."

The healer frowned as she inspected the victim. "You expect me to squander my magic on a white woman?"

Tisquantum spat upon the ground. "Your magic won't work on her? You once healed a dog with a broken leg."

"If the knife of a red man cut her," said Sho-na-goh, "then my magic can cure her. Why should I bother?"

Tisquantum studied his wife's aunt, an obstinate, proud woman, but an accomplished healer. "The white men across the bay will pay well for a white woman but only if she's alive! If you heal her, I'll reward you. If she dies, I'll slander your name."

"Your words are mere wind against my curses."

"Ha." He threw up his hands in disgust. "I wasted my time. She's beyond your power to heal."

"You have no idea of my power."

Tisquantum stomped away, happy to have lost the argument if Sho-na-goh would begin to work. He smiled at the status he would receive from a large reward for something discarded by the foolish Susquehanna. That would teach the more powerful *sachems* to respect Tisquantum, even though he was merely a minor leader of a small band for now.

* * * * *

With rheumatic fingers, the medicine woman poked and prodded the white woman's body. As usual, the troubles of others made her forget her own aches and pains. Most of the girls and young women in the village hovered around the platform and watched.

A hand's width of hair and skin had been yanked from the top of the skull. Most people were scalped after death, but young men were often hasty and careless. Sho-na-goh had seen several scalping victims recover. This wound, maybe a quarter-moon old, was already healing. She pushed aside the hair—an odd brown color—adjacent to the ear where a blade had bashed the skull before continuing down to slice into the shoulder. If the woman had survived this long, then perhaps her brain was not mush. Only the Great Spirit would know.

Mymy, Abba's adopted daughter of seventeen summers, peered closely. "Is she dead?"

"Not yet." Sho-na-goh placed a hand on the victim's forehead. "Abba, take this knife and hack her hair short so it doesn't stick to the scalped area. Then smear honey on it."

Abba pointed to the victim's half visible eyes. "Gray eyes! Is that a sign of death?"

Indeed the color was strange, but there were no signs of illness there. Sho-na-goh caressed a strand of surprisingly soft hair. "White skin, pale hair, weak eyes. I'm amazed these strangers survive at all. But her blood's red."

Sho-na-goh studied the shattered collarbone and shoulder wound, but they were not life-threatening. Where the intestines poked through the skin, she expected to see ruptured organs and imminent death but the organs were intact. She sniffed only a faint odor of foulness. Perhaps this white woman possessed her own powerful magic.

Most of the villagers lost interest in the nearly dead woman and drifted away.

"Mymy," said Sho-na-goh, "fetch me a hollow reed." The girl nodded, took the offered knife, and ran to the stream.

Sho-na-goh removed dead skin from the abdominal wound and smoothed the edges of the cut with her sharpest knife, the one made of obsidian that was sharper than the white man's iron. She dropped fine deer sinew into a tightly woven basket filled with water and added hot rocks to bring it to a boil to make the sinew flexible and easier to work. A nearby locust tree provided a thin thorn to use as a needle for sewing up the wound.

With an iron Dutch awl intended for punching holes in leather, Sho-na-goh drilled a small hole into the thorn. When Mymy returned, the healer said, "Cut the smoothest reed into three pieces half the length of a little finger. Then hold the reeds in the wound and I'll sew around them."

She sprinkled powdered herbs into the gap and sewed up the abdomen as though repairing a rip in a tanned hide. Mymy tried to peer through a hollow reed into the cavity.

Sho-no-goh laughed. "Silly girl. It's too dark to see anything. I smell what's happening inside. Now wrap the belly with rawhide to keep my needlework from ripping out."

Now that she thought the white woman might live, Sho-na-goh studied the shoulder wound. Her medicine had few weapons against meat-rot except the stamina and resilience of the victim, who was young and otherwise healthy.

"There," Sho-na-goh told the girl. "What do you see?"

Mymy peered intently into the bloody hole in the shoulder. "What a mess! It looks like a blind man tried to cut a deer haunch from a carcass."

"I want the maggots, alive, in this little basket," said the medicine woman. "Throw away any loose bone chips and trash. Don't make matters worse by tugging on anything."

Mymy inserted her slim, nimble fingers into the wound and examined everything she pulled out. "Maggot, bone, leaf, bone, maggot, sand, clotted blood, meat, bone."

"Stop, girl," said the medicine woman. "You're not digging a rabbit from its hole. Bend a piece of reed double and use it like a crab claw to retrieve the deeper pieces."

The girl giggled and searched the bloody cavity for more trash. Sho-na-goh crumbled several herbs together into a coarse powder she mixed with fresh honey and bear grease.

"That's everything," said Mymy. "Do you wish to see?"

"These old eyes could hardly find an acorn in there." Nevertheless, Sho-na-goh looked. "Dip this reed into the salve and coat the red spots where the meat-rot is the worst. Next, insert shredded willow bark to absorb the bodily fluids. Then place the maggots atop the bark."

"Won't they eat the flesh?"

"These are common fly maggots, not the screwworms you find in living deer. These only eat the corrupted flesh that, if not removed, causes those horrible smells that precede death."

The girl held up an insect and studied its shape and color. Then she placed six maggots into the wound. "Eat well, little worms."

"Good. With these straps bind her shoulder to her body to prevent movement of this joint."

Sho-na-goh steeped a piece of *garantoquen* root. Abba prepared a thin venison broth. Mymy gently massaged the white woman's arm to stimulate the flow of healing juices and soothed her feverish brow with a damp cloth.

As twilight darkened, Tisquantum carried the unconscious victim into the longhouse that was home to his subtribe of fifty people and laid her upon a raised platform that served as a bed. From beneath the bed platform Sho-na-goh pulled rabbit skins from wicker baskets used for winter storage. She instructed Mymy to cover the patient and to lie on the bed next to her body to still her restlessness with a soothing song—Mymy's name meant nightingale. Also she was to cool the victim's forehead with a wet cloth and give her broth and *garantoquen* decoction every few hours throughout the night.

Sho-na-goh's parting remark was: "Don't bother to wake me if she dies."

Chapter 19

Lenni Lenape Village

late summer, 1648

After two weeks of life in the aboriginal village, grunting noises startled Penelope awake, a dream still vivid in her mind. Penelope sighed as dim morning light revealed, not Greek warriors turned to pigs on Circe's island, but noisy aborigines in a primitive house of bent saplings covered with wide strips of bark.

She shut her eyes to avoid watching fifty naked bodies arise and greet the morning. No longer did she care who shared whose bed as long as none of them attempted to share hers. Having berated—privately in her mind, of course—the Amsterdam congregation for intolerance and excessive sanctimony, she was now the most narrow-minded and pious person in this village. The sins she saw each day would give Reverend Prince apoplexy.

How could she extricate herself from this captivity before she lost her soul? Or had she already? Matthew's family would curse her name for leading him to his death. Hadn't Hamlet argued a person could endure only so many slings and arrows of contemptible fortune before the will to live perished?

The noises subsided. She didn't want to be trapped alone with one of the male aborigines. She was ready to die but not to be ravished by one of the filthy heathen.

To test how stiff her injuries were, Pe-ne, as the *wilden* called her, stretched her muscles and joints as she slipped out of bed. Better than yesterday. She rubbed the scar on her abdomen where two days ago the medicine woman had removed leather threads like letting out a dress hem.

Her nightdress reached down almost to her knees. It was a worn blanket of Dutch duffel cloth with a hole she had enlarged to slip over her head, like the ponchos Dutch sailors had copied from Spanish sailors.

She yanked a second threadbare blanket from the bed and wrapped it around her waist. With her one good arm, she grabbed her day clothes and followed the procession of women and children to the nearby stream.

While the female aborigines scraped off yesterday's grease from their bodies and applied new lard, Penelope knelt behind a screen of low bushes a few yards away and washed her body. Once she had accepted Mymy's offer of body grease. Now she preferred the vermin rather than the oily ointment that attracted dirt like a street mongrel.

She dried herself with the bed blanket and donned her deerskin skirt, its hem immodestly hovering around her calves despite being the longest skirt in the village. Carefully she slipped her mutilated left arm into a soft leather garment—it was sleeveless, so she called it a vest—and then her right arm, and tried to lace it together over her bosom with one hand. It looked like appropriate attire for an Amsterdam harlot but it would suffice among the bare-breasted aboriginal women until Mymy could pull the gaping edges together and lace them tightly.

Penelope wondered again about the relationship of Mymy, the unmarried girl who assisted the medicine woman, to her rescuer Tisquantum. He treated Mymy like a daughter some days and like a concubine some nights. His wife, Abba, alternately treated Mymy like a daughter and then like a slave. Maybe Mymy was also an orphan.

Penelope shuddered at being adopted into this tribe and spending the rest of her life in slavery here.

The morning sky predicted another hot, dry summer day. With a sigh, she dunked her bed blanket and poncho into the stream and dashed them against rocks, hoping to drown or squash the tiny nits that bedeviled her restless nights.

On the return to the village the single file of women and children passed the garden, bigger than several Amsterdam city blocks. Jungle was a better description. Tall *maize* plants grew in randomly located hillocks with bean plants twining up the stalks. The broad leaves of *askutasquash* and other vines covered the soil wherever the weeds hadn't pushed through. Penelope hadn't yet reached a decision on whether this untidiness was better than weeding. Fifteen minutes a day tending her landlady's tiny flower and vegetable garden was hardly comparable to acres of work.

As the last person in line, she listened to the chattering women ahead of her, recognizing maybe one word in twenty. She had learned two hundred or so words of the language, enough for her to perform a smidgeon of useful work around the camp and to engage in odd conversations with small children intrigued by an ignorant grown-up.

She resisted a temptation to flee. The women and children never loitered in the deep woods where strange shadows flitted during daylight and frightening noises emanated at night, not to mention those terrifying snakes that rattled a warning like the one Abba killed in the garden last week. Alone in the forest, she would die. So what? Who would care?

A sharp stick penetrated her flimsy leather slipper and she hopped away, almost uttering a sailor's curse. Did a person ready to die curse at a simple pain? Fret at boredom? Fear wild animals? Maybe she wasn't ready to join her parents in Heaven yet. Even Hamlet lived long enough to avenge his father's murder. But she couldn't linger amidst these primitive *wilden* forever.

Back at the village, Penelope draped her wet poncho and blanket over a bush to dry and followed Mymy to a fire that had burned down to coals during their sojourn to the creek. Penelope selected several small clean rocks, positioned them in a corner of the fire pit, and half-filled a small woven basket with water. With her only intact fingernail she cut off a piece of the dried root the medicine woman had called *garantoquen* and dropped it into the water.

She sniffed the remaining root before returning it to Mymy's medicine pouch. It wasn't ginger although it looked similar. This tuber had originally resembled a misshaped human body with its protuberances for head and limbs. She had already steeped three crooked legs. Holding two sticks in one hand like she had often done with a pair of Dutch spoons, she deftly dropped hot stones into the basket until the water simmered. She put it aside to infuse and cool.

Meanwhile Abba had unfastened the cover to a ground pit, retrieved dried *maize*, and dumped a double handful into a depression in the center of a large boulder. Mymy pounded the yellow and red kernels into a powder with a rock like an apothecary's mortar and pestle. Flicking a willow switch to get Penelope's attention, Abba pointed to her own basket of water and shredded willow bark, into which Penelope dropped hot rocks—like an Amsterdam lady's lapdog with one adorable trick. Abba snatched the basket away as though afraid Penelope would overturn it.

"I'm not helpless," Penelope muttered to a blue and gray bird watching her from a few feet away as she combined *maize* flour, saltwater, fragrant berries, and stinky grease in a shallow wooden bowl held in her lap and stirred the paste with a stick carved into a rough semblance of a spoon. She ladled dollops of paste onto wet leaves, placed the bundles in the coals with a hot rock atop them, and waited for the *pone* bread to cook. At the adjacent fire pit, a seven-year-old girl performed the same tasks more quickly and more neatly.

Saltwater. Because the *wilden* men never did any work except hunt, surely a woman carried sea water to the village in a pouch made from the stomach of an animal, such as Odysseus used for wine. Therefore, the ocean had to be nearby. The sun and the North Star provided directions on land as well as sea. But in which direction was Manhattan? Shipmaster Andriessen had said the town was northeast from the shipwreck but the crew had started walking southwestward in a big circle because of the bay. How big was the bay and where was she now in relationship to the wreck site?

"Pe-ne!"

Penelope scrambled to remove the burnt *pone* from the fire with a stick, humiliated by the acrid smell of her mistake. The seven-year-old neighbor snickered. Abba swatted Penelope with a willow switch that left a red mark on her bare ankle. Mymy sighed and ground more *maize*. Penelope ladled more paste onto leaves.

How her world had turned upside-down! A few months ago, she was a respectable, married, literate woman in perfect health living in a brick house in the richest city in the Europe. Now she was a maimed widow and slave living in the wilderness in a wooden hut with wild heathens whose language she barely understood and grateful for one scandalous dress and scraps of leather for shoes.

After breakfast Penelope threw the dirty breakfast leaves into the fire and looked for a quiet place to sip her medicinal drink. While the women busied themselves with routine tasks, Penelope silently walked away from the village toward the meadow, pushing aside the dried twigs and grass with the toes of her leather slippers as the *wilden* children had instructed her rather than noisily crushing them. Ahead beckoned three majestic trees, situated fifty yards from the village and even further from the mysterious forest, their branches intertwining far above her head.

At the edge of the meadow, tall trees grew so close to-gether that the relationship of trunks to branches was impossible to decipher.

Alone in the meadow, she sat down and leaned against a huge trunk to conceal herself from the village. In vain she tried to recall the proper name of the bushy-tailed tree rats that chattered at her arrival. Amsterdam had an infinite number of wharf rats but few trees and no tree rats.

She couldn't escape the pattern of life from the village: children frolicking and arguing, the murmuring sounds of women sharing the morning's work, the smell of meat roasting. With her eyes closed, she could ignore the strange location, the unfamiliar clothes or lack thereof, the strangers who were becoming her new family. Hadn't Matthew's family accepted her in the same way: a stranger becoming part of daily life?

Music surrounded her as songbirds accepted her pres-ence and resumed their cheerful antics. She was amazed by the variety of birds within a few yards of her—big brown ones, little brown ones, brown with a red chest, big blue noisy ones and little blue silent ones. In addition to the edible birds of the fowl market, Amsterdam had rau-cous seagulls, silent storks, cooing pigeons, chattering house sparrows and an occasional hungry hawk but no songbirds except yellow ones from the Canary Islands kept in wicker cages by spoiled housewives.

She ransacked her memory of English plays and poems, searching for names for these delightful creatures: crow, owl, nightingale, dove, lark, wren. But which was which?

The meadow accepted her presence but no one, at least no European, could live in a meadow. The absence of song caused her to look up in time to see a hawk dive into the grass and fly off with a tiny creature clasped in its talons. Paradise was an illusion.

Matthew was dead and she had learned nothing about her father. Yet she wasted her time in this heathen village that was the opposite of an idyllic sojourn on Calypso's island. She—they—should have remained in Amsterdam. And if dreams were horses, even beggars would ride.

She recalled the first morning she had awakened from a dizzying fever to find herself in the native hut, wrapped in leather straps and surrounded by half-naked, curious strangers. She had retreated to the far edge of the bed like a cornered beast waiting to be slaughtered. The *sachem* of this small village had surprised her with his broken Dutch: "I save you. Get well. Go home."

Now she was well enough to go home, but how? What would wily Odysseus do?

A slithery feeling crept around her wrist. Penelope jumped and searched for a stick to strike the snake with. Instead, three *wilden* children snickered as they waved the feathery twigs they had used to tease her.

One girl pointed to the village and said "Abba," and many more words Penelope didn't catch and didn't need to.

She brushed grass and twigs from her ridiculously immodest attire as she accompanied the children back to the village like a captured escapee. With hands on her hips Abba shouted like an Amsterdam housewife berating a recalcitrant servant. The message was clear despite the unfamiliar language. Abba was the *baas*—a useful Dutch word that described the person in charge of the work regardless of who paid the worker.

But Abba wasn't the person in charge of the village. So Penelope did what Amsterdam housemaids did when angry at another maid and ignored the woman. She marched toward Tisquantum's fire pit, sat, and waited until the tribal leader acknowledged her presence with a grunt.

Penelope wished she knew the native's language better. In Dutch she asked, "Where is Manhattan?"

Chapter 20

Lenni Lenape Village

late summer, 1648

Life in the aboriginal village continued as though Penelope had never spoken. Tisquantum stared into his firepit.

She said sharply, "Manhattan." When he glanced up, she asked more politely in a mixture of Dutch and the aboriginal language, "Where is Manhatten?"

Tisquantum pointed vaguely to the north.

"How far?" she asked.

"Three days." As usual, he replied in barely intelligible Dutch. He needed as much practice in her language as she needed in his.

"When?"

"Soon." Tisquantum had never been in a hurry. Soon might mean years to him.

She shredded a dried leaf and threw the debris on the fire. "You save my life. Grateful. How pay you?"

"We go Manhattan. White *sachem* give *losgeld*."

Had she heard correctly? *Losgeld* was the Dutch word for release money? "Someone will pay a ransom—a *losgeld*—for me?"

"You well now. White *sachem* pay *losgeld*."

She had no relatives or friends in Manhattan. Who would be willing to reward Tisquantum for her return? "You get many guilder for me?"

"You worth much, yes?"

She encouraged his greed. "Yes, many guilder."

He grinned.

"You get blanket? You get iron?" she asked. Everyone in Amsterdam wanted something. What did he want? How soon did he want it?

He smiled. "Blanket good. Iron much good."

"Tisquantum get iron? Abba get blanket?"

"Abba? Hah!" He threw a pine cone at a dog that sniffed too closely.

The women were probably lucky to get trinkets like beads and mirrors. "You trade iron with Lenape?" She wasn't sure whether Lenape meant his tribe or all *wilden*, but she was sure the term excluded Europeans.

"Lenape go Manhattan, trade, get iron."

"You trade blanket with Lenape?" she asked.

The native scratched himself in an immodest part of his body. "I trade, get iron and blanket. Lenape trade, get iron and blanket."

Did every man trade for himself? Were there no companies? No organization? "Lenape trade good?"

"Lenape trade, drink beer. Come back. Hands empty." He wiggled empty fingers to emphasize his point.

She remembered stories about sailors who encouraged the natives to get drunk in order to swindle them. "You drink beer?"

"One beer. Trade good. Come back heavy." He pantomimed one swig of beer and a weighty load in his arms.

She paused to decide how to phrase a basic European business concept so the aborigine would understand. "You trade Pe-ne for small iron. One beer. You come back with small iron. You trade small iron with Lenape for big fur. You go Manhattan. You trade big fur for big iron. One beer. Come back with big iron."

His lowered brows and pursed mouth showed confusion.

Penelope excitedly used fingers to illustrate her points again. "You have one hatchet. You trade one hatchet to Lenape. You get one fur. You go Manhattan. You trade one fur. You get two hatchet. You drink one beer. You come home. You have two hatchet. Good, no?"

Tisquantum grinned. "One hatchet. Trade. Trade. Two hatchet. Good, yes!" He rocked back and forth. His smile widened as he held up one finger on his left hand and two fingers on his right hand.

Penelope sat and waited, hoping her continual presence would stimulate his greed.

A young aborigine man with a deer carcass on his shoulder strolled out of the forest. He dumped the meat at Mymy's feet and flirted with her as though they were shopping in Amsterdam's Westermarkt. With giggles, the pair soon disappeared into the forest.

Abba strung the dead animal on a tripod over a pit, where the blood dripped into the ground. She removed her skirt and necklaces before beginning the untidy task of butchering. With surprising speed and economy of movement, the naked woman cut the animal a few times with an iron knife and magically peeled the skin away.

Butchering in Amsterdam occurred in an obscure area at the beast market. Here it took place under Penelope's nose. Although her intestines rebelled at the sights and smells, she retained her position near Tisquantum and alternated her gaze between the butchering and the *sachem* whose greed controlled her future.

Two young girls received thin strips of meat from the butcher's knife and draped them over a framework of saplings lashed with vines and enwrapped in a smoky fire. The sticky-fingered youngsters turned the meat so it dried evenly without burning, their frequent glances indicating Pe-ne should assist them.

A dog chased a tree rat. Blackish birds tried to steal meat droppings. A cloud shadow came and went. Mymy, smiling, returned alone.

Tisquantun said, "We go white village."

Penelope could scarcely believe the words. "Now?"

Tisquantum studied the morning sky and pointed straight up. Did that mean noon? Then he told Mymy what to pack for the trip.

Penelope jumped up, ran to her laundry bush, and folded her damp poncho and blanket with one good hand. On her return to the sanctuary beside Tisquantum's fire pit, she dodged Abba's switch and stuck out her tongue at the old slave driver. All packed and ready to travel, she resumed her seat near her knight in a loincloth.

The *sachem* grunted and pointed at the sky again. Then he fiddled with his pouch of dried leaves and carved stick held between his teeth until the stick began to emit smoke. Somehow the man belched rings of smoke that attempted to encircle the gnats surrounding him.

It was still two or three hours before noon. Abba shouted crossly. They both ignored her and continued to sit, Tisquantum occasionally performing finger arithmetic, Penelope often glancing at the sun's excruciatingly slow climb toward the zenith.

A big brown bird cocked its head at Penelope as though echoing her thought: *when.*

* * * * *

In mid-afternoon, Tisquantum and Shonto hefted their packs and picked up spears, bows, and arrows. Penelope rubbed her scar. Was she strong enough to walk all the way to New Amsterdam carrying her blanket and poncho? Mymy followed with a sack slung over her shoulder, a comforting presence for their journey into the unknown.

Fifty yards into the journey, Tisquantum and Shonto dragged a twenty-foot-long tree trunk out of the brush. Were they going to build a boat such as Odysseus did to escape from Calypso's island?

She looked more closely. The log was hollow. Mymy placed the sack into the hollow log and hugged Penelope. Wasn't Mymy coming? Traveling with two men without a chaperone was highly improper but less shocking than living in a village of naked people.

The two natives shoved the log into the stream. Tisquantum knelt in the rear of the odd boat and used a short-handled oar to stabilize the strange vessel like an Amsterdam bargeman with a pole. "Pe-ne," he called.

With misgivings but no other options to get to civilization, Penelope cautiously climbed into the hollow log, which rocked frightfully. The young aborigine clutched the front of the boat and frowned at her clumsiness. She peered over the side to see how deep the water was.

The old aborigine said, "Pe-ne. Sit."

Shonto shoved the log further into the stream and climbed into the front. The watercraft started to float downstream. Mymy called goodbye. Penelope feared overturning the tipsy boat and called back without looking.

The stream was too narrow for full-length oars. Nor were there oarlocks. Shonto lowered his shovel-like oar vertically alongside the log and pulled it through the water. The strange vessel moved faster. Then he lifted the short-handled oar out of the water, reached forward, and stroked again. She assumed Tisquantum was doing the same but feared turning around to see.

For an hour the men propelled the odd craft down the creek. Becoming more confident in her situation, Penelope watched the meadows and forests slip by. Strange birds fluttered out of their way and unseen animals rustled the bushes. She examined the log. Both hatchet and fire had left their marks on the hollowed-out interior.

Canoe. That was the name one of the sailors on *de Kath* had once used for an aboriginal tree-trunk boat.

The sight of the wide bay with small waves reassured her—the first step from wilderness to civilization. Penelope almost fell out of the canoe when the men beached it without warning.

Tisquantum said, "Pe-ne, start fire."

"How?"

Tisquantum laughed. "Shonto, show fire."

Shonto grumbled as he rummaged in the sack Mymy had put into the canoe. He opened a clay bowl, blew into it, and offered her the pottery vessel. An ember glowed among some moss.

She refused to take it and raised her eyebrows at Tisquantum. "How?" she asked again.

Shonto threatened to smack her face with his hand like he did to the native women when angry. She backed away.

The young native ordered, "Fetch wood."

Penelope dragged over a large driftwood branch. This wasn't the beach she and Matthew had shared because wide-leaved trees were only twenty yards away. Where was their beach with its stunted pine trees?

"No!" Shonto shouted. "Small wood." He held his hands a foot apart.

She dropped the branch, trudged to the edge of the forest, and picked up small rotten sticks from the litter beneath the trees.

Shonto slapped the damp wood from her hand. She darted away before he hit her. Tisquantum burst out in laughter. Shonto turned toward his uncle and they exchanged rapid, angry-sounding words she couldn't follow.

Finally, Tisquantum repeated what sounded like, "Do it yourself."

Glaring back at her, Shonto strode to the boundary between beach and forest and snapped small dead branches off the nearby trees. With care, he arranged the materials and added the glowing ember from the pouch and blew. Quickly a fire started. He fed it more sticks. Ignoring her, he stomped off.

Penelope gathered larger sticks and fed the flames. She knew how to do that.

Tisquantum said, "More wood." Soon a large fire blazed.

In Mymy's sack, Penelope found bowls, maize flour, and a water bag.

Tisquantum said, "No maize."

What were they to eat? She looked at him blankly and rubbed her empty stomach.

"Shonto, show her."

Shonto stalked into the inlet where the stream met the ocean. Penelope followed at a safe distance. They spent an hour digging oysters out of the mud with sticks. Penelope had often bought oysters in the Amsterdam fish market, because they were inexpensive and Liesbeth was frugal. Like most of the food in the Westermarkt, she had no knowledge of its source. These American oyster shells were bigger, sharper, and more irregular in shape than the European ones and cut her fingers.

In the stream she washed off several dozen oysters and filled Mymy's pouch, which she dragged toward Tisquantum. She pointed to her maimed arm and then to the tightly closed shells. Back home in Liesbeth's kitchen sat a pair of pincers for breaking a hole in the lip of the shell and a thin-bladed knife for shoving between the two halves and cutting the muscle that held the oyster closed.

Tisquantum pointed at the tide line. "Fetch."

She looked at the beach littered with seaweed. "Fetch ocean grass?"

"Yes." He laughed. "Ocean grass."

She retrieved a clump of wet seaweed. Tisquantum wrapped an oyster in the damp vegetation, spread out a few hot coals with a stick, and placed a wrapped shellfish among the embers. A cloud of steam rose. He gestured for her to do the same with the remaining oysters.

When she attempted to rake a heat-opened oyster out of the coals, it fell into the sand. Tisquantum grunted his displeasure. Shonto laughed. The older man took Penelope's stick and quickly raked a dozen into a bowl. With his fingers, he yanked out the hot meat and greedily popped it into his mouth. Shonto did likewise.

Penelope carefully worked a few oysters to the edge of the fire and slipped them into her bowl. She ignored Shonto's angry glare that meant a woman should wait and eat after the men finished. She didn't expect him to leave any.

Penelope awoke at first light, still wearing yesterday's clothes because she couldn't undress and dress herself and would never ask the aborigine men for help.

Tisquantum had judged the weather well and the water in the bay was calm. She prepared a breakfast of corn pone cooked on rocks hot from the nightlong fire. Shonto selected a hot coal and carefully stuffed it into Mymy's clay pot.

The boat entered the broad empty bay, scattering seabirds. They traveled in their own morning shadows—west. But Shipmaster Andriessen had said Manhattan was northeast.

To speak to Tisquantum, she twisted carefully to keep from rocking the craft and pointed abeam on the starboard quarter—northeast. "Manhattan?"

His hand pointed the same direction as hers and pantomimed big waves. Then he pointed ahead—west—and his hand undulated in small waves. Penelope compared the size of his hand waves to how low the canoe rode in the water, the gunwales merely a few inches above the waves on this calm day.

Tisquantum kept parallel to the shore, about one hundred yards out. Away from both the incessant buzzing of the insects and the pleasant songs of the birds, it was deathly quiet. Only the occasional slap of the odd oars on the water disturbed the silence.

At the westward limit of the bay, they turned north into a narrow saltwater creek that separated the mainland from an island that Tisquantum said the Dutch called Staten Eijlant. They stopped to rest and eat pemmican, a mixture of corn, dried meat, and berries packed by Mymy. Late in the afternoon they reached the north end of the island at which point the creek turned east. In another hour, open water lay ahead of them. And land on the opposite shore, only a mile or two away!

She pointed east. "Manhattan?"

Tisquantum pointed northeast toward a hazy blob on the horizon that was several miles away. "Tomorrow."

With tears in her eyes, she stared toward her new home, a place she had never seen.

As the canoe moved out of the shelter of the large islands into the open bay, the wind and the waves increased until Penelope feared the craft would be swamped. But Tisquantum aimed for a nearby island, really just a big mudflat.

"*Kioshk*," Tisquantum said.

"What's that?" asked Penelope.

The old native pointed to a seagull and said, "*Kioshk*," and then pointed to the mudflat again. "I say, *Kioshk*. You say, *Oester Eijlant.*"

They camped for the night on Seagull or Oyster Island. Shonto started a fire. Penelope gathered oysters and driftwood, alone except for the company of dozens of noisy seagulls. Simply to know the correct English name of a bird brought her a soothing feeling of civilization.

The spectacle of a bright round moon rising in the east conveyed an unexpected memory. On her last morning with Matthew, the moon was nearly at its last quarter. Thus the attack had occurred about three weeks ago, give or take a day or two. It was now the end of August, maybe early September. Having counted fifteen days in the aborigine village, she calculated she had spent about a week on that terrible beach and had even missed her twenty-second birthday.

Alone in the twilight, she forced her thoughts elsewhere—toward Manhattan, toward civilization, and a language she knew, and fragrant soap, and a dress that covered her ankles.

And a chamber pot. And a bed with curtains and a feather mattress.

Chapter 21

New Amsterdam

Thursday, September 3, 1648

At sunrise, Tisquantum and Shonto inspected the cloudless sky above Staten Eijlant and grunted their approval of the calm waters in the bay. Penelope noticed a smile on Tisquantum's face and neither aborigine complained about the breakfast of overcooked corn pone.

She threw the breakfast remains on the fire and put her blankets and Mymy's pouch in the canoe. But Tisquantum sat. And sat. Finally he lumbered out of sight and returned in a few minutes, cleaning his hands with wet sand.

Soon the canoe headed northward, hugging the shoreline on the larboard side.

From her position merely inches above the waves, she searched the horizon across a mile of open water, straining for a glimpse of ship masts, buildings, or other signs of man's struggle against the wilderness.

A windmill? Yes, it was a Dutch windmill. Near it, a church steeple poked above a walled fort with the familiar orange, white, and blue tricolor flag atop a tall pole. As New Amsterdam drew closer, she noticed the windmill lacked two of its four vanes and cattle and sheep grazed on the earthen walls of the fort.

The log boat rammed the Manhattan beach at full speed and stopped with half its length on the shore, causing seagulls to scatter and nearly tumbling Penelope over-board. She carefully disembarked into the wet muck, surprised at the stability of the canoe, now stuck in a deep, muddy furrow.

Grateful to be on solid ground, Penelope moved aside and looked around. She laughed at the dilapidated earthen walls of the fort. Had she expected the thick brick battle-ments that surrounded Amsterdam? Above the crude ramparts loomed two large stone buildings, sturdy signs of Dutch civilization.

Together, aborigine uncle and nephew shoved the craft further onto the beach to resist the tide, leaving it next to three other canoes. The older man stuffed his meager possessions into a large pouch and handed it to his neph-ew, leaving the log empty except for the odd oars. Penelope adjusted her head scarf and arm sling and smoothed wrinkles from the tattered blanket-poncho that attempted to cover her immodest vest and calf-length leather skirt. She wrapped her other threadbare blanket around her waist to cover her legs and ankles.

At the fort's gatehouse a hundred yards away, the dis-tant sentry scarcely glanced at them. The trio skirted a mud hole defended by two hogs. Penelope snickered. Like Odysseus on his return home to Ithaca, she was indeed dressed as poorly as a beggar. Instead of meeting a swine-herd, she met swine. Then she frowned as she remembered that, like Odysseus, her shipmates had died. Certainly Matthew, and possibly Trijn, Dirck, their children, and the crew. *Have hope*, she told herself. *And courage.*

They turned away from the fort and walked down two city blocks with sturdy brick houses only on the landward side of the street.

Men noticed them and stared. What a sight they must be! Which aspect chiefly attracted their notice: that she, the female, was fully clothed despite the late summer heat; that she was walking beside the old native and not behind him; or that a woman wearing a headscarf fashioned from scraps looked around so brazenly? In a colony with five men for each woman, was each female worth studying?

Several men plus numerous seagulls trailed them like a parade. She restrained herself to avoid bursting into loud laughter at their perplexed looks and outmoded clothes not seen in Amsterdam in years.

She could not resist a soft, "*Goedemorgen, Korporal,*" to a startled soldier.

Tisquantum pointed to a one-story building, a warehouse or factor's office.

A tall man exited the factor's store. Ten years ago, her father had brought back a doublet like that from London. The man, looking down at a paper, mumbled to himself in English, "Forty five stuivers per hundredweight. It's not worth growing tobacco if they tax it that much."

Penelope smiled to hear English spoken again. Without thinking, she said, "Forty-five stuivers? That's only four shillings one and a half pence, sir."

The man started to tip his hat but froze in mid-action as he looked at her. Only his head moved to follow her as she entered the building. She giggled at his look of astonishment at a wild woman converting stuivers into shillings.

Inside, Tisquantum announced in his broken Dutch, "Where *Mijnheer* Loockermans?"

A crowd followed the three strangers into the factor's building and pressed them against the counter. Shonto struggled to free himself or perhaps to loosen the hatchet at his waist. Penelope clamped her hand around his wrist.

"Back away," Penelope shouted in Dutch. "You're frightening the *wilden.*"

A man shouted, "She's no aborigine. She's European."

In the words of her father, it was as though all the inmates of Bedlam broke loose at once and crowded into the room with them, shouting and shoving.

A large, burly man appeared from the back room, banged a belaying pin upon the counter, and screamed, "Avast!"

Tisquantum and Shonto sought the door, but the crowd blocked an escape.

In the silence, the big man demanded, "What's happening here?"

Twenty voices answered at once. He smacked his wooden club against his palm and glared around the room until his eyes stopped at Penelope. His mouth opened and shut like a dying fish. "What in blazes are you?"

Afraid for the wellbeing of the two natives, Penelope pointed at her companions. "These *wilden* saved my life."

A thump of the man's belaying pin restored order. "Who in blazes are you?"

"I'm *Mevrouw* Prince." She looked around at the curiosity seekers who elbowed each other for silence.

"I was on the ship *de Kath* out of Curaçao, the ship that wrecked a month ago." She blushed because everyone in the room stared at her. "My husband couldn't walk. We stayed behind. The *wilden* found us, killed my husband, and left me for dead." She displayed her arm in the sling.

"But not these *wilden*." She quickly put a hand on Tisquantum's shoulder. "They found me, took me to their village, healed me, and brought me here to safety. I must see his High Mightiness, the Director-General."

Several voices explained Pieter Stuyvesant was away, inspecting the settlements on the North River.

The man in charge interrupted the crowd, "You have the story. Now clear out of here. Give us room to breath, all of you. Except you." He pointed to a man who was soon introduced as Grovert Loockermans. The crowd departed reluctantly, helped by the brawny man's ferocious glare and upraised belaying pin.

"Coenraad," he yelled to an unseen clerk, "bring us a round of beer. Even the *wilden*, they look like they need it the worst. Make it the good stuff from Amsterdam, none of that local rotgut. And bring a chair for the lady."

The burly man introduced himself as Seth Verbrugge, son of the owner of Verbrugge and Company, factors handling all manner of trade with Amsterdam. Coenraad soon returned with the beers and a chair. Tisquantum, having experienced Dutch beer before, happily gulped his mug whereas young Shonto sipped his brew and grimaced at its bitterness.

"Coenraad, fetch whoever is acting for the Director-General."

The clerk opened the door and nearly bumped into the spectator for whom Penelope had converted stuivers into shillings. Coenraad reported back that the Englishman had volunteered to fetch the *schout-fiscaal,* a combination of sheriff and government prosecutor as in Amsterdam.

Savoring the familiar taste of warm beer, Penelope relaxed in one of civilization's greatest inventions—a rocking chair with armrests and thick cushions. She grinned at bolts of duffel—the familiar coarse woolen cloth from Amsterdam—and barrels labeled gunpowder, wheat, and stockfish while Loockermans explained the aborigine's business history to Verbrugge.

She closed her eyes, breathed deeply, and expelled a long sigh of pleasure. Discussions of Dutch commerce and both strange and familiar scents floated soothingly through the air. Safety and civilization at last! Unlike Odysseus, she had no need to shoot a swarm of usurpers. Being both Odysseus and Penelope at the same time was somewhat disconcerting. But the undeniable fact was that she had survived.

She studied a tall pile of smelly pelts adjacent to her chair and reached out her fingers to stroke the fur of an unimaginable beast. Its softness and color reminded her of a fur-lined hat her father brought back years ago from Riga and the Baltic forests. Could this be beaver? Sailors claimed a pelt could be used as money, although silver coins seemed much more convenient than a heavy bundle of fur that reeked faintly of rotten meat.

The return of the Englishman with a fat, pompous man who acted like a government official interrupted her reverie. Coenraad fetched another chair for the hefty official while the Englishman stood quietly a few feet away. The official pointed a finger at Verbrugge. "His High Mightiness issued an ordinance only four months ago against giving beer to the *wilden.*"

Verbrugge replied, "Some laws are more important than others."

The *schout* stared at the trader. "I could arrest you for that."

Penelope watched this contest of wills. Verbrugge chewed his lip and stared at the *schout* as though the man's dog had just pissed on his boot. The clerk, who had left the room upon the *schout*'s arrival, soon delivered a mug. The *schout* smiled before he took a long swig of beer.

Penelope was introduced to *Schout* Hendrik van Dyck, who apologized for her brutal arrival in New Netherland, assuring her that they had started a rescue as soon as ship master Andriessen arrived and were disappointed in locating neither her nor her husband.

Van Dyck stretched a fifteen-minute summary of her ordeal into two hours by asking dumb questions and slowly writing in his thick ledger. At the conclusion, the *schout* stood, thanked Tisquantum and Shonto for their services, and shook their hands. Shonto studied his empty hand as though counting his fingers to be sure none were missing.

Penelope interrupted his departure. "*Mijnheer schout,* Tisquantum rescued and delivered me. He expects the Director-General to reward that display of friendship."

With a hand on the door, van Dyck paused. "*Mevrouw* Prince, you and your husband weren't employees of the GWC. Why should the company pay a ransom for you?"

She observed his fancy clothes and smug eyes. Obviously his duties excluded charity and honor. "We traveled on a company ship which failed to deliver us to our destination."

"By declining to accompany the master of the ship, you voluntarily abandoned your voyage."

"The ship master abandoned my husband first."

Shrugging his shoulders and spreading his soft, fat hands, *Schout* van Dyck said, "The master has life and death power aboard the ship."

She glared at the supercilious official. "We weren't aboard the ship after it wrecked."

The *schout* grinned. "Of course, *mevrouw*, you could sue him for dereliction of duty."

"Gladly. Where's the scoundrel?"

He chuckled. "However, the case would be decided by his High Mightiness, who has already complimented ship master Andriessen on his admiral performance in difficult circumstances in saving the cargo."

Penelope didn't like to lose an argument, especially with a conceited officeholder more interested in the survival of cargos than people. "Doesn't the company have a responsibility to keep the *wilden* friendly?"

"Of course, but this situation is without precedent. We've often ransomed hostages from the *wilden* but never one already safely inside New Amsterdam. Perhaps, if you wait until the Director-General returns and reviews the situation, he might take the action for which I, as mere *schout-fiscaal*, have no authority." While talking to Penelope, he fiddled with the door handle behind his back.

Penelope rose from her chair and charged at van Dyck and waved a finger in his face. "You think I should return to the wilderness until the Director-General gets back!"

"No, no, *mevrouw*." He backed himself against the closed door. "I merely said any ransom money would have to be decided upon by His High Mightiness."

Penelope, weary with her journey and this tedious conversation, pointed at Tisquantum who stood there stoically amid the tempest of words, but she spoke to the *schout*. "If I had any money, I myself would gladly reward him. I think my life was worth saving, even if you don't."

The *schout* defended himself with another round of wretched excuses. He couldn't exit the building with his back against the door and an angry woman mere inches in front of him.

Tisquantum asked, "Pe-ne, you say reward?"

The aborigine's words caught her off guard but she noticed a bolt of fabric identical to the blanket-poncho she wore and pointed to it. "Duffel cloth."

"How many?" asked the native.

Twenty was the highest number she had experienced in the aboriginal village, usually demonstrated by ten fingers and ten bare toes. With her one good hand, Penelope displayed four sets of five fingers.

Tisquantum nodded vigorously.

She turned to the merchant. "May I have twenty ells of duffel on credit?" Belatedly, she remembered the English in America outnumbered the Dutch twenty to one. Did Verbrugge use the Dutch ell of cloth that was fingertip to armpit, about 27 inches, or the English ell of 45 inches?

The Englishman who had fetched the *schout* and then remained in the background stepped forward. "Mr. Verbrugge, I'll be pleased to pay for the blankets," he said in English. Sweeping off his hat in the best London fashion, he bowed low before her. "Madam, I am Stout. Richard Stout. At thy service."

"Mr. Stout," she replied in the same language, "I cannot accept your money but I'll be pleased to accept your offer of bond so that Tisquantum may have his blankets and be on his way. I promise I'll repay this debt."

"Madam. I learned long ago that a gentleman always loses, one way or another, whenever he argues with a beautiful woman. Whatever thou wisheth is my command."

She blushed at this unexpected compliment given to a filthy woman dressed in rags, and briefly doubted Mr. Stout's sense of judgment. Or maybe he was a kind minister since he spoke with "thou" and "thee" as though quoting the Bible, although a minister with money was as rare as hens' teeth. But she was in no position to reject favors. "Thank you, kind sir!"

From Verbrugge's smile, she assumed he understood English and asked the merchant, "*Mijnheer*, is that sufficient collateral for you?"

Matching gallantry for gallantry at no cost to himself, Verbrugge replied, "Your word, *mevrouw*, is enough for me." He bellowed, "Coenraad, twenty ells of the wool blanketing!"

"Wrapped in oiled cloth, please," she said, halfway between a request and a command. The blankets had a long journey ahead of them.

The factor regarded the woman more closely, grinned, and called to the storeroom, "Coenraad, wrapped in oiled cloth."

In this interlude, Mr. Stout addressed the *schout* in poor and hesitant Dutch. "*Mijnheer*. This woman is without a house. Will you ask *Mevrouw* Stuyvesant to be the host?"

The *schout*, obviously the type to calculate his advantage in any circumstance, hesitated only a moment. "As a personal favor to you, *mijnheer*, I will do my utmost to persuade the wife of His High Mightiness to extend her gracious hospitality to *Mevrouw* Prince."

Mr. Stout bowed slightly. "Thank you, *mijnheer*. We give *Mevrouw* Stuyvesant time. I take *Mevrouw* Prince to eat." He glanced at Penelope for approval.

She hesitated. He was an older man, about forty, the age of her father at his disappearance six years ago. Although he was a stranger, he was also a businessman— she remembered his complaint about taxes—and the only person trying to remove obstacles from her path instead of creating them. She searched his eyes for pity and found only concern, the disquiet any father would feel for a child in distress. He probably had a wife and children of his own and offered an act of Christian kindness to a hapless stranger. She accepted with a nod.

After Tisquantum and Shonto left happily with a bundle of woolen blanket and many words of friendship, Verbrugge said quietly, "The cloth is four guilders per ell for a total of eighty guilders."

"What?" Her jaw quivered. "It's only half that in Amsterdam!" Her passage across the ocean had cost as much.

"We're far from Amsterdam," the factor said. "Each item is double the price here. As you well know, it's a long and dangerous trip."

She couldn't argue with that fact. "I hope you're not in a hurry to be paid."

Verbrugge shrugged. "No one in Manhattan is in a hurry to pay his debts. However, *mevrouw*, you made a good bargain. When the GWC ransoms a captive, they usually pay 200 to 250 guilders in goods, which, of course, the family of the victim must repay."

Two hundred guilders was much more than Matthew had earned in a year in Amsterdam. Who could repay that much? How in the world could she repay even eighty guilders? She wasn't sure which was worse, being mutilated or being smothered by a huge debt. But if she could survive the *wilden*, surely she could survive civilization.

Coenraad provided two copies of the promissory note to Verbrugge who quickly scanned, signed, and presented them to Penelope.

She read the document carefully. Its format looked identical to the ones she had copied in a fair hand for her father six years ago, although at the moment, that seemed a lifetime ago. Mr. Stout cleared his throat and appeared ready to offer more assistance, assistance that in good conscience she could not accept.

"A question, *Mijnheer* Verbrugge." She pointed to a passage in the contract. "You've already doubled the Amsterdam price and yet are charging me four *percentum* interest from today. I would have expected you to have already factored time and interest into your prices."

Rather than engage in a staring contest, she laid the contract in her lap, bent over to study it more, and rubbed a fingernail over her teeth, a trick her father had used to feign a reluctance to sign an agreement. Her silence forced the opponent to say something.

"This is the standard contract," said the clerk.

Penelope maintained her silence and her pose, as though the clerk hadn't spoken.

Verbrugge sighed. "I could delay the interest for six months."

"Twelve months."

"Six months, madam. As you said, I should factor time into my calculations. Goods should turn over in a year and this cloth left Amsterdam a half-year ago."

"Very well. Six months," she conceded, trapped by her own logic. What difference would a few months of interest make to a penniless debtor?

She handed the papers to the clerk, who notated both copies in the margin, and handed them to Verbrugge, who initialed the changes. He handed the contracts to Penelope. She signed both and then stared at them, realizing bonds of paper could be as strong as bonds of iron.

Mr. Stout plucked both copies from her hands and scribbled his assurance of payment at the bottom and handed one to her and one to the clerk.

Then she collapsed into the rocking chair, the promissory note clutched in her fist.

So much for a quiet arrival into New Amsterdam. Everyone in this little village would know her story in an hour. No, they would hear about widowed Mrs. Prince. With Matthew dead, no one on this side of the Atlantic knew about John Kent. On the other hand, she was alone on this side of the Atlantic. The beer-guzzling *schout* would certainly be of no help.

She glanced around. Three men she had met an hour ago stared at her. She wanted to laugh. She wanted to cry. She wanted to shout at Mr. Williams and the other church elders, *I have no escort. What are you going to do: condemn me because God had mercy on my soul?* But the church elders were an ocean away.

"Mrs. Prince, art thou hungry?" asked the Englishman.

Hungry? She was a widow without money, without respectable clothes, without a home, stranded in a strange town on a strange continent, surrounded by strange men, any one of whom might have killed her father. Hunger seemed like a trivial difficulty, but it was the only problem with an immediate solution.

"Yes," she said. "I am hungry." She hoped she didn't have to dig and cook her own oysters.

Chapter 22

New Amsterdam

Thursday, September 3, 1648

Penelope said, "Thank you, sir," to Richard Stout, who held open the door of the factor's warehouse and escorted her down the street. She gazed around to orient herself as they continued further into the village and away from Tisquantum's canoe landing.

Every man on the street stared at her alone, not as one member of a trio of aborigines, as they had hours earlier. The crude poncho gapped immodestly in places and she rubbed her half-bare mutilated arm.

Distress must have showed on her face because Mr. Stout said, "Ma'am, thou shouldst wear my doublet around thy shoulders." He stopped on the street and immediately began to disrobe.

"But, sir, then you would be unseemly dressed."

"Phsaw, no one cares how I look, but thou art a lady."

She looked down at her make-shift garments and dusty aborigine slippers and rubbed her gritty forehead in wonderment at this second unexpected compliment from this strange man who apparently wouldn't permit her to refuse his offer.

He held his garment so that she could place her good arm in one sleeve and then draped the other sleeve around her injured shoulder. The padded jacket that fit him well hung loosely on her slender frame, but now strangers' glances were directly to her face as was proper, not to her body.

"Sir, how do I thank you?"

"No need. But I'm curious. Thou hast displayed a familiarity with contracts."

How much of her past should she reveal? "Sometimes I assisted my father with his business papers."

"Ah, here we are," he said at the entrance to a three-story building with the GWC emblem above the doorway.

She hesitated. She had never eaten in a tavern before, although she had stood in their doorways in Amsterdam on half a dozen occasions to deliver urgent messages to her father, but travelers had to eat somewhere. The aroma of a pot roast greeted them as he opened the door.

"*Mijnheer* Gerrit, a private dining room," said Mr. Stout in his poor Dutch.

The man at the doorway, obviously a Frenchman from his atrocious accent, waved his hands. "No, no, impossible."

"But the lady." Mr. Stout nodded toward Penelope and then pointed toward the loud babble coming from the main room. "S'*il vous plait.*"

Penelope peered around the two men at the interior of the dark, smoky tavern. Its small tables were crowded with men, mugs of beer, and plates of food. A maid passed by with a tray of steaming bowls, from which wafted garlic and onions. Probably carrots, beans, turnips and who knew what other fresh vegetables hid below the surface.

"The men, they play at cards yesterday." The Frenchmen shook his head. "They play last night. They play this morning. I ask when they leave. They point pistol at me."

Mr. Stout repeated, "But she's a lady."

Penelope whispered in English, "I have eaten with sailors and soldiers and aborigines." But she hadn't eaten fresh vegetables in months, excluding aboriginal ones whose names she didn't know. The aromas were irresistible.

Mr. Stout looked at her and opened his mouth to object but no words came out.

"Impossible," repeated the Frenchman.

Penelope edged around her companion for a better look and pointed to a corner, "Isn't that an empty table?" Almost empty, except for a ledger.

"Oui, madame, ma table est votre table." The tavern owner bowed slightly and signaled for them to follow.

"Is the food here good?" Penelope asked Mr. Stout, mainly to get him to recover from his paralysis and to move.

"Yes, the best in town," he said. He swept his hand in an invitation for her to precede him.

Penelope followed after the tavern host, who adroitly replaced his ledger book with napkins and spoons and signaled the serving maid. The disheveled girl sloshed two beer mugs onto their table and mouthed, "Food too?" If she spoke, Penelope never heard the words in the noise and simply nodded.

Penelope took a big gulp from her mug before she realized it wasn't the watered-down small beer that women and children usually drank but she didn't complain. As her eyes became accustomed to the dimness and the haze of tobacco smoke, she realized she was the only woman patron. And most of the men had realized that too. They nudged each other and pointed with their mugs.

She had believed the tavern keeper's table was in a discreet corner, but actually it was well placed to oversee the entire room and thus to be seen by all.

At least the men's lecherous hands couldn't touch her as they did the bedraggled serving maid. Of course, her low-cut bodice encouraged their advances just as it encouraged the ministers in Amsterdam to rail against such lechery. She blushed at the idea of the congregation's elders discovering her presence here.

"Mrs. Prince." Richard Stout had to nearly shout to make himself heard. "Mrs. Prince. I fear thou wilt be the subject of intense speculation for weeks."

Penelope blushed even more. "Why do they care?"

"Because thou hast survived. May I suggest thou tellest thy history once for all to hear rather than a hundred times. Otherwise, strangers will harass thee on the street."

"That's a wise suggestion, Mr. Stout. But how?" She pointed to her ear to indicate the noise gushing from the rowdy crowd.

Now Mr. Stout blushed. Was that the result of her compliment or the requirement that he be the center of attention to quiet the crowd? Nevertheless, he stood amidst the hubbub of the room and proclaimed in English, "Gentlemen, please. Your attention. If ye will give the lady, Mrs. Prince, your attention she will satisfy your curiosity."

The turmoil in the room slowly subsided.

Penelope rose and paused to gather her wits as fifty pairs of eyes fixated upon her. She spoke each sentence in Dutch, followed immediately by the same in English:

"When our ship wrecked in the storm, my husband broke his leg. The crew and other passengers immediately set out to march here, but my husband and I remained behind. The next morning a band of young *wilden* approached us. They seemed curious, not dangerous.

"Without warning, they attacked. My husband defended me. They killed him and left me as good as dead. Some days later, the aborigine Tisquantum found me, took me to his village where the medicine woman treated my wounds and saved my life. Then Tisquantum delivered me to Verbrugge's factory because he is known there.

"Some of the *wilden* were good Samaritans to me. I ask God's forgiveness on my unknown trespassers and thank Him for my deliverance. Amen."

In the ensuing silence, one inebriated patron raised his mug and shouted, "A salute to the lady's deliverance." Immediately, the City Tavern resumed its usual boisterousness.

Their meal of pot roast and vegetables soon arrived. Mr. Stout looked as relieved as she felt to have an activity that temporarily eliminated the need for conversation—nearly impossible amid the tumult. She contented herself with the hot, familiar food and a civilized spoon to eat it with and ignored stares of strangers. Mr. Stout was right—she would be the center of attention for a few weeks. She hoped Manhattan didn't have a newspaper.

* * * * *

The *schout* bulled his way to their table, helping himself to a mug of beer from the maid's tray, and invited Penelope to the Director-General's house. Happily she escaped the noise of the tavern. Despite the lack of an invitation, Mr. Stout accompanied her and the official through the dusty village streets toward Fort New Amsterdam.

"What happened to the crew and other passengers? Did they survive?" Penelope asked the *schout*. She hoped Dirck was already plowing a field, Trijn milking cows, and the two children tending farm animals.

"Ship master Andriessen saved everyone willing to accompany him."

She ignored his continued defense of the ship master and skirted a mud hole and the pig that occupied it. She shook her head at the contrast between Amsterdam and New Amsterdam and then chided herself for fickleness as she recalled her complaints about the Indian village.

"Where are they? I want to let them know I'm alive."

"The farm family went up the North River to Fort Orange as they were intended."

Would Penelope ever see them again after spending five months together? "If you know anyone going there, can you send a message?"

"That's a waste of time. Everyone at Fort Orange will know as soon as the next ship arrives." The *schout* pointed out the Director-General's stone mansion and boasted of its size, one hundred by fifty feet.

Mr. Stout whispered in English, "It was built by stone masons from Boston."

Adjacent was the Dutch Reformed Church that towered over Fort New Amsterdam's sod-covered walls. These were the buildings she had seen when the log boat had approached Manhattan. She looked toward the beach but Tisquantum's canoe was gone.

At the entrance to the fort, the *schout* dismissed Stout with a jerk of the thumb. Penelope was so surprised by the official's lack of tact that she almost forgot to return the doublet. As he retrieved his garment, he seemed to want to speak, but the *schout* hustled her into the fort.

At the door of the Director-General's mansion, the *schout* introduced *Mevrouw* Anna Bayard, the Director-General's sister, who dismissed the *schout* as brusquely as he had dismissed Mr. Stout.

Anna escorted Penelope to the parlor and introduced her to *Mevrouw* Judith Stuyvesant, a woman in her late thirties, who displayed the beauty that comes from expensive clothes and the careful application of cosmetic. Even while her husband was away and she had no social obligations, her hair was elaborately arranged in the French style of formal braids entwined with combs and other jewelry.

Anna called the maidservant, Sara, who agreed Penelope needed to bathe with the best soap and to sleep in a soft bed. Sara chattered as she led Penelope to a visitor's bedroom and soon Penelope knew much of the life story of the maid, her two daughters, and her husband, Stoeffel, who was the Stuyvesants's butler.

When Sara returned with two buckets of hot water, Penelope sat frozen at the dressing table holding a hand mirror, her ragged scarf still wrapped around her head. Penelope sniffled. "I haven't looked into a glass in a month." She pictured herself as a mangy street mongrel.

Sara said, "Don't fret, *mevrouw*. With many handsome young soldiers surrounding this mansion, my daughters experienced beauty crises every day. Here's a warm, wet cloth. Cleanse your face before you see yourself in the glass. I think you'll be pleased."

Penelope washed slowly, thinking Sara's daughters had never encountered a disaster this severe. At last she forced herself to look at her reflection. "My skin is so dark. Does that come from living with the natives?"

"No, *mevrouw*. That comes from the brighter sun. Men here think a woman with pasty white skin," Sara glanced around and whispered, "like the mistress and her cosmetic paint, is too pampered to survive."

At the outlandish concept of being too pampered to survive, Penelope blurted out, "Ha!" even though she knew the maid didn't intend to make such an awkward remark.

Sara gasped and her face reddened, but she continued quickly, "*Mevrouw*, if you'll put down the glass, I'll have the first look." Sara removed the homemade cap.

Silence from the garrulous maid worried Penelope. She asked softly, "How bad is it?"

"It looks like Stoeffel's bald head."

The description stunned Penelope at first. Then she burst out in laughter and picked up the hand mirror, the glass pointing away from her. "Like a man's bald head, you say? I expected worse." She rotated the handle back and forth several times before finally facing the truth.

Sara's analogy was apt. Reflected in the mirror was a four-inch-wide swath as hairless as the glass and surrounded by inch-long hair as raggedy as though cut by a three-year-old with dull scissors.

"*Mevrouw*, if you please, the water's getting cold."

Penelope peered into the huge, odd-shaped copper bucket, half full of warm water, that was entirely too big for washing clothes. Sara explained the "tub" was one of those French ideas that Mistress Judith suffered from, but it was quite pleasant.

Having a maid to undress you and to pretend not to stare at your naked body was another idea Penelope reserved judgment on. However, it was better than what she had survived in the *wilden* village. Reluctantly, she allowed Sara to assist her entrance into the copper bucket, feeling like a dirty platter being placed in a tub of hot soapy water.

Then like grease dissolving from a dinner dish, the dirt peeled away her skin. As the maid scoured her body with a rough cloth, Penelope felt both pain and pleasure.

"Oh, look at this filthy water!" said Sara, assisting Penelope out of the tub. "I'll fetch more and bathe you again."

"That's too much luxury."

"As you wish," Sara said in a disapproving tone while rubbing the guest dry, "but first you drink this." The maid removed a finger-tipped piece of root from a cup of hot water Penelope hadn't noticed. "The mistress brought this all the way from Amsterdam to use after childbirth. It takes away aches and pains and soothes the entire body. And Director-General uses it for pain in his absent leg."

"What is it?" asked Penelope, taking a sip of the warm liquid that tasted like the root the medicine woman had used. Did all root steepings taste the same? How would she know? This was only her second root, not counting the ginger of which she had chewed a tiny piece just to experience what Matthew was enduring.

"It comes from China and it's frightfully expensive," whispered the maid. "The mistress swears by it. Don't tell her or she'll deduct it from my wages."

Penelope fondled the hog bristles of a hair brush. She wouldn't need that tool for quite some time.

A young serving girl delivered a bowl of soup that smelled delicious. Even the silver spoon gleamed brightly. To be polite Penelope ate half the soup and then tested the bed. It was softer than Liesbeth's. Sara pulled the bed curtains and Penelope pretended it was night instead of mid-afternoon. She slept peacefully, having escaped from the valley of the shadow of death.

* * * * *

Penelope slept late in the morning, at least an hour after dawn, the latest she could ever remember.

The Stuyvesants's maid, Sara, knocked softly on the door, eased it open, and slipped a pile of clothes onto the dresser. Sara saw that the guest was awake. "What do you wish for breakfast?"

What a strange and wonderful question. Was this what being rich was like? "I'll eat what everyone else is eating," Penelope said, not wanting to cause more trouble for the servants. After the door closed, she grinned at the luxury of a chamber pot again, especially since someone else would empty it. She felt no guilt to relinquish that chore.

A bleached-white linen chemise and a black dress sat next to the mirror. Deliberately ignoring her reflection, Penelope ran her fingers over the expensive fabric and held up the mourning dress. She gasped at the black lace and embroidered flowers. If she wore such sinful clothes, her mother-in-law would have apoplexy and the church elders would banish her from the congregation without a trial.

The offensive garment slipped through her fingers. She backed away until her legs touched the bed and forced her to sit down. "An ocean away," she whispered at the lump of black fabric on the floor. "The congregation is an ocean away and I'm a bankrupt widow. What can I do?"

An ocean away, her father had often said, "Beggars can't be choosers." Penelope breathed deeply. If the elders had seen her in yesterday's immodest *wilden* clothes, they would likely have burned her at the stake. Who on this side of the Atlantic cared what she wore?

Slowly she bent down, picked up the dress—the lesser of the two evils when compared to the aborigine garments— and held it against her body. It seemed a reasonable fit. Besides, Sara with her needle and thread would surely insist on making it skintight, because a guest of the Director-General's couldn't be seen in wrinkled attire.

She inserted her injured body into the flexible chemise, but the stiff, heavy fabric of the dress defeated her until the maid returned and assisted.

Sara offered a maid's black cap that hid everything except Penelope's earlobes. The servant also produced a black scarf that worked well as a sling and was more practical than having her maimed arm strapped across the chest.

Penelope followed the aroma of fresh bread to the breakfast area and discovered cheese, cold smoked herring, buttermilk, and hot pancakes dripping in butter. Judith, saying she had already eaten, fed bits of pancake to her year-old son—Balthazar was his name, if Penelope remembered correctly.

The eldest of Anna's four children—a boy about twelve years old—joined them. Penelope, competing with an adolescent boy's appetite, stuffed herself with cheese and buttered pancakes. How much had Matthew eaten at this age?

"Tell me about the *wilden, mevrouw*," the boy asked. "Is it true they wear no clothes?"

"Balthazar!" said his aunt. "You embarrass our guest."

Penelope nodded at the baby and the adolescent. "Two Balthazars in the same family?"

"Of course. First cousins have the same grandfather."

Penelope rose uncertainly. If she and Matthew had had a baby, it would have been named after Matthew's father. "Thank you for a wonderful breakfast."

Judith asked, "What are your tasks for today?"

The question caught Penelope by surprise. What tasks did a new widow have? "I must write my husband's family and tell them of his death. Is the village safe?"

"Oh yes, quite safe, ever since my husband has been in charge. Except for the drunks."

Chapter 23

New Amsterdam

Friday, September 4, 1648

A few minutes after breakfast, with directions from the Stuyvesants's butler, Penelope left the Director-General's mansion inside Fort New Amsterdam to find a factor's office. Just beyond the guardhouse, she looked to her right toward the calm blue-green waters of the bay she had crossed in a canoe yesterday. Only yesterday! She turned her back on that part of her life, headed toward town, and skirted a placid cow. Why didn't the city watchman remove stray livestock from the streets?

With the three-story City Tavern building as a landmark, she headed in that direction, evading numerous deep ruts and mud holes. Never again would she complain of tripping over a loose cobblestone on an Amsterdam street if ruts and giant holes were the alternative.

Trees. Many fewer than in the forest, but there were trees—giant ones, medium ones, saplings—everywhere. And shrubs, weeds, and dead leaves. Such as contrast to the neat, treeless streets of Amsterdam.

Suddenly, she realized she needed no guardian to accompany her and rejoiced to be a trustworthy Dutch citizen again, free to accomplish her errands alone. Except she missed Matthew's company. She forced those notions away and concentrated on her errand to write a letter home. How would she explain her husband's death to his mother? Or rather to his grandfather since her mother-in-law didn't read or write.

Past the taverns, surprisingly busy this early in the morning, stood three warehouses in a row, their gables facing the street just like on the Damrak. The first factory displayed a faded sign "Pieter Gabry and Sons," a trading firm whose name she recognized from the wharves of Amsterdam. She opened its door and saw the profile of a potbellied, bald man laboriously writing in a ledger book. He waved his left hand in acknowledgement but completed his entry before he looked up.

He stared for a moment, hurriedly stood up, and greeted her warmly in English with a heavy accent, "Welcome, Mrs. Prince." He was not as old as his lack of hair implied, only in his early forties, about the age of her father.

She glanced at shelves stacked with furs. Like Verbrugge's factory, barrels occupied most of the floor space. "How do you know who I am?"

"A small village, madam, hides few secrets. How do I serve you?"

She blushed slightly, unnerved by his penetrating stare. "I need to write a letter. My husband's family doesn't know how or when he died."

The clerk asked, "This letter for you I write?"

"Oh, no, my writing arm's fine." She flexed the fingers of her right hand, thinking he was concerned about her maimed left arm. "I've much to tell, but I've no money to pay for paper."

* * * * *

The flutter of Mrs. Prince's fingers reminded the potbellied factor he had been gawking at his visitor. "Writing paper is my gift, madam." He assembled paper, inkwell, quill, and blotting sand on an empty desk near a window with good light and pulled out a chair.

The man returned to his desk and pretended to focus on his ledger but secretly studied the profile of his visitor, a woman worthy of staring at, single or married or widowed, maimed or whole. She dipped her quill in the ink but held it poised in the air. She grimaced as though in pain and gritted her teeth. How would she say she had returned to the land of the living?

Without looking up, Mrs. Prince asked in Dutch, "*Mijnheer*, the date? I've lost track of time."

"The fourth of September, *mevrouw*," he answered in Dutch, noting her two languages.

The factor studied the deep tan color her face and hands had acquired during her sojourn in the wilderness. He tilted his head and admired the profile of her face and then of her body and noted the graceful movement of her writing hand and the way she blew the excess blotting sand from the paper. He mused about painting her portrait. How would he handle the sling and bad arm? But her face— there was a lot of strength and character in her face.

As she finished the first page, his artistic mind yielded to thoughts of commerce and his attention focused on the writing itself. The quill was in constant movement, into the inkwell and out—how could a quill suck up ink so fast?— onto the paper without a pause and back to the inkwell. Never a hesitation. Never a correction.

Even from a distance, he discerned the ruler-straight lines of ink, the tight character spacing, the beauty of the finished page. Another page finished! She could write more in an hour than he could in a morning.

Then he recalled the rumor about her besting Verbrugge over a contract about her own ransom money. If such were true, how pleasant would be life for the manager of a remote trading post with a clerk like that! Without a doubt, she never got drunk or bet on horse races.

Could he hire her? Ach. She was in debt and thus in need of money. But should he? In Europe the minister would condemn him to hell for hiring a woman who wasn't a relative. But this was New Amsterdam. None cared if he hired a woman, except maybe his beloved Jannetje. This attractive, penniless widow would be married in a few months or on her way home—one or the other. How much work could she accomplish in a few months?

Arithmetic? Too much to hope for. Ach! The rumor claimed she complained about interest rates. And she was English. Could she do pence, shillings and pounds too? He smiled at his wishful thinking, probably the result of too much beer at the tavern last night.

The woman stood up, using her injured left hand cautiously to assist the right hand in organizing the papers. She looked down pensively at her work.

He stood, bowed, and said in English, anxious to improve his skill in the language, "Ach, my manners have lost themselves. I name myself Augustine Herrmann." Without further hesitation, he said, "If you perform sums as fast as you write, then you I hire."

Her eyebrows jumped and her forehead wrinkled. "I beg your pardon, sir."

"The task of company clerk to you I offer. Alas, a large surprise to you it is but not to me. With myself while you write I debate."

"A job? With pay? You can do that? You don't know me."

Herrmann stood a little straighter. "Mr. Gabry trusts me. You I trust."

"Well, sir." She paused and laughed. "I'm between positions now, having just been fired—in truth, sold—as slave of the heathens. What would the duties involve?"

"You consider? Excellent! All the correspondence. Manifests, bills of sale, contracts you copy." He paused. "Good sums you execute, no?"

"On the voyage I calculated the declination of the sun and the latitude."

"*Gut. Sehr gut.*" His head bobbed up and down. "Guilders? Pence and shillings?"

She nodded.

Last night he dreamed of good fortune, though these developments exceeded his imagination. "It settles itself then!" He clapped his hands together in glee.

"Almost."

"On Monday you start?"

"I can start tomorrow," she said, "but there are matters we haven't discussed yet: the first is wages. I find myself without assets at the moment and in significant debt."

He bowed deeply. "Many assets, you have, Mrs. Prince, many assets, but money no."

"How much do you pay a clerk?"

"Two and one half guilders a week I pay to clerk of whom last week I fire."

She paused. "Was he worth it?"

Herrmann smiled. "That clerk is worth to fire but is not worth to pay even two guilders."

"What's the most you've ever paid a clerk?"

Ach. She's even a good haggler. "Old Joachim, my best clerk ever, is dead these three years now. Three guilders a week to him I pay. Slow but precise he is when the room is warm and his joints are loose."

Mrs. Prince stood straighter and assumed a business-like demeanor. "Then I shall work for you for three guilders a week and I shall be worth it."

Without hesitation, he said, "Since a man's work you do, Mrs. Prince, then your hand I shake."

* * * * *

Penelope was surprised at her own audacity to accept a job from a stranger. And she had negotiated good pay, as much as Matthew had made in Amsterdam. Never before had she shaken a man's hand to seal a business transaction. In Amsterdam a handshake between merchants commonly indicated agreement on terms and that a written contract would soon follow. Nervously she wiped her hand on her dress. This was her second decision today that, across the ocean in Amsterdam, would have gotten her banished from Matthew's congregation.

She shook Mr. Herrmann's hand.

Good things came in threes, claimed the proverb. Buoyed by her success so far, she decided to take a first step in locating her father. After all, that was her purpose in coming.

"A question, Mr. Herrmann. Do you know a Mr. John Throckmorton?" That was the name of the man whom her father's letter had said would transport him from Boston to Manhattan.

"Oh yes, a sad story he is."

Penelope gasped. Had her only clue died?

"A large group from Providence Plantations—that's where one goes first when one is banned from Boston—a land grant here in Vredeland they obtain." Herrmann pointed to a spot on a hand-painted map on the wall. A creek separated the north end of Manhattan from the mainland near a picture of a house labeled Jonas Bronk's.

"The year later, yes, in the blood year of 1643, just before the harvest, the *wilden* invade from the north. Many in Vredeland they kill. Many here on Manhattan they kill. The villages on the long island they attack. If one lives, one flees to Fort New Amsterdam. The savages roam the woods for months while in fear we huddle."

Penelope's mind whirled. Her father had come in that same year. Death from these savages was so easy. She stammered, "What...what happened to Mr. Throckmorton?"

"To Providence Plantations, he returns. As far as one knows, there still he lives."

Penelope collapsed into a chair and rubbed her face with her hands. She had endured so much to get to New Netherland to begin her search. Throckmorton, the man who would know whether her father had even made it this far, had removed to another colony.

"You know Mr. Throckmorton?" Herrmann asked.

"No," she whispered. "He...he was a friend of a friend." Throckmorton might be alive. How much should she reveal to a man she had just met? In whom could she confide? She was too shocked to trust her own judgment.

Herrmann gently placed a hand on her shoulder, then quickly removed it. He shuffled his feet in obvious embarrassment. "My apologies, please. This talk of danger from the *wilden* for you is no good. Let me for you to get a beer."

"No, please, Mr. Herrmann. I'm fine." She dabbed at her tears with a black cuff of her sleeve. For whom was she crying—herself, her father, or Matthew? Or her plans. "After...after the last month, I thought New Amsterdam was a place of safety."

"Oh, the village is safe," he said hurriedly. "Quite safe, compared to the wilderness."

She sniffled again. Safe? Safe compared to the wilderness, where her father might have roamed and where Matthew had been murdered. "Were...were many people killed? Back then. Back in 1643, when Mr. Throckmorton was in danger." When her father may have wandered the forest infested with heartless wilden.

Herrmann shrugged. "Only a hundred or so. A dozen in the Hutchinson family, the neighbors of Mr. Throckmorton. Isolated farms. Some soldiers who battle them."

Penelope wiped her eyes again. A hundred had died in this tiny place and her father was probably among that number. Was this the Will of God: to bring her family to America to be killed one at a time by the savages? "Where were the hundred buried?"

Herrmann was silent. She looked up.

"Here...there...everywhere...nowhere." He blinked back tears.

Nowhere. She thought of Matthew's body, abandoned by the savages who killed him, abandoned by the wife who had promised to be faithful to him. The Anabaptist congregation didn't believe in funeral ceremonies. But her father was Anglican and she had come to find him, dead or alive. He deserved a grave and words said over his bones.

Herrmann said, "I fetch for you a beer," and hurried to the back of the factory.

Penelope sipped the drink in silence and pondered the dangers of the wilderness. She should abandon the search. What was the purpose of losing her life in an impossible task? Yet what else did she have to do with her life? To return to Amsterdam would require explaining Matthew's death to his family. She couldn't face this. She had even addressed the letter to Liesbeth rather than the Prince family, justifying to herself Liesbeth was easier to locate and better able to pay the delivery fee when the letter arrived.

The best she could expect in Amsterdam was a lifetime in the *Spinhuis*, the charitable workhouse that took in the penniless and the crippled, the widows and orphans—she was all four in one body.

She lifted the mug to drain the last of the beer and realized Herrmann still hovered around her like Stuyvesant's maid. "Thank you. That was good."

"You like it?" Herrmann beamed. "From my own brewery it comes."

"You own a brewery?" She examined the bald, pudgy businessman with soft hands stained with ink and paint and tried to imagine him stirring hops and yeast in a huge vat. Obviously he hired workers. He had certainly hired her quickly enough. The rumors that New Amsterdam was short of workers and the pay was high were obviously true.

"My grandfather brewed the best beer in Prague."

"Prague? In Bohemia?"

"Ach. My ancestry and name are German, but my birth belongs to Prague. The religious wars urge my family to Amsterdam when a boy I am. Rootless and impatient, the GWC I join, and years later, here I am."

"Prague?" She laughed. "You're further from home than I am."

"No. This is home now." He waved his arms to encompass the entire village. "Come. My pleasure is to show to you every street and every building in Manhattan."

Home. That had been her and Matthew's intention—to make New Amsterdam their home. How could it be a home without Matthew? But where else could she go? "That's a kind offer, but don't you have a factory to run?"

"The work I preserve for my new clerk, who starts on the Monday. Today we enjoy."

"Pardon me, but what day of the week is today?"

"Friday."

"Friday?" Giving names to the days of the week was a small symbol of civilization. Maybe New Amsterdam wasn't home but it was familiar. She laughed. A calendar. Wool and linen clothes that completely covered her arms and legs. Brick buildings with gabled roofs. Beer in a ceramic mug. She smiled and stood up. "Yes, let's enjoy Friday."

Chapter 24

New Amsterdam

Friday, September 4, 1648

Penelope and Augustine Herrmann exited the factor's office to begin the promised tour of Manhattan, a respite to take her mind off the shock of her father's probable death at the hands of the *wilden*. And she needed to learn more about her new home. No, it wasn't her home—merely her place of residence. She had no home and no family.

Herrmann pointed to a partly completed pier jutting into the water. "This names itself East River, which is better than Southeast River. On Pearl Street, we stand, for piles of oyster shells which slaves burn into lime. Good pearls only grow themselves in warm tropical oceans, yet hope burns always. A block to the left exists the City Tavern where such a sensation yesterday at lunch you make." They headed to the right. "Here's the bakery which unites with my beer to make me as broad as tall."

"Oh. A hat shop." Penelope stopped to look. The local fashions were many years behind Amsterdam.

Herrmann muttered something about women and hats under his breath. At the corner, he stopped. "To the right the market pasture where farmers bring their produce

weekly exists. The good improvements which Director-
General Stuyvesant has made are only this market and the
pier. To the left our beautiful church and our dismal fort
exist. After the problems with savages five years ago, is
anyone interested in repairing the fort? No, not a one."

"What problems?" She was intensely interested in dangerous savages.

"That is long time ago under another Director-General.
Some day to you I tell."

She restrained her impatience. She wasn't going anywhere. Time had no meaning. "It does look rather pitiful,
but at least it has cannon."

He shook his head. "Four cannons exist but have no gun
carriages to support themselves and with which to aim
themselves. Furthermore, the gunner consumes all gunpowder to celebrate the Director-General's arrival last
year. Just as well. Much of the powder is bad. Half of shots
misfire. Luckily, one is not injured or killed."

Penelope wrinkled her nose in disgust and stepped
around an odoriferous puddle. "Have they no self-respect—
letting an outhouse leak into the street?"

"Like Silver Leg you sound now."

"Silver Leg? Oh, you mean the Director-General. Why
doesn't he do something?"

Herrmann pantomimed signing a document. "Each
week, rules, edicts, ordinances, and more rules. Forbidden
to open tavern before two o'clock on Sunday. Forbidden for
outhouse to leak into street. One would think a minister he
is rather than Director-General he is."

"No one enforces the laws?" She decided New Amsterdam had a much different opinion of Director-General
Stuyvesant than the one widely held in Amsterdam.

"The *schout* enforces some of them, especially for the
taverns at nine o'clock to close. A quarter of all businesses
possess liquor licenses yet to sell beer and rum without
licenses is common. Many inspections are required. Sometimes to inspect a single tavern all night he takes."

She watched two mongrels tussle over ownership of a bone. "I saw yesterday how *Schout* Van Dyck enforced the one about not giving beer to the *wilden*."

"See. He forbids beer, the elixir of life." Herrmann shook his head and walked on. "Ahead and to the left exists the windmill to cut timber and to mill wheat."

She grinned. "I never saw a windmill with only two good arms."

"Ach. The holes in the roof. The timbers rot. With four sails, a strong wind tears the building apart. Stomachs growl even now because too slowly the wheat it grinds."

With enthusiastic gestures, Herrmann pointed out other features. "This broad highway leads past the company's orchards and through a pitiful wall into the countryside."

Penelope stared through a distant gate in a sagging wooden wall and into the undisturbed forests beyond, the forests where her father had sought his future. If he had gotten this far. New Amsterdam was small and Herrmann apparently knew everything that happened here. She was tempted to confess her secrets and ask his help. Except he was German, as was the man who started her father on his disastrous path. She would wait.

Herrmann stood near the edge of a narrow waterway. "Here exists the Begijngracht, which joins over there to the Herengracht." They walked to the corner.

Penelope frowned at a crooked watercourse that didn't look like a real canal. The banks were dirt, not brick, and meandering, not straight. She could even see the muddy bottom in many places. "They certainly didn't honor the Herengracht I know by naming this...this thing after it." She inhaled the familiar odor of algae and dead fish. "Though it smells like the real one."

"When the tide comes in, the creek fills itself. Then one poles small barges to deliver goods to the company warehouses."

Of course, a natural stream, like the one on which she had ridden in Tisquantum's canoe to the ocean. How many other things did these locals improvise? She noticed a house with bricks on the front side that faced the street and wooden boards on the sidewall.

"Hollanders love their canals," Herrmann continued. "Across 'The Ditch' one sees more homes, taverns, and stores and a better view of the pitiful wall."

She echoed Herrmann's combination of admiration and scorn. "Such a promising city—New Amsterdam."

"Ach. One will promise one anything here. If one doesn't deliver, one sues. For the best entertainment one attends the weekly court to see who sues whom for what. Money. Slander. Bastardy. Breach of contract. One sees it all."

At least that was similar to Amsterdam, she thought. "Do you go to court often?"

"Many contracts seek me. If one doesn't wish to appear before the Director-General, then me one hires."

She studied her employer, a man of many talents. "Are you a lawyer too?"

"No, no." He waved his hands in dismissal of the idea.

"No legal training? Aren't you at a disadvantage in an argument against a lawyer?"

"Ach, so it would be if it was so. But the lawyer is not allowed to speak in Director-General Stuyvesant's courtroom."

She raised her eyebrows. "That doesn't make sense."

"But explained it clearly you just did. Only one lawyer resides on island of Manhattan. Thus unfair it would be if the plaintiff hires the only legal counsel and defendant himself alone must defend."

After sorting out Herrmann's convoluted logic about New Netherland's single lawyer, Penelope had to agree. Hundreds of lawyers in Amsterdam earned rich fees arguing against one another on behalf of contentious businessmen. Why would they leave a lucrative city for a poor wilderness village?

Herrmann shrugged. "Besides, the lawyer *Meijnheer* van der Donck is too philosophical to argue well against Stuyvesant whose fixed ideas of right and wrong firmly he holds and fanciful ideas he distrusts."

The leisurely tour of Manhattan had taken an hour. Penelope complimented him on his knowledge.

Herrmann shrugged. "My recreations of geography and painting unite into map-making."

"Map making. Then, you would be interested to see my father's globe. Oh no! My globe! My father's globe! It was in my chest. I packed clothes all around it." She wiped tears from her cheek. "Gone. Gone forever."

"The cargo of your ship they recovered. Perhaps your chest hides itself within the GWC warehouse." Herrmann pointed. "One turns here on Brughstraat and there it is."

Penelope practically dragged her guide around the corner. Halfway down the block Herrmann led her into a walled compound that flew the GWC flag. She compared the small, crude yellow brick buildings to the large, sturdy red-brick structure that housed the company offices in Amsterdam.

Herrmann pushed open a door and called to the nearest clerk, "*Mevrouw* Prince has come to claim her chests from the wreck of *de Kath.*"

The clerk stammered, "*Mevrouw*, we thought that you...Please wait while I search."

After what seemed an inordinately long time, the clerk reappeared, dragging her chest. When she opened it, the odor of mildew gagged her. She rummaged through her trunk, abruptly arose and ordered, "Please deliver it to the Director-General's house, where I'm staying." Ignoring Herrmann, she swirled around and exited the office.

Herrmann caught up with her in the street. "Distressed you are. Why?"

She fought back tears. "My globe was not there."

"One suspects company clerks to pilfer. Such theft is commonplace"

"Stuyvesant is so strict about everything else. Why doesn't he stop theft in his own warehouse?" She wiped her eyes with a cuff of her dress, knowing she made a spectacle of herself in the street.

"To call the kettle black, the pot hesitates. One hears rumors the Director-General twists the rules to make money for himself. One hears smugglers are not punished if they smuggle for the Director-General."

"To whom can I turn for help?" She pleaded more to God than to her companion.

He lowered his voice, even though no one else was nearby. "If Lieutenant Nicholas Stillwell you meet, ask him."

"Stillwell? That's an English name." Surely she could trust a fellow Englishman and a military officer. She had to rely upon someone.

Herrmann blushed and patted his ample stomach. "Listen to how it rumbles. Let's go see what my betrothed's mother cooks today." He took her arm, encouraging her to accompany him.

"Your betrothed's family?" She pulled back. "We'll descend upon them with no warning?"

"Yes. Come. They will enjoy. Remember, this fortnight, the most famous person on Manhattan you are."

Reluctantly, she let herself be persuaded. "It'll be best for you if your betrothed meets me in person, rather than from gossip."

He smiled. "Ach! That too."

They crossed the so-called canal on a rickety wooden bridge. His enthusiasm cheered her spirits.

"You seem to like this place yet seem so critical." She studied his face.

"Quite perceptive. Manhattan I love like a son who has much potential but wastes his youth with wine, women, and song. Or in this case, one chases easy money now, instead of to develop a prosperous colony then. Such wasted opportunities depress me."

* * * * *

The wife of Caspar Varleth removed the lid from the heavy iron pot suspended from a chain in her fireplace, listened to the sizzle, and sniffed. Her pork roast needed another half hour. Hearing voices in the parlor, she called from her kitchen, "Jannetje, is that scamp Augustine sweet-talking you into a free meal again?" She would be insulted if Augustine ate anywhere else.

Jannetje called back, "Two free meals, Mother."

Mother Varleth peered around the doorjamb. Silhouetted against the light spilling through her front door were Augustine and a woman.

"*Mevrouw* Prince, this one is my betrothed, Jannetje Varleth, whose mother," Herrmann raised his voice, "is the best cook in America. And her father Caspar Varleth. And her sisters Ann and Judi and her brother Nicholas."

Mother Varleth grinned. Her daughter had picked such a polite man.

Caspar said, "My dear girl, what a catastrophe you've experienced!"

The young woman with her arm in a sling could only be the survivor everyone was talking about. Mother Varleth hurriedly basted the pork roast again, wiped her hands on an apron that barely covered her wide girth, and joined the crowd in the parlor. She noticed the uncertainty on the widow's face and gave her a strong maternal hug while avoiding pressure on the arm in a sling.

Caspar said, "Be careful, Mother. You may hurt her."

Mother Varleth stepped back, held the sweet, innocent girl at arm's length, and looked deeply into her gray-green eyes. "This one, I think, will not break. But she does need fattening."

"Ach, then her to the proper place I've brought," said Augustine.

Mother Varleth pinched Penelope's cheek. "Why does she honor you with her presence, Augustine?"

"Because her I've hired. My new clerk she is."

"You hired a female clerk?" Caspar stroked his chin as he often did when thinking. "What a stroke of genius, Augustine, since good help is so hard to find this far away from the fatherland."

Herrmann beamed. "Her father was an English businessman."

Caspar, Nicholas, Augustine, and Penelope immediately jumped into a discussion on the state of commerce in Amsterdam. Mother Varleth pointed to the table and Ann and Judi resumed arranging the dining table while whispering to each other.

"Oh, my roast. Jannetje, help me." The mother dragged her daughter into the kitchen but ignored the food. "It concerns me that Augustine stares at another woman like that."

"The eye of the artist, not the man, stares. Look." Jannetje pulled her mother to the doorjamb." See how he tilts his head to regard her from another angle. He does the same with the windmill near the fort."

"Are you that certain of your man?"

"Yes, I am." Jannetje tucked a loose strand of hair back beneath her cap. "Have you spent two hours watching him study a broken windmill? Have you seen the state of the archives in his office? Listen to her discuss interest rates."

Mother Varleth peeked through the doorway and stared discreetly at the young widow. "She has not grieved yet."

"It's the shock of a soldier experiencing battle for the first time," said Caspar, coming to the kitchen to refresh his beer. "The soul cannot comprehend."

"Jannetje, you tell Augustine to let her cry now and then, and not to scold." Mother Varleth lifted the lid of a pot and sniffed again. "But if she cries too much, send her to me. She's too young to be so far away from her mother at a time like this."

Caspar said, "Didn't you hear? She's both widowed and motherless."

Mother Varleth looked at Jannetje. "Even more so, she needs a mother's shoulder to cry on. Any mother's. You tell your Augustine that."

* * * * *

Penelope said goodbye and thanks to the Varleth family. Her single voice was overwhelmed by their six. Herrmann simply waved back to them and she did the same.

In the comparative quiet of the street, Penelope asked Herrmann, "My gallant knight from yesterday, Mr. Richard Stout, where does he live?"

"Mr. Stout lives in the Anabaptist village of the English. Across the East River at the long island's southwest tip it is. His village calls itself Gravesend. What an odd name that makes itself in English."

Penelope's eyebrows shot up. "Are there many Anabaptists around?" Matthew had sought a haven for Anabaptists. Why had God directed them to one of the few places in the world where such a site already existed and then let Matthew be murdered?

"His Highness complains of overmuch of everything, except devout members of his Dutch Reformed Church."

She forced herself not to think of Matthew. "What time do we start work?"

"This town slowly wakes up and lately goes to sleep. Nine o'clock is soon enough." Herrmann tipped his hat goodbye.

"I'll see you Monday morning." Penelope glanced up to spot a tall building to get her bearings as she used to do in Amsterdam. She turned in a circle. There were only two— City Tavern and the church. The Stuyvesant mansion must be behind the church.

She walked alone as she used to do in Amsterdam, observed the town and its inhabitants, enjoyed civilization, such as it was, and exchanged smiles and nods with strangers. At the fort's gatehouse, she stared at the nearby bay, whose shoreline marked the edge of civilization. She contrasted this crude village with her former abode, the richest city in Europe. Manhattan was nothing compared to Amsterdam but much better than Tisquantum's village.

The Stuyvesant mansion loomed ahead. Was it proper to knock on the door as a stranger or to enter as a resident?

The butler saw her coming and opened the door. "Your chest has been delivered to your quarters, *mevrouw*."

As Stoeffel shut the door, Penelope tried not to stare at his bald spot.

The trunk waited at the foot of the bed. She knelt before it but could not bring herself to look inside again, knowing Matthew's clothes occupied one quarter of the space. Instead she opened a paper lying atop the trunk—an invoice from the GWC for expenses on the journey.

Freight for two people: fl 64.0
Food for two people for 138 days: fl 101.10
Freight for 632 pounds: fl 31.12
Total: fl 197.2
Less deposit: fl 164.0
Less work credit: fl 30.18
Balance due: fl 2.4

She could not comprehend it at first. Four and a half months at sea, several weeks of Matthew's labor on Curaçao, a shipwreck, abandonment, Matthew's death, and a month with the savages, and still she owed two guilders and four stuivers to the GWC?

Chapter 25

New Amsterdam

Friday, September 4, 1648

Penelope had no idea how long she sat stupefied beside her unopened trunk before someone entered her bedroom.

Stuyvesant's maid, Sara, knelt beside Penelope, squeezed her good shoulder gently, and spoke in a voice as comforting as Liesbeth's. "Too many memories lie in that trunk."

Penelope touched her head. "Too many memories here."

"Hang unto the good ones, dear. Let the rest drift away."

"I wish I could."

Sara said, "I'll fix you a hot bath. That always cheers the mistress. The Director-General hasn't returned, but the ladies will dine at eight."

At eight, Penelope joined Judith and Anna and recognized an extra piece of silver cutlery near her Delft plate—the fork, the latest French fad among the rich Amsterdammers—but considered it odd that it sat alone on the left side. She had never used a fork and, with only one good hand, didn't intend to try.

In a typical Dutch family the children and servants ate with the parents. Where were Anna's four children? How

many strange customs did rich people have? Or was that a
French habit?

After Anna said the blessing, the butler served Penelope
first. She was relieved her food had already been cut into
small pieces and politely waited while he served the other
two women. Anna held the fork in the left hand, speared a
piece of meat that she cut with the knife, and immediately
popped the morsel on the fork into her mouth. That was
efficient. What else was the left hand good for except to
hold bread to sop up gravy and shovel peas into a spoon?
Not that her left hand was good for much any more.

"How do you like our quaint village, *mevrouw?*" asked
Anna after she and Judith had exhausted the day's gossip
about children, servants, and neighbors.

Penelope related her experiences with Augustine
Herrmann and the Varleth family but omitted mention of
her new job. Her rich hostess might be insulted for a
female guest to work or might even forbid it. If Penelope
had considered that complication earlier, she could have
asked Mother Varleth about renting a room in the home of
a respectable family.

Judith said, "Councilman Herrmann is one of the Nine
Men, the advisers to my husband."

Anna said, "The Varleths are a highly regarded family.
Caspar's brother is Amsterdam's representative to Virgin-
ia. I knew of them back in Holland. I can't understand why
Judith Varleth doesn't hire a maid and cook."

Penelope didn't explain that Judith loved to cook and
had three capable daughters.

The conversation turned to the absent Director-General.
Anna explained how her brother had lost his leg leading an
attack on the island of Sint Maarten. The wound had not
healed well and he had returned home to Holland to
recuperate. Judith, the sister of Anna's deceased husband,
had nursed the wounded soldier and they had fallen in
love.

It was as though a candle had been lit in Penelope's
brain. Anna had been born Anna Stuyvesant and now was

Mevrouw Bayard. Judith Bayard now called herself *Mevrouw* Stuyvesant. "Being English," Penelope said, "I should've noticed you had each taken your husbands' name."

Judith replied, "Yes, it's surely time the Dutch join the rest of Europe in properly recognizing a wife should share name of her husband."

Penelope expected Anna, a native Hollander, to be somewhat offended by the comments of her double sister-in-law, who was of French Huguenot descent.

Anna nodded. "The absence of a proper surname is so ancient as to be shameful. Though most of my countrymen don't appear to be humiliated in the least. I blame it on resurrection of this nonsense of Batavian heritage, as though nothing has changed in seventeen hundred years."

The mention of Batavia, the Roman name for Holland, reminded Penelope of catfights with her blue-eyed classmates in Amsterdam. When the Dutch girls poked fun at her green eyes, she had reminded them Julius Caesar had conquered Batavia but had been repulsed from Britannia. Too bad she hadn't had reasonable classmates like Anna.

When the three women adjourned to the drawing room, the butler poured each a small glass of Spanish wine.

Penelope admired Judith's wedding portrait that dominated one wall. "Is this by Rembrandt van Rijn? I hear his portraits are popular though I've never seen one."

"Of course not," said Judith. "He lives in the Jewish quarter and has a mistress. And he requires such an excessive number of sittings and takes forever to finish."

"This was done by a family friend, who does excellent work with only four sittings," added Anna. "And he charges even more than that scoundrel Rembrandt."

The clothes, Penelope thought, were so much more lifelike than the faces. But the clothes had "sat" for many more hours than the subjects.

She was tired, the happy weariness of a busy day. Tomorrow, Saturday, she would rest.

* * * * *

A strange thumping noise interrupted Sara's struggle to fit Penelope into another of Judith's fancy dresses for Saturday supper.

Sara said, "Listen. The Director-General's leg clumps happily tonight."

How would an angry leg sound?

Before departing Amsterdam, she had heard about Pieter Stuyvesant, the Director-General of New Netherland. The GWC directors in Amsterdam expected this experienced military leader to run a tight ship after the slack and incompetent Willem Kieft. If fact, his appointment was another factor supporting her decision to immigrate to New Amsterdam, a symbol of a better future for the colony.

She brushed dust off the hem of the black dress and allowed Sara to apply a heated flatiron to a few wrinkles.

At a quarter to eight she followed the sound of conversation to the drawing room. Bands of silver decorated the wooden leg of a man dressed in velvet and silk—obviously the Director-General—who happily played with year-old Balthazar.

This initial impression of a loving father conflicted with the stories she had heard the previous day about the tyrannical Director-General who ordered the taverns to close at nine o'clock and not to open on Sundays before two and required fences to keep livestock off the streets.

It also gave new meaning to his phrase, "I shall rule over you as a father over his children," which the inhabitants interpreted as a condescending message from royalty. Perhaps the phrase had been the sentiment of a new father who, Judith claimed, loved the people for whom he was now responsible and remembered how his father, Balthazar, had raised him in stern but loving righteousness.

Judith noticed the guest at the doorway and took the baby from her husband. "*Mevrouw* Prince, this is my husband, his High Mightiness, the Director-General, Petrus Stuyvesant. And this, my dear, is the widow Penelope Prince, the lost woman from *de Kath*."

He bowed. She curtseyed as her mother had taught her long ago.

"A pleasure to make your acquaintance, your High Mightiness. Your wife has taken good care of me." Whose idea was it to convert the good Dutch name Pieter into its Latinized version—Petrus? Did every high mightiness put on such airs?

The Director-General maintained a ram-rod straight posture. "The pleasure is mine, *Mevrouw* Prince. I am pleased that at least some person in my colony has treated you well. I believe *Schout-Fiscaal* van Dyck could have shown you more consideration. Had I been present, I would have paid your ransom to the savage myself."

From his tone and formality of speech, Penelope was half surprised he didn't use the royal "we" instead of "I." His silk stockings alone would have paid half her ransom.

"Thank you, sir. I would describe it as a reward for services rendered rather than a ransom and all the implications of that word."

The butler announced dinner and a nanny retrieved the baby. As the Director-General escorted his wife into the dining room, followed by Anna and Penelope, the scent of Dutch food with East Indian spices—nutmeg, cinnamon, and curry—greeted them. Stuyvesant said grace rapidly and without emotion as though he had said those same words a thousand times before. In contrast, the Separatists followed the Biblical instructions, "When ye pray, use no vain repetitions, as the heathen: for they think to be heard for their much babbling."

The four-course meal surprised Penelope. Was it in her honor or a typical dinner in the Stuyvesant household when the Director-General was present?

Stuyvesant said, "I understand you lived in a native village for a month. I would like to hear about your experiences there. My knowledge has come from common soldiers or fur traders who have a biased point of view."

She skipped the description of the attack on the beach, for fear it would upset Judith and Anna, and detailed the children's games and how the women stored food underground in tightly-woven baskets and pulverized maize into flour with stones.

Mevrouw Stuyvesant curled her upper lip. "You make them sound almost civilized."

Stuyvesant had listened with great interest. "I keep telling *Domine* Bogardus these *wilden* are a happy, peaceful people—not blood-thirsty savages. If he would learn their language and preach the Bible to them, I'm certain they could easily be converted to Christians."

Penelope restrained a giggle at the notion of naked Christians but she didn't argue with her host. He seemed to have an unreasonably high regard for his own beliefs and she might need a favor to learn what had happened to her father.

On their way to the drawing room after the meal, the butler whispered to the Director-General, who made his excuses about the press of business and hurried away.

His abrupt departure caught Penelope off guard. Although the Director-General could make things happen, what would he do personally to investigate the disappearance of her father? Nothing. Instead, she feared, he would refer the matter to a deputy and her secrets would scatter to the four winds. Matthew would have said the Director-General's departure was a decision made by God, but she felt her hesitation was due to prudence.

* * * * *

The arrival of Sunday morning accompanied the delivery of another of Judith's black dresses, this one formal enough for a king's reception. How many dresses did her hostess own? The true number would likely depress her spirits, so Penelope fretted over buttons instead.

"Why would anyone own a dress with buttons in the back?" she asked the maid. "How impractical." Not to mention inappropriate for an Anabaptist but she had already abandoned that fight. Apparently none of Judith's outer garments used hook or laces.

"Mistress," said Sara, "a dress like this proves you're rich enough to afford a maid."

Because the Reformed Church was the adjacent building, Penelope expected a leisurely stroll. Instead, the drawing room was full of military officers in formal uniforms. She was introduced to several Englishman, including Lieutenant Brian Newton, the secretary for English affairs. She asked him, "Are we preparing for battle or for church?"

He whispered, "Pretend you're part of the family at a fancy wedding and follow Anna's lead."

Lieutenant Newton's description was accurate. Except for a modest neckline, Judith and Anna's dresses were similar in style and expense to ball gowns that rich ladies wore in Amsterdam. Of course, it was customary to wear your best clothes to church, but God should set a limit.

His High Mightiness wore more silk than his wife but in blues and reds bold enough to strike down Reverend Prince with apoplexy. Arm in arm, husband and wife led the procession in a stately march to the slow beat of a drum. Next came Anna with her military escort, followed by her lavishly dressed thirteen-year-old daughter on the arm of another officer and then three sons in military uniforms. Next, as a guest of the household, walked Penelope escorted by Lieutenant Newton. Following were the household servants in order of rank, with two black slaves at the end.

Troops stood at attention, adjacent to a freshly sanded and raked path to the church and presented arms as the Director-General passed. Nearby stood townspeople who whispered and pointed at the procession as though it were a carnival parade. As at a formal wedding, escorts led the women to their reserved pews with purple cushions near the front of the church and withdrew. Then the dignitaries marched in—the Director-General, the burgomaster, the *schout*, the *schepens,* the military officers including Newton, and the minor officials—and sat on purple cushions.

Penelope recalled Reverend Prince's humble church in a former barn. How can one believe each man is equal in the eyes of God after participating in this spectacle?

The Dutch Reformed Church service was as she remembered it at Westerkerk, which she had often attended with her landlady when her father was away on a voyage. The Church of England congregation in Amsterdam was inconveniently located on the far side of town.

The *voorleser*, a combination clerk, assistant minister, gravedigger, and bell ringer, marked the beginning of the service by pounding his staff on the floor. After he read the Ten Commandments and another passage from the Bible, he led the singing of a hymn, during which *Domine* Johannes Bogardus entered, prayed silently, and climbed the stairs to the high pulpit, from which he preached for two hours. Fortunately in this church the benches had backs, although she noticed Director-General Stuyvesant sat so straight his back didn't touch the wood.

In two hours, the *domine* could have covered every sin. Instead he castigated the men of New Amsterdam for their manly transgressions, those mostly associated with drinking, swearing, and fornication. He omitted vanity.

In Amsterdam, if a *domine* preached too long, the *voorleser* would rap his staff on the floor three times as a reminder. Would the same happen here if Stuyvesant's military precision clashed with his religious ardor? After the sermon, the deacons collected the offering by extending leather bags on the end of a pole to each male, ringing a small bell if the deacon considered the contribution too miserly. She smiled at the notion of the deacon ringing his little bell at His High Mightiness.

Meanwhile, the *voorleser* collected written prayer requests, inserted them into the cleft of his staff, and thus passed them to the *domine* in his high pulpit. The domine admonished everyone to have regard for the poor and praised the generous. He concluded the service by reading the prayer requests, including one thanking God for his mercy in saving Penelope Prince. Penelope suspected Anna was responsible, caught her eye, and nodded her thanks.

* * * * *

The worshippers filed out of the church and socialized on the parade field of the adjacent fort. The elegantly dressed military officers reminded Penelope of the Arquebusiers of Amsterdam. The city hadn't been threatened during Penelope's lifetime, yet rich gentlemen, like Mayor Cocq and his cronies, paraded in colorful clothes and shiny muskets as though the city's survival depended upon their military skills

She met several more Englishmen. Where had they come from? Apparently Stuyvesant expected all persons employed by the West India Company to attend the Reformed Church.

Then she was introduced to Lieutenant Nicholas Stillwell, whom Herrmann had suggested she talk to. His military attire was somewhat threadbare, and his leather belt was nicked and gouged. That and his alert posture suggested he wasn't a parade-ground fancy-pants like most of the others.

How much should she tell this stranger? Herrmann had only suggested he could retrieve her globe, not find her father. She would be cautious.

The lieutenant introduced his two sons, Ricky and Nicky, and apologized for his wife's absence, explaining she wanted to meet Penelope, but there were babies at home.

Penelope complimented his sons' good behavior.

He confided, "It's part of their training."

"I beg your pardon?"

"When a savage stalks a deer or a man, he waits for hours, ignoring hunger and mosquitoes, observing everything, waiting for the right time to strike. I use the sermons to train the boys. Nicky only twitched thrice today."

She looked at him askance. "Do you jest?"

Lieutenant Stilwell frowned. "No, ma'am, I never jest about the savages!"

Penelope wasn't sure what to make of this man but his respect for the dangers of the *wilden* encouraged her. "Sir, at your convenience, I would like to talk privately. Would you meet me at Augustine Herrmann's factory, where I start my employment tomorrow?"

He replied, "I sail to Long Island in the morning. Since my sloop is docked at the pier in front of Mr. Herrmann's, it will be my pleasure to see you there before I leave."

"Until tomorrow then. Thank you, sir."

Lieutenant Stillwell moved away. She spied Andrieseen, the master of the ill-fated *de Kath* and the man who had abandoned her and Matthew on the shipwrecked beach. Merely the sight of him gave her nausea as well as sudden pains in her shoulder wound. She turned away in disgust and hoped he didn't see her. But already he pushed through the crowd.

"*Mevrouw* Prince, I'm divinely grateful you're alive. I'm truly sorry about your husband. Leaving you on that beach was the hardest thing I've ever done. I was responsible for the lives of all the people on the ship. I had to save as many as possible. I greatly feared taking your injured husband would get us all killed, especially the two children." He knelt on one knee before her and bowed his head. "Please, I beg your forgiveness."

Surrounded by scores of staring people and standing in the church's shadow, she felt compelled to be magnanimous although she would have preferred to borrow a sword and batter him over the head. However, he did save the other passengers and crew, either by luck or skill. Feeling like a Catholic priest, she placed her right hand on his shoulder and said, "I forgive you."

"Thank you. My soul is greatly comforted." He rose and merged back into the throng.

How much of Andriessen's performance was sincere and how much was to impress the Director-General and the public? Probably as much as hers. She felt like a hypocrite and didn't bother to notice if the crowd was impressed. Liesbeth had always said grudges interfered with living, although Liesbeth seemed to enjoy her little resentments against her three daughters-in-law. Some grudges were well-earned, despite sermons to turn the other cheek and to forgive your trespassers.

Deliberately, she turned her mind away from Andriessen and concentrated on tallying up the monetary value of the expensive fabrics worn to worship the Lord. Her attitude wasn't Christian but she believed a small sin was better than a larger sin.

The Director-General's family and guests returned home less formally. They ate cold food left over from yesterday since even the Director-General's slaves and servants did minimal work on the Sabbath.

However, the Director-General didn't return until evening, his arrival accompanied by angry shouts in the courtyard. Herrmann had said many people disliked him.

Chapter 26

New Amsterdam

Sunday, September 6, 1648

As twilight fell, the Director-General felt guilty working on the Sabbath but duty was high on God's list of virtues. He joined his wife, his sister, and the English woman in the mansion's dining room for a light supper. Then they adjourned to the drawing room, where he conferred with the butler about a bottle of Spanish wine.

As the guest chatted with his sister and wife about children and domestic matters, Stuyvesant wondered about her unusual background. Although she was English, she spoke perfect Dutch. She was well educated yet her late husband was a carpenter and they had paid their own passage, rather than being contracted to a *patroon*, or rich landowner. Like himself, she appeared to handle her injury with grace and dignity.

Anna left to investigate some noise from her four children. To explore his curiosity, he engaged the visitor in conversation. "*Mevrouw* Prince, will you add your name to the church roster?"

"Of course, she will," said Judith, smiling at the guest.

"What choice of churches do I have, Your High Mightiness?" The English woman held an erect posture despite the injuries he had heard about.

He studied her carefully. "There is only one legitimate church in New Amsterdam, the Dutch Reformed Church."

A frown quickly passed over her face before a smile replaced it. "Isn't there complete religious freedom here, as in Amsterdam."

Her question irked him. True Calvinists had all the freedom they needed inside his church. "Despite the heretics and backsliders here, the only approved worship is the Reformed Church. Are you a member?"

She paused before answering. "My father was English and took me to the Anglican Church in Amsterdam. When my father was at sea, I accompanied my landlady to Westerkerk."

"Yes, the new church in the western suburbs." He nodded in approval. Perhaps merely her Englishness and not her religion irritated him. Those New Englanders continued to cause trouble, encroaching upon Dutch territory along the Fresh River, which they insisted upon calling the Connecticut. Yesterday he had read a report about another group of English starting a village without his permission at the distant eastern end of his long island, which they fraudulently claimed was English territory.

His wife said, "The Director-General has always preferred the Old Church. But then, he is rather traditional."

The butler refilled their glasses.

Being the daughter of an English merchant explained some of her strange background. Her family was probably not rich, since she had a landlady. He continued, "I suspect this continuing conflict between the Puritans and the Church of England distresses you."

She hesitated again. "My husband's family was English Separatist."

His wife put a calming hand on his arm.

He maintained a neutral voice. "I've heard about those English Brownists and how vexing they are to Church officials in Amsterdam."

Mevrouw Prince studied the wine in her glass, obviously reluctant to admit her sins. "Well, Brownist is the general term applied to a wide group of beliefs. I understand Reverend Brown has been dead for many years."

"What do you believe, *mevrouw?*" He looked directly at her, suspecting another backsliding heretic and ignoring his wife's subtle gestures of disapproval. Religion was too serious a subject for politeness to interfere with.

The widow stared at him for a surprisingly long time for such a simple question before saying, "When I married, I joined my husband's church."

Stuyvesant relaxed his grasp on his wine glass less it shatter. "What is the everlasting attraction of these heresies? Mennonites! Brownists! Hutterites! Ancient Brethren! Every *domine* worth his salt has warned false beliefs prove the sinner has not been elected to salvation and will wind up in the darkness of eternal damnation."

Judith pulled on his coat sleeve again. He shoved his empty glass into her hands.

"Your High Mightiness," *Mevrouw* Prince asked politely, "what's the purpose of teaching all Protestants to read the Bible if they aren't allowed to believe what they read?"

Was she amenable to admitting the errors of her ways? He released a slow breath to calm himself. "Without proper guidance from an educated minister, people easily misinterpret the Word of Jesus and fall into the lap of the devil. Is that what your soul seeks?"

"In my husband's church," she said, "there was much discussion and interpretation, but people generally reached the same conclusions. Depending upon one's personal circumstances, they merely emphasized different aspects of Jesus' message."

"That's my premise exactly." Perhaps, there was a chance to rescue her soul from heresy, though she resisted staunchly. "By following the *domine's* explanation, people will not waste time thinking but will spend more time obeying the Word of God. Most of these so-called ministers are nearly illiterate and create trouble to exalt themselves."

"Since I haven't had the proper training, perhaps you can explain this Biblical passage." Her tone of voice sharpened noticeably.

He had found a sore spot in her armor. Likely she knew deep in her heart her Brownist minister was a false prophet. "I will humbly attempt to assist you." He was confident of his ability to explicate any Biblical passage for her.

The widow began, "Then a certain young ruler asked Jesus, saying, 'Good Master, what must I do to inherit eternal life?'"

Stuyvesant immediately recognized the passage and knew how it ended. His pulse raced. He clenched his fists to restrain his fury. Judith continued to pull on his sleeve. He shook his arm to free himself.

"Jesus said unto him, 'Sell all that ever hast thou, and distribute unto the poor and thou shalt have treasure in heaven, and come follow me.'"

His body trembled. He wanted to slap the impudent wench even though she was a guest in his mansion and injured and recently widowed. Yet she insulted him with the words of Jesus.

"But when he heard those things, he was very heavy, for he was marvelously rich."

Stuyvesant sputtered, fumed, and clenched his fists. Finally he turned on his heel in his own parlor and stormed away—stomp, thump, stomp, thump.

Halfway down the hallway, he stopped, turned, and stared at the heretic. "*Mevrouw*, you will be gone from my house in the morning."

* * * * *

Anna returned just in time to hear this last exchange and to watch her brother struggle to maintain his dignity and restrain his fury. To surrender any battlefield was humiliation to him.

Penelope, also barely controlling her anger, turned away, fumbling with her drink. She found herself face-to-face with Judith, whose trembling hands dropped an empty glass that shattered on the floor. Judith fled after her husband.

From the doorway, Anna watched until Penelope had mostly regained her composure. "You certainly threw the cat into the yarn." She stepped around the broken shards and signaled a servant to remove the mess. "It has occurred to me, *mevrouw*, your recent difficult experiences could try a person's faith in God."

The young woman's face indicated a need to confide in someone but probably not the sister of Petrus.

Penelope twisted the stem of her wineglass. "I questioned God's intentions for me, not my faith."

Anna studied the young woman who had challenged her powerful brother—and won. "I'm sure Petrus usually skips over that part when he reads his Bible. He can be quite obstinate about religion."

Penelope sighed wistfully. "I feel like I've given away all that I have. In the native village everyone shared equally. But in civilization, everything has a price and I've no money."

Anna changed the subject. "I do wish to assure you there's complete religious freedom here as long as you don't do it in public. Most of the English have private religious meetings in their homes. I don't pry but I hear there's quite a variety of beliefs among the English."

Penelope trembled slightly as she put her wineglass on a nearby table. "That was Reverend Prince's experience in Amsterdam—once you acknowledge a man has the right to interpret scripture for himself, then one hundred men will interpret it one hundred different ways. Unfortunately, many will argue about it endlessly."

"I never heard it described this way but I can see your logic. So where does it end?"

"So far, it hasn't."

Anna gave a fleeting smile. "Liberty of conscience, I believe, is the English term. My brother doesn't recognize
this concept. He simply doesn't understand why anyone
refuses to believe in the Calvinist tradition. After all,
Holland is peaceful whereas wars have swept over the
Germanies for a hundred years."

Penelope looked at the floor.

There was little else Anna could say. "I can often change
my brother's mind but it usually requires several days.
However, that is of no benefit to you in your current
distress."

Penelope displayed a sad, though not unfriendly, smile.
"I appreciate your and Judith's hospitality. My former
landlady often said fish and houseguests stink after three
days. It's time to leave anyway."

"I'll inform Sara and Stoeffel to assist you in the morning after the Director-General leaves. If your situation
doesn't work out, let me know privately. As a widow, I have
much freedom as long as my brother doesn't know."

Where would this widow go? No *Spinhaus* or almshouse
assisted penniless women as in Amsterdam yet the monetary temptations of taverns and brothels were numerous.

"Thank you, *mevrouw*, for all you've done. I'll be fine."

Brave sentiments, thought Anna, or foolish pride.

* * * * *

After a restless sleep, Penelope heard the unmistakable
thump of Stuyvesant's wooden leg heading to the front
door. She preferred not to chance another encounter, so she
stayed in her room until he clumped his way out of the
house.

Sara packed the trunk while Penelope went to the
breakfast table where she displayed little appetite. Stoeffel
introduced the Angolan slave Domingo, who would carry
her chest anywhere she wished. She held her head high
and smiled bravely, as she departed the mansion and the
fort, trailed by the slave.

She turned left onto the dusty street. Her pace slack-
ened as she realized the direness of her situation: home-

less, moneyless, friendless. Also maimed and ugly. Would Herrmann let her sleep on the floor of his factory or would he fire her? Judith had said Herrmann was one of Stuyvesant's advisers, one of the Nine Men. How could Herrmann defy such a tyrant? Or would Stuyvesant even care once she was out of sight? A man who called himself Petrus instead of Pieter was too proud to forget an insult.

She stopped to look back across the waters of the bay, from whence she had come only a few days before. Could she find Tisquantum's village again? The wild, heathen, barbarian savages had treated her with much more kindness and charity than the civilized Christians of New Amsterdam. No, that wasn't true. Only the leaders of the government had spurned her.

In vain, she searched the harbor for a tall-masted vessel to carry her back to Amsterdam to an admission of failure to find her father and to accusations of murder from Matthew's family. The North River was empty of ships.

She trudged toward Herrmann's factory on Pearl Street, for she could think of no other option. Her feet moved without conscious effort. Cruel images filled her brain. Matthew's mother accosted her, "I entrusted my son to your care." His father said sadly, "Mr. Blossom's son died in Holland, not in America." Her father gaily waved goodbye. "It's merely a trip to Danzig."

She should start her search for her father, not feel sorry for herself, but she had no idea how to start and no spirit.

From the wobbly railing of a bridge over a canal, she stared at the muddy stream and its few inches of water. How had she fallen so far so fast—from a comfortable house along the bank of the true Herengracht with its stone bridges to homelessness adjacent to a muddy imitation of a canal with a rickety wooden bridge in a pitiful village perched on the edge of a savage wilderness? She ignored Domingo's polite cough and the sound of his lowering the trunk to the street.

In Shakespeare's play, Ophelia fell into a pool of water when things looked hopeless. Matthew would've said it was the Will of God that there wasn't enough water in the canal for Penelope to drown herself. *Oh, Matthew, where are you? I'm so lonely. God, Matthew, Father, anyone, please send a sign that you still care.*

"Good morning, Mrs. Prince."

Chapter 27

New Amsterdam

Monday, September 7, 1648

Penelope's head jerked up from its position of self-pity. Was she dreaming? Or gone mad? She turned, expecting to see a neighbor on a cobblestoned Amsterdam street. But this vacant road was made of dirt. She was on Pearl Street near the door to Herrmann's factory.

"Good morning, Mrs. Prince."

The English voice came from behind her, from the East River, from Lieutenant Nicholas Stillwell on his boat with his two sons. She had to look twice to recognize him in a coarse linen shirt and a straw hat, clothes suitable for a farmer. Plus a sword. Her appointment to meet him here this morning had flown her befuddled mind. "Lieutenant Stillwell," she said in surprise, thankful that she had not yet been reduced to tears.

He jumped from the craft onto the pier and approached her.

Putting her other problems aside for the moment, she concentrated on the reason she had asked him to come. "Thank you for meeting me, good sir. I hope I'm not delaying your journey." By reflex, she admired his one-masted sloop, appraising it well maintained and capable of carrying three or four tons of cargo, merely a coastal vessel for protected waters.

"No trouble at all, Mrs. Prince. The weather's good and I give the boys extra responsibility this morning." Something in the boat clunked. A non-descript dog barked. He briefly looked at his two sons and turned back to his visitor.

"I need a nettlesome favor," she began. "It has been suggested you could help. I'm a stranger here with no friends."

"No trouble at all, ma'am, as long as it's entertaining and I don't get caught." His mouth smiled and his eyes sparkled.

His jesting on this matter strangely reassured her. She gestured vaguely toward the trunk next to Domingo. "In my sea-chest was a special item from my late father. It was missing when the company delivered my trunk."

Lieutenant Stillwell widened his eyes. "What was it?"

"A globe. A map of the world upon a round ball." She spread her hands a foot apart as though holding a sphere, not wanting to embarrass him if he were not familiar with the term.

"I've seen no globes lately," he said. "Be unwise to sell it here—too much gossip. Anything else missing?"

"A bag with a few coins, but that's of no significance."

"I've heard people say, 'He who steals my purse steals trash,' but I've never understood that sentiment." His voice carried compassion.

"I'm a woman in turmoil, Lieutenant Stillwell. Money seems...seems irrelevant lately." She looked away because money was never irrelevant but often dangerous. Her father had surely met his death seeking it. Matthew had died defending their chest of iron tools and the money it represented. And she had contracted herself to a lifetime of debt to ransom her worthless life. Indeed, many people said greed was the most deadly of the seven infamous sins.

Lieutenant Stillwell clasped his hands behind his back and paced up and down the street, mumbling to himself. "I imagine some West India clerk thought you to be dead and stole your globe and money during inventory." He looked up. "Do you want to prosecute the guilty, or just recover your property?"

"I merely want my globe." She also wanted her father and husband back but no human could accomplish that.

He gave a brief salute, a formality like a handshake between men. "It'll be my pleasure to assist you though I cannot promise success. Fond memories are indeed a treasure far more valuable than coin."

From another person, his optimistic manner might've seemed like arrogance but to Penelope it appeared genuine. Never before had she met a man who appeared confident in both drab farmer clothes and military splendor.

He turned away, paused, and turned back to her. "Excuse my impudence, ma'am. But your countenance upon your arrival seemed sadder than your tale would justify."

How much should she tell? What difference would it make? She would be the main topic of gossip at the City Tavern again today. "I insulted my host last night and he expelled me. I was considering my options."

"Well," he said with a straight face except for the raising of his eyebrows, "I've been exiled from much better places than the Governor's house. I'm *persona non grata* in both Virginia and Maryland." Then he bowed low. One hand swept off his farmer's cap and held it toward her as though he were an actor on the stage waving a plumed cavalier's hat. His other hand pivoted his sword sheath so that it extended backwards.

His cheerful demeanor raised her spirits as his acquaintance with Latin raised her opinion of him. She felt a small smile creep upon her face. "Both colonies?"

"Indeed." He straightened his body and adjusted his hat. "Both at the same time. It's quite a tale. I imagine if I went to Boston, they would exile me from there too."

"From what I've heard, that would be no challenge to a man of your aptitude." She recalled numerous tales of banishment from that self-righteous Puritan city. That was another reason she and Reverend Prince had chosen New Amsterdam as the destination.

"Probably as much of a challenge as your insulting the Governor."

His wide smile was contagious, causing her first to grin, then to smile, and then to emit guffaws of laughter to relieve stress bottled inside her soul from last night. She might've collapsed on the street but instead she sat on the chest.

"Oh, by the way," he said, "my wife, Ann, would be pleased if you would visit. The little ones keep her close at home these days. Mr. Herrmann can give you directions."

"I'm not sure if Mr. Herrmann will even talk to me, now that I'm *persona non grata* with the Governor."

He shrugged. "Most of the Governor's closest advisors despise 'His High Mightiness.'"

Her fingers tightly clutched her dress fabric. "If Mr. Herrmann doesn't fire me, perhaps, he will take pity and allow me to sleep on the floor of his factory."

"Then you don't jest about the Governor kicking you out. And this chest you're perched on contains all your worldly possessions?"

She tapped the trunk with the heel of her worn-out boot, also a discard from Mrs. Stuyvesant's wardrobe. "Unfortunately, yes to both questions."

Stillwell turned away from her and looked toward his boat. "I recollect several times in my life when I didn't have a chamber pot to piss in. But now I own a small boat and may buy a house. Fortune is a fickle mistress."

Penelope appreciated his gentlemanly gesture of averting his face while alluding to her poverty. His words of hope instead of pity also lifted her spirits. "I observed the aborigines survive without chamber pots."

He chuckled. "Yes, I've noticed that too. Impecuniousness, like a broken arm, is merely a temporary nuisance." He waved to the boat and called, "Boys!"

The two boys and dog immediately jumped onto shore and raced up.

Stillwell instructed the younger boy, "Nicky. Guide Mrs. Prince to our house and introduce her to your stepmother. Tell Ann she has my permission to let Mrs. Prince stay as long as she likes." He pressed a coin into Nicky's hand and whispered further directives.

"Lieutenant Stillwell, that's too much." Penelope rose and faced him. "You can't impose a stranger upon your wife."

"Mrs. Prince?" He looked at her with complete seriousness. "Did you insult Stuyvesant in less than a half hour of private conversation?"

His question confused her but she answered honestly. "Perhaps, a quarter hour."

He raised his eyebrows and allowed himself a slight grin. "And do you regret it?"

"No. He deserved it."

His grin broadened into another infectious smile. "Then, you and Ann will enjoy each other's company. She too was once an orphaned waif deposited upon an unfamiliar shore. The boys and I will be gone all week and she gets lonely. If my wife kicks you out, then ask to sleep on Herrmann's floor."

To Nicky, he said, "Go."

To the slave, he said strange words, some of which sounded almost like Dutch and some almost like English. Domingo picked up the chest and followed Nicky.

"But Mr. Herrmann expects me." She glanced over her shoulder at the factory where she was supposed to start work this morning.

"Don't fret about Mr. Herrmann. I'll explain the situation to him. Now, go." He doffed his hat as if to dismiss her.

He turned and spoke to the dog, "Munkey. Sit! Stay! Guard!" He clapped a hand on the shoulder of the older boy. "Ricky, a small errand of mercy for a damsel in distress before we leave. Now, I'll show you how to use the rumor mill to our advantage. We start with a true story: family heirloom is stolen from poor widow. We add something false that everyone will believe: Stuyvesant needs a scapegoat for company pilferage. We'll mix it up properly, stir it into suitable ears, and wait to see what happens."

Father and son disappeared into a nearby decrepit building she suspected was an unlicensed waterfront tavern that never closed despite Stuyvesant's directives.

* * * * *

Penelope had no option but to follow Nicky, Domingo, and her trunk from the pier to the Stillwell house. Penelope and the slave waited outside while Nicky rushed through the doorway. A five-year-old boy played tug-of-war with a piglet in the street. Nicky ignored the boy so he was probably not Ann's. The top half of the Dutch door was open to let in air and light. The bottom half was closed to keep out piglets and stray children.

Again, Penelope had second thoughts about imposing herself upon a stranger and searched for another option.

A friendly voice floated out of the doorway: "Mrs. Prince, please come in! Watch out for toys on the floor!"

Devoid of choices, Penelope opened the rest of the Dutch door, took a step or two, and paused to let her eyes adjust to the dim light.

"I'm over here in the corner." An attractive woman of perhaps twenty-five nursed a six-month-old baby and watched a five-year-old girl play with a poppet of stuffed cloth with charcoal eyes and mouth. "Come, sit beside me."

Mrs. Stillwell sat in the only chair, liberally furnished with small cushions, and pointed to a bench next to the table. The house was reasonably clean and neat for a home harboring two small girls and two rowdy boys. "I'm Ann. This," she said, pointing to the happy chubby infant, "is Baby Alice. On the floor is Annie."

Nicky directed Domingo to set the chest in a corner, flipped him a coin, ruffled Annie's hair, and called "Good-bye" to everyone as he rushed out the door. Domingo backed and bowed himself out of the house.

Penelope looked at Ann and shook her head. "I feel like I was rescued from a shipwreck again."

"Nicholas likes to take charge of chaos." She looked kindly at Penelope. "Once upon a time, I too felt like Jonah: swallowed by the whale and then spit out on an empty beach. And then Nicholas rescued me."

Penelope smiled and nodded her head. "That's a good analogy, except I believed I was obeying the Will of God, not running away from it."

"Life is forever taking unexpected twists. So, what has Nicholas promised to do for you?"

Penelope explained the disappearance of her father's globe to this stranger who was quickly becoming a friend.

Ann chuckled. "You found the right man for the job. Not much happens in this town, legal or illegal, that Nicholas doesn't know about." She patted Baby Alice on the back until the child burped. Then Ann stood up and placed the infant in Penelope's lap. "You two, get acquainted while I rustle up some food."

A surprised Penelope sat rigid with her left hand grabbing the baby's chubby leg and her right arm around her back, afraid the tiny human would fall and break. Ann expertly tossed a soft rag into Penelope's lap just before milk dribble soiled her dress.

"Haven't had much experience with babies, have you?"

"I was an only child." Penelope was afraid to move her eyes from her unexpected responsibility even though the baby cooed her satisfaction with the arrangements. "Don't fix any food for me." Penelope's stomach churned at the kitchen sounds. "I've no appetite."

"Oh, no. This is just to keep the children quiet while we talk. How was life in the mansion?" Ann substituted a dish of finger food for the bone the five-year-old nibbled on.

"I feel like a butterfly in a tempest."

"I've felt that way myself." Ann wiped drool from the baby. "Now, I feel like a butterfly in a garden, flitting from flower to flower with two small children chasing me."

She scooped up her baby and the cloth in one fluid motion, flipped the cloth onto her shoulder, burped the baby again, and replaced her into Penelope's lap before the startled visitor moved her hands. Ann sat, giving Penelope the freedom to talk about whatever distressed her.

"I went to services with the Stuyvesant family yesterday, where I met your husband. Then the Governor and I had a brief discussion of religion. I fear I insulted him."

"What did you do? Tell him the truth?" Ann asked.

Penelope recalled games she had seen others play with babies. She was afraid to release her grip on the child so she touched noses with Baby Alice. "After he insulted my husband's grandfather, I applied one of Jesus's parables to him."

"Aha, it must've fit if he expelled you. You're lucky not to be banished from the colony." Ann chuckled.

"Banished?" Penelope recalled the long-ago sight of English exiles in the Amsterdam harbor. Long ago? It was only six months. She shuddered and almost dropped the baby.

"Don't fret." Ann wiped the baby's mouth. "Banishment requires a trial at which your insult would be made public and embarrass the Governor again. He won't do that."

Penelope asked the baby, "Does anybody like the Governor? Do they?"

"Like him?" Ann shook her head. "No. Those who have tangled with him respect his authority. He's better than his predecessor but that's a weak compliment. Nicholas respects his military leadership. But no, none like him."

There was an awkward pause. "But enough of that." Ann offered to retrieve the baby but her guest declined. "Let's talk about us. Why did you leave the luxuries of Amsterdam for the simplicities of the wilderness?"

Penelope related a brief version of her life and Matthew's vision, omitting any mention of her father.

"Ah, another 'Seeker of the Truth.' That's one reason we're moving to Gravesend."

"Seeker of the truth! Are you Anabaptist?'

"In Gravesend, I can be whatever I wish to be and change every week. I don't have the courage to seek deeply for the truth right now, because if you find it, then you must obey it."

Penelope watched Ann's pensive face. The baby cooed for attention. The guest looked at the baby to give her hostess some privacy and said softly, "We both have things that are too difficult to think about. It's comforting to know there's someone to share those things with. When the proper time comes."

"Amen." Ann wiped absently at spots on the table.

How does one play with a baby without injuring it? She found another topic of conversation, "When are you moving to Gravesend?"

"If Nicholas actually buys the land today, he and the lads will harvest the standing crops and finish the house. They'll work during the week over there, and come home Saturday and Sunday. The sloop he won in gambling a few months ago is a true gift from God. It only takes ninety minutes in a boat against eight hours on a horse or all day in a cart on that wretched excuse for a road.

"When we got serious about moving to Gravesend, the sloop appeared. God and Nicholas work in mysterious ways. It does no good to question either."

"Tell me about the house," Penelope said.

"To live in Gravesend, you must build a house, but the original owner never finished his. I plan to go over monthly to make sure Nicholas is still working. You know how easily men can get distracted. Come with us next time."

"Oh, I would love to." Any excuse to remove herself further from Stuyvesant's reach sounded good, even though a trip delayed her search for clues. How does one delay a search that hasn't started? A few days wouldn't matter.

Ann retrieved Baby Alice who was happily smearing drool over Penelope's hand.

"I'm so glad you're moving in with us," Ann said with what appeared to be true sincerity. "With Nicholas and the lads over on the island, there's plenty of room here. The baby and I certainly enjoy your company and we still have plenty to talk about."

How lonely was Ann that she would instantly scoop up an orphan off the street? Good manners dictated Penelope should refuse such a generous offer. And then what? Sleep in an alley? "But I would be in the way when Lieutenant Stillwell and the boys come back. You wouldn't have any privacy in this house at all."

"There could be some advantages to that." Holding up the baby, Ann chuckled. "From some of the late night conversations with his drinking cronies when they think I'm asleep, I imagine he wouldn't be embarrassed in the least with you upstairs or downstairs or in our bed. Your biggest problem up in the loft is that the lads will pester you continually for stories about the savages. No arguments. End of discussion."

"Oh, thank you so much," Penelope blurted. "This is such a great relief."

"You'll fit right into this crazy house. We're going to have a good time."

Ann Stillwell's friendship soothed Penelope's soul as well as Liesbeth's wisdom could have. How could she repay Ann's kindness?

Beer was the answer. Herrmann was a brewer. Surely she could buy the household's beer from her employer at a discount. If she still had a job.

Chapter 28

New Amsterdam

Monday, September 7, 1648

After the simple noon meal with Ann, Penelope decided she must go to work and explain everything to Herrmann. Losing the only job she was likely to find was too stressful to even consider.

When she arrived at the factor's office, Herrmann assured her he often disagreed with Stuyvesant.

Papers overflowed the filing cabinets in the back office and cluttered every horizontal surface. She remembered he was an artist trapped in a business. They spoke Dutch because commercial and legal contracts contained so many arcane phases derived from Italian, Spanish, and Portuguese that even she couldn't translate them into English.

"Wait," she said. "This'll take weeks. We should start with the current business affairs. It would be foolish to miss a deadline tomorrow because I was organizing last year's papers."

They returned to the front office and its much smaller volume of current paperwork. Herrmann picked up a stack and said, "I've worked on these lately. This is a power of attorney I registered last week from Hans Fomer. He's from a small town in Prussia, didn't speak much Dutch when he started working several years ago. His friends persuaded him the GWC owes him eighty-one guilders in back pay, but he doesn't have the documents to prove it. Write the company office in Amsterdam to get his pay records. Hans provided a list of all the places, job titles, and dates that he worked, so it should be straightforward. In a few months we'll get a reply from Amsterdam."

The type of person most likely to stow away on a ship was a sailor. She would look for more German sailors as she worked her way through Herrmann's files. This was a safe and private way to begin her search for clues.

"How can you have Power of Attorney without being a lawyer?" Penelope asked.

"Ach, here in Manhattan, we make do despite the absence of lawyers."

The office bulged with contracts, lists of shipments expected to arrive at any day in the next six months, and lists of things people wanted to buy or sell when the next vessel arrived. Penelope worked steadily for an hour, before she had a question worth getting up for. She found Herrmann in a tiny back office, happily engrossed in painting. The outline of a woman showed on his canvas, perhaps his betrothed. That paper could wait with a multitude of others. Time passed quickly.

After work, Penelope walked to the Stillwell house, knocked on the door, and called out, "Annnnnne? Hello?"

"Come on in, Penelope. This is your home too. You don't have to knock."

The concept of home left Penelope momentarily speechless. "I haven't become accustomed to the idea yet."

"We'll make it official. Kneel down. Humor me." Penelope knelt. Ann wet her fingers, placed her fingers gently on Penelope's bonnet, and proclaimed in solemn voice, "I pronounce you, Penelope, adopted sister of Ann. Now we are sisters, and this is your home." They hugged, with Baby Alice squeezed between them.

Penelope grinned at her adopted sister. "I had a sister-in-law I liked, but I never had a sister. It feels good. Although my father-in-law would never have approved of your ceremony."

"I can't believe God doesn't have a sense of humor, especially after feeling your head through this bonnet."

Penelope changed the subject. "Tell me about your husband."

"Nicholas doesn't look for trouble, but whenever trouble finds him, he greets it as an old friend. I knew that when I married him.

"He's like a wild animal. Can't be kept in a cage. Has to roam sometimes. My job is to make sure he returns to me afterwards. I make him laugh. But I have to laugh. I have to keep laughing."

Ann's eyes glistened with tears. She paused to recover her composure. "Sorry, I get into these moods sometimes. Don't let me stay in one of them." She recovered her good spirits quickly. "What do we do first? Hang your good clothes in the wardrobe? Do you have any other black dresses in your trunk?"

"All my Anabaptist clothes are rather drab but this one is Judith Stuyvesant's. She said to keep it—too old and too small for her, the maid said."

"I once fit into a dress like that, two babies ago." Ann passed her hands over her matronly figure.

The leather tunic was on top. "I like your native garment. Did you make it?"

"Well, I was there when it was made and assisted a little. I did some of the embroidery."

"How did they get the leather so soft?"

"They don't consider this soft. You should've seen the ceremonial garb the chief wore when a bigger chief arrived. I didn't know the language well enough to ask for an explanation on leatherwork. However, it involved many hours of hard work by women."

"Some things are the same in every culture. Scut work and having babies." Ann slammed the trunk closed. "Your husband's clothes are in there. Somebody washed them."

Penelope nodded. "Sara, Mrs. Stuyvesant's maid."

Ann said gently, "You could save those clothes for another husband."

After no response, Ann asked, "Hide them in this trunk forever?"

Penelope shook her head.

"Down to two choices: sell them to strangers or donate them to strangers."

"If I sold them," the impecunious widow asked, "what could I spend the money on that would feel right?"

"Since the *Domine* complains about spending money on foreigners, the church poor fund would be good."

Penelope nodded.

Ann put her hand on the chest and paused. "Some people keep a reminder of a loved one. Is there something that has good memories for you?"

"An almost new leather carpenter's apron." Her voice was hoarse, the memories, raw. "I'd like to keep that as a reminder of how we were going to build a new life here, together, in a new world."

Penelope looked away while Ann searched by feel in the almost closed trunk.

Penelope whispered. "They say a person's not truly gone as long as you remember his name. Matthew, I'll always remember you." Silently she added, *and you, Father.* She held back her tears.

Ann whispered, "Go ahead and cry."

Penelope hid her head in her hands. "You must think me a fool to be unable to weep."

"No, you remind me of myself when I first arrived here."

Penelope remembered Lieutenant Stillwell had hinted his wife washed up on this shore too. "Were you also shipwrecked?"

"Only metaphorically."

Penelope looked up with wide eyes.

Ann explained her brother and her father took opposing sides but both had perished in the first battle at Edgehill six years ago. Her mother had fled with seventeen-year-old Ann on the first ship to leave for any place where Puritan or royalist didn't matter. When they disembarked in Manhattan, her mother was ill, whether from melancholy or fever, Ann didn't know. The stone church in Fort New Amsterdam had been converted into a hospital and place of refuge for the survivors of an aborigine uprising. There she met and clung to the young sons of Lieutenant Stillwell, who recovered from his battle wounds. Her mother died, leaving Ann orphaned and alone in the midst of chaos. She attached herself to the Stillwells and soon married the lieutenant.

Tears ran down Ann's cheeks.

"Does weeping help?" Penelope asked.

"Yes, if you weep for loved ones who await you in Heaven, not for yourself."

Penelope wiped away a tear and stared at her damp finger. Suddenly the dammed-up tears burst loose and they sobbed together.

* * * * *

On Tuesday evening Penelope returned from work to the Stillwell house, tired but pleased. Herrmann certainly received his money's worth from her toil, paperwork that a one-armed woman with a sharp mind and knowledge of shipping could easily handle.

Penelope put bowls and spoons on the table while Ann ladled porridge into one side of the bowl and vegetables into the other side. Penelope sniffed the food. "It's similar to what the aborigines cooked. The onions definitely improve this *askutasquash*."

"We simply call it squash. My husband learned from the natives and taught me."

"The lieutenant is a good man to have around in a crisis," Penelope said between bites.

"That is what the Dutch officers thought back in '43 just after we married. They put every able-bodied man they could find into the army and made Nicholas a lieutenant because of his experience in Virginia. Of course, he told the Dutch officials his opinion of their stupid war with the savages, a war which they had caused."

Penelope dropped her spoon when Ann mentioned war with the *wilden* in 1643. "How clumsy of me." She ducked to retrieve the spoon and her composure. Surely a lieutenant would know who had been killed by the savages. "What did your husband do?"

"The army needed him and the people needed him, so he stayed. When Lady Moody arrived a few months later, I think they wanted to get Nicholas out of their hair, so they assigned him to escort and advise Lady Moody."

"A lady? You mean English royalty?"

"Yes, her late husband was a lord." Ann continued the tale of the early days of Gravesend during supper.

Penelope was confused. Where was Lieutenant Stillwell during the fighting? How much did he know? How much could she trust him?

Tomorrow she would write to John Throckmorton in Providence Plantations, asking what he knew of John Kent. Better yet, she would pretend to be Augustine Herrmann and say an acquaintance asked about Kent. With luck, she would intercept Throckmorton's reply in a few weeks and Herrmann would never know.

After Annie climbed into the loft to bed down, Ann nursed the baby. The two women discussed kitchen chores and exchanged receipts for stews and soups. Penelope had seen the primitive kitchen and volunteered she was a better maid than cook.

Ann quickly accepted the offer. "But you must learn the vagaries of American cooking. For example, if we want to eat corn tomorrow, we need to parboil it overnight or else we'll break teeth on it tomorrow."

How many times do I need to be tutored in cooking? Penelope asked herself.

"What kind of corn?" Corn was the English word for grain of any type but she had never heard of boiling grain in advance of cooking it, except to make beer.

Ann lifted a handful of colorful kernels from a cloth sack and let them slip between her fingers into a black kettle hung from a chain over the fireplace.

Penelope said, "The *wilden* call it maize."

Ann nodded. "I suppose nobody knew its name forty years ago when they first ate it."

Ann put Baby Alice in a cradle and then worked to extract Penelope from her dress. In their chemises, the two women climbed into a narrow wooden bedstead.

In the morning, Ann ground the parboiled corn, sifted it through a loosely-woven basket, and combined salt, water, and yesterday's bacon drippings. Adding more grease to a hot skillet, she dropped in the corn paste and shaped it with a wooden spoon. Bacon went into another skillet. She removed both pans and placed the bacon atop the corn bread to absorb the grease and to cool. Holding out their aprons to catch the crumbs, they ate the bacon and warm crumbly cornbread, then scooped up the crumbs with their fingers, and ate them too.

Penelope contrasted the *wilden*'s pone bread made with bear fat to Ann's made with pork fat. She decided both were good as long as someone else cooked it.

Chapter 29

Gravesend

Friday, September 11, 1648

On Friday morning, Penelope cleared the breakfast table and put the scraped plates into a pot of boiling water suspended from an iron hook in the hearth. If she couldn't cook, at last she could clean. A boisterous noise in the street drew her attention.

Into the house burst a man and two boys.

"Nicholas!" Ann screamed in delight. "Did you buy the house?"

Lieutenant Nicholas Stillwell hugged his wife and waved papers in the air behind her back. "Signed, sealed, and soon to be delivered to the city hall."

Annie ran up and clung to her two stepbrothers.

Penelope whispered to Ann, "I'm going to work now to get out of your way."

Lieutenant Stillwell released his wife, bowed to Penelope, and picked up Annie as he rose. "Ah, Mrs. Prince. I knew you and Ann would get along fine. Going to work? Nonsense. You'll come with us to Gravesend to celebrate."

Penelope put her hand over her gaping mouth. She was curious about this haven of Anabaptists and wished to thank the mysterious Mr. Stout for his kindness. But today was the fifth day of her job, minus a half day on Monday. "Oh, no. I couldn't impose on you."

Ann laughed. "You have to come. Otherwise, you'll be locked up in that dress for three days." She said to Stillwell, who had raised his eyebrows at her remark. "A lady's dress isn't designed for invalids. Where I go, she has to go."

"Ann? No," Penelope protested again.

Stillwell called out loudly to his sons, "Nicky, get your sisters ready. Ricky, find your mother's trunk. We leave as soon as I get this deed recorded." He kissed Ann, handed her the baby, and was out the door.

Ann laughed. "You're a butterfly in the whirlwind again. Get used to it."

Soon the lieutenant and the boys were loading supplies into the sloop at the pier outside Herrmann's factory. Penelope stepped into the building to explain she had to go to Gravesend because her hostess was going, she had nowhere else to stay, and she couldn't extricate herself from her dress alone. Herrmann blinked twice.

Ricky steered under his father's watchful eye.

Nicky introduced Penelope to the other member of the family. "This is Munkey, short for the Panmunky River and the Panmunky tribe of Virginia. She's friendly, if properly introduced."

Penelope was accustomed to the small housedogs of Amsterdam, though her house never had one. But Munkey weighed sixty pounds and had correspondingly big teeth and a disconcerting habit of licking her hands even though she had just washed them with soap.

Nicky explained his father had rescued Munkey from a hastily abandoned native village where the emaciated puppy had been left tied to a tree. The bitch always whimpered and growled when she smelled natives, a useful trait for the dog of an Indian fighter. "Did you know the heathens eat their dogs when food is scarce?"

Penelope would've preferred not to know.

The trip across the water took ninety minutes plus twenty minutes to trek through the woods. Ann explained Gravesend was so isolated each visitor was a celebrity.

Introductions were made first to Lady Deborah Moody, the founder of Gravesend. Names, faces, and more English dialects than she had imagined mixed together as villagers swarmed out of houses to introduce themselves

Lady Moody suggested a noon picnic in the clear warm September weather. Sundry boys with wooden spades removed the cow dung from a grassy area outside the palisade. Women spread old cloths on the ground and fussed over the arrangements and complained they'd had no time to prepare fancy fixings.

After lunch, the women gossiped and shared stories. They appeared to have no qualms in forsaking the drudgery of housewifery for an extra hour or two of gossip, though most of the men returned to their tasks. One order of business was deciding where the guests would spend the night. Elizabeth Applegate was most outspoken and insisted on hosting Penelope. None could persuade her otherwise. Ann and her two daughters accepted an invitation to stay with another family while Lieutenant Stillwell and the boys camped out in the unfinished house.

Penelope saw Richard Stout on the edge of the crowd and gestured to him to approach. She publicly thanked him for the kindnesses he had shown her upon her arrival and bragged to everyone that Mr. Stout had arranged for her to stay in the Governor's house for a few days but failed to mention her ignominious departure. He appeared both embarrassed and pleased with the recognition. The women's conversation quickly moved on to the Governor's house, his seldom-seen wife, and her beautiful clothes.

Penelope asked, "Mr. Stout, where's your family? I haven't met them yet."

Mr. Stout answered, "I've never married."

His lack of a family surprised her. "May I prepare you a plate of food? There's so much here."

He blushed, a rare sight on a grown man. "I've worked in the fields since daybreak. I must look like something the cat dragged in."

"Nothing soap and water can't fix," she said lightly, regarding his mud-splattered garments and thankful she didn't have to wash them.

"Allow me to don clean clothes and I'll be delighted to share a meal with thee."

He returned in twenty minutes with wet hair and clean garments: a russet velvet doublet, brown breeches, gray stockings, and boots that reached far up his calf. She had deemed such boots a vanity in Amsterdam, but here they seemed appropriate for the rough land.

His doublet was the same as he had worn on her first day in New Amsterdam—probably his best one—and again reminded her of her father.

Because he had worked all morning in the fields, she prepared him a well-laden plate. He appeared to be slightly taller but slenderer than Matthew, who had had a voracious appetite. She gestured to Lady Moody's old blanket on which she was sitting and he joined her, murmuring his appreciation and acknowledging the greetings of several neighbors with a nod or a single word.

Penelope looked around to introduce him to the Stillwells but they had disappeared.

Mr. Stout ate hungrily with his fingers as the others had done, wiped them occasionally on a linen cloth, and drank from the mug of beer she offered. She let the warm sunshine and the murmur of friendly voices speaking English wash away her problems for a few minutes.

Mr. Stout interrupted her reverie. "Wouldst thou care to see the village?"

The women mostly gossiped about people and events she didn't know. She nearly refused because the church elders wouldn't approve before she realized they were far away. She accepted his invitation but intended to remain in public view the entire time. Reputations were too easy to lose and too hard to reclaim.

They picked their way around cows and dung in the rough meadow back to the village gate. She glanced at the noon sun. "It's so hot for the first week in September."

Mr. Stout swept his arm in a wide arc. "We cut the trees. It's important to keep the land near the palisade free of hiding places for the enemy."

"Enemies?" She automatically scanned the horizon. "You mean aborigines?"

"We've had no problems for five years, but still ..."

He didn't elaborate on five years ago but she recalled Ann saying every able-bodied man had been impressed into the army then to defend Manhattan.

As though he had read her mind, he asked, "Didst thou feel safe within the walls of Fort New Amsterdam? Or wouldst thou prefer a strong wooden palisade?"

"A wall that can't keep out goats isn't much of a wall. This one looks solid."

"Each resident is responsible for the repair of a section of the palisade." He pointed. "My responsibility is two chains in length near this corner."

How long was an English chain, a new measurement to her?

They passed through the palisade's gate and entered the village. Mr. Stout explained the layout. The village's two streets crossed at a right angle to divide the community into four blocks, each containing ten lots. The central intersection, like a village square, hosted the flagpole, stocks, and board for official notices. Penelope admired the outside of Mr. Stout's house, across the square from Lady Moody's. He made it clear he lived alone except for his male farmhand. She peeped inside the front door to see a neat but nearly empty room but declined an invitation to enter without a proper chaperone. In such a small village, just like on her block beside the Herengracht, nothing passed unnoticed.

Mr. Stout said, "Our town charter gives us the right to elect the *schout* and magistrates and to make local ordi-

nances. Lady Moody encourages Lieutenant Stillwell to
run for magistrate in January."

"Oh, do you know him?"

"Yes, the lieutenant planned to be one of the original
settlers before the Indian troubles five years ago delayed
our plans."

So Mr. Stout was also here when her father disappeared. Could she trust him? What did he know? Penelope
said, "They tell me many Anabaptists live here."

Mr. Stout said, "Lady Moody negotiated liberty of conscience into our charter. We have a variety of believers,
many of whom are Anabaptist."

"Are you the minister here?"

"No. Why dost thou ask?"

"You always speak as though quoting the Bible."

"I canna help being born in the East Midlands where
near everyone talks this way or much worse if they've non
been to London."

"Are you Anabaptist?"

He said, "Lady Moody argues well against infant baptism. How can God condemn an infant for the parents'
failures or accept a soul based upon the parents' promises?
I canna say for sure exact what I am. But Anabaptist is
close enough."

How strange to cross an ocean and blindly stumble upon
a group of Anabaptists. "Seek and ye shall find," said the
Bible, yet that was Matthew's dream, not hers.

He interrupted her reverie with a question, "Wouldst
thou care to see my crops?"

She didn't know one plant from another but, in the direction he pointed, beyond the palisade wall, she saw the
tops of tall trees and readily accepted his invitation. This
village seemed less straight-laced than Reverend Prince's
congregation. And she would remain in public view the
entire time.

They walked down the perpendicular street to another
gate in the palisade. He pointed out his back garden with
its pigsty and small barn and the common grazing area in

the center of each square of ten lots. They brought cows and horses inside the village walls each evening to these small common areas for protection.

Protection? She looked out the gateway in the palisade at nearby fields and wilderness in the distance. For all she knew, an aborigine village could lie five hundred yards away, hidden among the trees.

Each purchase of one of the forty shares of the village, Mr. Stout explained as they walked alongside the fields, included a town lot, a meadow area, and ten Dutch morgens equal to twenty English acres of farmland in a wedge radiating from the village.

He pointed to five acres he and his farmhand had planted. "The land with the tallest trees is obviously the best soil, but removing the trees is a huge chore. I plant tobacco seedlings amongst the stumps and roots the first two or three years for they need the richest soil and provide the most revenue. Stumps are easier to extract from the ground after they rot for a few years."

Her farming experience was looking down at straight rows of distant fields from the town wall of Amsterdam and two weeks in an aborigine village garden. She recognized maize and squash. "Has it been a good year?"

Mr. Stout said, "Yes, we expect a good harvest."

She searched for something to say about crops. "Where did you learn to be a farmer?"

"My father owned a farm in Nottinghamshire."

Her knowledge of English geography was sadly lacking, but this name sounded familiar. Nottinghamshire had a famous forest, the home of Robin Hood, according to stories told by her father.

Mr. Stout waved his arm to encompass the horizon of trees. "If thou couldst have seen this wilderness five years ago, thou wouldst be amazed. Grain ripens where forests stood. Someday, our tiny village will be a town, although never as large as Nottingham."

His passionate voice and enthusiasm for the future reminded her of Matthew. Here was Matthew's vision, spread before her—a village of Anabaptists in the New World—yet his bones were scattered in the lonely sand as though he had never existed.

She was reminded of Trijn and Dirck, even in the midst of the ocean passionately in love with land they had not yet seen. Surely, their vision was coming true in their new home up the North River.

A small trail of smoke wafted from a stack of logs. "Is that wood on fire?"

"No. That's my barn where tobacco is cured over a slow fire. The leaves must be picked when they have the proper color of green and yellow and are moist and pliant. Then dried slowly. Too wet—they rot in the barrel. Too dry—they crumble in shipping."

She had never before considered the husbandry of tobacco, the enjoyment of which was becoming ever more popular in Amsterdam.

"Your barn. Is it a Finnish house of logs?" she asked as they came closer. "My father tried to describe one to me years ago. Now I see what he meant about the ends of the logs being notched to prevent rolling and shifting."

"Did thy father voyage to America?"

She continued to examine the log house in order not to reveal the concern on her face. Was it an innocent question? Or did he suspect something? She stuck to the partial truth. "He was in the Baltic trade—Danzig, Riga, Stockholm. How did you know how to build such a structure? Have you been to Finland?" Could he have known the mysterious German who lured her father to America?

"Lieutenant Stillwell told me about such houses and barns in New Sweden down on the South River."

She poked her finger between two logs and raised her eyebrows.

"If it were a house, the tops and bottoms of the logs would be adzed flat. Or stuffed with clay. But a tobacco barn needs a draft."

Beyond the fields stretched a forest of tall trees with a canopy of dark green with just a few hints of autumn color.

Her suspicion of Mr. Stout was overcome by the nearness of the forest. Somehow these trees, as tall and dense as the ones around Tisquantum's village, were less threatening. Did the presence of European women enjoying a picnic in a nearby meadow embolden her?

"May I go see your trees? My father told me wondrous stories of the dense woods of Poland when I was a child."

Penelope picked her way across a rough field to the trees. "Surely, this is one of God's most magnificent creations!" she whispered as though in the soaring tower of the Westerkerk. She stroked the bark of a tall tree and then smelled it. "Do you think me strange?" she asked without looking at Mr. Stout.

"A woman without passion is merely a painting of the real creature."

"Passion?" She shook her head. "Recent happenings have removed my passion, left me empty. Yes, lifeless, like a poor painting. But these trees..." She picked up an acorn and stared upward, transfixed by a majestic oak. Surely fearsome creatures lurked here too but also friendly ones. "What is the name of this noisy tree rat?"

"Hast thou never seen a squirrel?"

"Amsterdam has few trees and no tree rats." She turned to face her host. Was his lack of fear encouraging her? "Do you know the names of all the trees?"

"Most of them, but some I never knew in England."

"Name them, please?" She felt some passion now.

Mr. Stout picked up three branches from the ground. "Here, smell the wood."

He snapped a branch she recognized both by the cone and the resinous scent that reminded her of the Damrak and its odors of pitch and tar and new masts. Matthew often came home from work with pine shavings in his clothes. Her father had brought similar cones home from Finland one fall. She and Liesbeth had transformed them into candleholders for Christmastide.

"That's easy. Pine."

He broke another branch and held it six inches from her nose.

"Cedar." Liesbeth had a clothes trunk of this aromatic wood to discourage wool moths.

He nodded and smiled like her father had done when she had answered a particularly hard question.

He snapped the third branch over his knee and held it up. The faint scent was familiar. She put her hand on his to steady the wood and bent over to sniff it. His fingers were calloused from daily work as Matthew's had been.

"Oak?" she asked.

"Hickory. Very similar."

She flitted like a butterfly from tree to tree, heard the name and merits of each, stared upwards at the dark green canopy of leaves, fingered fallen leaves and fruits, sniffed the bark and rotting leaf litter, oblivious of Mr. Stout's regard for her or the passage of time.

Penelope stopped at a recently chopped tree with wilted green leaves. Some branches dug into the dirt and some stretched heavenward. She twisted a leathery leaf between her fingers like Liesbeth tested yarn. "Why did you cut down a living tree?" Sadness deepened her voice.

Mr. Stout answered, "We cut them down whenever we have the time—summer or winter."

"Isn't it easier to girdle the green trees first and then cut them down when the wood is dry?"

"I'm a farmer, not a woodsman. One canna cut trees in Nottinghamshire because the forest belongs to the king. What dost thou mean by girdling?"

She told him a long story her father had told her of woodsmen who cleared dense forests like these in Poland, near Danzig, and burned the wood into ashes to make potash to ship to Amsterdam. She pointed out those woodsmen found it more efficient to remove a swath of bark from around the trunk of a live tree, causing it to die, and then cut down the dead tree several months later.

He listened well, even though she rambled. She felt comfortable in his presence, safe even though surrounded by a dense forest.

His eyes surveyed a fallen tree. "Let it die standing up? What an interesting idea. A felled tree occupies a huge acreage of ground until it dries enough to burn."

He started to remove his doublet but stopped and blushed. He called to a man working in a nearby field.

Penelope watched the approach of a large dark-skinned man, whom Mr. Stout introduced as his servant Emil. She was accustomed to the GWC's ownership of *neger* slaves but didn't realize an individual could own one.

Mr. Stout pointed to a large oak and explained with hand gestures and simple Dutch words.

Emil studied the tree. "Yes, *baas*. Kill tree slowly."

Penelope suspected Emil spoke better Dutch than Mr. Stout, though neither spoke well because each had been born in other countries. The slave yanked an axe from a nearby stump and quickly removed a foot of bark from the circumference of the large oak.

Mr. Stout rubbed his chin. "Mid-September is somewhat late in the season for a tree to bleed to death, but girdling a tree is wonderful quick compared to chopping."

At Mr. Stout's words, Penelope went to the beautiful oak, still boasting a full canopy of green leaves, and put her fingers into the lifeblood of its sap oozing from the fresh cuts. She recalled Trijn saying she cried when a cabbage plant died.

Penelope felt like a murderer, a judas goat leading its flock to slaughter. Clearing forests in Poland was merely a tale. This was true. The death of ancient Trojan soldiers was merely a tale. Matthew's death was true.

"I've made a mistake. I've brought death and destruction." She turned with tears in her eyes and slowly walked to the village, refusing to look backwards.

Mr. Stout trailed behind her. She ignored his words. He had been a soldier. He had killed men and he killed trees. He might have killed her father. No, that was her sadness confusing her. Mr. Stout was a man who built things. But he killed a forest to build a tobacco field.

Penelope recovered her composure by the time she reached the wooden palisade. Living trees might become ships and masts, even the planks such as Matthew had used to build houses on the mud flats of Amsterdam. Soaring trees deserved a more fitting end than black ashes.

She thanked Mr. Stout, turned, and rejoined the women around Lady Moody. How rare and refreshing it was to find a man who had a dream of the future and knew how to accomplish his vision. How unfortunate that his vision chiefly centered upon the killing of God's magnificent creations in order to grow ugly, smelly tobacco plants.

Chapter 30

Gravesend

Friday, September 11, 1648

As the afternoon waned, Gravesend families dispersed for supper. Penelope's hosts, Elizabeth and Thomas Applegate, invited several couples to join them and their daughters and guest after supper for more beer and socializing.

There was more noise, activity, and beer at the gathering than Penelope was accustomed to. She complimented Mrs. Applegate on the festivity, then drifted to a quiet spot by a window, and stared at the friendly scene of the Applegate's cow returning to the back fence and mooing softly. She admired the adjacent houses and gardens, remembering how it felt to be utterly alone.

Isn't that what she and Matthew had dreamed of—a calm, quiet, friendly location where a family could live peaceably, prosper, and worship God as they pleased?

The movement of a woman sitting down on a stool to milk the Applegate's cow destroyed her reverie. *Who's that?* It couldn't be Elizabeth Applegate, whom she had just talked to her a moment ago. Maybe it was Mrs. London, but she couldn't remember the woman well.

She half turned to the men adjacent and asked softly, "Is that the wife of Ambrose London milking the Applegate's cow?"

Rodger Scott, conversing with Thomas Greedy, wasn't paying attention to her. "What about Ambrose London, Mrs. Prince?"

Mr. Greedy answered for her. "She said Mrs. London is milking the Applegate's cow."

"What?" asked Mr. Scott, "Why would she do that?"

Both men crowded up to the window to see such a scandal. Twilight was fading rapidly. The small window had not been washed in months. Applegate's daughter Emilie passed by and asked what was happening.

Mr. Scott said, "The widow says London's wife is milking your cow."

Emilie looked out into the dimness. "If she steals our milk, we'll sue her. Mrs. Prince, you're a witness. Where's my father?"

Emilie quickly found her father and they raced outside to confront the thief and discovered the milker was Elizabeth Applegate, not the neighbor.

Penelope cringed each time Mrs. Applegate, breaking into gales of laughter, told the story that night: The cow's mooing had reminded Mrs. Applegate that she had forgotten the milking in the evening's socializing and had come out into the dusk to relieve the cow. The visitor had mistaken fourteen-stone Mrs. Applegate for eight-stone Mrs. London.

* * * * *

On Saturday morning, Mrs. Applegate prepared a hearty English breakfast of eggs, ham, griddle corn cakes, and buttermilk. Before Mr. Applegate went to the barn to gather tools for the harvest, his wife reminded him of the monthly town meeting at noon.

Penelope thanked her hostess and left to find Ann and assist her to prepare her house for its new family. Penelope was interested in the differences between an English colonial household and a Dutch urban household. This information she hadn't been able to learn in Amsterdam for none of the sailors had ever noticed.

Ann prepared the noon meal. How many ingredients had she dumped into the stew pot? Merely sniffing the delicious odors made Penelope hungry. At least there would be only one pot to clean.

Lieutenant Stillwell and his two sons came into the house noisily.

Ann said, "Just in time. Dinner will be ready in a jiffy."

Stillwell said, "I need a clean shirt. I forgot today was the town meeting."

"Now?"

"In a few minutes. They just rang the bell. A head of household is fined a guilder for non-attendance. Besides, I must set a good example since several men have proposed I run for magistrate in January."

"It'll be in the stew pot when you get back." Ann laughed. "Penelope, let's eat. We women won't be fined for being late."

After the meal Penelope, Ann, and her two daughters edged to the back of the crowd in the middle of the town square. Surely everyone in Gravesend was there. Some stood but most sat on benches in the beautiful September weather.

"What's happening?" Ann whispered to a neighbor.

"It's a trial," whispered the woman. "Ambrose London accused Elizabeth Applegate of slandering his wife."

A man promised the magistrate to tell the truth.

Ann whispered, "Did you ever notice a Dutch court expects a witness to tell the truth and an English court makes a man swear to tell the truth?"

"My name," said the witness, "is Thomas Greedy of Gravesend. Last night in Thomas Applegate's house, I discussed the price of wheat with Rodger Scott. The widow Prince stood near us and looked out the window, and I heard her say, 'Ambrose London's wife is milking Applegate's cow.' We both looked out the window. I could see someone was milking the cow but couldn't tell who in the gloaming. When Emilie passed by, we called her to the window and told her what the widow said. Then Emilie and her father ran outside and discovered Mrs. Applegate was milking her own cow and everybody laughed."

The magistrate excused the man and called the next witness. The crowd informed him Emilie had returned to the village of Flushing that morning.

The magistrate called loudly, "Mrs. Penelope Prince of Amsterdam, come forward."

Penelope clutched her heart in surprise. She whispered to Ann, "I can't speak before these people about this embarrassment."

People in the crowd turned and stared at her. The magistrate banged his gavel and called her name again.

Ann whispered, "You must. Do you want to be placed in the stocks for disobedience?" She pushed Penelope forward. The crowd opened a path for her as she slowly walked forward, head bowed.

The magistrate said gently, "Mrs. Prince, please tell us what happened Friday night."

Penelope was sure her face was as blushed as a pink stork. Relating a tale from the Odyssey to a dozen friends was one thing, but confessing an embarrassing blunder to a hundred strangers was another. As Macbeth had said about murder, it was best to do it quickly and be done. She took a deep breath and squeezed her legs together to avoid trembling.

"My name is Penelope Prince. I'm a visitor to your village and I was introduced to so many people yesterday that I couldn't keep names and faces straight. At the party at Thomas Applegate's house, I was staring out the window and thinking. I've had a lot to think about lately."

There were murmurs of sympathy.

"Suddenly this woman came out of the twilight and began to milk the cow. I didn't think it was anyone from the Applegate's house. I tried to identify the woman. The notion of stealing milk never crossed my mind.

"I asked the gentleman next to me whether it was Ambrose London's wife. He thought I stated a fact, rather than asked a question. Then everyone made such a big ado about nothing I was embarrassed at causing such a ruckus. I hoped by not saying anything else, it would all go away." She hung her head in shame. "Obviously it didn't go away. I'm sorry for all the trouble I caused. I hope everyone involved will forgive me."

Penelope looked around wildly for a friendly face. Where was Ann?

The audience digested this apology with murmurs and loud whispers.

Richard Stout began to clap. People joined in and soon everyone was clapping.

The magistrate banged his gavel and said, "I find the defendant not guilty. Case dismissed." The town clerk finished summarizing the proceedings and closed the ledger.

Penelope felt she was the victim of this lawsuit and tried to escape from the crowd of well-wishers, but she was surrounded. Tears blurred her vision.

Mr. Stout took her arm and led her away. "People didn't mean any harm. They got carried away." He ushered her into his house, the nearest refuge, and showed her to a bench. He disappeared and immediately came back with Ann and the girls.

Ann sat on the bench with an arm around her friend's shoulder. "Nicholas says these villagers are truly nice people, except for the Applegates who have a reputation as troublemakers. Surely, you won't have ill feelings for an entire village."

Penelope's face was still wet but at least she had stopped crying. "Oh, the entire thing was so ridiculous. A mountain out of a molehill. I've never been so ashamed in my life. I must leave. I can't face these people after this."

Mr. Stout disappeared again and returned with Lieutenant Stillwell and the boys.

Annie sat in Penelope's lap, hugged her, and kept whispering, "I love you," a trick she used to soothe her mother when Ann was feeling distraught.

Penelope sat and hugged little Annie, scarcely listening to what the others said about her: "distraught; needs time; overmuch excitement; too soon; take her home; she'll recover soon."

* * * * *

An hour later, they all plodded down the path toward Coney Island and the sloop.

Richard Stout had not planned to accompany Penelope back to New Amsterdam but under the circumstances, he felt he must. For most of an hour he told her about other silly court cases in Gravesend. The people used the magistrate court for entertainment. He tried to coax a smile. Ann helped prompt Richard's memory of some of the cases she had heard second hand.

By the time the boat reached New Amsterdam, Penelope smiled. Richard hoped he would never see her cry again. His soul hurt to see her normally happy face in tears. He decided what he loved the most about her was the way her mouth and gray-green eyes were usually on the verge of breaking into a smile. Yes, she smiled with her eyes. Did other women do that? How could she smile after such ordeals?

On the return trip, Stillwell asked Richard. "Are you aware you're in love with her?"

After a long silence, Richard gave a brief nod.

Stillwell asked, "What are you going to do about it?"

Richard replied, "I've no idea."

* * * * *

Ann and Annie helped Baby Alice wave goodbye to her father and stepbrothers as the boat departed from New Amsterdam. Penelope watched. Then they all turned toward town and home.

Ann asked Penelope, "What did you think of Mr. Stout?"

Penelope hesitated. "He's a gentleman."

Ann giggled. "What a rare compliment. Not many men in Manhattan fit that description."

Penelope hung her head. "I fear I made a fool of myself."

"Tsk. Tsk. Tsk. The entire trial was foolish. It's over and will soon be forgotten."

"No, before that, crying over trees he cut down."

Ann laughed. "Trees, phsaw. Mr. Stout seemed quite infatuated with you."

"Infatuated? Why he's nearly as old as my father! And I'm a grieving widow."

Ann wrapped an arm around Penelope's shoulder. "Men are supposed to be old and rich, women young and beautiful. When you were presented to society at age sixteen, weren't most of the men a dozen years older?"

"Presented?" Penelope laughed. "Not without a dowry."

"Nevertheless, Mr. Stout couldn't keep his eyes off of you. Didn't you notice?"

Penelope shook her head. She had paid more attention to his trees. She flapped her injured arm a few inches. "Why would any man be interested in me?"

"It's customary here in the wilderness for a widow, rich or poor, to remarry exactly a year and a day after the death of a husband—a year of mourning followed immediately by a wedding and a day of celebration."

"A year and a day?" What a strange custom.

Ann laughed. "Manhattan teems with bachelors, but most of them prefer a tavern over a field. Mr. Stout would be a good catch."

"His farm is nice. Not that I know much about farms."

Ann leaned over and whispered, "How long did he talk to you? I don't mean how long did the two of you converse? For how many minutes did words come from Mr. Stout's mouth directed to you?"

Penelope sighed. Perhaps it was best to humor Ann until she tired of this silly sport of matchmaking. Penelope recalled the tour of the town, the fields and trees, comforting words on the boat. "About two hours, total."

Ann pounced like an Amsterdam lawyer. "One hundred and twenty minutes of speech to you! Do you know how many minutes Mr. Stout has spoken to all other women in the past year, including 'Hello', 'Good Morning' and 'Good Evening'? I would say thirty minutes. He has never said more than three sentences at one time to me in his life."

"Is he truly so quiet?"

"He certainly is quiet and shy around women. And not much more talkative around men, unless he has something worth saying. Think about this: four years' worth of conversation in two days. I'm surprised the man is not hoarse! Now can you deny the man is obsessed with you? Is truly in love with you? Is uncontrollably, well, no, wrong word for Mr. Stout. I've never seen him lose control. Can you deny the man is totally in love with you?"

Deny it? Penelope preferred to ignore it.

Triumphantly, Ann said, "Case settled. Now, we have to reckon how you feel!"

Penelope frowned. "You can figure that out by yourself because I've no idea and no interest." She didn't have time either. She had made no progress in unraveling the circumstances of her father's disappearance. Because she needed help, she would have to confide in someone. So far, she had two choices—Lieutenant Stillwell or Mr. Stout. She had no reasons to trust or distrust either of them.

Ann opened the door of their house. "You should be interested. You have less than a year to find a man."

Penelope ignored that remark too. She was already looking for a man—her father.

* * * * *

Work went smoothly the next week. Herrmann coaxed a few details out of Penelope and assured her that there was nothing personal in the Gravesend trial. He showed her a book, actually a collection of pages in his usual halfway random order, that was a copy of the Secretary's Register and contained some of the typical cases in New Amsterdam. He explained, "Drinking and gossiping make themselves our entertainment. When either gets out of hand, the Register reveals it. Those cold dreary days of winter, the worst they are."

Later in private moments Penelope searched the Register for indications of her father. Mostly the ledger recorded domestic squabbles, disturbances of the peace, and business disagreements, including a few incidents of get-rich-quick schemes of dubious legality gone wrong. But nothing revealed clues about a newly arrived Englishman.

What if her father never reached Manhattan and she wasted her time searching in the wrong colony?

Chapter 31

New Amsterdam

Friday, September 18, 1648

Late Friday afternoon Lieutenant Stillwell, the boys, and their dog arrived home. Penelope observed a warm and lengthy greeting between the three females, three males, and one canine.

The lieutenant greeted Penelope, "I invited Richard Stout to come. He wasn't sure how he would be received."

Penelope froze, caught off guard by this mention of the subject Ann had harped on all week. Was there to be no end to the planning of her future?

Ann asked, "Why did you ask Mr. Stout?"

Stillwell kissed his wife again. "Because he's in love with Mrs. Prince. Didn't you know that?"

"Of course, I knew, but how did you know?"

"I asked him." He hung up three muskets on pegs high on the wall, well out of reach of small children.

"What did he say?" Ann winked at Penelope.

"Yes," said Stillwell, taking off his coat.

"What do you mean 'Yes'?"

"Am I going to have to tell you the whole conversation before I get anything to eat?"

Ann placed her hands on her hips. "Yes."

Penelope was embarrassed anew by this conversation of her personal affairs. She was tempted to leave the room. But she didn't.

Stillwell picked up Annie and swung her in a circle. "As the boat left the pier, I asked Richard, 'Do you know you're in love with Mrs. Prince?' He nodded.

Then I asked him, 'What are you going to do about it?' and he answered, 'I've no idea.' Now, what's for supper?"

"That's the entire conversation? What else did you talk about all the way to Gravesend?"

"I told him I thought a whale spouted by the Narrows."

"Oh, men!"

"What's for supper?"

"What did you bring?"

"Three rabbits and six geese."

"Then we're having three rabbits for supper. Did the boys shoot them?"

"One shot by each of us for the rabbits. We let Munkey pull the trigger for the geese." He chuckled. "Now that autumn is nigh, the flocks are so thick there's no need to aim. We got all six with one load of scattershot." He went out back to wash.

"Well, Penelope, did you hear that?" Ann untied the rough hempen sack containing three rabbits.

Penelope nodded but said nothing. She didn't want to encourage Ann.

Ann echoed her husband's words, "'What was he going to do about it?' 'I've no idea.'" Then she echoed their earlier conversation, "'What are you going to do about it?' 'I've no idea.' At least you two have something in common—a scarcity of ideas."

Penelope changed the subject. "What'll you do with six geese? We can't eat this many before they spoil."

"I'll send Annie to trade with the neighbors for butter or cheese or vegetables or fruit or whatever they have."

Penelope was accustomed to domestic rabbits killed by a quick blow to the head from a Dutch butcher at the market. "What mangled the heads of these rabbits?"

"A lead ball. If the bullet hits the intestines, it makes a horrid mess over the meat. Dig the lead out and save it. The boys'll re-melt it."

Penelope learned another skill she had never needed in Amsterdam.

Nicky overheard their conversation. "We use half a charge of powder to keep the lead slug from coming out the other side of the rabbit and getting lost."

At supper the boys described their week on Gravesend in detail while Ann extracted an occasional tidbit from Lieutenant Stillwell.

Annie was too animated at her usual bedtime so she stayed up until the boys were sent to bed too, with instructions to leave room for Penelope. The adults talked, or rather, the two women chatted idly, while Stillwell more or less listened and drank beer.

When the village watchman called out nine o'clock, the women went outside to relieve themselves at the privy. Then Ann explained to her husband the women needed privacy in order to extract Penelope from her dress.

Penelope climbed the ladder into the loft for the first time. The ascent was awkward and only a little painful.

She found Annie and snuggled beside her, but the child had knobby knees and sharp elbows that poked everywhere.

Noises from the couple downstairs distracted Penelope. She shifted restlessly. Why would Mr. Stout be infatuated with her? Ridiculous. He scarcely knew her. She reviewed their conversations, but his only suspicious sentence asked if her father had ever voyaged to America.

* * * * *

Saturday and Sunday were filled with inconsequential but pleasant family activities that reminded Penelope of busy households in Amsterdam. She tried to hold onto the happy memories.

At one point when Lieutenant Stillwell and Penelope were alone, he opened the conversation abruptly. "Considering what happened after the shipwreck, if you had it to do again, would you have remained with your husband?"

Penelope was astounded at the lack of tact, but she knew the lieutenant was a direct man. "Of course, what other choice does a person have?"

"To leave."

She stared at him, her anger and color beginning to rise. "Under those circumstances would you abandon Ann, or the boys, or the girls?"

"Of course not," he said calmly.

"Then why did you doubt me?"

"I like to know what kind of person shares my wife's bed when I'm not here." He raised his eyebrows and smiled until her anger turned into a giggle.

He saluted her with his beer mug. "Friends?"

"Yes, friends." She looked around to be sure they were still alone. "Do you have many friends?"

"The few I have are dependable. Want more beer?"

She believed both parts—the few and the dependable. "Yes, I would like more beer." She would also like more friends, especially dependable friends.

"No trouble. No trouble at all, for a friend. Speaking of which, I've heard some rumors about your globe, but I must tread carefully or the thief will destroy it to protect himself."

Penelope studied him over her mug of beer. Perhaps she should confide her second problem to her newest friend. Then Ann returned. Penelope feared that telling Ann would be the same as telling the entire island. Actually two islands now.

* * * * *

On Monday morning after breakfast, Penelope straightened the kitchen as Lieutenant Stillwell prepared to leave with the boys.

He asked her, "Should I invite Mr. Stout to come with me next Saturday?"

"No," said Penelope. Was the husband involved in matchmaking as well as the wife?

"Yes," said Ann, an instant later.

Stillwell grinned at the two women but said nothing.

Ann looked at Penelope and spoke to her husband. "What Penelope means is Mr. Stout is shy and you can't pressure him to come. It has to be a neutral invitation, from us, not from her. Tell him that I, as your wife and his future neighbor, invite him for supper Saturday evening."

Penelope walked with Stillwell and the boys to the pier and Herrmann's factory. Halfway there, Stillwell asked, "Any messages for Mr. Stout?"

She almost blurted out, "No," but Ann's persistent discussions had persuaded her to consider her future. Curiosity and good manners finally overrode her inclination to hide from the world. "Tell him, 'Thank you for the tour last weekend and for his kind words on the boat.'"

* * * * *

When Penelope arrived home from work that evening, she noted a lack of the usual gaiety in the Stillwell house. What could have happened?

Annie pouted. "Mommy, why won't you tell me what three and three is?"

"Because you must learn to do sums yourself. Just hold up three fingers on one hand and hold up three fingers on the other hand, and then see how many fingers you're holding up."

Annie put down the bark and charcoal she was practicing on and held her fingers as instructed and then asked crossly, "How can I count my fingers when I'm already using my fingers to count?"

Ann said, "Just in time, Penelope. Do you wish to teach arithmetic to a pouting child or clean a stinky baby?"

"Arithmetic."

"Wrong answer. You need the experience. I see the future Mrs. Stout having half a dozen babies and changing diapers with one hand."

Surely Ann jested, at least the part about half a dozen babies. With a scarred abdomen and one useful arm, Penelope would be lucky to have one baby and overwhelmed with two. Why she was even thinking about babies—some other man's babies—while Matthew had been dead only a few fortnights. It felt disloyal, shameful. Although her voice had promised until "death do you part," she had anticipated "forever."

Ann said, "The men here believe that letting a good woman go fallow is a waste of rare resources, that a woman needs a man's protection."

Penelope ignored her.

Ann continued, "The women hold the opinion men think a widow's money and property need more protection than her person does."

The widow forgot she wasn't interested in this topic. "I have neither money nor property."

"Some men feel an unmarried widow gets too uppity, with Lady Moody being the prime example. Some wives feel a widow is a luring temptation to their husbands."

"I don't feel uppity or tempting."

"Oh, silly, I didn't mean you, personally. I meant widows in general. People will expect you to remarry in a year for many reasons."

"Remarry in a year," she echoed with no enthusiasm.

"In a year or three, when you're ready, what would you look for in a husband? Are you interested in handsome? Rich? Well-respected?"

"You're prattling like my old landlady now."

"What did your landlady advise?"

"Beauty is only skin-deep."

"Answer the question."

Penelope sighed. Distracting Ann from her game of match-making was too difficult. It was easier to participate until she tired. "She advised me to find a man who appreciated me for my own fine qualities and ignored my meager dowry. Ha. As if such men were common in Amsterdam."

Ann added, "A man who can make you laugh."

"Sober. Protective," countered Penelope.

"A man who always comes back home. Alone and alive."

"A man who doesn't gamble."

"A man who doesn't lose at gambling," amended Ann.

Penelope shook her head at Ann's priorities. "A man of quality."

"Good in bed."

"What?"

Ann laughed. "It's important a husband should make his wife happy. A woman spends much of her life in bed."

Penelope covered her reddening face with her hands. "That may be, but some qualities are harder to evaluate than others."

Ann giggled. "Especially before the wedding."

Penelope required a few moments to regain seriousness. "I remember quite a few sermons addressed to people who were evaluating that quality before the wedding. Some ministers and gossip-mongers are fond of talking about other people's fornications."

"Is that because it's rare or because it's so common?"

Penelope raised her eyebrows at Ann. "Based upon the quantity of gossip and length of sermons, it must be common."

Ann made a few additional ribald comments.

Hours later as Ann slept peacefully inches away, Penelope tried not to toss and turn in the narrow bed as she considered the topic of remarriage. Mr. Stout had the necessary virtues and she respected him as a gentleman. Men were numerous in Manhattan, but gentlemen were scarce. Knowing that Mr. Stout loved her offered both comfort and discomfort.

On the other hand, many people advised a marriage based upon passion soon burned out, whereas a marriage based, like a business contract, upon mutual advantage and specific responsibilities enjoyed a lasting foundation. She understood contracts better than passion. But she couldn't marry a man she addressed as mister. Henceforth, she would think of Mr. Stout as Richard.

Only two months had passed since Matthew's death. Myriad upheavals in her life made it seem much longer.

In half consciousness before sleep, she saw two men who looked alike: nearly six feet tall, around two hundred pounds, muscular build, calloused hands, brown hair. But they were completely different: Matthew's smooth, boyish face and boyish dreams versus Richard's mature, rugged face and mature visions. She fell asleep with both watching over her.

* * * * *

On Tuesday, the reply from John Throckmorton arrived with two letters from Boston. Because Herrmann in the back office concentrated upon the proper colors for a sunset in his latest painting, he never learned of the additional communication. She extracted the proper coins from Herrmann's purse to pay the messenger for the legitimate correspondence and added her own coin for the third letter.

The young man was a common seaman from Boston eager to complete his errand and experience the frivolities of New Amsterdam that, if available in Boston, would be severely punished.

She took the letter to her writing desk near the front window where the light was better and intercepting messengers was easier. With one of the ubiquitous knives intended for trading with the *wilden,* she popped the sealing wax from the paper and flattened the single sheet on her desk. She inserted the knife back into her sling. Carpenters and housewives might wear an apron with its convenient nooks and crannies but not clerks.

After the polite greeting the clear handwriting was short and to the point. Just before Easter of 1643 John Throckmorton had escorted John Kent and a German-speaking servant through the forests from Boston to Providence Town and then across Long Island Sound to Vredeland. Mr. Kent was excited by the forest but the servant was fearful. After three days at Throg's Neck, the name of Throckmorton's plantation, Throckmorton's servant rowed the two visitors across the creek to Manhattan. Mr. Throckmorton never saw either of them again.

Penelope rose and studied Herrmann's map. Vredeland was at the northnortheast end of Manhattan Island whereas New Amsterdam was at the southsouthwest end, a distance of ten to fifteen miles. The Broad Way ran a half-mile from Fort New Amsterdam to the wall and quickly narrowed to a trail. The island averaged two miles in width. Somewhere between Vredeland and the wall, somewhere in those twenty to thirty square miles of green wilderness, her father had disappeared.

At least he had arrived in New Netherland.

Was the German a murderer or a fellow victim?

Like the Anabaptists, the Puritans in Boston didn't recognize Easter. Mr. Throckmorten and her father probably wanted to leave Boston before Easter so they could observe the holy day without being thrown into the stocks.

The *wilden* didn't attack until August. Where was John Kent between April and August? Four months was a long time for a merchant to live in a forest. Had he found what he sought and left, only to die elsewhere? If so, did he sail straight to Amsterdam or via Boston? She had bribed the smiling young clerk in Curaçao to check the incoming and outgoing passenger lists there and found nothing.

She folded up the letter and stuffed it into her sling next to the letter-opening knife.

Chapter 32

New Amsterdam

Friday, 2 October 1648

Richard Stout stood outside the Stillwell house and again questioned why he had accompanied the lieutenant to Manhattan when crops remained in the fields. The Stillwell boys shoved the deer haunch into his hands when Annie ran out to greet her half-brothers. With envy, he watched the male and female halves of the Stillwell family greet each other warmly and noisily.

On the opposite side of the Stillwell cluster stood Penelope, an outsider like he was. Although she greeted Lieutenant Stillwell formally, she greeted the boys and dog with gaiety.

Richard trailed the Stillwells into the house and found himself three feet in front of Penelope with no idea what to say or do.

Ann relieved Richard of the venison and surprised him with a chaste kiss on the cheek. He felt his face warm.

Penelope raised a hand to her mouth to hide a giggle. Yielding to a sudden impulse, Richard bowed, grasped Penelope's hand as she lowered it, and kissed it. Then he watched her face blush, though he knew his was even redder.

Ann snickered. "Oh, to be sixteen again..."

Richard overcame the urge to run away and stood quietly on the edge of the group for several minutes.

Fortunately, the lieutenant entertained the women with news about game, crop conditions, and fishing. "I hear rumors of an oystering day for the entire village of Gravesend next Saturday. Anyone interested?"

Ann said, "Sounds like a gay time."

Penelope said, "Not me."

Ann whispered to Penelope, "Would you rather spend time with Judith Stuyvesant?"

"Anything would be better than being near Elizabeth Applegate!"

The lieutenant said, "I almost forgot. Lady Moody extends her invitation to Penelope."

Ann looked at her husband. "Is it true Lady Moody owns three dozen books?"

Richard surprised himself by answering, "Probably more. Her neighbors have borrowed some."

"What kind of books?" Penelope asked.

Richard recalled Penelope had once mentioned Shakespeare. "She has a volume of plays from London though she doesn't boast of it."

Ann said to Penelope, "I'm sure Lady Moody would lend you a book."

Penelope rolled her eyes at Ann and sighed. "If I can avoid Mrs. Applegate. If everyone forgets that horrid trial."

Ann clapped her hands. "It's settled then."

Contrary to the usual custom, there was a light lunch because the main meal would be in the evening today. Richard mostly listened as lively conversation washed over him like ocean swells. Then Annie demonstrated her arithmetic skills and her mother was quick to give Penelope due credit. Penelope demurred, saying using pebbles instead of fingers for counting was as old as the abacus.

Ricky Stillwell posed his half-sister a word problem. "If I had five pieces of molasses-candy, and Nicky stole one, how many would I have left?"

Annie held up her fingers. "Four."

Ricky shook his head sadly and said, "No. I would still have five, because I would hit Nicky on the head and take it back."

Nicky looked at Annie and nodded. Together they jumped on their big brother, who slumped to the ground. Annie knew where her elder half-brother was most ticklish and her tiny fingers dug deep between his ribs. Ricky giggled so hard he couldn't hold off his little brother, who tried to pin his shoulders to the floor. Between paroxysms of laughter Ricky managed to speak, "If I had five pieces of candy and gave one to Nicky and one to Baby Alice and gave two to you, how many would I have left?"

Annie paused in her torturing to compute the answer. "One! And I would have more than each of you! You're forgiven." Ricky was now able to devote full attention to his brother. The body wrestling switched to arm wrestling.

Long ago, Richard and his elder brother had a relationship like that—teasing and tumbling together. Long ago, he had been a mirthful boy amidst a happy, though stern family.

Ann held the attitude that the happy sounds of children weren't noise. The children's gaiety engendered in Richard regrets for the family he had never had.

When the floor was safe, Baby Alice showed off her toddling skills. The lieutenant announced he had business to attend to in town. Richard said likewise and the two men went off together, agreeing to return around five o'clock.

Their passage to town was delayed by a typical Saturday afternoon game of *ganstrekken*, or "Pull the Goose." A man tied the legs of a live goose, greased well the head and neck, and securely tied the bird to a rope that was stretched across the street. The goal was for a man to gallop on horseback, grab the greased neck of the shrieking, frantic goose, and pull the head off the bird. Betting, drinking, and shouting accompanied this recreation.

Lieutenant Stillwell was readily persuaded by several cronies to pull the goose. Had Richard spent too much of his life watching instead of participating? Not that this was the sort of activity he enjoyed—drunken games by grown men—but again he was on the side of the street while life proceeded at full speed down the center.

Shouldn't the civil authorities fine the participants? Then Richard noted the *schout* was already present and was betting noisily against the lieutenant.

* * * * *

After the two men left the house, Penelope stared at the deer's haunch and wistfully recalled the muscular butcher from the Beast Market in Amsterdam and even Tisquantum's spiteful wife from the aborigine village. While Ann sharpened on a whetstone two long knives that looked more like swords than kitchen tools, Penelope decided her one good arm was better suited to butchering rabbits than deer.

The men returned together, Stillwell carrying a bottle of wine and Richard wearing a new doublet of dark green velvet.

"Is it too bold and extravagant, dost thou think?" Richard asked. "The merchant said it's the latest fashion."

"Oh, no. It's well made and quite becoming on you." Penelope didn't mention it was the latest style in Amsterdam five years ago. Her father had bought a similar one the summer before his last voyage. "The upturned white cuffs add a nice contrast. Don't you agree, Ann?"

"I would've expected such a fine doublet to come with silver buttons," Ann said.

"Silver is overmuch gaudy for me. I prefer pewter," Richard said.

Indeed, thought Penelope, doesn't apparel proclaim the man? Prosperous but self-effacing. He would never fit into Amsterdam society. But neither would she.

"Silver buttons make a shiny target for a savage," said Lieutenant Stillwell.

The men shared the news they had separately learned while the women continued with meal preparation and Annie set the table. A ship had arrived from Boston via New Haven. Governor Stuyvesant had issued new rules that none were likely to obey. Tobacco prices held firm.

By the end of supper, the bottle of wine was empty. Richard invited Penelope to stroll in the cool twilight. Before she could decline with a defense of dirty dishes, Ann pushed Penelope out of the house. Ann's cleaning up alone after the meal would be due punishment for her interference in another person's life.

Penelope hoped a walk would clear her head of two glasses of wine. She and Richard picked their way around the rough streets but said little. Upon rounding the block and returning to their starting point, Richard explained he usually sat outside on a bench to enjoy the appearance of the stars and the quietness. She nodded. He borrowed Ann's kitchen bench, set it next to the wall of the house to provide a backrest, and invited Penelope to sit.

Automatically, she chose the left side and sat near the center of her half of the bench. He sat so far away from her he was almost off the plank. When she lifted her body slightly to bunch her dress to create more space for Richard, the bench tipped. Richard caught himself and moved his body a few inches closer to the center, but still left a four-inch gap between his body and her dress fabric.

He was as shy and modest as Matthew. The memory of her late husband reminded her of the year and a day that Ann claimed a colonial widow was allotted before remarriage.

If Penelope didn't return home—to Amsterdam, that is—she had few choices but to remarry. Marriage was merely a contract, she reminded herself, or perhaps the wine was speaking. The husband provided food, clothing, and shelter. The wife cleaned, cooked, and bore children.

God provided better or worse, sickness or health. And the couple provided love or hate, friendship or apathy.

She and Matthew had shared a mutual determination to travel to America as well as friendship, which the Separatists argued was a better foundation than love. She glanced at Richard, who fiddled with his pipe. He was a shy but persistent man. Some day, she would have to choose whether or not to marry him. She needed to decide how she felt about this man because he was unlikely to do much besides sit and stare.

As it darkened, Richard pointed out a few constellations. They discussed Greek mythology, followed by some vague references to his time in the Royal Navy and the way the stars were different in the Caribbean than here.

"Where is the North Star?" she asked. "I don't see it." She knew it was behind a neighbor's chimney.

Richard scanned the heavens. "We should be able to see it from the street."

They moved away from the candlelight escaping from Ann's window for a more vivid view of the stars from the dark streets of Manhattan. She stumbled on the unpaved street. He quickly grabbed her elbow to steady her and as quickly released it. He pointed out several constellations and how the angle of the North Star above the horizon was also the latitude.

She enjoyed the quiet confidence of his voice as he explained things she already knew. "The stars shine so brightly here in Manhattan whereas Amsterdam was so foggy or smoky one could scarcely see the moon, much less Orion. Shouldn't it be rising now?"

"No, the constellation Pleiades has barely risen."

"Oh, the Seven Sisters. Where are they?"

He pointed but she couldn't find it.

"It's quite faint and just over the roof of that house." Richard moved behind her, put his head over her shoulder, and picked up her right hand to point to the sky. Together they sighted down their joined fingers to the seven faint stars. In a few seconds, he released her hand. For a man who was supposedly infatuated with her, he seemed afraid to touch her. Reverend Prince would approve.

Maybe she had drunk too much wine at dinner. Maybe she had listened to Ann too much. Upon their return to the bench, Penelope pretended to stumble and grasped Richard's hand for balance. Not releasing his hand after she sat down, she forced him to sit a little closer to her than before. Their clasped fingers rested in the neutral territory of the bench. Their shoulders occasionally brushed briefly as they shifted positions on the hard plank.

Penelope looked down at their shadowy hands clasped together. For sixteen years she had held her father's hand. Then he had disappeared. She had taken Matthew's hand and held it for less than a year. Then he had died. Now she held Richard's hand. Would that kill him? Should she yank her hand free? She was surprised she cared enough to save his life, despite it being a silly superstition, merely her mind playing tricks. Would she care in the morning after the wine had worn off?

At least she cared about something tonight. Most of the time, she tried to avoid feeling. Apathy—a strange new word she had heard just before leaving Amsterdam— described her situation well. What would the adjective be? Was she both pathetic and apathetic at the same time?

Ann's call through the window that it was bedtime startled Penelope. Richard carried the bench back into the house, apologized for the late hour, and made a hasty exit. Ann invited him to return in mid-morning. Ann's husband excused himself so Ann could help Penelope undress.

Penelope twisted her good arm so far she feared it would break. "Surely there exist clothes I can handle alone, even if they're ten years out of style. "

Ann grinned. "The wooing must be going well if you're worried about style."

"A courtship at Richard's pace is like watching a tree grow."

"Hah! So there is a courtship."

Penelope declined to reply, thankful her blushing face was turned away from Ann.

Up in the darkness of the loft, amid the sleeping children, Penelope tired to imagine what Richard Stout saw when he looked at her. Her body still had the strength, grace, and curves of a twenty-two-year old in the prime of womanhood despite being too skinny. The ugly summer color was fading from her skin. Her face was still attractive, more so when she smiled. Thanks to Ann, she did smile often these days. She removed her cap, ruffled her two-inch-long hair, and touched the bald spot. No man would see her lack of hair until after a wedding.

She raised her left arm a few inches, as far as pain allowed. Never again would she handle heavy tubs of hot laundry water or stir clothes in the kettle with a large stick but she grinned at those limitations. She could neither hoe a garden nor fold a quilt. Nevertheless, she had demonstrated she could prepare food, cook, clean up, handle a baby, sew, knit, and do a hundred other household tasks.

Surely Richard courted her, but was she courting him? Or was the wine courting?

At least she didn't compete with the spoiled daughters of rich Amsterdam burghers whose milky skin was protected by parasols with silver handles. In this savage land hard living and few conveniences made women look old before their time. As a widow in a strange city with no relatives and no assets, remarriage was her best option, truly her only option.

When? And to whom?

Ah, those were good questions. Two and a half months of "a year and a day" had passed. But she had to find her father or his body. One day at a time was sufficient for now. Sometimes, one day at a time was almost too much.

She despised the feelings of helplessness and despair that sometimes tried to overwhelm her. She lay down on her pallet next to Annie's bony limbs. Her hosts were not as noisy tonight.

How much did she care? Another knotty question. The purpose of courting was a chance to learn a person slowly. She recalled the ancient warning carved into the lintel over the Old Church in Amsterdam, "Marry in haste. Repent in leisure."

She had many acquaintances in her former life, but few friends. You didn't need friends in Amsterdam if you were wealthy. At least she had several true friends here. She knew they were true, because she had no money.

The phrase "a year and a day" echoed in her mind as she fell asleep.

Chapter 33

New Amsterdam

Saturday, 10 October 1648

On the next Saturday Lieutenant Stillwell arrived at Manhattan alone because the boys had made an early start at harvesting oysters. Penelope was loath to go to Gravesend again but even more reluctant to stay alone. She stuffed half her clothes into one of the lieutenant's rucksacks, dropped the bag onto the floor below and carefully descended the ladder.

Ann had Annie and Baby Alice ready to go. They all hurried to the pier and into the sloop for a pleasant sail. Since the boat had a shallow draft, Stillwell anchored in the channel separating Coney Island from Long Island.

Penelope surveyed the scene from the boat.

Contrary to Ann's flippant remark of a few days ago that the women were invited to do the work, shoeless men and boys waded in water so shallow that their trousers, conveniently ending just below the knee, seldom got dampened. Younger children, including several girls under ten who were stripped to their shifts, alternately helped and splashed in the water. Were they frolicking?

Women sat further up the shore in the shade of awnings made from former sails, obviously attired in their finest clothes as though enjoying themselves in a garden in London or Amsterdam, except for the sand.

Richard Stout and the boys arrived to help unload the passengers. One brother carried Baby Alice while the other assisted Annie. Penelope watched Richard watch Lieutenant Stillwell grab Ann by the waist, lift her over the gunwales, and swing her around to touch on damp sand.

Richard looked at Penelope. "Art thou sure?"

In his presence she wasn't sure of anything. "I prefer not to get my shoes wet."

He reached up and put his hands around her waist as though he held a delicate flower.

With her good hand on his shoulder to steady herself, she said, "I'm not a basket of eggs. I won't break."

He started to lift her but his foot slipped in the mud. He regained his balance but not his composure as evidenced by his reddening face.

Ann snickered. "Mr. Stout, she's not a bag of flour either."

He shuffled his feet in the mud and looked up at Penelope. "Art thou true certain of this?"

She ignored Ann's remark but felt embarrassed at his embarrassment. "I've survived worse."

His hands froze in mid-air and his eyes widened.

She giggled. "Don't you have a sense of humor?"

Richard nodded. "I did when I was a boy. A hundred or so years ago." Holding her waist firmly, he swung her with overmuch vigor onto the beach.

There they stood, face to face, their bodies only a few inches apart.

She avoided his eyes and noticed a small cut on his chin from his shaving razor. She thought he held onto her a trifle longer than necessary. "Thank you for keeping my shoes dry."

As though her words broke his trance, he instantly released her and turned to assist with the boat.

Lunch consisted of fresh oysters, baked oysters, roasted maize, and beer. Meanwhile, more oysters dried over smoky fires. The older men preferred political discussions, the younger men contests of strength and agility. Girls too old to frolic in the water watched the younger men while the wives analyzed food receipts and ingredients with more civility than Penelope expected, remembering the accusations and gossip from the slander trial. Ann was right: those little animosities were merely entertainment to be put aside while taking pleasure in today's diversions.

A favorite topic was the upcoming bird migrations in which enormous flocks of geese, ducks, and pigeons would darken the skies before descending upon nearby Jamaica Bay. The deliciousness of eating fowl was offset by the labor of plucking feathers that was offset by the pleasure of soft pillows and warm quilts. Penelope developed friendships with the women, except for Mrs. Applegate, whom she avoided, and Mrs. London, who avoided her.

Lady Moody quickly stifled a competition among the villagers concerning who would offer the visitor a bed. Ann's house was finished enough for all the Stillwells to sleep in it for one night.

Penelope noted the stack of muskets under a tree and the occasional departure of an armed man toward the empty village a mile or two away. A third of the males remained on the beach all night to tend the smoky fires that still dried the oysters, while the rest of the populace straggled back to their houses.

* * * * *

Late on the Sabbath morning, half the village gathered in Lady Moody's parlor for worship, over-filling the house, the largest in Gravesend. Several families brought a bench. Children sat on the floor.

Penelope took the opportunity to study Lady Moody's home. Velvet curtains decorated the windows and Turkey carpets covered much of the floor. Walls of wood instead of plaster seemed odd when combined with furnishings reminiscent of rich Amsterdam houses.

Because the town had no minister—wasn't allowed to have a church or minister—Lady Moody was the hostess. She welcomed the group, made sure Penelope had been introduced to everyone, and asked about illness in the village and if anyone was in need. Harvest season approached and James Hubbard led the singing of the Sixty-Fifth Psalm. The voices were ragged but enthusiastic.

Then Hubbard read the third chapter of Ecclesiastes that described a season for everything. He sat down next to a young woman who smiled sweetly at him. Penelope considered it odd that men and women sat together. But they were in Lady Moody's home not a church.

Richard Stout recited Psalm 107.

One verse stuck in Penelope's head and would not go away: "Then they cried unto the Lord in their trouble, and he saved them out of their distresses."

James Bowne rose slowly. "I thank Lady Moody for allowing me to read her copy of the *Book of Martyrs*. I have pondered why God allows his faithful followers to suffer so much. I think God uses our temporary bodies to test our immortal souls. We mortal men prize our bodies highly. Yet to God, they are as dried leaves blowing in the wind. When a martyr says 'I believe' as his body burns at the stake, he believes his soul is on its way to heaven. I look into my soul. I try to see such faith. I cannot find it."

Lady Moody said, "I think the story of Job illustrates the same principle. If God considered a body to be equal to a soul, surely He would not sacrifice a dozen bodies to test one soul."

Penelope was astounded a woman spoke openly, even if it was in her home.

"What's a body good for?" asked another.

Penelope ignored the ensuing discussion as she contemplated her own problems.

By undertaking his journey, Mathew had proven he loved his church more than he loved his body. Without doubt, his spirit was with Jesus now. Was the purpose of Matthew's death to test her soul? So far, she was certain, she had been found wanting. She had journeyed for selfish reasons, nor for the glory of God. She had mourned Matthew's death because of the distress it caused her. She had survived, but to what purpose?

Lady Moody closed her Bible and said, "Mrs. Prince, do you have a favorite verse?"

Penelope looked at the men surrounding her. Their faces were pleasant and encouraging. In a low voice, she said, "I was recently comforted by the Twenty-Third Psalm."

Lady Moody smiled. "That's a favorite of mine too. Let's all stand and recite that psalm as our benediction."

Benches scraped, clothes rustled, voices spoke. The people slowly departed.

* * * * *

After church services Lady Moody requested Penelope and Richard Stout to join her for lunch, along with Hubbard and his betrothed. The Sunday meal was cold venison, bread, cheese, and beer plus tea for Lady Moody. Rumors claimed the residents of Gravesend didn't respect the Sabbath, but this meal had a Puritan simplicity, except for Lady Moody's tea, an expensive drink that had recently become popular among Dutch merchants in Amsterdam.

As a recent traveler from Europe, especially one who had spent several days in Stuyvesant's house, Penelope was expected to be full of news. However, she could add little to their obsolete Boston and Amsterdam newspapers. They were more informed about the war in England than she. And more interested.

After the guests departed, Penelope helped the serving girl clear the table.

"Good Heavens, child," said Lady Moody. "That's not why you're here. Come join me in the parlor."

The front window held four large panes of glass, each at least a foot square. How could such fragile items be shipped safely across a stormy ocean while she had arrived in such a wretched condition? Then she remembered that some colonies produced glass to ship to England because glass-making required huge amounts of heat and wood that was free for the taking here.

Through the window, Penelope watched Richard Stout converse with Hubbard. Where was Richard when her father died? Richard was once a sailor and the German stowaway was most likely a sailor. Did they know each other?

"Lady Moody," she asked, still staring outside, "what do you know of Mr. Stout's history?"

"He's the second son of a gentleman farmer," Lady Moody said. "And a gentleman himself, don't you agree?"

"Yes, he has acted quite proper to me."

"And quite an eligible bachelor. More tea, dear?"

Penelope swirled around, feeling a blush coming to her face. "I...I'm a recent widow. That...that is not my interest." Embarrassment was safer than revealing secrets.

"Tut, tut, child. I'm an old widow, yet I pay attention to men, as a drowning person pays attention to water. Sometimes you need to attract men, sometimes to repel them, sometimes to flatter them, sometimes to keep them just out of reach. But you always need to know where they are, what they're doing, and what they want."

"Well, then." Penelope smiled and sat. "Why is Mr. Stout in Gravesend?" She sipped the hot infusion of green leaves Lady Moody had called tea. "Oh, how bitter. What kind of medicine is this?" She sniffed it.

"Medicine for the soul. A pleasurable drink made of leaves from faraway islands, a rich lady's drink. So humor me and add some sugar."

Penelope pulled out pinchers from a bowl and scooped up a tan lump. "My landlady in Amsterdam was suspicious of such luxuries. How much sugar is enough?"

Lady Moody smiled. "One lump for those unaccustomed to luxuries."

Penelope stirred the tea and sipped again. She could taste the sweetness like an Amsterdam confection.

"Mr. Stout," said Lady Moody, "is here because I'm here."

Penelope's eyebrows rose.

"Tut, tut, child. Don't jump to conclusions. I'm here because I made some wise decisions and some foolish decisions. When my husband died and I was allowed to think
for myself, I decided England wasn't the proper place for a
proper woman who didn't believe in the proper religion
anymore. My son and I sold the estate and we took ourselves and our money to the Massachusetts Bay Colony
because that's where I thought people who no longer
believed in the proper religion were supposed to go."

Penelope said, "Religion is so complicated these days."

Lady Moody nodded in agreement. "In Salem we were
flattered by officials more interested in our wealth than in
our religion. Acreage was so cheap that we bought too
much and neglected to notice American land doesn't come
with labor."

"Is that why you left?" Penelope sipped more of the
strange concoction.

"No. After we entrapped ourselves with too many acres,
the same officials began to inquire about our religion.
Massachusetts only tolerates one improper religion and we
believed in the wrong one. Alas, we heard of the battle of
Edgehill. If the Puritans of old England were bold enough
to declare war on the king, what protection did I have from
the even more aggressive Puritans of New England?"

Penelope clearly recalled the day in the fall of 1642
when she learned of the battle of Edgehill and of Matthew's dream.

"I began correspondence with Governor Kieft," Lady
Moody continued, "the former governor of this colony, who
promised we could believe anything as long as we didn't
flaunt our beliefs in public."

Penelope grinned, "Spoken like a true Amsterdammer."

"We rented a boat, invited a few like-minded friends,
such as Mr. Hubbard, to join us and sailed south. We
discovered this isolated and fruitful spot where we hoped
government officials would be reluctant to venture. Governor Kieft insisted we needed enough people to defend a

remote settlement so we invited local Englishmen, such as Mr. Stout, to join us."

"When was that?"

"We left Salem in April of '43." Lady Moody refreshed her cup with more of the hot infusion from a pot on the table.

What a coincidence, thought Penelope, refusing her hostess's offer of more tea, nearly the same time her father left Boston. "Is Salem near Boston?"

"Thirty miles north as the seagull flies. We had enough trouble with Puritan ministers already and Boston was out of the way because we sailed around Cape Cod."

That geography confused Penelope, for her father's globe had been made before Boston was settled. She noticed Lady Moody analyzing her but pressed on anyway. Hopefully, the old lady was merely an inveterate match-matcher. "Where did you meet Mr. Stout?"

"Mr. Stout had been impressed into His Majesty's Navy. By chance, his warship was in New Amsterdam when his seven years' term expired. He chose to be set ashore in a foreign land amidst an Indian war—that, likewise, was early in 1643 —rather than continue back to England."

Penelope swirled the cup. Everything came back to the spring of '43. How does one sift fact from fancy? "How does Mr. Stout spend his time?"

Lady Moody smiled. "He's a planter. He works."

Penelope nodded. "He said he cleared the most land here. Does he ever leave the village?"

Lady Moody laughed. "Before you arrived, my dear, he left the village twice a year. Once in September to arrange to sell his tobacco and again in December to deliver it. I assure you he has no entangling alliances to interfere with your opportunities."

Penelope understood her hostess referred to female en-tanglements, but that also meant none with a German sailor or the sailor's former comrades or enemies. If anyone could keep her secret, it was the taciturn Mr. Stout.

She was reluctant to share secrets with Lady Moody. In Amsterdam, the maids who collected the most gossip also revealed the most.

At least Lady Moody vouched for Mr. Stout's history and whereabouts. Penelope thanked Lady Moody, strolled to Ann's house, and pondered the best way to ask for assistance to search for answers to her father's disappearance.

Chapter 34

New Amsterdam

Sunday, 11 October 1648

At the Stillwell house in the tiny village of Gravesend on the long island, Ann and the baby napped. Nicky and Annie invited their guest to hunt mushrooms. Penelope reckoned a walk in the woods was an excellent place to think.

Once again huge masses of trees surrounded her and soared skyward as though she stood inside the tall, new church in Amsterdam. Had her father died in a forest like this? With almost no progress in solving the mystery of his disappearance, she resolved to ask for help. But how?

In the woods Nicky plucked a plant from the forest floor and handed it to Penelope. "Look at this mushroom carefully. Most of them are poisonous. We only want this type."

She examined the spongy brown mass. "You trust me with your life?"

"Mother always checks them. Especially the ones Annie picks."

Annie stuck out her tongue at her brother.

Penelope took a basket and wandered beside the girl, who pointed out a fearless red-breasted robin, a gray and white mocking bird that imitated other birds' songs, and a red bird whose head feathers resembled a Catholic cardinal's red hat. Penelope spent more time admiring majestic trees and cheerful birds and pondering life's problems than she did gathering mushrooms.

"No!" Annie screamed and pointed where Penelope's hand was reaching.

Penelope jumped back and dropped the basket. Her heart raced. Her eyes searched the ground for snakes.

With a stick Nicky touched a small plant with dark green leaves. "That's the poisonous ivy plant. "

"Poisonous?" Penelope stared at the innocuous looking greenery. "It looks like the ivy Amsterdammers plant around new houses to make them look old."

"I don't know anything about European ivy," said Nicky. "I was born in Virginia. But touching these leaves gives Annie a horrible rash and the itching drives her mad."

"Leaflets three, leave it be," chanted Annie.

"What a dangerous continent!" Penelope recalled shipwrecks, deadly savages, and a missing father as well as snakes and toxic plants. She bent down to retrieve her dropped basket and froze.

"That one's safe," said Nicky.

"What is it?" Penelope stared at a plant with bright red berries and leaflets of five.

Nicky squatted beside her. "The world's full of worthless weeds. Father taught us the useful and dangerous ones."

"My father taught me about this one." Penelope knelt down until her eyes were inches from leaflets with finely serrated edges, identical to the dried specimen in her father's letter.

Had John Kent, respected merchant of Amsterdam, sailed across the ocean to get rich from this spindly little herb? If she trusted her father, she must trust his business judgment, however illogical it seemed at the moment.

Annie plopped down on the ground. "What's it good for?"

Penelope's finger traced around a leaflet. "I don't know."

"Most red berries taste bitter. Why did your father teach you about this one?" asked Nicky.

"I don't know."

"Which part is useful? Berries, flowers, leaves, roots?"

"I don't know."

Nicky sighed. "Mrs. Prince, you make no sense."

"I know."

"What do we do, Nicky?" asked Annie.

Nicky shrugged. "We ask Father." He picked up a forked limb, broke off the ends to make a stubby shovel, and dug up Penelope's plant. The main stem was four inches long and an inch in diameter.

"It's a body," said Annie. "See. A head. Two arms."

"And three legs," added Nicky. "With rheumatism. Look how gnarly it is."

"Is it ginger?" Penelope finally snapped out of her trance. "Let me smell it." She took the plant and sniffed the root. The faint odor wasn't ginger.

"Wash it off in the creek," said Annie. "Mother doesn't like dirty mushrooms."

Penelope dumped her few mushrooms into the girl's nearly full basket, rinsed the dirt off the roots of her treasure, and carefully arranged the wet plant in her basket as though it grew there. She turned around in a complete circle twice, searching for landmarks.

The trees all looked alike. Well, not alike. Each one was different but unfamiliar, like being led blindfolded into a strange section of Amsterdam and recognizing none of the buildings. She looked up but no church spires soared into the sky. Only trees. "Where's home."

Nicky and Annie pointed in the same direction. Penelope walked and scarcely noticed the children soon led her.

Ann greeted them at the door. Penelope walked in without speaking, sat down on a bench at the table, and stared at her plant.

Ann said, "That's no mushroom."

Penelope whispered what she felt in her heart, "That's what killed my father."

"You're talking nonsense," said Ann.

"She's been talking nonsense ever since she thought it was the poisonous ivy," said Annie.

"You imagined this was poisonous ivy?" Ann laughed at the plant with the red berries. "You would think you'd never been in the woods before."

"I haven't. At least not before the shipwreck."

A frown replaced Ann's laugh. She sat next to her friend and put an arm around her shoulder. "Tell me about it."

Before Penelope could speak, Richard Stout and Lieutenant Stillwell entered the kitchen. Annie, Nicky, and Ann all tried to explain at the same time. While Richard stood motionless with his mouth open, the lieutenant hung guns on pegs high on the wall, shucked his muddy boots, filled two mugs with beer, and sat in the only chair at the table, his chair.

A smile played across Stillwell's face. He rolled his eyes from one speaker to another to another and back again. His calmness and good humor cheered Penelope.

When the noise died down, Stillwell said to Penelope, "They don't know what they're talking about, do they?"

She shook her head.

"Then tell me." He pushed a mug of beer across the table to her.

She took a sip. "Tell what?"

"Everything." He gestured to his wife. "Eventually you'll tell Ann and she'll tell me. Save time and tell me directly."

While Penelope sipped the beer, she searched for nonexistent alternatives. "This knowledge might kill you."

Stillwell shrugged. "Our days are numbered. Forewarned is forearmed. Misery loves company. Take your pick. My first wife had a proverb for every occasion."

Penelope had already decided she could trust Stillwell and Richard. "I was told my father died in a shipwreck in the Baltic Sea in November of 1642. In April of '44, I received a letter written by him in Massachusetts the year before." From memory she recited the contents of the letter to her silent, attentive audience and explained what she had deciphered.

Stillwell rose and refilled his and her beer mugs. "Quite a story. Have you contacted John Throckmorton? He's an honest man."

Penelope recited the letter from Throckmorton word for word. Speaking was easier than thinking.

"John Kent," Stillwell mused. "John Kent."

"Did you meet him during the Indian wars?"

"No," Stillwell said. "At least not by that name. But you implied he might have been in disguise."

Richard said, "I knew some men of dubious character in the navy who changed their names. But they usually kept the same initials."

"J.K." Stillwell leaned back in his chair and sipped beer. "That sounds familiar."

Ann pointed to the plant in the basket. "What does this plant have to do with your father?"

Penelope picked up the plant as though it would break. "A dried leaf like this was in the letter I just told ..."

An abrupt movement and a loud crash made Penelope nearly spill her beer.

Stillwell had jumped up and knocked over his chair. "A brass locket! With the initials JK!"

"Yes!" cried Penelope. "My father carries...carried a tiny portrait of my mother in a brass locket. Did you see it?"

"I have it," said Lieutenant Stillwell.

"Did you kill him?" Penelope covered her mouth with her hand and stared at Lieutenant Stillwell and then at his wife.

Chapter 35

Long Island

Sunday, 11 October 1648

The Stillwell house was as silent as an empty forest. Penelope searched for a way to retrieve her accusation. Feet scraped the floor. Someone coughed.

Ann whispered, "Nicholas?"

"No," Nicholas Stillwell said. "Of course not. I found his body. Nicky, go retrieve the brass locket from that worn-out musket-ball pouch."

"I didn't mean that." Penelope hid her face in her hands.

"Of course, you didn't." Ann patted her shoulder. "This is all so sudden. You're merely overwrought."

Nicky returned and dumped out the contents of a leather pouch.

Penelope's hand plucked out the locket from a jumble of metal items. "I had an identical one—my mother's—but I lost it in the shipwreck." Her fingers instinctively worked the tiny clasp that opened her father's locket. The portrait of her mother was a water-stained lump of rubbish. She dropped the case.

Ann squeezed Penelope's shoulder. "Nicholas, tell us everything."

Stillwell righted his chair and drained his beer mug. "I'll start at the beginning. An Indian war began here in New Amsterdam in the fall of '42, about the same time the civil war started in England. Several tribes of Indians raided the entire colony and drove most of the survivors into Fort New Amsterdam for safety. By spring we thought it was over. That's when Private Stout and I accompanied Lady Moody to settle here in Gravesend, but attacks resumed and we abandoned Gravesend."

Richard nodded, confirming the events.

Stillwell continued, "Near the end of summer in '43, we saw smoke from a new set of attacks. I led a rescue party to Vredeland. A few of Throckmorton's people were killed along with almost all of the family of his neighbor, Mrs. Ann Hutchison. While we escorted the survivors to Fort New Amsterdam, Munkey scented two long-dead bodies in a blackberry thicket. Most people assumed the Indians had killed them back in the spring, but it was murder."

Silence fell over the room.

Penelope whispered, "How did you know?"

Ann squeezed Penelope's shoulder again. "She doesn't need to hear any more of this."

Penelope shook off Ann's comforting hand and said in a low, intense voice, "I know how aborigines kill people. I want to know how Europeans kill."

Stillwell glanced at Richard, who shrugged. The lieutenant intertwined his fingers, placed them on the table in front of him, and stared at them. "One man was stabbed in the back. One was stabbed in the heart. Both knives—the cheap trade knives—were left behind. The bodies were still clothed except the boots were missing."

"The *wilden* are fond of European clothes but they don't wear boots," Penelope said.

Richard added, "They don't leave iron knives behind."

"They don't hide dead bodies under bushes," Nicky said, "that shed leaves in the fall."

Stillwell continued. "Therefore, they were killed in the spring or summer. Probably in the springtime since that's when your father arrived at Throckmorton's. I doubt a European could have hidden his presence for long."

"Thou hast kept the locket for identification?" Richard asked.

Stillwell nodded. "It was next to an empty money belt."

Ann asked, "What did you do with...with..."

"The Throckmorton survivors were distraught and in a hurry." Stillwell looked Penelope in the eye. "I came back a few days later with a squad of soldiers and two coffins. We buried them in the cemetery behind the fort beside the other victims." He lowered his voice. "I can show you."

Penelope nodded, feeling numb. "Did you say words over my father?"

"Yes, we did."

Ann tried to escort her from the room. "Maybe you should lie down."

"No," Penelope said, "My mind already knew. I just needed proof to quell a doubting heart." The locket, made of brass to withstand ocean voyages, had been carelessly tossed aside when the robber determined it was not gold. She visualized a murderer thrusting a knife into John Kent's beating heart. The last thing her father saw was the discarded portrait of his wife.

Her sorrow transformed into anger at the murderers, into a determination to bring them to justice or to death, whichever came first. Their death or hers.

Richard asked Lieutenant Stillwell, "Couldst thou identify the other man?"

Stillwell shook his head. "Dead for months."

How did Stillwell know they had been dead so long? She didn't want to know. She knew enough.

Richard pointed toward the plant in the basket. "Is that what Mr. Kent searched for?"

She stroked a leaf. "It must be."

"What's it good for?" asked Ann.

"I wish I knew." Penelope fondled a red berry. "His letter said it would make him rich."

"May I see the roots?" asked Stillwell.

"It's not ginger." Penelope pushed the container across the table.

Stilwell lifted the plant from the basket and snapped a small piece off the end of the root. The inside of the pale yellow root had many concentric rings like a tree stump.

He sniffed it. "I never saw it fresh but it reminds me of the dried roots the Panmuncky medicine men in Virginia traded for. They steeped it and claimed the decoction helped the sick and injured recover faster. Indian runners chewed it to increase stamina on long trails. Let me think. What did the medicine man call it?"

"If it grows here," Ann asked, "why doesn't it grow in Virginia?"

Richard said, "Each plant has its preferred range. Wheat grew well in Nottinghamshire but poorly two hundred miles north in Cumberland, where oats and barley dominated."

Penelope sat up straight. "The medicine woman steeped a medicine for me from a root like that. She called it *garantoquen.*

Stillwell nodded. "Yes, that's the name. Means man-shaped. There's a similar bluish root called fever root."

"How," asked Ann, "can an Indian root make a white man rich?"

Richard said, "The same way an Indian weed like tobacco can make a white man rich. Ye ship it from where it's common and cheap to where it's rare and expensive."

Penelope regarded Richard with new respect. How had he acquired his business knowledge?

"Lieutenant, where didst thou find...find them?"

"In the craggy rocks above the Collect Pond, about a mile and a half north of the wall."

Richard nodded. "That's eight miles from Throckmorton's and rather close to the village for men trying to hide."

"They couldn't find the berries." Nicky pointed to the plant in the basket. "They searched in the spring or summer, but berries appear in the fall."

Stillwell slapped his thigh. "The boy's got a point. The pond and crag are obvious landmarks, good places to meet with people."

"Meet with whom?" asked Ann.

"The murderers," replied Richard.

"And the names of those murderers?" asked Ann.

Blank faces met blank faces.

"Mr. Kent wasn't accustomed to the woods," said Lieutenant Stillwell. "They picked a landmark anyone could find."

"Even a merchant and a sailor." Penelope remembered being disoriented after a few minutes in the forest. Without the children to guide her, she might still be wandering. Anything visible above the trees made a good guidepost.

"They threw the bodies into a blackberry thicket near the pond," added Stillwell. "If it hadn't been for the Indian scares, they would have been found much sooner. Nobody picked berries in the woods that summer."

"Sailors," said Ann. "Friends of the German sailor."

"New Amsterdam is a port." Penelope compared Manhattan's empty harbor upon her arrival with the bustling wharves of Amsterdam with hundreds of ships and thousands of seamen. "There are dozens of sailors here."

"Scores." Richard fiddled with a pipe and tobacco pouch.

"Over a hundred, including former sailors from five or six years ago." Stillwell pulled out his pouch, shook it, and turned it upside down. Crumbs fell out.

Ann asked, "How much would one pay for a root?"

Richard pushed his tobacco pouch across the table.

"If you're rich and sick, you would pay any amount." Penelope's father had frantically searched throughout Amsterdam for a doctor able to cure her mother and infant brother of childbed fever.

"Does it work?" Ann rubbed a leaf between her fingers.

Penelope pointed to her shoulder. "I survived."

Ann said, "This root's too valuable to let rot. You must either dry it or store it in a root cellar."

"What's a root cellar?" asked Penelope.

Richard grinned behind his tobacco smoke. "Where didst thou grow up? A root cellar is a hole in the ground to keep roots from either freezing or sprouting during the winter."

Penelope laughed. "I grew up in a marsh. In Amsterdam, a hole in the ground fills up with water."

The sound of pile drivers had been almost constant in Amsterdam as tree trunks that had been floated down the river from German forests were pounded deep into the swampy mire of a construction site. Houses in Amsterdam floated on mud, except when pilings slipped and a house tilted. Penelope sighed. She knew how houses were built in a swamp but not what to do with a root.

Stillwell said, "The Indians dry most botanicals so they'll keep beyond spring."

"How do you dry a root?" asked Penelope.

"I'll show you." Ann plucked the *garantoquen* plant from the basket, sliced off the leafy stems, tied threads around the root pieces, and hung them over a nail protruding from a ceiling beam near the fireplace. "Give it a few weeks. If you have a bunch of roots, a fish net works well."

Penelope picked up the greenery from the table and stowed it in an apron pocket. These leaves formed her only surviving link to her father because his leaves and letter were in the secret compartment of the missing globe.

* * * * *

At work the next week, Herrmann approached Penelope's desk and hovered behind her. She dropped her quill and looked up at him, noting the way he nervously shuffled several papers he carried.

"A report that concerns you," he said while avoiding her eyes, "but might distress you yesterday I heard."

She looked at him warily, trying to keep her thoughts neutral. Sundry matters had troubled her mind lately.

"The preliminary report on the salvage of *de Kath,* it is ready. The salt that was recovered is enough to pay wages to the sailors. God receives blame for the wreck."

Without thinking, she pulled the papers from his hand. Over two hundred barrels of salt owned by the GWC and one half-chest of ginger consigned to Jansen and Company had been salvaged.

Eureka. Each barrel had an owner. She merely needed to learn who shipped plant material from New Amsterdam, besides tobacco and ginger.

"Mr. Herrmann, how can I see every manifest of every ship that sailed from New Amsterdam in the last six years?"

"Why? That information I don't need."

"But I do." She stood up and glared at him. "I need to see it now."

He took a step back as though in fear. "But...but."

Penelope sat down and buried her face in her hands, trying to regain her composure. "Please."

"The papers," said Herrmann, still keeping his distance, "keep themselves in the *fiscaal*'s office but papers are confidential. Without a valid reason one can't see them."

She looked up. "What's a valid reason?"

He looked at her as though she were mad and must be humored. He was probably correct. "To be sure inventory records are correct, to make a copy of lost documents."

"I just spilled beer on a stack of documents. I need to make copies."

"What beer? Where?" He looked around alarmed.

"In my imagination," she said. "As an excuse to rummage through the tax files. How can I get two hours alone with the records?"

"Through van Dyke's official papers, you wish to rummage? Are you mad?"

"No, not mad, but angry and determined."

Herrmann rubbed his chin. "One still thinks it mad but the tax office just before lunch we visit. A tax rate on a manifest we contest. That his paper is incorrect makes the wager with *Fiscaal* van Dyck. The file he pulls. The wager I lose. The file you straighten while my purse pays for a lunch and three beers."

"Won't there be a clerk in the office?"

"No. The clerk weds two weeks ago. Every day for lunch with his wife he goes."

She stood up. "Let's go now."

"Now? But Jannetje with lunch awaits me. Today her mother cooks lamb chops. Furthermore, today a trial makes itself. There van Dyck finds himself."

"Tomorrow then." Penelope was too excited to sit. At last, she had some clues to work with. She merely had to learn who exported roots from Manhattan.

Chapter 36

New Amsterdam

Wednesday, 14 October 1648

The next day Augustine Herrmann's scheme worked as planned. As soon as Penelope promised to re-file the documents, *schout* Hendrick van Dyck put on his hat and dragged Herrmann out the door and toward a tavern.

Fortunately, the numerous oak filing cabinets were clearly labeled with date ranges. Penelope opened the drawer with the most recent documents.

The first manifest was for the ship *de Witte Paard,* or *White Horse,* sailing in a few days. Verbrugge was shipping a huge number of furs, a score of barrels of smoked oysters, and a dozen barrels of sugar. Where did Verbrugge obtain sugar? Jansen and Company paid export duty on five chests of ginger. GWC listed twenty barrels of salted cod. They must have traded some of *de Kath*'s salt to New England fisherman for stockfish. It was too early for tobacco. How could the ship make any money a third loaded? That's probably what the Nineteen Gentlemen continually asked Director-General Stuyvesant.

She scolded herself for snooping into other people's business when she needed to catch a murderer. She searched more rapidly, being careful to keep the papers in order. January was prime shipping season for tobacco, March for furs and feathers, salt in the fall and early winter. Sugar could arrive at any time. Salt and sugar were exempt from export duties because they originated elsewhere in the GWC domain and were merely trans-shipped. One year New Netherland must have enjoyed exceptional good weather to explain the export of one hundred barrels of wheat and barley to New England.

She was disappointed practically nothing was exported in 1643, the year her father arrived. But the Indian wars explained that. She went back one more year and stopped.

Except for furs and tobacco, New Amsterdam exported little except occasional grain, dried peas, and salted meat to the Caribbean islands, and barrels of smoked oysters and a few chests of ginger a year to Amsterdam. Smuggling likely explained the absence of records.

"What are you doing?" From behind her came a pleasant voice trying to sound gruff.

"Who? Me?" She glanced over her shoulder at a young soldier, thankful he wasn't the clerk, and deliberately avoided eye contact and easy identification. Not that a woman with a bad arm could disguise herself.

"Yes, you," the soldier said, "the stranger poking around in the official records."

She chattered like a tiresome cook Liesbeth had fired after a week. "Merely doing what a woman always does—cleaning up after men. They tell me to file this while they go to lunch. At least, I don't have to cook or wash up. Doesn't anyone here know the order of the alphabet? Who's responsible for this mess? A blind dog could do this better. Ha. That explains it. When the letter P looks more like an E, what can you expect?" She yanked out some papers and stuffed them back in the same place, hoping her body hid the details of her deception.

She turned around, put her one good hand on her hip, and glared around the *fiscaal*'s office. Van Dyck's desk was a muddle. She waved a finger in disgust. "Look at that mess. Thank the good Lord, I don't work here." She paid attention to the soldier for the first time and pointed a finger at his shirt. "Look at you. Don't you know anybody who can wash and iron decently? Your mother would be ashamed."

She tsked, tsked as she walked around the soldier and out the door and maintained her stance of indignation until out of sight.

Mostly she had detected an absence of information. How was she to detect smugglers if the Director-General and his soldiers couldn't? Lieutenant Stillwell would know.

* * * * *

Several days later, as soon as Penelope entered Herrmann's factory, she spotted an object swathed in oiled cloth. Its shape made the contents obvious. She knelt on the floor and unwrapped a globe, her father's globe, complete with its wooden stand. She stood, took a step back, and held onto Herrmann's arm for support. Together they admired the thirty-year-old globe.

How in the world had Lieutenant Stillwell caused her globe to reappear? Ann was such a fortunate woman to have such a wonderful husband.

"I've prepared a place of honor for it," said Herrmann, artist and flat mapmaker. Near a front window where it could be admired from inside or outside, but out of the path of traffic and of the bright morning light that would fade the colors, Herrmann had placed a small, ornate table with turned legs that matched the turnings of the wooden stand. He reverently placed the masterpiece on its shrine.

Penelope ran her fingers over the familiar surface of the globe again. "I loved to hear my father tell of his adventures. The forests around here make me think of potash."

Herrmann said, "One reminds me. A month ago Seth Verbrugge and I drink beer. To start a potash business he talks. To hire you as advisor he should."

Penelope said, "If he'll relieve my debt, I'll advise him: Don't let free wood and a high price for potash blind you to the absence of cheap labor."

Mention of her debt brought back a memory of two let-ters and three coins in a bag under the stand. *Where they still there?*

She said to Herrmann, "There's a weak spot on the stand. Please hold the globe while I check it."

Herrmann lifted the globe while Penelope felt under-neath. She opened the secret compartment and felt inside. Empty. She pulled out the drawer, turned it over, and rapped it on the table. Still empty. She exhaled a long breath and ignored Herrmann's raised eyebrows.

Had the thief thrown the letters away? She had memo-rized the contents, contents that would be meaningless to anyone else. Anyone except her father's murderer, who would now know the owner of the globe was the daughter of the Englishman who scoured the forests of Manhattan for a spindly plant in the company of a traitorous German.

How could she be a credible threat when she didn't know the name of the plant or the name of the murderer or how his smuggling worked? But did the murderer know she knew so little? Would he interpret the ostentatious placement of the globe in Herrmann's window as a chal-lenge or an admission of her ignorance? Nothing risked, nothing gained.

She shifted her chair and writing table so the globe was in view whenever she lifted her head to recall memories of good times during her former life in Amsterdam.

Every man who walked past the window earned a stare. On the street, she looked behind her at every odd sound and evaluated every stranger.

* * * * *

The rest of October passed much the same for Penelope—work with Herrmann, wariness on the streets, peaceful weeknights with Ann and the two girls, busy weekends in Manhattan or Gravesend. Her meaningless existence mostly involved marking days off a calendar, an activity that aptly suited her soul. Would time soften the harsh memories of the past and open a door to a future?

Lieutenant Stillwell had advised patience. Smuggling was plentiful and questions about it were delicate. When asked, "Who is involved?" he answered, "In smuggling? Who isn't?"

On a Monday she turned the page of Herrmann's calendar to November of 1648. On a November day six years earlier she had begun to understand death. First newspaper accounts of a thousand Englishmen dead at the battle of Edgehill. Then the report of her father's death.

Now an Englishman offered her a chance at happiness, or so Ann claimed. Surely a promise of bliss was a trick of fate, as had happened so often to Odysseus. When the Greek wanderer finally returned to Ithaca, he came alone, for all his companions had perished along the way.

Matthew had called her an angel. Was she an angel of death?

Yesterday, she had ignored snatches of conversation borne on the wind. Thirty yards away, Ann talked to Richard Stout while the Stillwells prepared the sloop on a Sunday afternoon to return to Gravesend. Penelope preferred to stand alone and stare at the East River. The overcast day, irritating cries of seagulls, and a chill breeze matched her dismal mood.

Richard Stout wrote his own death warrant by courting her. Her conscience couldn't bear the responsibility for another death. She could save Richard's life by sending him away.

Or should she go away? Was she afraid to return to Amsterdam because it required an ocean voyage and possible shipwreck? Or admitting failure to find her father's murderer? Or because it required confessing her responsibility for Matthew's death to his family? Which type of coward was she?

"Mrs. Prince?" Richard's voice startled her. "Mayhap this is an awkward time for discussion."

She frowned at his brash interruption. He made more noise than a dozen seagulls. Couldn't he tell she wanted to be alone with her thoughts?

Richard twisted his hat in his fingers. "My tobacco yielded well. I'm prepared to pay thy debt to Verbrugge."

Penelope stiffened and almost replied inappropriately with the adage: s*peak not of my debts unless you mean to pay them.* Instead she stared at him until he dropped his eyes. "That's a kind offer but I'll extricate my own debt."

"I dunna comprehend how thou canst achieve that goal?"

"It doesn't concern you."

He rotated his hat in slow circles. "I care deep about thy welfare."

"Then care about my feelings. I'll not be bought and sold like a cow."

"I dunna intend to offend thee." He twisted his cloth hat into a knot.

"Is that why you're silent so often? You're afraid of offending me with your words?"

Her challenge hung in the air.

Richard looked up from his pitiful hat. "Yes, for I...I...I love thee."

"Love? You're either blind or a fool." She was surprised her own sarcastic remark was delivered calmly, even kindly. She had never confronted such a stubborn man. At least not a stubborn man she respected.

"Some say any man in love is a blind fool." He revolved his hat between his fingers in small, slow circles.

"Mr. Stout, I like you." She directed her eyes and her words to his feet to spare his feelings. "I do not love you."

"Not yet."

The simple words hung in the air, not as a question but as a statement of fact.

Penelope raised her head and tried to look through his eyes into his soul. She saw pain. And hope. She could not see beyond. In his face, she saw endurance. And courage. And forgiveness. And a glimmer of happiness as he returned her close regard.

"Not yet," she echoed with ambiguity, wondering about the future.

"The Bible says there's a season for everything under the sun." He held her stare.

How could she discourage him? How could she save his life? She straightened her posture, folded her arms beneath her breasts as best as she could, and forced a neutral expression onto her face.

"The Bible says many things, Mr. Stout, but I must warn you. There are some things my husband—if I ever take another husband—must never say to me. My husband must never say, "Goodwife, you shall not.' God has already told me what I shall not do. My husband may say, 'Goodwife, it would displease me.'"

He continued to regard her carefully. Was he trying to see into her soul? But she was explaining her soul to him.

"My husband must never say, 'Goodwife, I order you.' The *schout* and the magistrate may order me but not my husband. My husband may say, 'Goodwife, I request you.'"

Strangely, the glimmer of happiness in his face seemed to increase.

"Mr. Stout, as you well know, I'm in debt for a large sum of money."

"I've money enough for the two of us."

What would it require to discourage him from this foolish notion of marriage?

"I was raised Dutch, Mr. Stout. I expect a Dutch marriage of partners, not husband and slave. My name will never be Mrs. Richard Stout." She recalled sitting in Matthew's church in a row populated with old Mrs. Prince, younger Miss Prince, Mrs. Prince, the future Ms. Prince, and elder Miss Prince. "Mayhap, my name could become Mrs. Penelope Stout. If you were to have sons, they would take wives and I refuse be another hen in a flock of Mrs. Stouts."

The glimmer of hope in his face multiplied as he held his ground before her onslaught of discouraging words. She had erred grievously by mentioning sons.

"I'm a person and I'll remain a person. My husband may take charge of my meager possessions. I shall remain in charge of my soul and my life and my name." She found his steady gaze discomfiting.

She frowned. "I know men who would've slapped my wicked face for those remarks."

Richard smiled. "I know men who would gladly throw thee into gaol for thy remarks."

She chewed on her lip. "I know men who would walk away and never look back."

His smile widened, if such were possible. "I know one man who's standing here, still in love with thee despite thy remarks. Mayhap he's in love with thy soul and thy person and desires to preserve them and share them."

"Mr. Stout, I still fear such a man to be a fool." There was no jest in her voice.

"I was a fool thirteen years ago. I had sentiments like thine. My father said to me, 'Thou shalt not.' We argued. He didna relent. I abandoned my home in anger. But I also abandoned what I was arguing for. I was a fool thirteen years ago."

She had been too consumed with her past to speculate about another's. Now she confronted his person, his unknown history, and his loneliness and suffering. He had willingly talked about the present and the future but never the past of which he now hinted.

"Mayhap you have requirements for your next wife?"

"There's mere one thing the woman who will be my wife must do, Mrs. Prince."

Her body stiffened at the word. "Only one must?"

"She must willing say, 'Yes.' Is that such a difficult requirement?"

She had no reply for it was a thorny question, one requiring long consideration.

He made no effort to depart but remained there looking cryptically at her.

Would she ever be rid of him, so she could enjoy her despair in private?

Recklessly, she spoke again. "Mr. Stout, a husband and a wife should have no secrets." She removed her cap to reveal her short, wretched hair and then tilted her mutilated head downward to clearly display more ugliness.

She capped her head and faced him again. "That's a reminder of God's punishment of me."

"It's a reminder God spared thy life." His lips held a mere glimmer of a smile.

"Mr. Stout, what are you thinking now?"

He blushed. "My second thought is not seemly."

"Do you withhold a secret from me?" She stepped back.

"Since you insist, ma'am. Though thou mayest regret it. A proverb I heard long ago in a tavern in Nottinghamshire says, 'A wise man weds a bald woman for she will be eternal grateful.'"

They continued to regard each other solemnly.

"I tried to warn thee," he said.

She raised her hand into the air. "You're standing too far away for me to reach your cheek, for such a remark deserves a slap." But she had commanded him to tell and thus lowered her hand. "Or a kiss."

He immediately stepped forward, within reach.

"Do you often take bold risks, Mr. Stout?"

"Only when the reward is well worth the risk."

She stared at this peculiar man who was not discouraged by harsh words or harsh sights. Who didn't shirk hard work. Who looked ahead to a future.

A future. She didn't have a future. Is that what she needed? Hope for the future implied life and purpose. They seemed distant memories, like childhood dreams.

She gently reached out her hand to his cheek and stroked it, felt the afternoon stubble of his shaven face, the warmth of his flush, his stolid boldness.

From the distance came Lieutenant Stillwell's call, "Are you coming?" and Ann's faint scolding, "Not now, you fool."

Richard said, "I'll hold thee to thy promise of passion—a slap or a kiss." He turned his head slowly, forcing her motionless hand to slide across his face and his mouth. He kissed the palm of her hand, stared into her eyes, mayhap into her soul, turned, and walked away.

Passion? She stared at his retreating figure. That was long gone, chased away by sadness and guilt.

Back in Herrmann's factory, she pulled out the dried *garantoquen* root and stared. Being indebted to Richard instead of Verbrugge would complicate her already confused situation. She would feel like Richard's slave, bought and paid for. He already owned one slave. She refused to be his second.

In her hands, the root seemed poised between life and death: old, gnarly, wrinkled. Or was she describing her soul? She shook her head to clear it. How much could one root be worth? Would Herrmann know? How could he know its value when she didn't know its name?

If she revealed it to the world, the murderer would be forewarned. How could one small root make such a difference? On the other hand, would ten roots matter? Or a hundred? What if she gathered roots from the forest to sell, as her father had planned?

She didn't know its name, what it was worth, or how to sell it. But she had faith in her father's judgment. If he were alive now, he would gather *garantoquen* roots. She looked forward to next weekend in Gravesend where she and the children would rummage around the woods. Already she felt her father smiling down upon her.

Chapter 37

New Amsterdam

Sunday, 8 November 1648

Upon the return from Gravesend to Manhattan three weeks later, Lieutenant and Ann Stillwell announced they expected to remove to Gravesend in the first week of December, less than a month away. Ann invited Penelope to come with them.

Penelope turned her back on her friend, gripped the gunwale of the lieutenant's sloop, and studied the passing shoreline. She had long ignored the inevitability of this event because she was forced to choose and all her options involved drastic change. She had no place to hide, either on the small boat or in life.

If she removed to Gravesend as a part of the Stillwell household, then she would lose her job at Herrmann's and become what—a housemaid and a nursemaid in exchange for room and board. Her accumulated wages were far from adequate to pay off her debt to Verbrugge. Her stash of *garantoquen* roots grew slowly because the plants were harder to find than expected.

After two months of organizing Herrmann's accumulation of years of office chaos, she could see the end in another month or two. He might continue her employment but at lesser hours and lesser pay since she could keep up with the incoming workload in a few hours per day. Perhaps, she could rent a bed from Jannetje Varleth's mother?

Change. Change was going to happen—one way or another. It always did.

Or she could return to Amsterdam. A note from Liesbeth would buy passage and her debt would transfer. If Liesbeth lived and was willing. Return home maimed, in debt, and broken in spirit! How could she explain to Grandfather Prince that Matthew's death was meaningless? How could she forgive herself for abandoning the search for her father's murderer?

No, she would sooner go to the nearest tavern and become a barmaid.

Or she could marry Richard Stout—or someone. Why did she save that as the last option?

Mrs. Stout, she whispered to the waves to test the words. Bland. No enthusiasm. No dread either. Maybe she wasn't feeling anything today, except worry.

Marrying would hinder her search for the murderer. How could she make progress being stuck in Gravesend at the edge of New Netherland? Not that she was making any headway in Manhattan. She was becalmed and merely drifting in a circle, as though stranded in the Sargasso Sea with no chance to escape.

Good sensible advice from Liesbeth was what she needed. Her letter had been dispatched less than three months ago. With luck, Liesbeth would be reading it now and writing a reply—a reply that might arrive in another three months, with luck.

One of the boys called, "Land, Ho." After an hour of lonely moodiness Penelope pretended to cheer her up as they said their goodbyes to the men. She volunteered to carry Baby Alice through the treacherous footing of the muddy streets to force her mind to concentrate on the precious little bundle rather than her bleak future. At least she had a future, bleak or otherwise. Matthew didn't. Her father didn't.

* * * * *

When Penelope arrived at Herrmann's factory earlier than usual Monday morning after a sleepless night, the door was locked. She sat on the stoop and waited. A pair of small brown birds dropped from the sky, cocked their heads, and stared at her. She began to sob.

She scarcely noticed Herrmann's hand on her shoulder or his questions. He led her down the street and entrusted her to Jannetje's mother.

Mother Varleth sat beside Penelope and took both her hands. "Penelope, you've never truly grieved for your husband, have you? You've not wept like this before, have you?"

Amidst the tears, she whispered, "Once."

Mother Varleth, still holding Penelope's hands, pressed them against her breast. "Feel the heart of a woman who knows God loves her and comforts her after the world hurts her. You should accept God as you accept life: health and sickness, life and death, rich or poor, always knowing comfort is just a prayer away."

"Accept life and death? No, I can't." Penelope bowed her head. "I blame myself for everything that happened. I'm responsible we voyaged across an ocean to disaster. I blame God for punishing Matthew in order to punish me." She wanted to admit blame for her father's death too but kept silent on that sin.

Mother Varleth lifted Penelope's chin and looked directly into her eyes. "A God of Love lets us make our own mistakes. If he rescued us from all our follies, then we would never grow to maturity, but remain helpless babies. He's sad at our mistakes, and grieves at our errors, rejoices at our triumphs for He loves us like a parent."

Penelope blinked away tears. "God didn't punish me?"

"No, God loves you and wants you to live. You must be strong enough to grieve, to forgive, to live."

"I can grieve for Matthew, but I can't forgive myself. Or God." The word "forgive" was easy to say, difficult to do.

"Now, tell Matthew farewell by telling me how you miss him. Remember him but let him go. God has received him. God does not blame you. Do not blame God. Now you pray for Matthew while I prepare sassafras tea."

Penelope bowed her head and tried to let the spirit and voice of God enter as Matthew had said he often did. But she only felt guilt for Matthew and despair at her failure to solve her father's death. Murder, she corrected herself.

Jannetje served two cups of steaming liquid that smelled faintly of lemon. "Careful. This sassafras tea is hot."

Penelope stirred the tea, her spoon swirling around bits of roots. "What's sassafras?"

"We can't afford the newfangled tea from China that's all the rage back home. This is the root of a local tree. The *wilden* say it will calm you and restore your spirits." Jannetje blew on a spoonful and sipped it. "It's not as powerful as ginseng but who except the Director-General can afford ginseng or real tea?"

"Ginseng?" asked Penelope, remembering a cup of hot tea that *Mevrouw* Stuyvesant's maid had served her and said was expensive. "What's that?"

Mother Varleth joined them with a cup. "According to Chinese legends or perhaps the boasts of Amsterdam merchants, ginseng's a magic elixir that cures whatever ails you. Ha. If you have enough money. I've heard it sells for its weight in silver. But nothing is too costly for a Chinese emperor or the wife of the Director-General of New Netherland."

"Does *Mevrouw* Stuyvesant really have some?" Penelope asked. To many people, anything worth its weight in precious metal was worth killing for. Could the roots hanging beside Ann's fireplace be ginseng?

"She has anything she wants." Jannetje made a face. "Why not ginseng?"

Penelope grasped Mother Varleth's wrist. "What does ginseng look like?"

The older woman chuckled. "You might as well ask me what the King of Spain's crown looks like. Who needs ginseng? This sassafras has certainly perked you up."

Penelope sipped her sassafras tea. After being ejected from the Director-General's mansion, how could she contrive an opportunity to see *Mevrouw* Stuyvesant's ginseng to determine whether her root was the same?

Excusing herself as quickly as politeness allowed, Penelope hurried down the street toward Fort New Amsterdam and bumped into a woman with a basket of eggs. She apologized, hurried on, then stopped. "Wait, *mevrouw*. How much for the eggs?"

The housewife smiled. "How many? I have two dozen."

Penelope said, "The entire basketful."

"Four stuivers."

"If you come by the factory of Augustine Herrmann tomorrow, I'll give you six stuivers. But I need these now." She practically yanked the basket out of the woman's hand and resumed her hasty approach to Fort New Amsterdam.

At the gate house to the fort, she smiled, held up the basket for inspection, and continued walking. The guard scarcely noticed. As she approached the mansion, she searched for the rear door, the one for servants and tradesmen. A *neger* raked a gravel path that headed in a likely direction. She followed it and accepted the slave's slight bow. The path curved around the stone building and branched into three lanes. She took the one to the kitchen that was separated from the main house by twenty feet.

Penelope leaned over the open half door. "Where is Sara?"

The cook, busy with lunch preparations, looked up and nodded toward the mansion. "In the dining room."

Penelope quickly approached the house, climbed the three steps, and hesitated. Through the glass, she saw a young *neger* girl ironing shirts. Penelope knocked on the door and hid the basket of eggs behind her. In her best imitation of Judith Stuyvesant's tone of voice, Penelope said to the girl, "Don't stand there gawking. Fetch Sara immediately."

The girl gave a brief curtsy and disappeared. Penelope sighed, thankful Stuyvesant's servants obeyed first and never asked questions.

The girl returned with Sara and pointed to Penelope. Sara scarcely looked at her. "I'm busy. What do you want?"

Penelope held up her arm in its sling, displayed the basket, and whispered, "Shh. Pretend I'm selling eggs."

Sara stared at Penelope, looked over her shoulder, and finally said, "Are the eggs fresh?"

Penelope said, "Of course. Come and see."

Sara exited the house, shut the door, and peered into the basket.

Penelope spoke softly, "On my first night here, you steeped a root to make me feel better. You said it was expensive. What is it called?"

Sara asked, "*Mevrouw* Prince, are you in trouble?"

"Only if someone recognizes me. Was it called ginseng?"

"Yes, that's the name. The mistress brought it with her from Amsterdam."

Penelope forced her mouth into a sad pout. "Please, Sara. I need to see the ginseng. I don't want to take any of it. I just need to see it and touch it and smell it. Please."

"Smell it? Why?"

"It's complicated. Do you love your daughters?"

Sara nodded. "Of course."

"I love my father just as much. It's to help him. Please. Just to touch it and smell it."

Sara hesitated.

Penelope thrust forward the basket. "Take the eggs. Bring back the ginseng hidden in the basket. I need to see it."

"Only half is left." Sara accepted the basket.

"That's enough."

Sara went inside. To Penelope it seemed like hours before she returned though surely it was only minutes.

Sara said, "Sorry. The mistress insisted upon an errand. Here."

Penelope pulled back a linen cloth and stared at the dry, gnarly root that looked like a yellowish snowman with an elongated belly, a small round ball for a head, and one skinny arm. She pinched it. It felt spongy but solid. She lifted it to her nose and sniffed. The earthy odor was much fainter than the aroma from her freshly harvested plant but it was the same.

Her father's treasure from the earth was ginseng.

She smiled broadly, tenderly pulled the cloth over the root, and pushed the basket into Sara's hands. "Thank you. And forget you saw me. I'm merely a woman selling eggs."

"But I didn't pay you."

"Yes, you did." Penelope touched Sara on the forearm. "By being a friend."

Penelope turned and walked away, her mind whirling.

Someone had killed her father because he tried to harvest ginseng that grew wild in the forest. Most likely the German sailor had sneaked into New Amsterdam either to betray her father or to ask an old comrade for help. Either way, the German led the enemy to her father and they both paid for that mistake with their lives.

If her father's murderer still harvested ginseng and sold it for its weight in precious metal, he should be rich. A rich sailor? That should be a rare, but noticeable, occurrence. Or else he spent money like a drunken sailor, like the treasure-finders from *de Kath*. And like them, spending ill-gotten treasure would be his downfall.

How could she identify this unknown and get him arrested? Ha! An arrest was unlikely because the *schout* was lazy, corrupt, and incompetent. She would have to identify, locate, and trap the killer.

* * * * *

Outside Ann Stillwell's kitchen that afternoon, Richard Stout sat on the bench in the mid-November sunshine, entranced by the dexterity of Penelope's fingers. Her maimed shoulder was no hindrance as she rapidly shelled the bushel of beans he had brought as his contribution to the household economy.

Occasional glances at her face brought Richard no pleasure because her countenance was downcast, not from looking at the work in her lap, but surely from tormented thoughts. A quick half-smile crossed her face as she bent toward him to retrieve more beans from the reed basket.

He concentrated on her right forearm, visible because her sleeve was still rolled up for kitchen tasks and because she always positioned herself to his left. The smooth skin shifted with the motion of tendons and muscles underneath. Fine hairs glistened silver in the afternoon light. To watch her thrilled his heart. His thoughts drifted to the pleasure of stroking that supple skin. He jerked his mind back to morality and stared at his own calloused fingers.

A moderate breeze cascaded yellow leaves from a nearby maple tree. A minute later a single leaf fluttered down and landed a foot from his boot—golden, symmetrical, fragile. Like her face as the golden rays of the setting sun gilded it.

Why did that leaf fall now in the stillness and not earlier in the breeze? The Bible claimed there was a time for everything. Would he recognize the right time or let it slip by, to drift away on a breeze like an autumn leaf?

Bold and decisive action won the fair maiden, Lieutenant Stillwell recommended. Or led over the abyss, others advised. He was more experienced at waiting. Too experienced at waiting. Weary of waiting.

He wanted to converse with her now, yet attempts to engage her produced short, distracted answers. He appreciated a woman who could hold her tongue but her silence today was too much. He waited. Patiently. Too patiently.

* * * * *

At work on Tuesday, Penelope wrestled with the option of moving with her friends to Gravesend, marrying Richard Stout, or remaining in Manhattan.

The debt to Verbrugge still hung over her head. If she made quick money by offering ginseng for sale, she would alert the murderer and put her life in danger. However, if

Herrmann offered ginseng for sale and claimed it was shipped from Amsterdam, then she could observe who was interested.

Would a murderer connect her to ginseng merely because her employer offered it for sale? Or connect her to a friend who inquired about smuggling? Or identify her as the daughter to whom a man wrote a letter about finding a fortune in the woods?

Herrmann's job was to import and to sell. Lieutenant Stillwell was famed for knowing all rumors. Neither was doing anything unusual. Maybe the letter had been thrown away unread.

She walked to Herrmann's desk and dropped ginseng upon the ledger he perused.

He picked up the root. "What's this?"

Only the two of them were present, yet she whispered, "Ginseng."

"How—"

"Shh. Don't ask questions. And never reveal the source. Say it came with a shipment of botanicals from Amsterdam. Display it for sale and see who is interested."

Herrmann scratched his nearly bald head. "In all of New Netherland, it exists only three men with the money for an entire ginseng root."

She leaned closer and whispered, "I'm more interested in men who display an interest in its source, not its price."

Herrmann frowned. "Not interested in price? To converse with Jannetje's mother do you need? Your behavior, it is not usual."

She retrieved a discarded canvas from his painting room and wrote on the reverse with his black paint, "New Botanicals. Make offer." She deliberately omitted the word ginseng. The person she wished to identify already knew what the root was.

"Any time again *Mevrouw* Varleth is happy to see you."

Penelope walked past him and plopped sign and root in the dusty window. She accomplished only half the usual work that day because she glanced at each person who passed by the window and stared at everyone who paused. She washed the little panes of glass to improve the display of botanicals and her view of passers-by.

* * * * *

A week later, Penelope noticed a well-dressed woman stop to examine the ginseng in the window. Not so much well-dressed as colorfully dressed in the style frequently found in the evening a few blocks from the piers. The proverb said one caught more flies with honey than with vinegar.

Out of curiosity, Penelope rose to greet the customer. The woman looked Penelope over thoroughly and asked without preamble, "How much is the ginseng?"

Penelope offered her rehearsed speech. "The supplier didn't set a price. He wanted to test the market here."

"How do I know if it's any good?"

Penelope answered truthfully, "It's the same quality as the ginseng found on the docks of Amsterdam."

"May I smell it?"

The question indicated the woman was well acquainted with the medicinal. Penelope removed the tuber from the window and handed it to the woman, who wore red colorant on her lips and a pinkish powder on her cheeks. Penelope had seen harlots from a distance in Amsterdam but never this close, nor smelled one. Strangely this woman favored violet water, much as Liesbeth did. Perhaps that was the only fragrance that grew in her garden.

The woman sniffed and squeezed it. "Why, this root seems fresher than what I bought in Amsterdam. I'll give you ten guilders for it. If it works, I'll buy more."

"If it works?" Penelope tried to estimate if the root weighed as much as ten silver coins.

The harlot glanced around the empty factory. "My gentlemen sometimes need help. Not that I imagine you would know anything about such problems yet."

Penelope felt her face grow warm. "Really, *mevrouw*?"

"A pretty widow with a bad arm will do better to marry an older man. They expect less and are more grateful." The woman peered intently at Penelope's cap, as though trying to inspect what was left of her hair. "And they die sooner."

"*Mevrouw!*" Penelope studied the harlot's reddish tresses half covered by her outrageous hat. Was henna a hair dye as well as a painting color?

"Many house maids get into trouble for free and then need to feed a baby. I encourage a woman to marry. That way she removes only one of my clients." The woman laughed. "And often not for long. Tell your handsome Augustine to put this on my account. The name is Mirjam."

Mirjam, usually a nickname for a baby or a lover, departed with ginseng in her bag.

The wrong fish had taken Penelope's bait. The freshness of the new ginseng drying over Ann's fireplace would be an obvious telltale of its local origin. So much for that stratagem!

"Is she departed?" Herrmann peered around the door jamb of the back office.

Penelope turned. "Does Mirjam have an account?"

"Yes, but Jannetje approves not. That woman," he nodded toward the street, "the word 'no' is not understood."

"I'll debit her account ten guilders for ginseng." Penelope grinned at Herrmann. "She'll want more if it works."

"Ten guilders! Do you have more?" Herrmann asked. "Works for what?"

Chapter 38

New Amsterdam

Tuesday, 17 November 1648

"Excuse me, Penelope." Ann stood up. "I have to clean up and put Annie to bed."

Penelope looked around. Where had the daylight and early evening gone? Had she, Ann, Richard Stout, and Lieutenant Stillwell discussed the mystery of how to smuggle ginseng out of New Amsterdam that long? She had run out of daylight just as she was running out of days before the Stillwell household relocated to Gravesend.

Penelope started to rise to assist her hostess.

"Aunt Penelope," asked Annie, "is a ginger a fish?"

"No, sweetie." Penelope invited the girl to climb into her lap, suspecting an attempt to stay up a little longer. The child deserved a little spoiling because she had patiently played with her poppet during the adult's long conversation. Penelope extracted a needle and thread from her sling. The poppet needed a few stitches before all its straw leaked out. "Why do you ask?"

Annie wrinkled her nose in concentration. "You remember when Jesus took one fish, and it become lots of fishes, and fed all the people."

"Yes, I remember."

"Then how did one ginger become five gingers?"

"What do you...oh, oh yes." One half-chest of ginger, Penelope recalled, had been shipped from Curaçao on *de Kath,* shipwrecked, and recovered. Now five full chests of ginger were on a manifest to be shipped to Amsterdam. What a miracle! Half a chest of ginger became five. Or had someone disguised ginseng root from New Amsterdam— worth its weight in silver—as ginger root from Curaçao— worth its weight in copper?

Penelope kissed Annie and shouted, *"Eureka."*

"What?" asked Richard.

Penelope explained how Jansen and Company exported ten times more ginger than they imported and how ginseng root looked much like ginger root. "Now we merely need to find Jansen and Company."

Ann laughed. "I don't know much Dutch, but I know Jansen translates as Johnson. If one Englishman in twenty is Johnson, how many Dutchmen are named Jansen?"

Richard said, "For sure, Jansen and Company is a false name. It could be anyone."

"No," said Penelope. "Someone paid the export tax on the ginger. We have to find the receipt in the *fiscaal's* office and see who paid the tax."

"Where is the *fiscaal's* office?" asked Richard.

"The *schout* and *fiscaal* are the same person," Penelope said. "Mr. Herrmann took me to the office a few weeks ago to look up old records."

"When does it close?" asked Richard.

Stillwell said, "The *schout's* office never closes, but it's always guarded."

"The *schout's* not cooperative." Penelope rested her elbow on the table and placed her chin in her palm. "Mr. Herrmann had to trick him for me to see certain records."

Ann removed dishes from the table. "How did he trick him?"

"Deliberately lost a bet and had to take him to lunch."

"Ha," said Stillwell. "A bribe might have been cheaper, considering the fat bastard's appetite. Can we trick him again tomorrow?"

Ann smiled. "How much does it take to bribe van Dyck?"

"Not much." Her husband removed his leather pouch and shook it. Two or three coins clinked. "But I'm sure he doesn't take copper coins or promissory notes for bribes."

Richard shrugged. "My money is in a ledger book at Verbrugge's."

Penelope sighed. She had money in two ledgers. Her meager unspent wages were in a column in Herrmann's ledger. Her monumental debt was in Verbrugge's ledger.

The night watchman's whistle sounded faintly in the distance, signaling nine o'clock and time for the taverns to close. Penelope glanced at the window to see if the candle was lit and then remembered this wasn't Ann's night of the week to provide light for the street.

Stillwell said, "Van Dyck is no longer in his office. He's gone to inspect closed taverns."

Richard asked, "When will he return to the office?"

Stillwell chuckled, "Not any time soon. The inspiration behind visiting a closed tavern is that the tavern owner either gives the *schout* free beer or gets fined."

"We have to break into the sheriff's office," Richard said.

Penelope's chin slipped off her palm and almost hit the table. She might have expected such a remark from the lieutenant but never from Richard.

"This will be a first for me: breaking into a gaol." Stillwell belched. "Good dinner, dear. Don't wait up." He stood and looked at Richard, "You ready, Private Stout?"

"Wait!" Penelope stood. "Let me get my wrap."

Richard placed a hand on her forearm. "Where dost thou think thou art going?"

Penelope shrugged off his hand and threw a dark-colored shawl around her shoulders. "Do you know where to look? Do you read Dutch? Do you comprehend manifests and tax records? You'd waste your time without me."

Stillwell buckled his sword, stuck a huge knife in his belt and a smaller one in his boot, and walked to the chimney where the muskets and pistols hung. "Private Stout, what's your weapon of choice?"

"Lieutenant, art thou going to tell her no?"

Stillwell removed a pistol from the wall. "Like the woman said, it'd be a waste of time without her."

Richard looked at Ann, who mouthed the words: "a waste of time."

Stillwell tamped powder and ball into the muzzles of both a pistol and a musket. "You do prefer the musket, don't you? Not a good choice in an alley at night, but it'll do. Makes a nice club." He handed it to Richard, bent to fetch an ember from the fireplace, and lit a piece of slow match for each man.

In a few minutes the trio approached the *schout*'s office, which was barely lit by a single candle. A man stood guard in the shadows outside the door. Stillwell gestured Penelope and Richard to stay back, then walked boldly toward the *schout*'s office, and peered through a windowpane. "Where's that fat bastard?" he mumbled in Dutch, loud enough for the guard to easily hear.

The guard, a private too young to shave, watched Stillwell but remained near the doorway. "He's out making rounds."

Stillwell looked at the guard. "Which tavern should I try first?" He stepped closer. "Do you think the Three-legged Dog?" Suddenly Stillwell held a knife to the private's throat. "Son, are you willing to die to protect some papers?"

The private shook his head slowly.

"Smart answer." Stillwell smiled, handed the soldier's gun to Richard, but kept the knife near the soldier's neck veins. "Now come with us into the office, sit down, and be quiet. We aren't going to steal anything, merely examine some papers."

Penelope hurried in. From the single taper burning in the office, she lit a candle in a reflective metal shield. As she tried to juggle the candle lantern and search the wooden filing cabinet with one good hand, Richard took the lantern and directed its light to the best advantage. She murmured thanks.

Stillwell talked softly to the hostage in Dutch. "When we leave in a few minutes, you have two choices. If you raise an alarm at once, I'll kill you. Or you can pretend nothing happened here tonight. You think about it while the woman looks through yonder files.

"If you did raise the alarm long after we left, what would you tell the *schout*? That you allowed us to search his office and did nothing? Van Dyck would make you ride the wooden horse for two weeks. That pine plank will shove splinters so far up your arse you'll cough them out your nose."

Penelope hoped Stillwell didn't intend to carry out his threats against the young man. Surely logic made the soldier's decision to do nothing irresistible. "Aha. Here it is. Josef Laurensen paid the tax. Who's he?"

Stillwell danced the knife in front of the soldier's eyes. "Do you know Josef Laurensen?"

The soldier quickly denied knowing any man by that name.

Richard asked, "How do we find Josef Laurensen?"

Her eyes remained fixed upon the document. "We'll have to locate the *fiscaal's* clerk, who witnessed this signature, and ask him."

Stillwell said, "That could be awkward."

"Wait, this is odd." Penelope turned the paper this way and that way, trying to coax more candle light onto the bottom of the page. "It's not the usual signature. Someone else witnessed this transaction."

"Who?" Richard looked over her shoulder.

"Someone with illegible handwriting." She shoved the paper in the private's face. "Who signed this?"

"I don't read or write too good." The private looked at her sheepishly.

Stillwell jiggled the knife by the soldier's neck. "Take a close look, son."

The soldier looked at Stillwell, then at his knife, and then at the paper. "Oh, that there's my squiggle."

"What do you mean, 'your squiggle'?" asked Stillwell.

"I told the paymaster I don't write. He told me to invent a mark I can remember and nobody else can copy so other soldiers don't forge my pay records."

Lieutenant Stillwell removed the knife a few inches and smiled. "That was quite smart of you and the paymaster, son. Now tell us. Who is Josef Laurensen?"

"Sorry, sir. I don't know. Honest, I don't."

Penelope waved the paper in his face. "But your squiggle says you watched him sign."

"Sure I signed, but they didn't give me no names." The soldier's voice pleaded with Penelope to believe. "People signed papers and then the *schout* told me to sign."

Penelope asked, "Why you? Where was the clerk?"

"Ever since he got married, he takes himself a long lunch. You know, enjoying his moon's worth of honey."

"Lad," Lieutenant Stillwell sighed deeply. "Do you know who the clerk married?"

"Sure. The beer maid from the City Tavern. You know, the one with the big ..."

"I know the beer maid, lad, so let this be a lesson to you." Stillwell shook his head slowly and spoke in a sad voice. "The clerk goes home at lunch to be sure no other man is dipping into his jar of honey."

The soldier's jaw dropped.

Penelope recalled her lunch with Richard upon her arrival in Manhattan. She thought she had seen men drop coins down the low-cut bodice of a beer maid when she leaned over to place a mug on a table but had hoped the dim, smoky air had clouded her vision. Perhaps not.

Thankfully, Richard aimed the candle lantern toward the young soldier and the darkness covered her embarrassment while revealing the soldier's.

"Forget the beer maid," said Stillwell. "Describe the man who signed."

"Which man? There were a dozen or so this week."

Penelope collapsed into a chair. What could they do with the signature of an unknown man? It might not even be his real name. Why should it be? The *schout* didn't care who paid money, only who owed money.

Stillwell sighed. "I feel like slitting this boy's throat because of his stupidity."

"Wait," pleaded the soldier. "I don't read but I remember real good. Tell me what the paper was about. Maybe I can remember that man."

Richard said, "It's worth a try."

Penelope took a deep breath and let it out slowly. "This man." She waved the paper. "He paid export tax on five chests of ginger."

"Oh, that's easy. He was Beanpole."

Penelope shoved her face inches from the soldier's. "You mean the runty sailor who whittles all the time?"

"Yeah, he whittled me a harlot."

The lieutenant laughed so hard he almost dropped his knife. "Son, that's the only way you'll ever get one."

The baby-faced soldier blushed again, a deep red visible even in the dim candle light, and looked at the floor.

Penelope collapsed into the chair again and stared at the papers in her hand. "Beanpole was on my ship from Curaçao. He was a friendly man."

Stillwell said, "Most devils are. Like the serpent in the Garden of Eden."

"Ask him where we can find Beanpole," said Richard in English. He understood Dutch better than he spoke it.

"At one of the taverns that's still open, no doubt." Stillwell looked at the soldier. "Where do think we should look for Beanpole?"

"At the Three Small Pigeons?" the soldier said eagerly. "Or the Blue Grape? The Wooden Horse?"

Richard shook his head. "The boy doesn't know. We'll have to check them all and we'll have to take him along to identify Beanpole." Richard grabbed the young man by the back of his shirt and lifted him from the chair.

"No," said Stillwell. "Dereliction of duty by a soldier of the guard will bring too much attention, perhaps even a search of the taverns."

"I can identify Beanpole," said Penelope.

"Ha," said Richard. "Thy presence in a tavern will bring even more attention."

"Beanpole will be the shortest sailor in the tavern." She held a hand about five feet above the floor.

"Is he still short when he sits?" asked Stillwell. "A man with short legs can sit tall."

Penelope smiled at the soldier. "How does Beanpole usually dress?"

"He likes to be noticed," the soldier blurted. "He often wears a jacket with red and white stripes."

Lieutenant Stillwell stared at the soldier, who shrugged and said, "The sooner you leave, the safer I feel. Can I get my musket back? I got to pay for it if you take it."

Stillwell brought the gun forward and brushed the powder out of the flashpan. The soldier grabbed the weapon but Stillwell didn't let go. The soldier grinned. "All this talk makes me sleepy. I think I'll take myself a nap." He sat down, closed his eyes, and continued to lightly grasp the musket.

When Stillwell released the gun, the soldier continued to pretend to nap. "The boy's not as stupid as he looks. I should buy him a beer the next time we meet."

The soldier smiled but kept his eyes closed.

The threesome moved off into the darkness that was only slightly disturbed by a candle in the window of every seventh house. Stillwell led them directly toward a nearby building. Although the curtains were drawn, noise identified its function. Penelope suspected Stillwell knew the locations of all the taverns.

At the door Stillwell said, "I'll draw the least attention." He walked in, looked around, and said over his shoulder as he left, "Just looking for someone who owes me money."

At the fourth tavern, Penelope noticed a curtain was crooked and peeked in. Stillwell whispered to a short man in a red and white jacket, then half dragged the man toward the door by one arm.

Beanpole kept shouting, "I don't owe you no money."

The other patrons ignored the two of them.

At the exit, Richard grabbed Beanpole's other arm and clamped a hand over his mouth. The two lifted Beanpole off the ground and carried him around the corner. There was just enough light to see Stillwell's knife gleam in front of Beanpole's nose.

"Whisper," whispered Lieutenant Stillwell, "or I'll cut out your tongue."

Beanpole, staring cross-eyed at the huge knife, nodded slowly and often. Richard released his hand from the sailor's mouth.

"Wait," whispered Penelope. "He always carries a small carving knife in an ankle strap." She knelt down, searched the man's boot and ankle blindly, and found the knife. She stood up and displayed the two-inch blade before inserting it into her sling for storage.

"That's a child's toy. Where's your real knife?" the lieutenant inserted the point of his nine-inch blade into Beanpole's nostril.

"It's big enough for whittling," Beanpole whispered. "Don't kill me for two guilders."

"I'll kill you for five chests of ginger," whispered Stillwell.

"I don't have any ginger," said Beanpole. "Honest. I don't even—"

Stillwell grabbed Beanpole's tongue and rested the knife on it. Beanpole grunted and wriggled. The whites of his eyes shone.

"Then why," asked Penelope, "did you pay export tax on it?"

Beanpole quit struggling and mumbled, "Pnnnlll?"

"Yes, I'm *Mevrouw* Penelope. Let him speak."

Beanpole spat on the ground twice, frowned at Stillwell's knife that jutted from a hand that rested heavily on

Beanpole's shoulder, and doffed his hat in a slow, friendly gesture. "I congratulate you on your survival, *mevrouw*."

She smiled at the prisoner and hoped Stillwell was bluffing about cutting out the man's tongue. Beanpole's face indicated less confidence. "I hope you survive tonight too." Pretending wasn't so hard. Stage actors did it all the time.

Beanpole flashed a grin at Penelope. "I'm just a small fish surrounded by hungry sharks. I don't mean these two land sharks. I mean ocean sharks."

"Tell me about the five chests," she said sweetly through the heavy aroma of beer.

"He gives me money to pay taxes on five chests. I pay taxes. I don't ask no questions."

"What's in the chests?"

"Ginger roots."

"Ha!" Penelope wagged a finger in the sailor's face. "You didn't bring that much ginger from Curaçao."

"I'm a seaman. I know ropes, not roots. If they ain't carrots, I don't know what kind of roots they are."

She laughed. "Who gives the money to pay the taxes?"

"Turk does."

"You mean Anthony Salee, the Turk?" asked Stillwell. "Lives on Long Island near Gravesend and argues with everyone."

"No, that turk looks like a turk. This Turk is a Dutchman who will slit a Christian throat with as little regard as any heathen."

"What's his name?" asked Stillwell.

"He has lots of names. Sometimes he calls himself Jan Jansen, but nobody believes that's his real name."

"What's he look like?" asked Penelope.

"You know him." Beanpole nodded at Penelope. "He was a sailor on *de Kath*. Light hair. Tall. Two arms. Two legs. He looks like anybody. By His bones, I don't pay attention to what men look like."

"Did he kill a man five years ago?" she asked.

"If anybody's dead, Turk likely killed him. Like he's going to kill me for talking to you."

Stillwell smiled, his teeth gleaming as brightly as his knife blade in the faint light. "We won't tell."

"I won't neither but he'll find out anyway."

"What do you know about smuggling ginseng?" asked Penelope.

Beanpole swiveled his head toward Penelope. "How can you call it smuggling when I paid taxes on it?"

"Ginseng is worth twenty times more than ginger."

Beanpole grinned. "So that's his game? I wondered why he wasted his time on smelly roots."

Penelope doubted Beanpole's protestations of ignorance. "You sailed to the East Indies? Didn't you encounter ginseng in the port of Batavia?"

"By His wounds." Beanpole placed his hand over his heart to prove the truth of his words. "As if they paid me enough to buy spices and rubies."

Stillwell bounced his knife blade on Beanpole's shoulder, merely an inch from a bulging vein in his neck. "Where can we find this Turk?"

"Tonight? At a musico. Tomorrow night—on *de Witte Paard*. He sails to Amsterdam to sell the ginger. I mean ginseng."

"Which brothel?" asked Stillwell.

"How do I know?" asked Beanpole. "He don't invite me. But not the one he went to last night. He likes variety."

"Eleven o'clock and all is well." The distant voice startled all of them.

"Shh," whispered Richard. "The night watchman is coming."

"Back into the shadows," Stillwell ordered.

After the watchman passed, Richard asked, "Dost thou have more questions for Beanpole?"

"Where is he?" Stillwell blew on the slow match to create a tiny amount of light and moved it around. "I thought you had him."

"I thought thou hadst him," answered Richard.

"Of twelve sailors on *de Kath*, we're to find a fair-haired Dutchman who continually changes his name and frequents *musicos*," said Penelope into the darkness. The description of tall meant nothing. To Beanpole, everyone was tall. "Beanpole and Turk are both as slippery as live eels."

"Drat," said Stillwell. "We'll never find him again tonight."

"Can't you search the brothels?" asked Penelope.

"Too numerous. The large, noisy ones have guards at the front door and secret back doors. I don't know where the quiet, private ones are..." He grinned at Penelope. "Because I haven't visited any in six years."

Richard quit blowing on the slow match. The darkness seemed even darker.

Penelope stomped her foot in disgust. "Drat. The ship will be gone by the second sunrise." Thirty hours to find and identify her father's killer. Thirty hours.

Chapter 39

New Amsterdam

Wednesday, 18 November 1648

Breakfast among the adults in the Stillwell house was quiet and moody. The lieutenant and Penelope had told Ann everything that had transpired the previous evening. They had discussed various options and discarded them all, except to find Beanpole again and ask him more questions. But none had a good suggestion for locating the slippery little eel.

Penelope's mood was sour. In twenty hours, the ship and the murderer would sail away. And she still didn't know the murderer's identity.

A knock on the door interrupted the silence. Munkey barked. Stillwell whistled her to silence.

Ann said, "If that's the delivery man, Penelope, two barrels of beer and one of water will do us until we move."

When Penelope opened the top half of the door, morning sunlight streamed in along with a booming voice, "Nicholas Stillwell, you're under arrest." She stared at the *schout* and half a dozen armed soldiers in the street.

Lieutenant Stillwell leaped up and shoved Penelope away from the doorway and to safety beside the wall. "Is that you, *Schout* van Dyck?" he called from the shadows beside the door jamb, while gesturing to Ann to seek cover and to hold onto the dog.

"Nicholas Stillwell, you're under arrest," called the *schout*. "Come out peacefully."

Penelope whispered, "It's my fault. Let them arrest me."

"What's the charge?" Stillwell called.

"Murder!" rang out the voice of *Schout* van Dyck.

Stillwell laughed. "I was acquitted of that trumped-up charge years ago. You disturbed my breakfast for that?"

Penelope stared at her host. How could a man laugh at a charge of murder?

The *schout* called back, "You're charged with the murder of Josef Laurensen, commonly known as Beanpole."

Stillwell frowned. "He was alive when I last saw him."

"Drat," Penelope muttered to herself. She'd have to reveal her secrets in order to vouch for Stillwell's innocence. She owed him that much loyalty and much more.

The *schout* called back, "Half a dozen witnesses saw you kidnap him from a tavern last night. No one has seen him alive since."

"You know me better than that, van Dyck," called Stillwell. "I don't kill people who owe me money. It makes it hard to collect."

"Where did you hide the body, Stillwell?"

"If you don't have a body, do you accuse me of murdering a ghost?"

"We found Beanpole's cap and jacket floating in the East River near the pier on Pearl Street. We suspect foul play."

"Suspect all you want. Come back when you have a body that doesn't owe me money."

"I have a warrant for your arrest. We can discuss this in the gaol."

Penelope heard the rattling of paper in the street.

Stillwell asked, "Is that warrant signed by Petrus Stuyvesant?"

"There's no need. As *schout*, I have enough evidence to sign a warrant."

"Your signature alone isn't good enough to arrest Lieutenant Nicholas Stillwell, officer in the militia of the GWC. That requires the Director-General's signature."

"You're no longer an officer."

"I have a commission issued by Director-General Kieft in '42 that was never rescinded. Just because I haven't been paid in five years doesn't mean I'm not an officer. That reminds me. Since you're the *fiscaal* as well as the *schout*, you owe me sixty guilders for my last two months of active service in '43."

"Go to hell, Stillwell."

"That's Lieutenant Stillwell to you, *Schout-Fiscaal* van Dyck."

"We have you surrounded, Stillwell."

"Yes, van Dyck, but you're in the open. I'm behind wooden walls. My two sons and I are the best marksmen in New Netherland and you are the biggest and slowest target. You have an illegal warrant and I have the legal right to defend myself and my home. You owe me sixty guilders and you interrupted my breakfast. I'm becoming mightily pissed at you, *Schout-Fiscaal* van Dyck."

A scuffling of boots proved that van Dyck and the soldiers believed Stillwell's claims of marksmanship if not his innocence. Van Dyck's conciliatory words came from a much further distance. "Lieutenant Stillwell, I declare a truce until the Director-General returns and signs a warrant. Don't leave the village."

"Thank you, *Schout-Fiscaal* van Dyck. In the meantime, I suggest you obtain some grappling hooks and go fishing by the pier."

Penelope heard the schout order his men to return to Fort New Amsterdam. Did the *schout* intend to try to trick Stillwell? Van Dyck was sneaky but probably not that dumb. He knew how big and tempting a target his beer-swilling body was.

"Ahoy the Stillwell house!" came a voice minutes later.

"Is that you, Private Stout?" called Stillwell.

"The deck is clear," called Richard. "Thy bluff worked."

"Hell, Private Stout, that was no bluff. Come on in."

A sleepy voice called out, "What's the commotion about?"

Ann laughed, "I hope you never assign guard duty to ten-year-olds."

* * * * *

Through a long morning of discussion that stretched toward lunch, Penelope, Richard, and the Stillwell family pondered the problem. Penelope explained how the sailors on *de Kath* changed nicknames as readily as *Mevrouw* Stuyvesant changed dresses. Turk could be any one of them, if Beanpole told the truth.

The conclusion was that Turk, one of the sailors from *de Kath*, had killed Beanpole for talking and had taken refuge on *The White Horse*. If Turk were smart, then he would sell his ginseng in Amsterdam and disappear rich.

Images of sailors from *de Kath* floated through Penelope's brain. She would recognize Stinky, Bucket, Four-Toes, and the others if she saw them again in daylight, but she could remember only one seaman clearly enough to describe accurately: red-headed Rusty. But he didn't fit Beanpole's description.

How could they capture Turk before the ship sailed? The *schout* would refuse to issue a search warrant on the ship for lack of evidence and because he would suspect a ruse to shift blame away from Stillwell. Penelope proposed to sneak aboard but Stillwell claimed secretly boarding a busy ship in daylight was impossible.

Richard said, "I know one way to get every sailor on deck so we can look at them."

Penelope said, "Quickly, Mr. Stout. How?"

Richard blushed. "A lady of the evening."

"That might work." Lieutenant Stillwell lifted his beer mug to congratulate Richard.

Ann said, "I only know one lady: Lady Moody. Why would sailors be interested in meeting a lady?"

The lieutenant spewed beer onto the floor and collapsed onto a bench, laughing and choking.

Penelope whispered to Ann, "A doxy, a harlot."

Ann stammered. "Oh, how? Why? Oh."

Lieutenant Stillwell grinned at his wife as he spoke, "What's your plan, Private Stout?"

Richard continued to blush. "Thou, me, and a woman row out to the ship at dusk. One of us shouts to the watch that we'll auction off the services of the woman. The sailors lower the master's chair and we suspend the woman in the chair while the auction occurs. That way she'll be safe. The first man openly climbs on board to conduct the auction. The second man steals aboard the ship, conceals himself in the shadows, and watches the sailors."

Penelope said, "What good would a doxy do? She couldn't identify Turk."

Richard said, "I expect Turk to be the high bidder."

Stillwell grinned at Penelope. "We don't need a real harlot. Just a woman to be a decoy."

"What kind of scheme is this?" she asked. "I'm the only one who can identify sailors from *de Kath*."

Stillwell refilled his beer mug. "So true."

Penelope looked around. All eyes were on her. How red was her face? "Pretend to be a harlot? What would Reverend Prince and the church elders think?"

Ann giggled. "I'll never tell."

"Excuse me. I must visit the privy." Penelope escaped out the back door and hurried to the outbuilding.

Pretending, like acting, was not exactly lying. The ninth Commandment forbade lying under oath, not ordinary lies. Anyway, Stillwell would perform the falsehoods, not she.

She stayed in the privy longer than her business required to think of some other way to trap the killer. She stood up and dumped a scoop of lime down the hole.

Outside the building, she paused to straighten her skirts. The role of lady of the evening didn't begin until sunset. Surely there was another option.

A hand clamped around Penelope's mouth and another around her waist. Her attacker pulled her body off balance and against his. He mumbled, "Be quiet or die."

She tried to butt him with her head but his head was safely buried in the nape of her neck. She tried to kick him but he pulled her backwards around the privy. Her screams were too muffled to be heard. Her attempts to bite his hand were thwarted by his cupping his fingers away from her teeth and twisting her head.

She lost her footing from being dragged backwards and almost fell. Her good hand stretched out toward the ground to catch her weight, but the attacker jerked her back upright. A shiny object slid out of her sling and without thinking, she grabbed for it. It was Beanpole's whittling knife from last night.

She plunged the two-inch blade into the forearm that wrapped around her waist.

Her attacker shouted obscenities and threw her down.

She screamed even louder when she landed on her maimed shoulder, rolled over, and clambered to her knees. She glanced backwards but the assailant was bent over double in pain, hiding his face. Shouting bloody murder, she turned and scrambled for the Stillwell house.

Above her own shrieks, she heard the pounding of heavy boots inside the house and saw, through the upper half of the Dutch door, a body racing toward her. She had the presence of mind to drop to ground. Stillwell crashed through the lower half of the door and bounded over her prostrate body into the yard, a three-foot saber waving in the air.

All she could think of was an ancient warning from Liesbeth not to run with scissors.

Richard followed behind with a stick of firewood. She pointed toward the privy. No one was there.

"What happened?" Richard asked.

"He grabbed me. I stabbed him," she said from the ground.

"With what?" asked Stillwell, searching the area.

"With Beanpole's whittling knife."

"Well, no wonder there's no blood and no body." Stillwell knelt and studied the ground. "One person." He looked up. "Where did you stab him?"

"In the arm."

"Which arm?"

She paused to think. "He grabbed me from behind with his left arm around my waist and right hand over my mouth. I stabbed him in the left forearm."

"Who was he?" asked Ann, shooing Annie away from the splinters of the busted door.

"I didn't see his face," Penelope said, "but he smelled like lilac water. I'm sure he's the brothel-frequenter who killed my father."

"Then, thou art fortunate." Richard helped her to rise.

Stillwell walked back and studied Penelope. "How seriously do you think you pricked him with that toy knife?"

"It went in all the way to the hilt and struck the bone."

"To the bone? The coward'll remember that for a long time. Not bad for a toy knife. Here's a real one for next time." Out of his belt he pulled a hunting knife with a nine-inch blade, flipped the weapon, and presented her the hilt.

She stared at the blade. The beef butchers in Amsterdam used smaller knives. "Bless the good Lord, no. That thing would have gone all the way through his arm and halfway through me."

Stillwell smiled. "A good soldier understands weapons. Well done, Private Prince."

She would have saluted if she had known how. Instead, she warmed with pride.

Ann chuckled. "Some women will do anything to get out of preparing lunch."

"Where is thy toy knife?" asked Richard. "I don't see it on the ground."

Stillwell stared at the footprints in the dirt. "Probably still in the rogue's arm. It's better not to extract a blade until one is prepared to handle the bleeding."

* * * * *

A few hours later, Penelope sat cautiously in the stern of a rowboat headed into the sunset for the only ship in the harbor. She still couldn't believe she had agreed to do this and none of her friends had tried to stop her. Would she have let them stop her?

Richard sat in the middle, facing Penelope, and rowed while Lieutenant Stillwell sat in the bow and gave an occasional course correction. *De Witte Paard* loomed darkly ahead, a silhouette against the last pinkish clouds in the west. Even the seagulls had abandoned the scene.

Three-inch waves gently slapped against the wooden sides. Richard leaned toward her, the oars skimming above the murky water and then swirling into the depths as he pulled backwards.

She stared ahead at the flyboat, the type her father had often traveled on from Amsterdam into the Baltic, where she had once thought he and his ship had drowned in a storm. She shuddered at a vision of him disappearing beneath the waves. Despite having lived most of her life twenty feet from the Herengracht, she couldn't swim. Like a typical sailor, she was happy to sail the seas and yet fearful of water.

She had doubts about this expedition but Richard and Stillwell were confident. As darkness deepened, she worried about identifying the man. What if he recognized her despite her disguise? Having traveled so far and lost so much, how could she turn back so close to learning the truth? In the morning the ship would sail away with Turk.

She adjusted the uncomfortable English-style bonnet and Ann's colorful dress. Ann had even fashioned a sling out of the same fabric, so that in dim light, the sling would not be noticeable.

No one in New Amsterdam had seen her dressed in anything but a black dress and cap, except the day of her arrival. Surely her disguise would work.

A familiar sound from the ship marked four bells, or six o'clock in the evening. She estimated its distance at thirty fathoms, automatically reverting to nautical terms in the presence of the environment where she had spent much of the last six months.

"Ahoy the ship!" called Stillwell.

An indistinct, hostile answer floated across the water.

At five fathoms, Stillwell told Richard to hold position. "Ahoy the ship!" Stillwell repeated.

"Go away," said a voice from the deck. "We have adequate provisions."

Penelope stared up at the ship. The voice sounded like First Mate Eriksen's. What was he doing on the ship? As a sailor, he had a good excuse, but why this one? She pulled the bonnet closer to her face.

Stillwell laughed. "A sailor never has enough of what I'm selling." He gestured to Penelope to stand up.

She released her arm from its sling, stood and, as they had rehearsed, spread her arms slightly to reveal the contours of her body, thereby proving she was a female. She almost lost her balance, quickly sat down, then slipped her left arm back into its sling.

The hoots and hollers from the ship confirmed she made a good impression. Her face grew warm. She looked away from the sailors and straight at Richard. Her face grew even warmer.

Why had she ever agreed to this ridiculous masquerade? Why hadn't they hired a man to pretend to be the harlot like they did in plays?

Richard gave her an encouraging smile. Thankfully the darkness hid her embarrassment.

"Only one? Where are her sisters?" sounded a louder voice than the others.

Stillwell shouted back, "Quality, my good man, always triumphs over quantity."

"Not if you don't have none," shouted another. Several mates shouted their agreement.

"I propose an auction. The highest bidder gets an hour with this virgin runaway from New Haven."

"How do we know she's a virgin?"

"I only know one way to prove it. But then she's no long-er a virgin."

The sailors howled with laughter and coarse comments.

"We can leave," Richard said. "We don't have to do this."

Penelope was tempted to agree, but she had come too far to learn the truth to quit now. "I've heard worse on the docks of Amsterdam." But not directed at her personally.

She shivered and looked back at the shore, nearly a hundred fathoms away. *"The wife of Caesar must be above suspicion,"* Shakespeare said, and Reverend Prince would certainly agree.

The water beckoned her to drown herself to preserve her honor. But she was no longer a wife. She was a widow and an orphan on a mission as irresistible as Matthew's.

"You can't bring her on board," Eriksen called down to them. "She'll cause a riot."

"My plan," called Stillwell, "is to let the high bidder join her in the rowboat."

"And where will you be?" a sailor asked.

"I'll be on deck auctioning the second hour."

Penelope squirmed. Stillwell hadn't mentioned a second hour. Of course, the first hour wouldn't occur either. The purpose was merely to flush out Turk, a man with money and a desire for prostitutes. What if he felt pity for a virgin runaway? She emitted a harsh laugh. How could a man who killed her father feel pity for anyone?

Eriksen conferred with another man, presumably the ship's master. "As long as she doesn't come on board."

Penelope finally agreed with Eriksen on something.

Chapter 40

New Amsterdam

Wednesday, 18 November 1648

Richard Stout rowed the boat adjacent to the ship. A rope ladder dropped down and splashed its last few rungs into the water. Stillwell scrambled onto the ladder and pushed the rowboat away. The shove made the little boat rock. Penelope shrieked and grabbed for the gunwale.

As Stillwell climbed the ladder, he looked like a pirate with two pistols stuck in his belt and a long military sword swinging from his waist.

Once on board, Stillwell argued with Eriksen for a minute. Then the sailors scrambled to erect a small mast and its boom, attach the master's chair to ropes and pulleys, and swing it out over the water, where it rapidly descended toward Richard and Penelope. Richard helped her into the chair.

She had hardly wrapped her skirts securely around her ankles before she was jerked into the air. The support ropes were invisible in the darkness so she grasped onto a wooden arm with her good right hand.

Sailors cranked the windlass until her chair was two fathoms above the deck, then wrapped the rope around a cleat. Below her, Richard tied his boat to the ship's ladder and ascended. The sailors ignored Richard and shouted obscene comments at her. At least that was part of the scheme.

Carefully, because she sat in a slippery wooden chair several fathoms above the water and two fathoms away from the gunwale, she leaned forward to peer down at the crowd of fifteen or so, a sea of upturned faces that shouted and laughed. The whites of excited eyes were their only distinguishable feature among their shadowy countenances. Which pair of eyes belonged to Turk?

Stillwell started his pre-auction speech. She doubted he could increase the sailors' enthusiasm but Richard needed time to shuck his overcoat and to blend into the back of the crowd. She felt like a Christian in the Roman Coliseum, about to be thrown to the hungry lions. Two fathoms from the rowdy men hardly seemed enough distance for safety. The master and first mate also watched eagerly, but she dared not look at Eriksen for fear he might recognize her.

Instead she ignored Stillwell and watched the sailors. The crescent moon and a few lanterns shed scant light. She hoped her face was as shadowy as theirs. How much money did sailors have left after visiting the taverns of Manhattan?

The answer was less than two guilders. The spirited bidding quickly tapered off after the price exceeded a guilder and was stuck at a guilder fifteen stuivers. In the dimness, Richard silently raised a hand that showed two fingers. Stillwell picked up the new bid of two guilders and began to exhort the crowd to do better.

Gradually the sailors shifted their focus from the object of the auction to a sailor near the gunwale, as though they expected him to win the bidding and were curious to see how high he would go. He said, "Two guilders five."

Penelope leaned forward in the master's chair and frowned. Five stuivers? A quarter of a guilder? Sixpence? This sailor was making a fortune from ginseng and that's all he would raise: a quarter of a guilder. Even though he was one of the closest sailors, his face was turned toward the others.

To better see the man she was sure was Turk, she leaned forward more. The suspended chair lurched on its ropes and tilted. She screamed.

All eyes were on her as she scrambled to restore her balance. "Three guilders," shouted Richard from the rear of the group.

The sailors turned toward the source of the last bid.

"Three guilders five," said the sailor whom she presumed to be Turk.

The sailors between Richard and Turk melted away. She saw the fierce look on Richard's face and assumed Turk looked just as evil.

"Four guilders," said Richard.

"Who in hell are you," asked Turk.

"The high bidder," answered Richard.

"Five guilders," shouted Turk.

"Fifty guilders," shouted Richard.

"No sailor has fifty guilders," said Turk. His left hand reached behind his body and grasped a belaying pin from the row along the gunwale, while his right hand pulled a knife from the back of his trousers. Penelope screamed a warning. Turk charged toward Richard.

Richard brandished a short sword he had kept hidden behind his leg.

Turk used the belaying pin like a shield and the knife like a sword.

Richard grabbed his overcoat and looped it around his arm for protection.

Turk and Richard circled each other.

Penelope swung helplessly above the fracas, afraid to shout anything for fear of distracting Richard. Not that he could have heard her because the sailors screamed encouragement to both combatants.

Meanwhile, Lieutenant Stillwell pulled his long sword out of its scabbard, held the blade high above the crowd, and tried to force his way through the mob of sailors to assist his friend. The sailors pushed him back, shouting "Fair fight. Fair fight." Several of them lit torches and held them up for a better view of the combatants.

Lieutenant Stillwell pulled back from the crowd and fumbled to light a piece of slow match from a nearby lantern.

Turk lunged at Richard. Richard knocked the blow aside with his saber but slipped on the deck and fell. He rolled away as the Turk crashed a belaying pin onto the deck.

A pistol shot sounded like a clap of thunder. Everyone froze. Lieutenant Stillwell lowered the pistol he had fired into the air and raised the second one. The sailors cleared a path between him and the fighters.

The lieutenant slowly approached Turk. "By the authority vested in me as a lieutenant of the New Netherland militia, I arrest you in the name of Petrus Stuyvesant for the murder five years ago of the Englishman John Kent."

Turk threw the belaying pin at Lieutenant Stillwell, leaped into the rigging, and began to climb. His fingers and naked toes clung to the ropes like a monkey or an experienced sailor. How could he climb with a severely wounded arm? Surely this was the same man who had assaulted her this afternoon. As if in answer, Turk paused and massaged his left forearm where a white cloth shimmered in the faint light.

Lieutenant Stillwell took careful aim at the stationary seaman and fired. Turk nearly fell, but hung on and screamed curses at the lieutenant. With one arm dangling by his side, he continued to climb, though much more slowly.

Richard said, "Damned clodhoppers" and ripped his farmer's boots from his feet. He thrust his short sword into his belt, grabbed a rope on the mainmast, and began to climb.

Lieutenant Stillwell hunched over his pistols and reloaded as fast as he could.

Dangling from the master's chair, Penelope held her breath as she watched Richard ascend, slip, and grab again, ascend, slip, and grab. He was going to fall and break his neck. How many years had passed since he had been a sailor? Five? Six? After a minute or two, he regained his skills and climbed confidently, a little faster than the wounded Turk.

Meanwhile Turk had reached the end of the rigging where it attached to the spar that held the topsail.

"No," Eriksen shouted at Lieutenant Stillwell and pushed his pistol aside just before he could fire. "You're more likely to damage the ropes than to hit a man at that distance."

"Damn pistol's no good beyond fifteen feet." Stilwell lowered the weapon. "I should have brought a musket."

Turk clung to the end of a spar five fathoms above the deck. Richard reached the point where the spar attached to the mainmast, straddled the pole, and began to advance. Turk jumped up and down in the rigging but the spar only swayed a few inches.

Penelope looked down at Lieutenant Stillwell, who had taken up a position at the bottom of the rigging. She looked up at Turk, mostly a dark shape against an almost black sky. Turk's eyes and teeth twinkled in the light from the sailor's torches on the deck. His eyes looked down at her and then at the gantry that supported her chair. Meanwhile, Richard, another black shadow, who was halfway down the length of the spar, paused and pulled out his sword. Its blade reflected the scant moonlight.

Turk moved to the extreme end of the rigging and reached out for the block and tackle on the gantry. He repositioned himself, held on with his good arm, and stretched out with his wounded arm, his hand only two feet shy of the boom supporting Penelope's chair.

Richard reached the end of the spar and clambered into the rigging. He was still too far from Turk.

Turk leaped for the gantry and clung to its ropes. From ten feet away, she heard him gasp with pain. His teeth grinned evilly at Penelope as he consolidated his hold and began to climb toward the boom with one arm.

The ship rolled a little more than usual, throwing more moonlight into the rigging and onto Turk's face. She stared at a face that seemed familiar. His grin reminded her of Beanpole's friend with the nickname Rusty. If Gimpy could be rechristened Bucket, why couldn't Turk change his name and his appearance too? Now that she thought about it, his hair had been an unnatural red color, like that of Mirjam, who bought her ginseng.

Penelope shifted in the master's chair but she had no escape, except to fall to the gloomy waters several fathoms below. She grabbed one of the four ropes that supported her perch and tried to pull herself securely back into the chair. But that sent the chair slowly twisting. She squirmed again to face Turk, feeling defenseless. This part wasn't in the plan.

If she had known she would be stalked by a wild animal, she would have accepted Stillwell's offer of a hunting knife with its nine-inch blade. Even Beanpole's whittling knife would have been better than nothing.

Turk was eight feet above her and eight feet to the side. He moved cautiously on the gantry as though he prepared to jump. Was he going to jump into the water or jump into her chair? If he landed on her, they would both fall to the water, where she would surely drown.

In his hand, metal gleamed erratically in the lantern light. Did Turk hold a knife or a gun?

How would she prefer to die—gun, knife, or water?

She curled the fingers of her good hand like a cat stretching its claws. Beneath her voluminous skirts, she bent her knees in preparation to kick Turk away if he jumped onto her. The shift in weight caused her swinging perch to tilt backwards.

An explosive sound nearly dislodged her from the chair. A cloud of dark smoke billowed upward from the deck. Burnt powder stung her eyes and nostrils. She stared down at Stillwell's upraised arm and its smoking pistol. Stillwell jumped back as Turk's body fell through the smoke and into the ropes that controlled the gantry.

The noise of the gantry's splintering wood accompanied the jerking of her chair. A rope that suspended her above the water sought its freedom.

The chair lurched.

Penelope screamed.

Her body slid out of the chair.

She grabbed the nearest support rope with her good hand. Dangling twenty feet above the water, she spun in slow circles and tried to lift herself back into the chair. But the chair was tilted even more because her weight was entirely on a single rope. The rope burned her palm and pinched her hand against the wood of the chair.

Fifteen feet above her, Richard screamed, "Hang on!"

"I can't." She wiggled her fingers to get a better grasp and fell feet first into the ocean.

Cold saltwater enveloped her legs. She tried to suck in a breath of air but her mouth filled with fabric as air trapped under her dress billowed the fabric up to cover her head. Water poured down upon her and washed away Ann's bonnet as she sank into the ocean.

She popped back up like a cork but could hardly move her arms. Her left shoulder felt on fire because her maimed arm pointed skyward, pushed there by the ballooning dress. Looking up, she saw Richard's terrified face staring down at her.

Her right arm, tangled in her dress, slid free. The fabric soaked up water and uncovered her face but pulled her lower into the water. A wavelet washed over her lips. She sputtered and flailed her legs and good arm, but the water-logged cloth pulled her deeper. She kicked her legs frantically and managed to get her head above water for a moment and gasped for air.

An object fell from the ship and splashed beside her just before she went under again. Had Turk survived his fall and jumped into the water to finish his task of killing her?

Something grabbed her around the waist. Not knowing whether it was Turk or a sea monster, she pounded at it with her good arm but she had no force underwater. She grasped it and dug her fingernails into the soft flesh as it pulled her upward.

Her head popped above water again. She clawed the flesh that encircled her body and thrashed about, trying to keep her head above water, trying to breathe but ingesting as much water as air.

"Don't," an English voice panted into her ear, "struggle."

She twisted to face this unknown danger that refused to let go of her body.

"Penelope, hold still. I've got thee."

She recognized the voice, swung her good arm around Richard's neck and squeezed.

"Trust me," he sputtered.

She felt him kick his legs and twist his body. They rose a few inches and then sank beneath the surface. She released his neck and flailed the water to reach the surface. She hardly noticed he let go and then grabbed her again from behind with both arms. He jerked upward. Her head was above the surface. She spat out water and sucked in air.

She reached out to grab Richard but he was behind her, with arms around her waist and, like the outhouse assailant had been, out of reach.

He kicked vigorously.

She looked out into an empty sea. Where was the ship? She twisted her head and saw a black shape nearby.

"Trust me," Richard panted again. "I've got thee."

Trust? How could she trust anything? She spat out water and breathed again.

Then hands grabbed her good arm and pulled upward. Richard put his hands around her hips and pushed. She felt the gunwale of the rowboat dig into her abdomen. Someone put his hands under her armpits and pulled. Richard's arms encircled her thighs and pushed her further into the boat. She had to choose between slapping Richard for taking such liberties or using her good hand to keep her face from scrapping against a wooden thwart.

At last she was fully in the boat. Water drained from her clothes until she feared the rowboat would fill and sink.

"Where in hell," Lieutenant Stillwell called from the deck, "did a sailor learn to swim?"

"In a fishpond," Richard gasped, "a hundred miles from the ocean."

Penelope tried to imagine Richard as a happy youngster frolicking in a fishpond, whatever that was. There weren't any ponds in Amsterdam. Only smelly canals.

"Turk's neck is broken," said Lieutenant Stillwell, "so justice is served. However, I arrested him and I must deliver him, dead or alive, to the gaol."

"But it happened on this ship," said First Mater Eriksen. "We'll bury him at sea."

"But the ship is anchored in Director-General Stuyvesant's harbor."

"By His bones, Lieutenant Stillwell," shouted Erkisen, "that fool van Dyck will delay us for weeks with his legal incompetence. It's late in the season already and winter storms grow worse each day."

Penelope recalled van Dyck's leisurely and incompetent inquisition in Verbrugge's store and the scandal trial in Gravesend. She couldn't bear the thought of more public humiliation. She whispered to Richard, "Take me home. Now! Please!"

"Lieutenant Stillwell?" called Richard. "Upon thy honor as an officer and a gentleman, I ask thee to choose between hanging a dead man or helping me take a cold, shivering, frightened widow to warmth and safety."

"Mr. Eriksen," said Stillwell, "I accept your offer to bury this murderer at sea. But no scripture and no words to be said over his body except 'Good riddance.'"

Penelope imagined Lieutenant Stillwell and Eriksen saluting each other.

"Gangway," called Lieutenant Stillwell, clambering down the rope ladder to the rowboat. "All aboard who're going ashore."

The boat rocked as the lieutenant boarded and the sailors departed.

Richard sat beside Penelope and held her.

Lieutenant Stillwell assumed the middle seat and picked up the oars. "What's the world coming to when the private gets the woman and the officer gets the oars? Oh, before I forget, I found this in the dead man's pocket. To the victor belong the spoils."

In the darkness Penelope's fingers felt an engraved leather pouch. She dumped the contents into her hand. Three images of the King of Spain glittered in the faint torchlight from the ship. She searched the pouch more thoroughly. Empty. The notes from Liesbeth and her father had been discarded. Why not? How many sailors knew how to read? Especially English. Carefully she inserted the golden coins back into the pouch, tied the drawstring into a knot and wrapped the remainder of the drawstring around her fingers.

With more noise than effectiveness, Stillwell pushed off from the flyboat and splashed the oars into the water.

Chapter 41

New Amsterdam

Thursday, 19 November 1648

The next afternoon, Penelope traded three gold coins, a basket of dried ginseng roots with a reminder that Mirjam wanted it, and her ledger entries of unpaid wages to Herrmann for seven and two-thirds fathoms of sewan, legal tender in New Amsterdam. She walked to Verbrugge's factory with 2640 good quality, well-strung white and purple shells in several loops around her neck and shoulders, ignoring the pointing fingers and whispers, and settled her debt of eighty guilders in full, glad to have paid before interest began to accumulate.

She should have been pleased with herself for bringing her father's murderer to justice and freeing herself from her obligations. Instead she was listless and picked at the supper Ann had cooked. Even after the meal was over, conversation dragged as the Stillwell children begged their father and Richard to relate the story again. Each retelling by Lieutenant Stillwell was filled with more and more exaggeration of the death she had caused in avenging her father.

She covered one ear with a hand to try to shut out the noise. Seldom did she regret the uselessness of her left arm, but today she wished it functional so she could plug her other ear.

Richard whispered across the table, "Mrs. Prince?"

When she ignored him, he whispered her name again. She shoved her bench away from the table, nearly upsetting two of the children, and stumbled out the door into the cool evening darkness and an empty Manhattan street.

Richard followed behind her, not touching her but not leaving her in peace. "Did I say something wrong? Art thou angry with me? What's wrong?"

"What's wrong?" She directed her anger to the sky. "Nothing's wrong. Except my life is a shambles, that's all. Bankrupt. Living on the charity of friends. Trying to both forgive and forget the past. No future. Responsible for killing my husband, killing my father."

He took her hand and resisted her feeble attempt to jerk free. "Thou didst not kill anyone. Thou art non capable."

"No, I killed Matthew. He was just a dreamer. He dreamed of a new life here. I was the difference between dreaming and doing. I bought the passage. I made him come with me. I picked the ship that killed him." It was the truth.

He held onto her hand and faced her. "That's not true. Don't speak such things."

"I killed my father. He took a dangerous voyage to make enough money to give me a good dowry and it killed him too. I've killed everyone around me." She stared at her feet. "You should leave while you're still alive."

Wrenching her hand free of his, she snatched the linen napkin still stuffed into his doublet. She daubed her eyes, then burst into tears, and buried her head in his shoulder. Holding onto him with one arm around his waist for support, she sobbed uncontrollably, her body convulsing, her breath wheezing.

He reached both arms around her and held her close. His body was warm against hers. His hands patted her back. His soothing words flooded around her. Time had no meaning as she wept.

At last, between sobs, she choked, "I've ruined your new doublet with my tears."

"Thou art non alone," he said. "I'm here. Ann's here. Annie's here. We all love thee. Thou art non alone."

"Alone. Ha! What do you know about being alone?" She jerked herself free and turned away from him.

"I know thirteen years of being alone," he said to her back. "Of abandoning the people I loved. Of watching my friends die. Dost thou think thou hast a monopoly on loneliness? Everybody on this island has a sad tale. People don't come here unless they are running away from something. Or from themselves."

"Thirteen years?" She turned and stared at him. "How do you endure it for thirteen years? It has been four months and I can't tolerate it."

"I learned from my mistakes. I asked God to forgive me. I worked. I tried to remember the good and forget the bad."

She faced him, tears streaking her face. "What are you running away from?"

"I was a coward." His usually steady voice trembled. "I should've stayed, should have fought for the woman I loved. Instead I ran away."

Penelope caught her breath. Is that what she had done? Had she run away from Amsterdam? Is that why she was reluctant to even think about returning to the city of her birth? She breathed and sniffled again.

No. She was afraid to return to Amsterdam and admit her mistakes. What had Richard advised—ask God to forgive? Even if she couldn't forgive herself, maybe she could forgive God and ask God to forgive her. It would be a start. She felt her anger begin to slip away. Only her anger receded, not her guilt.

What had Richard run from? She was so consumed with her own fears she had scarcely considered that other people suffered from loneliness, guilt, and self-doubt too.

"Tell me about it." She took his hand and led him to the spot where they often placed the kitchen bench, but it was inside now.

They sat on the ground and leaned against the house. She asked again, but he could not start. She took his hand, held it in her lap, gently stroked it, and asked, "Whom did you love?"

The words started slowly, hesitantly, dredged up from the distant chambers of the heart where they had been locked up. He told about a beautiful girl named Jessica to whom he had never confessed his love, to whom he could talk for hours, except about what was truly important. He spoke of a confrontation with his father over the suitability of Jessica as a wife, of anger, of abandonment. He confessed to writing her a dozen letters he had never finished, never posted. He recalled comrades dying on Caribbean islands, in Virginian forests, on uncaring ships. He described sitting alone outside his house in the evenings, thinking, remembering.

After a long silence, he said into the darkness, "Since I met thee, I've been a coward again. Afraid to tell thee I love thee. Afraid thou wouldst abandon me. I knew thee would be hurting. That thou wouldst be afraid to love again. If I pressed thee, thou might run away. So I resolved to be near thee. To watch over thee. To let thee know thou hast a friend to share the loneliness with."

She continued to stroke his calloused hand in her lap. "No, Richard. I don't want to share loneliness."

Richard tried to pull his hand away from her.

She refused to let go. "I want to share joy and hope. I want a future."

His fingers entwined with hers. "I love thee. I loved thee the first moment I saw thee."

"You saw me in that savage garb and fell in love?"

"I fell in love with thy smile, thy spirit, thy soul. I don't remember what thou worest."

"Typical man."

The town bell rang, interrupting a long comfortable silence and announcing nine o'clock, time for the Manhattan taverns to close.

"Wilt thou marry me?" he asked.

Penelope stared at Richard. Although expecting this question, she was still surprised by it and hesitated. What did she know about being the wife of a farmer? Yet what good had her knowledge of shipping and commerce done?

Her own words echoed in her mind: I don't want to share loneliness.

"Ahem. Excuse me," said a voice in Dutch from the darkness.

Richard jumped up and stepped forward, placing his body between Penelope and the intruder. "Who goes there?"

"I want to thank you for saving my worthless life." A short man stepped out of the darkness into the meager light streaming from Stillwell's window.

"Beanpole?" Penelope stood up. "Is that you? I thought you drowned."

Beanpole nodded. "That was my scheme."

"To drown?"

Beanpole laughed. "No. To make people think I was dead."

Penelope stepped closer for a better look. He really was Beanpole. "Why?"

"Why?" he echoed. "Because people don't murder a dead man. You and that fellow with the biggest knife I ever seen threatened to kill me if I didn't talk. Turk would kill me if I did. Pretending to be murdered was the only way not to be murdered."

Penelope smiled. "I wouldn't have killed you."

"You I believe." Beanpole frowned at Richard. "Your friends, I'm not sure about."

"Why didn't you tell me Turk was the sailor I knew as Rusty?"

"Rusty?" Beanpole grinned. "I done forgot about that nickname. You see, just before that voyage a jealous harlot dyed Turk's hair while he slept. He didn't notice a thing for two days."

"Now, will you tell me the truth about my father's death?"

Beanpole sighed. "It was Karl's stupidity what killed him and your father. You see, Karl stole ginseng from Turk and tried to run away. But the ship's rats done found his hiding place and ate it. He were a damned fool to come back for more."

"I fear my father persuaded this Karl to come back," said Penelope, glad to finally know the name of the mysterious German.

"More likely, Karl convinced your father. Anyway, Karl and your father searched them woods for a month or two but couldn't find no ginseng and ran out of food."

"Were they looking for red berries?"

"Of course they was, but the berries don't turn red until fall." Beanpole shrugged. "I should know. They made me do most of the looking because my eyes are already so close to the ground.

"Anyway, Karl and your father camped at the Collect Pond outside the wall and Karl came into the village for supplies. But Ignaas spotted Karl, fetched Turk, and followed the traitor back to the pond.

"You know the strange thing, *Mevrouw* Prince? Your father found some ginseng near the pond, even without any berries. When he heard Karl coming back, your father yelled the good news to Karl. That's when Turk stabbed Karl in the back."

Penelope gasped. Had her father's shouts of eureka been responsible for Karl's death? No, Karl was doomed the minute he set foot in Manhattan. "Did my father suffer?"

"According to Ignaas, who drowned a few years ago in a storm, your father died like a man. He stood up to Turk and claimed he and Karl was the only ones what knew anything. Of course, Turk never trusts nobody. So he stabbed your father in the heart."

Her father had not told a lie, because at that time his daughter had not yet received the letter and its tiny clue.

Beanpole shook his head slowly from side to side. "I can't believe Turk is really dead."

Penelope said, "According to Lieutenant Stillwell, Turk had a broken neck from a fall, a musket ball in the liver, and the snapped-off blade of a whittling knife in his lung. The broken neck killed him immediately but the other two would have killed him in a week."

"My whittling knife in Turk's lung?" Beanpole bowed to Penelope. "Well, bless His bones. There is justice in the world after all."

Penelope felt herself blush in the darkness. "I only stabbed him in the arm with your knife. He must have kept it to use on me and landed on it in his fall."

Penelope rubbed the scars on her abdomen with the fingers of her maimed arm. Did she doubt Stillwell's diagnosis of slow death because of her survival or because she didn't want to be responsible, even indirectly, for another person's death? Even the slow death of a murderer?

"*Mevrouw* Prince." Beanpole pantomimed doffing his drowned hat. "Please keep my survival a secret. I'm gonna take my chances in Indonesia where it's safer."

Penelope reached a hand to stay him. "Why didn't Turk kill you long before this?"

"No one believes my stories." Beanpole smiled. "Neither giant red rabbits nor snakes that eat boars nor roots with red berries. Turk trusted a liar, even a liar who always told the truth."

Penelope believed him for she had seen an island of pink storks. "Then why leave? Aren't you safe now?"

"I'll never be safe. Eriksen thought up the whole scheme. He's the one what got the money." Beanpole slipped away into the darkness.

Penelope hoped Eriksen had enough wealth and enough sense he would never need to return to Manhattan. Surely,

after seeing Lieutenant Stillwell and Richard Stout in
action, he would be reluctant.

"Ahem," Richard said. "About the question I asked
thee."

Epilogue

Gravesend

25 March 1649

According to the Dutch, the day was March 25, the day the English with their obsolete Roman calendar said was the first day of the year. Except their obsolete system said today was only March 15, the Ides of March, a fatal day for Julius Caesar, but a happy day for Penelope. After three months of marriage, she knew she carried a child.

Was she smarter than wily Odysseus? She had needed less than a year of adventure, not twenty, to learn the value of peace and contentment, of life and love.

A tap, tap, tap outside the front window announced that a neighbor tacked a paper onto the notice board and agitated a wren that explored their eaves for a nesting site. Spring rains turned the streets of Gravesend into mud, again. Despite the weather, people would come to read, talk, and discuss. These English enjoyed arguing, expostulating, complaining. Endlessly. Like blue jays and crows arguing over a squirrel carcass.

Penelope drifted to the window to listen to her neighbors discuss the news, still moderately surprised to hear English instead of Dutch spoken in the streets.

The idea of a life inside her womb was strange. She needed a long conversation with Ann, a mother twice over.

Richard Stout followed behind her, gently wrapping his hands around her hands atop her still flat belly. He whispered into her ear, "What are thy thoughts, Mother Stout?"

The phrase "Mother Stout" sounded odd, but pleasant, and reminded her of how blessed she was.

"Liesbeth always said I was a strange mixture of English and Dutch." She reached out a finger and spun the globe dangling from hemp strings from the rafter for she had no sturdy table to support it. "I often wondered where my niche in the world would be."

"Here beside me. Here in our home, in our tiny corner of the world." He nuzzled her right ear lobe, trying to free it from her omnipresent cap.

He would have to wait until dark with the candles extinguished before she removed that cap.

The neighbors outside in the rain exclaimed their passions about King Charles and Cromwell. The English Civil War and its causes were the reasons most were now living in New Netherland. Penelope, the only adult in the village who had not grown up in England, ignored them.

She twisted within the comforting confines of his arms to face him. "Will our baby be a strange mixture of English and Dutch too?" she asked her English-born husband living in a Dutch-run colony on the edge of the wilderness.

"Yes. A strange mix called American."

A strident voice outside the window came through clearly. "Look at this London newspaper. Behold! The Puritans have beheaded the king."

"'Tis the work of the devil," said another man.

"Nay. The hand of man has executed the Will of God."

"What is the future of England now?"

Six years ago, Penelope had been stunned by news of the start of the Great Rebellion and, shortly after that, by Matthew's quest, the quest that had ultimately killed him and delivered her to Gravesend. Now, an hour after telling her new husband of the life stirring within her, she heard of the beheading of the king and the end of that war.

Some said fifty thousand Englishmen had died for their faith—fifty thousand and one, including Matthew. Yet, by the grace of God, she had survived. Surely Jesus had watched over her despite her doubts.

What a tangled path she had traversed to arrive at her destiny! God hadn't picked her to help Matthew. Instead God had used the deaths of her father and Matthew to send her to America to bear another man's child.

God works in mysterious ways.

Her husband hugged her firmly without putting undue stress on her left shoulder. "Who cares about King Charles and the future of England? We live an ocean away."

She closed her eyes, stretched up on her toes, and leaned her face toward his. In front of the window where all the residents of Gravesend could see, he kissed her lips.

Then he kissed her again.

Historical Notes

Although this is a work of fiction, it includes numerous historical persons, ships, and events, including Penelope, my great-great-great-great-great-great-great-great-great grandmother, who reportedly had 502 direct descendants when she died at the age of 110. If 1648 was the year she sailed to America, then this may be how it happened.

In the novel each character (except Penelope) who is introduced before her ship (fictional) reached the Atlantic Ocean is fictional save Thomas Blossom.

After Penelope's ship reaches Curacao, each new character with both a first and a last name is historical except for Josef Laurensen (alias Beanpole). Also the ships introduced at Curacao are real as was the capture of the *Nuestra Senora Rosario* and the dispute over its pearls and pieces of eight. The ship *de Witte Paard* is fictional.

Of course, all events are dramatized for your enjoyment.

In the eighteenth century Canadian priests reported the discovery of ginseng in America.

For more history details, consult my website at www.jim-mcfarlane.com.

Jim McFarlane